PRAISE FOR QU

Pride and Prejudice and Zombies
By Jane Austen and Seth Grahame-Smith

"A delectable literary mash-up . . . might we hope for a sequel?
Grade A-."
—Lisa Schwarzbaum of *Entertainment Weekly*

"Jane Austen isn't for everyone. Neither are zombies. But combine the
two and the only question is, Why didn't anyone think of this before?
The judicious addition of flesh-eating undead to this otherwise faithful
reworking is just what Austen's gem needed."
—*Wired*

"Has there ever been a work of literature that couldn't be improved by
adding zombies?"
—Lev Grossman, *Time*

"Such is the accomplishment of *Pride And Prejudice And Zombies* that
after reveling in its timeless intrigue, it's difficult to remember how
Austen's novel got along without the undead. What begins as a gim-
mick ends with renewed appreciation of the indomitable appeal of
Austen's language, characters, and situations. Grade A."
—*The A. V. Club*

Legend

1. Norland Park
2. The Middleton Archipeligo
3. Pestilent Isle
4. Deadwind Island
5. Allenham Isle
6. Sub-Marine Station Beta
7. Former site of Sub-Marine Station Alpha
8. *The Cleveland*
9. Combe Magna

DEVONSHIRE COAST

Sense and Sensibility and Sea Monsters

BY JANE AUSTEN AND BEN H. WINTERS

ILLUSTRATIONS BY EUGENE SMITH

QUIRK BOOKS

PHILADELPHIA

This book is dedicated to my parents—
lovers of great literature and great silliness.

Library of Congress Cataloging in Publication Number: 2009931290

ISBN: 978-1-59474-442-6

Printed in Canada
Typeset in Bembo

Designed by Doogie Horner
Cover illustration by Lars Leetaru
Cover art research courtesy the Bridgeman Art Library International Ltd.
Interior illustrations by Eugene Smith
Production management by John J. McGurk

Distributed in North America by Chronicle Books
680 Second Street
San Francisco, CA 94107

10 9 8 7 6 5 4 3 2 1

Quirk Books
215 Church Street
Philadelphia, PA 19106
www.irreference.com
www.quirkbooks.com

LIST OF ILLUSTRATIONS

CHAPTER 1

THE FAMILY OF DASHWOOD had been settled in Sussex since before the Alteration, when the waters of the world grew cold and hateful to the sons of man, and darkness moved on the face of the deep.

The Dashwood estate was large, and their residence was at Norland Park, in the dead centre of their property, set back from the shoreline several hundred yards and ringed by torches.

The late owner of this estate was a single man, who lived to a very advanced age, and who for many years of his life had a constant companion and housekeeper in his sister. Her death came as a surprise, ten years before his own; she was beating laundry upon a rock that revealed itself to be the camouflaged exoskeleton of an overgrown crustacean, a striated hermit crab the size of a German shepherd. The enraged creature affixed itself to her face with a predictably unfortunate effect. As she rolled helplessly in the mud and sand, the crab mauled her most thoroughly, suffocating her mouth and nasal passages with its mucocutaneous undercarriage. Her death caused a great change in the elderly Mr. Dashwood's home. To supply her loss, the old man invited and received into his house the family of his nephew Mr. Henry Dashwood, the legal inheritor of the Norland estate, and the person to whom he intended to bequeath it.

By a former marriage, Henry had one son, John; by his present lady, three daughters. The son, a steady, respectable young man, was amply provided for by the fortune of his mother. The succession to the Norland estate, therefore, was not so really important to John as to his half sisters; for their mother had nothing, and their fortune would thus depend upon their father's inheriting the old gentleman's property, so it could one day come to them.

The old gentleman died; his will was read, and like almost every other will, gave as much disappointment as pleasure. He was neither so unjust, nor so ungrateful, as to leave his estate from his nephew—but Mr. Dashwood had wished for it more for the sake of his wife and daughters than for himself or his son—and to John alone it was secured! The three girls were left with a mere thousand pounds a-piece.

Henry Dashwood's disappointment was at first severe; but his temper was cheerful and sanguine, and his thoughts soon turned to a long-held dream of noble adventure. The source of the Alteration was unknown and unknowable, but Mr. Dashwood held an eccentric theory: that there was discoverable, in some distant corner of the globe, the headwaters of a noxious stream that fed a virulent flow into every sea, every lake and estuary, poisoning the very well of the world. It was this insalubrious stream (went Henry Dashwood's hypothesis), which had affected the Alteration; which had turned the creatures of the ocean against the people of the earth; which made even the tiniest darting minnow and the gentlest dolphin into aggressive, blood-thirsty predators, hardened and hateful towards our bipedal race; which had given foul birth to whole new races of man-hating, shape-shifting ocean creatures, sirens and sea witches and mermaids and mermen; which rendered the oceans of the world naught but great burbling salt-cauldrons of death. It was Mr. Dashwood's resolution to join the ranks of those brave souls who had fought and navigated their way beyond England's coastal waters in search of those headwaters and that dread source, to discover a method to dam its feculent flow.

Alas! A quarter mile off the coast of Sussex, Mr. Dashwood was eaten by a hammerhead shark. Such was clear from the distinctive shape of the bite marks and the severity of his injuries, when he washed up on the shore. The cruel beast had torn off his right hand at the wrist, consumed the greater portion of his left leg and the right in its entirety, and gouged a ragged V-shaped section from Mr. Dashwood's torso.

His son, present wife, and three daughters stood in stunned desolation over the remains of Mr. Dashwood's body; purpled and rock-battered upon the midnight sand, bleeding extravagantly from numerous gashes—but unaccountably still living. As his weeping relations watched, astonished, the dying man clutched a bit of flotsam in his remaining hand and scrawled a message in the muddy shore; with enormous effort he gestured with his head for his son, John, to crouch and read it. In this final tragic epistle, Mr. Dashwood recommended, with all the strength and urgency his injuries could command, the financial well-being of his step-mother and half sisters, who had been so poorly treated in the old gentleman's will. Mr. John Dashwood had not the strong feelings of the rest of the family; but he was affected by a recommendation of such a nature at such a time, and he promised to do everything in his power to make them comfortable. And then the tide swelled, and carried away the words scrawled in the sand, as well as the final breath of Henry Dashwood.

Mr. John Dashwood had then leisure to consider how much there might prudently be in his power to do for his half sisters. He was not an ill-disposed young man, unless to be rather cold hearted and rather selfish is to be ill-disposed: but he was, in general, well respected. Had he married a more amiable woman, he might have been made still more respectable than he was. But Mrs. John Dashwood was a strong caricature of himself—more narrow-minded and selfish.

When he gave his promise to his father, he meditated within himself to increase the fortunes of his half sisters by the present of a thousand pounds a-piece. The prospect of his own inheritance warmed his heart and made him feel capable of generosity. Yes! He would give them three thousand pounds: It would be liberal and handsome! It would be enough to make them completely easy, and offer to each the prospect of making a home at a decent elevation.

No sooner was what remained of Henry Dashwood arranged in some semblance of a human shape and buried, and the funeral over, than Mrs. John Dashwood arrived at Norland Park without warning, with her

AS HIS WEEPING RELATIONS WATCHED, ASTONISHED, THE DYING MAN CLUTCHED A BIT OF FLOTSAM IN HIS REMAINING HAND AND SCRAWLED A MESSAGE IN THE MUDDY SHORE.

child and their attendants. No one could dispute her right to come; the house with its elaborate wrought-iron fencing and retinue of eagle-eyed harpoonsmen was her husband's from the moment of his father's decease. But the indelicacy of her conduct, to a woman in Mrs. Dashwood's freshly widowed situation, was highly unpleasing. Mrs. John Dashwood had never been a favourite with any of her husband's family; but she had never before had the opportunity of showing them with how little attention to the comfort of other people she could act when occasion required it.

"It is plain that your relations have an unfortunate propensity for drawing the unwelcome attentions of Hateful Mother Ocean," she muttered darkly to her husband shortly after her arrival, "If She intends to claim them, let Her do it far from where my child is at play."

So acutely did the newly widowed Mrs. Dashwood feel this ungracious behaviour that, on the arrival of her daughter-in-law, she would have quitted the house for ever—had not the entreaty of her eldest girl induced her first to reflect on the propriety of going and second on the madness of taking leave before an armored consort could be assembled to protect them on their journey.

Elinor, this eldest daughter, possessed a strength of understanding which qualified her, though only nineteen, to be the counselor of her mother. She had an excellent heart, a broad back, and sturdy calf muscles, and she was admired by her sisters and all who knew her as a masterful driftwood whittler. Elinor was studious, having early on intuited that survival depended on understanding; she sat up nights poring over vast tomes, memorizing the species and genus of every fish and marine mammal, learning to heart their speeds and points of vulnerability, and which bore spiny exoskeletons, which bore fangs, and which tusks.

Elinor's feelings were strong, but she knew how to govern them. It was a knowledge which her mother had yet to learn, and which one of her sisters had resolved never to be taught. Marianne's abilities were, in many respects, quite equal to Elinor's. She was as nearly powerful a swimmer, with a remarkable lung capacity; she was sensible and clever, but eager in everything. Her sorrows, her joys, could have no moderation. She was generous, amiable, interesting; she was everything but prudent. She spoke sighingly of the cruel creatures of the water, even the one that had so recently savaged her father, lending them such flowery appellations as "Our Begilled Tormentors" or "the Unfathomable Ones," and pondering over their terrible and impenetrable secrets.

Margaret, the youngest sister, was a good-humoured, well-disposed girl, but one with a propensity—as befit her tender years more so than the delicate nature of their situation in a coastal country—to go dancing through rainstorms and splashing in puddles. Again and again Elinor warned her from such childish enthusiasms.

"In the water lies danger, Margaret," she would say, gravely shaking her head and staring her mischievous sister in the eye. "In the water, only doom."

CHAPTER 2

MRS. JOHN DASHWOOD now installed herself mistress of Norland; and her mother and sisters-in-law were degraded to the condition of visitors. As such, however, they were treated by Mrs. Dashwood with quiet civility—she reserved for them the gills of the tuna at nuncheon—and by their half brother with kindness. Mr. John Dashwood pressed them with some earnestness to consider Norland their home; and, as no plan appeared so eligible to Mrs. Dashwood as remaining there till she could accommodate herself with a house in the neighbourhood, his invitation was accepted.

A continuance in a place where everything reminded her of former delight—except for the patch of beach where Henry's blood still stained the rocks, no matter how often the tide washed over them—was exactly what suited her mind. In sorrow, she was carried away by her sorrow; conversely, in seasons of cheerfulness, no temper could be more cheerful than hers, or possess that sanguine expectation of happiness that is happiness itself.

Mrs. John Dashwood did not at all approve of what her husband intended to do for his sisters. To take three thousand pounds from the future fortune of their dear little boy, would be impoverishing and endangering him to the most dreadful degree. She begged her husband to think again on the subject. How could he answer it to himself to rob his child of so large a sum? "Why was he to ruin himself and their poor Harry," she asked, "whose little life was already horribly imperiled by living in a coastal county, by giving away all their money to his half sisters?"

"It was my father's last request to me," replied her husband, "Arduously written out, letter by letter, using a bit of waterlogged beach-timber clutched 'twixt the digits of his sole remaining hand, that I should assist his widow and daughters."

"He did not know what he was about, I dare say, considering the amount of vital fluids that had spilled upon the beach by the time he wrote it. Had he been in his right senses, he could not have thought of such a thing as begging you to give away half your fortune from your own child."

"He did not stipulate for any particular sum, my dear Fanny; he only requested me, in general terms, to assist them, and make their situation comfortable. As he required the promise, and as I was clutching at bits of his ears and nose to give his face some form of face-shape while he required it, I could do no less than give my word. Something must be done for them whenever they leave Norland and settle in a new home."

"Let *something* be done for your sisters; but *that* something need not be three thousand pounds! Think of the number of life-buoys such a sum can purchase!" she added. "Consider that when the money is parted with it never can return. Your sisters will marry or be devoured, and it will be gone forever."

"Perhaps, then, it would be better for all parties if the sum were diminished one half. Five hundred pounds would be a prodigious increase to their fortunes."

"Oh, beyond anything great! What brother on earth would do half as much for his sisters, even if *really* his sisters! And as it is, only half-blood! But you have such a generous spirit! Simply because a man is mauled by a hammerhead does not mean you must do everything he tells you to before he dies!"

"I think I may afford to give them five hundred pounds a-piece. As it is, without any addition of mine, they will each have above three thousand pounds on their mother's death, which will furnish a very comfortable fortune for any young woman."

"To be sure it is; and, indeed, it strikes me that they can want no addition at all. They will have ten thousand pounds divided amongst them. If they marry they will be sure of doing well; and if they do not, they may all live very comfortably together on the interest of ten thousand pounds."

"I wonder therefore whether it would be more advisable to do something for their mother while she lives, rather than for them; something of the annuity kind, I mean. A hundred a year would make them all perfectly comfortable."

His wife hesitated a little in giving her consent to this plan. "To be sure," said she, "it is better than parting with fifteen hundred pounds at once. If Mrs. Dashwood should live fifteen years, we shall be completely taken in."

"Fifteen years! My dear Fanny! Her life cannot be worth half that purchase! Even strong swimmers rarely make it that long, and she's weak at the hips and knees! I've glimpsed her in the bath!"

"Think, John; people always live forever when there is any annuity to be paid them; and old ladies can be surprisingly quick in the water when chased; there is something porpoiselike, I think, in the leathery wrinkliness of their skin. Besides, I have known a great deal of the trouble of annuities; for my mother was charged by my father's will with the payment of one to three old superannuated servants who had once dragged him from the mouth of a gigantic phocid. Twice every year, these annuities were to be paid, and then there was the trouble of getting it to them; and then one of them was said to have been lost off the Isle of Skye in a shipwreck and cannibalized; and afterwards it turned out it was only his fingers above the knuckles that had been eaten. Her income was not her own, she said, with such perpetual claims on it; and it was the more unkind in my father, because, otherwise, the money would have been entirely at my mother's disposal, without any restriction whatever. It has given me such an abhorrence of annuities, that I am sure I would not pin myself down to the payment of one for all the world."

"It is certainly an unpleasant thing," replied Mr. Dashwood, "to have those kinds of yearly drains on one's income. One's fortune, as your mother justly says, is *not* one's own. To be tied to the regular payment of such a sum on every rent day, like Odysseus lashed to the mast, is by no means desirable: It takes away one's independence."

"Undoubtedly, and you have no thanks for it. They think themselves secure, you do no more than what is expected, and it raises no gratitude at all. If I were you, whatever I did should be done at my own discretion entirely."

"I believe you are right, my love. It will be better that there should be no annuity in the case; whatever I may give them occasionally will be of far greater assistance than a yearly allowance. It will certainly be much the best way. A present of fifty pounds, now and then, will prevent their ever being distressed for money, and will, I think, be amply discharging my promise to my father."

"To be sure it will. Indeed, to say the truth I am convinced that your father had no idea of your giving them any money at all. The assistance he thought of, I dare say, was only such as might be reasonably expected of you; for instance, such as looking out for a comfortable small house for them."

Their conversation was cut short by the clang of the monster bell; the servants were arriving in a mad panic and bringing up the drawbridge. The front coil of a fire-serpent had been spotted by the night watchman through his spyglass; the beast was some leagues out to sea, but it was uncertain how far inland such creatures could deliver a fireball.

"Perhaps it is best we cower in the attic for the time being," suggested John Dashwood to his wife, who most readily agreed, pushing past him as they rushed up the stairs.

This conversation gave to Mr. Dashwood's intentions whatever of decision was wanting before; and by the time they emerged to find, to their relief, that only a small woodland parcel on the outskirts of the estate had been singed, he had resolved that it would be absolutely unnecessary to do more for the widow and children of his father than he and his wife had determined.

CHAPTER 3

MRS. DASHWOOD WAS INDEFATIGABLE in her enquiries for a suitable dwelling in the neighbourhood of Norland, somewhere at a similar remove from the shoreline, if not the same elevation, as their current residence; for to remove from the beloved spot was impossible. But she could hear of no situation that at once answered her notions of comfort and ease, and suited the prudence of Elinor, whose steadier judgment rejected several houses as too large for their income, or too hard by the water's edge.

On the tragic night that Henry Dashwood was murdered by the hammerhead, Mrs. Dashwood had glimpsed what her mutilated husband scrawled in the sand and heard John's solemn promise in their favour; she considered that it gave what comfort it could to her husband's last earthly reflections. She doubted the sincerity of this assurance no more than he had doubted it himself, and she thought of it for her daughters' sake with satisfaction. For their brother's sake, too, for the sake of his own heart, she rejoiced, and she reproached herself for being unjust to his merit before, in believing him incapable of generosity. His attentive behaviour to herself and his sisters, stopping by their rooms in the evening to run his hands along the window frames, feeling for the tiny, blight-bearing water bugs that would sneak their way in through the smallest opening, convinced her that their welfare was dear to him. She firmly relied on the liberality of his intentions.

The contempt which she felt for her daughter-in-law was very much increased by the further knowledge of her character, which half a year's residence in her family afforded. She was astonished to hear Margaret harshly scolded for helping herself to a second generous portion of crawfish stew; where Fanny Dashwood saw a gluttonous and unmannered girl-child, her mother-in-law saw a young woman taking appropriate enjoyment in every opportunity to dine upon the hated foe. In short, the two Mrs. Dashwoods had as much mutual antipathy as two barracudas trapped in the same small tank. They might have found it impossible to have lived together long, had not a particular circumstance occurred to give still greater eligibility to their continuance at Norland.

This circumstance was a growing attachment between her eldest girl and the brother of Mrs. John Dashwood, who was introduced to their acquaintance soon after his sister's establishment at Norland, and who had since spent the greatest part of his time there.

Some mothers might have encouraged the intimacy from motives of interest, for Edward Ferrars was the eldest son of a man who had died very rich, having amassed a vast fortune from the manufacture and sale of sterling-silver lobster tongs; and some might have repressed it from motives of prudence, for the whole of his fortune depended on the will of his mother. But Mrs. Dashwood was alike uninfluenced by either consideration. It was enough for her that he appeared to be amiable, that he loved her daughter, and that Elinor returned the partiality. It was contrary to every doctrine of hers that difference of fortune should keep any couple asunder who were attracted by resemblance of disposition; life was too short, and too many dangers lurked under every sea-slimed rock, to act otherwise. Of course, that Elinor's merit should not be acknowledged by everyone who knew her was impossible to comprehend.

Edward Ferrars was not recommended to their good opinion by any peculiar graces of person or address. He was not handsome and his manners required intimacy to make them pleasing. But when his natural shyness was overcome, his behaviour gave every indication of an open, affectionate heart. His understanding was good, and his education had given it solid improvement. But he was neither fitted by abilities nor disposition to answer the wishes of his mother and sister, who longed to see him distinguished—as—they hardly knew what. They wanted him to make a fine figure in the world in some manner or other. His mother wished to interest him in political concerns, to get him into government, perhaps, or into aquatic engineering on the great freshwater canals of Sub-Marine Station Beta. Mrs. John Dashwood wished it likewise, but in the meanwhile it would have quieted her ambition to see him managing a gondola fleet.

But Edward had no turn for great men or gondolas; his ambition was more modest. All his wishes centered in domestic comfort and the quiet of private life. He was an avid scholar who had spent many years elaborating a personal theory of the Alteration. Edward Ferrars was skeptical of the poison-stream theory, which had seduced Mr. Henry Dashwood to set off, with such tragic results, in search of the mythic headwaters; he believed the calamity's origins could be located in the time of the Tudors, when Henry VIII turned his back on the Holy Church. God in his vengeance, thought Edward, had smote the English race for this impertinence and set the beasts of the sea against them.

Such scholarly theorizing was dismissed by Fanny and their mother as a waste of time and potential; fortunately Edward had a younger brother who was more promising.

Edward had been staying several weeks in the house before he engaged much of Mrs. Dashwood's attention. She was, at that time, in such affliction as rendered her careless of surrounding objects. When at last she noticed him, she saw only that he was quiet and unobtrusive, and she liked him for it. He did not disturb the wretchedness of her mind with ill-timed conversation.

She was called to observe and approve Edward further by a reflection which Elinor chanced one day to make on the difference between him and his sister. It was a contrast which recommended him most forcibly to her mother.

"It is enough," said Mrs. Dashwood, as they sat at the breakfast table one morning, "to say that he is unlike Fanny. It implies everything amiable. I love him already."

"I think you will like him," replied Elinor, "when you know more of him."

"Like him!" replied her mother with a smile. "I can feel no sentiment of approbation inferior to love."

"You may esteem him!"

"I have never yet known what it was to separate esteem and love."

Mrs. Dashwood now took pains to get acquainted with Edward Ferrars. Her manners were attaching and soon banished his reserve. She speedily comprehended all his merits; the persuasion of his regard for Elinor perhaps intensified the natural process of her affection, were slightly less unsettling when she knew his heart was warm and his temper affectionate.

No sooner did she perceive any symptom of love in his behaviour to Elinor than she considered their serious attachment as certain, and looked forward to their marriage as rapidly approaching.

"In a few months, my dear Marianne," said she, as they sat one day, carefully skinning catfish flanks and cutting the meat into bite-size chunks, "Elinor will, in all probability, be settled for life. We shall miss her, but *she* will be happy."

"Oh, Mama, how shall we do without her?"

"My love, it will be scarcely a separation. We shall live within a few miles of each other, and shall meet every day of our lives. You will gain a brother, a real, affectionate brother. I have the highest opinion in the world of Edward's heart. But you look grave, Marianne; do you feel some burden of sympathy for the beasts we painstakingly prepare and are soon to consume? Never forget that each bite represents a victory that must be savored, exactly as *they* would savor a victory over *us*. Or is it that you disapprove your sister's choice?"

"Perhaps both," said Marianne. "I may consider the match with some surprise. Edward is very amiable, and I love him tenderly. But yet—he is not the kind of young man—there is a something wanting—his figure is not striking. It has none of the grace which I should expect in the man who could seriously attach my sister. His eyes want all that spirit, that fire, which at once announce virtue and intelligence. And besides all this, I am afraid, Mama, he has no real taste. Music seems scarcely to attract him; and, though he admires Elinor's driftwood statuettes very much, it is not the admiration of a person who can understand their worth. He admires as a lover, not as a connoisseur. To satisfy me, those characters must be united, like two sea horses amorously intertwined in their watery rendezvous. I could not be happy with a man whose taste did not in every point coincide with my own. He must enter into all my feelings: the same books, the same music must charm us both. Oh Mama, how spiritless, how tame was Edward's reading to us of the diary of those shipwrecked sailors last night. Even during the passage where the doomed sun-mad protagonist realises with a start that the fellow seaman upon whom he has relied for comfort and protection is but a bucket balanced on the end of a mop! To hear those haunting lines, which have frequently almost driven me wild, pronounced with such impenetrable calmness, such dreadful indifference!"

"He would certainly have done more justice to simple and elegant prose. I thought so at the time; but you had to give him the diary of the shipwrecked sailors!"

"Well, it really is my favourite. But we must allow for differences. Elinor has not my feelings, and therefore she may overlook it, and be happy with him. But it would have broken my heart, had I loved him, to hear him read with so little sensibility. Mama, the more I know of the world the more am I convinced that I shall never see a man whom I can really love, and rely upon to protect me! I require so much!"

"I know, dear."

"The man I choose must have all Edward's virtues, and his person and manners must ornament his goodness with every possible charm."

"Remember, my love, that you are not seventeen. It is yet too early in life to despair of such a happiness. Why should you be less fortunate than your mother?"

CHAPTER 4

"WHAT A PITY IT IS, Elinor," said Marianne, "that Edward should have no taste for fashioning attractive miniatures out of driftwood."

"No taste for it!" replied Elinor. "Why shouldn't you think so? He does not whittle driftwood himself, indeed, but he has great pleasure in observing and admiring the efforts of other people; and I assure you he is by no means deficient in natural taste, though he has not had opportunities of improving it. Had he ever been in the way of learning, of instruction on the handling of a long bent knife, I think he would have whittled very well. He distrusts his own judgment in such matters so much that he is always unwilling to give his opinion on a model of a building, or vessel, created out of a lump of raw flotsam; but he has an innate simplicity of taste, which directs him perfectly right. I do think that given proper instruction, he could whittle, and be a great whittler indeed."

Marianne was afraid of offending, and said no more on the subject, but the kind of approbation which Elinor described as excited in him by the driftwood figurines crafted by other people was to her mind very far from that rapturous, wide-eyed delight which could alone be called taste. Yet, though smiling within herself at Elinor's mistake, she honoured her sister for that partiality towards Edward which produced it.

"I hope, Marianne," continued Elinor, "you do not consider him as deficient in general taste. For if that were your opinion, I am sure you could never be civil to him."

Marianne hardly knew what to say, and she was additionally attempting to dislodge a catfish bone from where it had become lodged in her throat since lunch. She could not wound the feelings of her sister on any account, and yet to say what she did not believe was impossible. At length she coughed, pounded a bit on her breastbone, and replied:

"Do not be offended if my praise of him is not in everything equal to your sense of his merits. I have not had so many opportunities of estimating the minute propensities of his mind, as you have; but I have the highest opinion in the world of his goodness and sense. I think him everything that is worthy and admirable."

"I am sure," replied Elinor with a smile, "that his dearest friends, could not be dissatisfied with such praise. I do not perceive how you could express yourself more warmly."

Marianne hacked three times vigorously and—a-ha!—out came the catfish bone. It ricocheted against the opposite wall and went skittering across the floor.

"Of Edward's sense and his goodness," Elinor continued, "no one can be in doubt who has seen him often enough to engage him in unreserved conversation. He has favoured me with his most intriguing theory of the Alteration, and he possesses a wide range of knowledge of that which is most important to our common safety. He can list most species of cirripedes, to provide just one example, and classify them by phylum and subphylum. The excellence of his understanding and his principles is concealed only by his shyness, which too often keeps him silent. I have seen a great deal of him, have studied his sentiments and heard his opinion on subjects of literature and taste; and, upon the whole, I venture to pronounce that his mind is well-informed, his enjoyment of books exceedingly great, his imagination lively, his observation just and correct, and his taste delicate and pure. His abilities in every respect improve as much upon acquaintance as his manners and person. At first sight, his address is certainly not striking; and his person can hardly be called handsome, and yet—I am sorry, dear sister, but that is most distracting!"

Marianne, who had become involved in an effort to pick her teeth with the newly ejected catfish bone, smiled.

"I shall very soon think him handsome, Elinor, if I do not now. When you tell me to love him as a brother, I shall no more see imperfection in his face than I now do in his heart." She smiled and renewed her attack upon her back molars.

Elinor, meanwhile, started at Marianne's use of the word "brother" and was sorry for the warmth she had been betrayed into. Edward stood very high in her opinion, and she believed the regard to be mutual. But she required certainty of it to make Marianne's conviction of their attachment agreeable to her. She knew that what Marianne and her mother conjectured one moment, they believed the next—that with them, to wish was to hope, and to hope was to expect. She tried to explain the real state of the case to her sister.

"I do not attempt to deny," said she, "that I think very highly of him—that I greatly esteem, that I like him."

Marianne here set down her catfish bone and burst forth with indignation—

"Esteem him! Like him! Cold-hearted Elinor! Oh! Worse than cold-hearted! Snake-hearted! Lizard-hearted! Ashamed of being otherwise! Use the words such as 'esteem' again, and I will leave the room this moment."

Elinor could not help laughing. "Excuse me," said she; "and be assured that I meant no offense to you by speaking in so quiet a way of my own feelings. But I am in no means assured of his regard for me. There are moments when the extent of it seems doubtful; and till his sentiments are fully known, you cannot wonder at my wishing to avoid any encouragement of my own partiality, by believing or calling it more than it is. In my heart I feel little—scarcely any doubt of his preference. But there are other points to be considered besides his inclination. He is very far from being independent. What his mother really is we cannot know; but, from Fanny's occasional mention of her conduct and opinions, we have never been disposed to think her amiable; and I am very much mistaken if Edward is not himself aware that there would be many difficulties in his way, if he were to wish to marry a woman without an estate sufficiently inland to protect against whatever bloodthirsty selachian might one morning drag itself out of the tide."

Marianne was astonished to find how much the imagination of her mother and herself had outstripped the truth.

"And you really are not engaged to him!" said she. "Yet it certainly soon will happen. But two advantages will proceed from this delay. I shall not lose you so soon, and Edward will have greater opportunity of improving that natural taste for your favourite pursuit which must be so indispensably necessary to your future felicity. Oh! If he should be so far stimulated by your genius as to learn to whittle himself, how delightful it would be!"

Elinor had given her real opinion to her sister. She could not consider her partiality for Edward in so prosperous a state as Marianne had believed it. There was at times a want of spirits about him, as if he was constantly recovering from the ingestion of bad chowder—if it did not denote indifference, it spoke of something almost as unpromising. Without sure knowledge of his feelings, it was impossible for Elinor to feel easy on the subject. She was far from depending on that result of his preference of her, which her mother and sister considered as certain.

But Edward's regard for Elinor, when perceived by Fanny, was enough to make her uneasy and uncivil. That lady took the first opportunity of affronting her mother-in-law, talking expressively of her brother's great expectations, and of Mrs. Ferrars's resolution that both her sons should marry well, and of the danger attending any young woman who attempted to *draw him in like a tidal pool*. Mrs. Dashwood gave her an answer which marked her contempt, resolving that, even if they had to go live in an undersea grotto, in a very nest of sea-squids, her beloved Elinor should not be exposed to another week of such insinuations.

In this state of her spirits, a letter was delivered to her from the post, which contained a provision particularly well timed. It was to offer their use of a rickety seaside shack belonging to a relation of her own, an aging eccentric monster-hunter and adventurer who had lately returned from the waters off Madagascar, where he had trapped and slain the infamous Malagasy Man-Serpent; he had, upon his return, laid claim to his ancestral inheritance, a chain of small islands off the coast of Devonshire. Sir John (for that was his name) understood that Mrs. Dashwood was in need of a dwelling. And though the waters off Devonshire were well-known to be among the most beast-bedeviled swaths of English ocean, and the house he offered was merely a haphazard shanty, built atop a jagged promontory on the windward side of Pestilent Isle, the smallest island in the archipelago, he assured her that everything should be done to it which she might think necessary. Sir John himself, being vastly experienced in the ways of the hateful denizens of the inky deep, assured her that while she and her family lived on his island every possible measure of security would be offered them. He urged her to come with her daughters to Deadwind Island, the place of his own residence, from whence she could judge for herself whether Barton Cottage—as the tiny, wind-rattled shack on Pestilent Isle was called—could be made comfortable to her. Well, not comfortable, he continued, given the amount of mosquitoes that swarmed the house at all hours, comfort was not really feasible. But she could judge whether it could be made *tolerable*. Despite this cavil, Sir John seemed really anxious to accommodate them; the whole of his letter, though composed in the crabbed, spidery script of a man used to composing treasure maps and desperate pleas for help rather than warm invitations to distant kin, was written in a most friendly style.

Mrs. Dashwood needed no time for deliberation or enquiry. Her resolution was formed as she read. To quit the neighbourhood of Norland was no longer an evil; it was an object of desire; it was a blessing, in comparison of the misery of continuing as her daughter-in-law's guest. She instantly wrote Sir John Middleton her acknowledgement of his kindness, and her acceptance of his proposal.

As she laid down her pen and called to Marianne, Elinor, and Margaret to pack up their dunnage, lightning crackled in the sky, and a cloud hid the face of the moon.

CHAPTER 5

MRS. DASHWOOD SHORTLY INDULGED herself in the pleasure of announcing to her son-in-law and his wife that she was provided with a coastal shanty, and should incommode them no longer. They heard her with surprise. Mrs. Dashwood had great satisfaction in explaining that they were going off the coast of Devonshire. John Dashwood gasped and clapped his hand before his mouth. "Not the Devonshire coast!" he exclaimed, growing very pale, while his wife smiled cruelly at the corners of her mouth, sure in her intuition that her mother-in-law would very shortly pose no future inconvenience, save perhaps to the digestion of some ravenous, bottom-dwelling devil.

Edward Ferrars turned hastily towards her and, in a voice of surprise and concern, which required no explanation to her, repeated, "Devonshire! Are you, indeed, going there? So far from hence! There? Of all places?"

Mrs. Dashwood, too suffused with pleasure at finding a situation for herself and her family, did not hear the shock and horror in his normally even voice. Calmly, she explained the situation.

"Barton Cottage is but a haphazard two-story shack, tottering on a rocky promontory above the sea," she continued, "But one under the protection of the ancient defenses employed by the sagacious Sir John. I hope to see many of my friends in it. A room or two can easily be added; and if friends find no difficulty in travelling so far to see me, and if they can bribe a ship's captain to undertake the journey, I am sure I will find no difficulty accommodating them."

She concluded with a very kind invitation to Mr. and Mrs. John Dashwood to visit her at Barton Cottage, to which they did not bother to pretend enthusiasm; and to Edward she offered an invitation with still greater affection. To separate Edward and Elinor was as far from being her object as ever; and she wished to show Mrs. John Dashwood how totally she disregarded her disapproval of the match.

Mr. John Dashwood told his mother again and again how exceedingly sorry he was that she had taken a situation at such a distance as to prevent his help in removing her furniture from Norland. He really felt conscientiously vexed on this occasion, and all the more so when the furniture was sent round by water, meaning that its likelihood of actually arriving at their new residence was exceedingly dim.

Mrs. Dashwood arranged to take the house for a twelvemonth; as she had reported to her son and daughter-in-law, it was already furnished with the netting, drain-plugs, and alarum bells that any seaside domicile must reasonably employ against the threat of ravagement, as well as those more esoteric devices known to Sir John's wisdom, which he had assured her were unobtrusive but effective. Elinor's good sense limited the number of servants they would take to four: a maid, a musket-man and two torchbearers, with whom they were speedily provided from amongst those who had formed their establishment at Norland. The servants left immediately to prepare the house for their mistress's arrival.

Mrs. Dashwood began to abandon any hope that her son-in-law would abide by his promise to his dying father. He so frequently talked of the increasing expenses of house-protecting, what with the coming of spring tide and the return of Highest Danger Season, and of the perpetual demands upon his purse, and also of the high likelihood that she and the girls would die either en route or soon after their arrival at the coast of Devonshire, and his having to bear their funerary expenses; in short he seemed rather in need of more money himself than to have any design of giving money away.

Many were the salty tears shed by them in their last adieus to a place so much beloved. "Dear, dear Norland!" said Marianne, as she wandered alone before the house, a pounding rainstorm soaking her pelisse. "When shall I cease to regret you!—when learn to feel a home elsewhere!— Oh! happy house, could you know what I suffer in now viewing you from this spot, from whence, perhaps, I may view you no more! You will continue the same, unconscious of the pleasure or the regret you occasion, and insensible of any change in those who walk under your shade! But who will remain to enjoy you?"

CHAPTER 6

THE FIRST PART OF THEIR JOURNEY was simple; in a post-chaise they travelled to the dock at Brighton, where they changed from their lightweight, pointed-toed travelling shoes into thick galoshes to protect their extremities if by some grievous mishap they ended up in the water. The Dashwoods lined up upon the dock to receive the attentions of a prelate, following the long-established custom of administering last rites to anyone embarking on a journey by sea. Gulls circled overhead, seeming to cry piteously for them as they stepped aboard a three-masted, heavily armored schooner called the *Tarantella*, which would take them to the coast of Devonshire.

Elinor felt a twinge of horror as the Sussex coast disappeared behind them and they were surrounded on all sides by the churning sea. As for

Marianne, she swooned with anticipation of their new life and looked upon the captain of the *Tarantella*, a stern and weathered personage with a rheumy step and a corncob pipe, as a charming harbinger of the romance and adventure that awaited them.

Elinor's apprehensions soon proved prescient; for, as they bore to the starboard after passing Dorset and piloted into the narrow inlet that would lead them to Sir John's chain of islands, that same captain hollered throatily to his men to take their stations. At once the dozen hardy sea salts of the crew were scrambling grimly about the foredeck, and from a sea chest at the schooner's waist, were rapidly unloaded blunderbusses and flintlock muskets.

Before the Dashwoods could ascertain the nature of the threat, something thudded powerfully against the hull; the mainmast snapped from its moorings and tilted forward at a perilous angle, sending the bosun's mate, who had been on duty in the crow's nest, pitching forward wildly; in an instant the unfortunate sailor was holding desperately to the cross trees, dangling beside the bowsprit just above the surface of the waves. The ship, its mainsail flapping uselessly, yawed heavily to port. The Dashwoods clutched each other in fear as a vast mouth appeared at the waterline, opening wide to display two jagged rows of razor-sharp fangs, which rose from the water and chomped down effortlessly on the bosun's mate.

It was Mrs. Dashwood who acted first, even as the sailors were still loading their blunderbusses and the coxswain was pulling the tarpaulin off the Ship's cannon. She grasped a spare oar from its rigging, snapped it in twain upon her knee with a swift motion, and plunged the sharp, broken point into the churning sea—piercing the gleaming, deep-set eye of the beast. "*Up*, mother! Drive it up!" shouted Elinor, and leant hard upon the flattened oar end to push the sharp point into the brain of the sea serpent. The beast relaxed its grip upon the shattered corpse of the bosun's mate; it pitched; it rolled; and then it was still, floating belly up upon the surface of the water, its scales glittering blue and green in the sunlight, blood streaming from the punctured eye.

MRS. DASHWOOD GRASPED A SPARE OAR FROM ITS RIGGING, SNAPPED IT IN TWAIN UPON HER KNEE, AND PLUNGED THE SHARP, BROKEN POINT INTO THE GLEAMING, DEEP-SET EYE OF THE BEAST.

"Dear God," said the old captain, flabbergasted, his pipe hanging limply in one hand. "You've slain it."

"Surely 'twas it or us!" cried Marianne in response, her breast heaving from the excitement of the moment.

"Aye. Aye, it was."

In the profound silence that followed, their ears were filled with a low thrashing sound, as the corpse of the bosun's mate was noisily consumed by devil fish. At length the captain drew upon his pipe and spoke again.

"Let us only pray that this is the worst such abomination you encounter in this benighted land; for such is but a goldfish when compared to the Devonshire Fang-Beast."

"The . . . *what?*"

But further conversation was impossible. The first mate announced that they had crossed the third line of longitude and entered the realm known and feared as the Devonshire coast. The captain apologised that his superstitious crewmen would take them no farther. The Dashwoods were gingerly lowered into the sea in a cockleshell, which pitiable vessel was cut loose and shoved in the general direction of Pestilent Isle; as the schooner disappeared behind them, the captain called out "God be with you" and turned away; the gesture had a certain coldness to it, as if the whole world was turning its back on them along with the man. This disheartening impression was reinforced by the head of the bosun's mate slowly drifting by, a twist of seaweed caught in its eye socket.

They arrived—thanks to Mrs. Dashwood's clever hand upon the rudder and Elinor's sure understanding of the coastal map that Sir John had included with his letter—at Pestilent Isle: a rocky and uneven spit of land, not more than nine miles across, patchworked with desolate plateaus, copses of crooked deadwood trees, and fenny marshes; with a single craggy hilltop standing stanchion at the centre of the isle.

Barton Cottage was situated on the windy north face, set back in a kind of smallish bay or cove that slashed into the northwesterly section of the island like a cruel mouth. The Dashwoods, as they struggled out of their cockleshell onto the rickety dock that jutted out into the cove, were somewhat cheered by the joy of the servants upon their arrival. But their cottage was small and compact—in comparison to Norwood, it was small indeed! It sat perched atop a rugged granite ridge, some forty feet above the waterline, with a rickety wooden stairwell leading from the front door to a small, creaking dock. There was no village or neighbours anywhere— no building on the island but their own. Sloping mudflats, here and there pocked with dense thickets of unfamiliar vegetation, surrounded the house in all directions.

All of them got busy in arranging their particular concerns and en-deavouring, by placing around them books and other possessions, to form themselves a home. Margaret, whooping with the characteristic excite-ment of her adventuresome spirit, swiftly set off down a miry trail to take the bearings of her new environs. Marianne's pianoforte was unpacked and properly disposed of; Elinor unpacked her set of thirteen driftwood knives and was pleased to hear from the servants that flotsam was in plen-tiful supply along the island's shores.

In such employments as these they were interrupted by the entrance of their landlord, who called to welcome them to Barton Cottage, and to offer them every accommodation from his own house and docks in which theirs might at present be deficient.

Sir John was an imposing figure, weathered and burnt nut-brown by years of trekking in tropical heat. He held the lifelong conviction that the Alteration resulted from a curse laid by one of the tribal races who had come under England's colonial dominion over the centuries, and he had spent the better part of two decades in search of the culprits. Never had he found proof of his belief, let alone any amelioration of his homeland's peril, but he had in the meantime accumulated a lifetime of wondrous ad-ventures. Sir John had led troups in search of the heart of the Nile, up the slopes of Peruvian volcanoes, and deep into the impassable jungles of Bor-neo. Except to bed, he invariably wore upon his belt a glinting machete; in his boot a five-inch quicksilver dagger; and 'round his neck a chain beaded with human ears. He bald head was round and cratered as the new moon, but his eyebrows and beard were thick as the Amazonian undergrowth and white as the snows of Kilimanjaro.

In his current state of semi-retirement from the life of adventure, Sir John kept prizes zoological, herbivorous, and mineralogical; the various islands of his archipelago were dotted with secret treasure pits, apiaries, and gardens filled with orchids and rare flowering shrubs plucked from Zanzibarian soil. In his den, among the musty, dark leather furniture, was a chess set carved from rhinoceros bone, shelves of dusty tomes revealing the ancient lore of various African, Incan, and Asiatic tribes, and exemplars of 112 distinct species of butterfly, each pinned to a board, their multihued or zebra-striped wings forever stilled.

But his greatest prize was the island maiden Kukaphahora, now Lady Middleton, a six-foot-two-inch, jewel-bedecked princess of a tribe indigenous to a far-flung atoll. Her village had worshiped Sir John as a god—until they discovered their new deity, in the dead of night, digging a pit from whence to strip-mine the diamonds that glittered in ore deep beneath the village. They nearly castrated him along with all his men, but he and his company fought loose, razed the village, murdered the men most triumphantly, and dragged away the women in their nets.

The arrival of the Dashwoods seemed to afford Sir John real satisfaction, and their comfort to be an object of real solicitude to him. His manner was thoroughly good-humoured, if somewhat eccentric to their more civilized tastes, and he delighted in sharing with them his expertise on all manner of monster lore and legend. He said much of his earnest desire of their living in the most sociable terms with his family and pressed them cordially to dine on Deadwind Island every day till they were better settled at home. His kindness was not confined to words; for within an hour after he left them, there arrived a large basket full of edible exotica from Sir John's various arboreums; this gift was followed before the end of the day by a brace of freshly caught sturgeon; and that by a big bag of opiates. He insisted, moreover, on conveying all their letters to the post-frigate, which delivered letters to and from the mainland; Sir John additionally would not be denied the satisfaction of sending them his newspaper every day.

Lady Middleton sent a very civil message by him, denoting her intention of waiting on Mrs. Dashwood as soon as she could be assured that her visit would be no inconvenience; and as this message was answered by an invitation equally polite, her ladyship arrived the next day on a handsome pirogue rowed by two sturdy oarsmen, their muscles oiled and glistening in the noonday sun.

The Dashwoods were, of course, very anxious to see a person on whom so much of their comfort on Pestilent Isle must depend, and the elegance of Sir John's concubine was favourable to their wishes. Lady Middleton was not more than six or seven and twenty; her face was handsome and her imposing figure was draped in long, flowing robes of distinctive tropical hues. Her manners had all the elegance which her husband's wanted. But they would have been improved by some share of his frankness and warmth. She was reserved and cold, as if having been stolen from her native village in a burlap sack and made to be servant and helpmate to an Englishman many years her senior, for some reason sat poorly with her. She had nothing to say for herself beyond the commonplace inquiry or remark.

Conversation however was not wanted, for Sir John was very chatty, and Lady Middleton had taken the wise precaution of bringing with her their eldest child, a fine little boy about six years old, with Sir John's same eyes and nose, but with Lady Middleton's imposing stature and bearing. They had to enquire his name and age, admire his beauty, and ask him questions which his mother answered for him, while he hung about her and held down his head. On every formal visit a child ought to be of the party, by way of provision for discourse, or in extreme cases, if someone needs to be thrown overboard to satisfy the piranhas trailing the boat. In the present case it took up ten minutes to determine whether the boy was most like his father or mother, and in what particular he resembled either, for of course everybody differed, and everybody was astonished at the opinion of the others.

Sir John and Lady Middleton would not leave the house and be rowed back to Deadwind Island without securing their promise of dining there the next day.

CHAPTER 7

A TEAM OF BRAWNY OARSMEN was thoughtfully dispatched by Sir John to convey the Dashwoods to Deadwind Island, about six mile's steady row due east from Pestilent Isle; the ladies had passed near it in their inbound journey, and Elinor had even remarked upon the enormous, ramshackle estate, marked around its perimeter with tiki torches and the skulls of alligators set upon pikes.

Lady Middleton piqued herself upon the elegance and extravagance of her table, and of all her domestic arrangements; she loved to surprise her English visitors with displays of hospitality native to her homeland, such as flavoring her soups with monkey urine and not telling anyone she had done so until the bowl had been drained. But Sir John's satisfaction in society was much more real; he delighted in collecting about him more young people than his house would hold, and the noisier they were the better he was pleased. He was especially fond of relating long tales of his days at sea, stories of riding recalcitrant crocodiles even as he throttled them, or of the time he got scurvy and had to be held down on the deck while his rotting front teeth were knocked out with a spyglass.

The arrival of a new family in the islands was always a matter of joy to him; and in every point of view he was charmed with the inhabitants he had now procured for his rickety little shanty on Pestilent Isle. The Miss Dashwoods were young, pretty, and unaffected. It was enough to secure his good opinion; for to be unaffected, or to have one of those facial piercings that grotesquely extends the lower lip, as he had seen in Africa, were the two things he found most captivating in a young girl.

Mrs. Dashwood and her daughters were met at the dock-end by Sir John, his pate glistening in the sun, laughing jovially, leaning casually on his oaken cane, and stroking his waist-length white beard. He welcomed them to Deadwind Island with unaffected sincerity as he settled each into an oversized sealskin-leather sofa; the only suspension in his cheerful attitude came upon hearing the tale of their inward journey and of Mrs. Dashwood's dispatching the monster that attacked them; "I hope," he muttered, "That you did not invoke the wrath of the Fang-Beast."

"The what?"

"Never mind, never mind," he muttered into his beard, and changed the subject to a favourite concern, that of being unable to get any smart young men to meet them. They would see, he said, only one gentleman there besides himself; a particular friend who was staying on the island, and who was—and here Sir John paused, and took a long, uncomfortable breath—a bit *unusual* in his appearance. Luckily, Lady Middleton's mother, who had been abducted at the same time and from the same Edenic tropical homeland as Lady Middleton, had arrived at Deadwind Island within the last hour; she was a very cheerful, agreeable woman. The young ladies, as well as their mother, were perfectly satisfied with having two entire strangers of the party and wished for no more.

Lady Middleton's mother was referred to as "Mrs. Jennings," simply because Sir John thought it amusing; her real name was some fourteen or more syllables in length, containing a series of consonant strings impregnable by the English tongue. She was an elderly widow who talked a great deal; her dialogue was peppered with bits of her inscrutable native language, accompanied by a wide supplementary vocabulary of winks, nudges, and suggestive hand gestures. Before dinner was over she had said many witty things on the subjects of lovers and husbands and hoped laughingly that the

Dashwood sisters had not left their hearts (or possibly their genitalia—the relevant hand gesture was not entirely clear) behind them in Sussex. Marianne was vexed at this inarticulate teasing for her sister's sake, and turned her eyes towards Elinor to see how she bore these attacks, with an earnestness which gave Elinor far more pain than could arise from such commonplace raillery as that leveled by Mrs. Jennings.

Colonel Brandon, the friend of Sir John, suffered from a cruel affliction, the likes of which the Dashwood sisters had heard of, but never seen firsthand. He bore a set of long, squishy tentacles protruding grotesquely from his face, writhing this way and that, like hideous living facial hair of slime green. There was, in addition, some odd aura about him, indefinable but undeniably disquieting, even beyond these perverse appendages; one sensed that to look him in the eye would be to catch a terrifying glimpse of all the terrors that lie, unknowable and unimaginable, beyond the world that we can see and feel. Otherwise, he was very pleasant. His appearance, besides the twitching tentacles that overhung his chin, was not unpleasing, despite being an absolute old bachelor; for he was on the wrong side of five and thirty. He was silent and grave, but his countenance was sensible and his address was particularly gentlemanlike.

There was nothing in any of the party which could recommend them as companions to the Dashwoods; but the haughty diffidence of Lady Middleton was so particularly unpleasant, that in comparison to it the gravity of Colonel Brandon, the squidishness of his visage notwithstanding, was interesting. Elinor leveled a silencing glance at her sister when she sensed Marianne's intention to indecorously enquire of their new acquaintance how he came to bear his peculiar facial stigmata. Such physiognomic eccentricities were variously whispered to result from one's mother drinking sea-water while confined, or a hex, laid upon the bearer by a sea witch. It was not, in any case, a topic appropriate to polite company, and certainly not in the presence of one so afflicted.

Margaret returned from a long ramble on the grounds of Sir John's estate, out of breath and bursting with wild-eyed excitement. "I—I—I

COLONEL BRANDON, THE FRIEND OF SIR JOHN, SUFFERED FROM A CRUEL
AFFLICTION, THE LIKES OF WHICH THE DASHWOOD SISTERS HAD HEARD OF,
BUT NEVER SEEN FIRSTHAND.

have seen . . . *something*!" she shouted. "Something . . . *incredible* . . . upon the island!"

"Tell me, then, dear girl, and I shall explain," offered Sir John. "I know Deadwind Island, and all its odd crevices, as I do the scars on the back of my own hand."

"No," replied Margaret. "Something upon *our* island—on *Pestilent Isle*. I saw, as I wandered along the shore here, a thick spiral of steam, shooting up from the mountain that sits in the centre of Pestilent Isle."

All laughed merrily. "The *mountain*?"

"Well, the hill is more like," said Margaret, blushing. "But as I gaze upon it from my window at night, I have taken to calling it a mountain. Mount Margaret, I have dubbed it, and it is there that—"

"Upstairs, young lady!" interrupted Mrs. Dashwood. "And clean yourself for dinner. No more talk of mountains, or queer spirals of steam, or other childish fantasies." Reluctantly, Margaret obeyed.

Shortly thereafter, Marianne was discovered to be musical and invited to play. At their request she performed a ballad in thirty-seven verses that Sir John had composed about his discovery of, infatuation with, and subsequent abduction of Lady Middleton. The performance was highly applauded. Sir John was loud in his admiration at the end of every verse, banging his cane on the ground, and as loud in his conversation with the others while the verses continued. Colonel Brandon alone, of all the party, heard Marianne sing without being in raptures. He paid her only the compliment of attention, and she felt a respect for him on the occasion, which the others had reasonably forfeited by their shameless want of taste. He sat in silence, his tentacles writhing; his hands folded in his lap, making only the low gurgling noise that his sinuses always emitted, unbidden, from his lunatic's nightmare of a face.

CHAPTER 8

MRS. JENNINGS WAS A WIDOW, her husband and male children having been ruthlessly slaughtered in the same raid during which she and her daughters were carried off in a sack by Sir John and his men. She had now, therefore, nothing to do but to marry all the rest of the world. In her promotion of this object she was zealously active, as far as her ability reached; and missed no opportunity of projecting weddings among all the young people of her acquaintance. Mrs. Jennings also possessed a vast trove of island lore relating to getting and keeping male attention, which she vigorously recommended to such ladies as she drew into her circle.

"Only cause by some wile a man to shed tears," she recommended to the astonished Dashwood sisters, "and catch three of his teardrops in an emptied jam jar. Mix these salty effusions with your own sputum, and smear the resulting ointment on your forehead before taking to bed. His heart shall soon enough be your own."

She was remarkably quick in the discovery of attachments. This kind of discernment enabled her, soon after her arrival on the Barton Isles, to insinuate that Colonel Brandon was very much in love with Marianne Dashwood. She rather suspected it to be so, on the very first evening of their being together, from his listening so attentively while Marianne sang to them; and when the visit was returned by the Middletons' dining at the cottage, the fact was ascertained by his listening to her again. It must be so. She was perfectly convinced of it. It would be an excellent match, for *he* was rich and *she* was handsome. Mrs. Jennings had been anxious to see Colonel Brandon well married, ever since her connection with Sir John first brought him to her knowledge; and she was always anxious to get a good husband, even one marked by a bizarre octo-face, for every pretty girl.

The immediate advantage to herself was by no means inconsiderable, for it supplied her with endless wet-lipped, cackling amusement against them both. At the Deadwind Island she laughed at the colonel, and at Barton Cottage to Marianne. All in all, it was perfectly annoying to both of them. And when the object of raillery was understood by Marianne, she hardly knew whether to laugh at its absurdity, or censure its impertinence. It seemed an unfeeling reflection on the colonel's advanced years and preposterous appearance, and on his forlorn condition as an old bachelor.

Mrs. Dashwood, however, could not think of a man five years younger than herself so exceedingly ancient as he appeared to the youthful fancy of her daughter.

"But you cannot deny the absurdity of the accusation, though you may not think it intentionally ill-natured. Colonel Brandon is old enough to be my father, and if he were ever animated to be in love, surely he has long outlived every sensation of the kind. In addition, he has to clothespin his tentacles to his ears in order to eat; it is perfectly nauseating. When is a man to be safe from such wit, if age and infirmity and the chance of him strangling his accuser with his rage-stiffened face-appendages, will not protect him?"

"Infirmity!" said Elinor, "do you call Colonel Brandon infirm? Deformed, maybe; repulsive, certainly. More fish than man, face-wise, it cannot be argued. But infirm? I can easily suppose that his age may appear much greater to you than to my mother, but you can hardly deceive yourself as to his having the use of his limbs! In a way, he has more limbs than all of us put together."

"Good point," agreed Mrs. Dashwood.

"Did you not hear him complain of cartilage rot?" Marianne protested. "And is not that the commonest infirmity of declining life for a person with his affliction?"

"My dearest child," said her mother, laughing, "at this rate you must be in continual terror of my decay; and it must seem to a miracle that my life has been extended to the advanced age of forty."

"Mama, you are not doing me justice," said Marianne, who could not be driven from her theme. "I know very well that Colonel Brandon is not old enough to make his friends apprehensive of losing him in the course of nature. He may live twenty years longer, long enough for those fleshy maxillae to turn green-grey and droop with age. But five and thirty has nothing to do with matrimony."

"Perhaps," said Elinor, "five and thirty and seventeen had better not have anything to do with matrimony together. But if there should by any chance happen to be a woman who is single at seven and twenty, and, say, visually impaired somehow, I should not think Colonel Brandon's being five and thirty any objection to his marrying *her*."

"A woman of seven and twenty," said Marianne, "can never hope to feel or inspire affection again. If her home be uncomfortable or her fortune small, I can suppose that she might bring herself to submit to the offices of a nurse or a ship's wench. In his marrying such a woman, therefore, there would be nothing unsuitable. It would be a compact of convenience, and the world would be satisfied. In my eyes it would be no marriage at all; to me it would seem only a commercial exchange, in which each wished to be benefited at the expense of the other."

"It would be impossible, I know," replied Elinor, "to convince you that a woman of seven and twenty could feel for a man of five and thirty anything near to love. But I must object to your dooming Colonel Brandon, merely because he chanced to complain yesterday (a very cold damp day) of a slight cartilage rot in his face."

"But he talked of flannel waistcoats," said Marianne; "and with me a flannel waistcoat is invariably connected with aches, cramps, rheumatisms, and every species of ailment that can afflict the old and the feeble."

"Had he been only in a violent fever, you would not have despised him half so much. Confess, Marianne, is not there something interesting to you in the flushed cheek, hollow eye, and quick pulse of a fever? It is imminent danger that excites you! I swear by the northern lights, when that bosun's mate was being consumed by those devil fish, you looked upon his rapidly disappearing corpse with a blush of interest upon your cheek."

Soon after this, upon Elinor's leaving the room, Marianne spoke again. "Mama," she began, "I have an alarm on the subject of illness which I cannot conceal from you. I am sure Edward Ferrars is not well. We have now been here almost a fortnight, and yet he does not come. Nothing but real indisposition—perhaps Asiatic cholera?—could occasion this extraordinary delay. What else can detain him at Norland? Must we assume he was dispatched by a giant serpent, perhaps cousin to the one that launched itself against us on our inward journey?"

"Had you any idea of Edward's coming so soon?" said Mrs. Dashwood. "I had none. On the contrary, if I have felt any anxiety at all on the subject, it has been in recollecting that he sometimes showed a want of pleasure and readiness in accepting my invitation to visit. Does Elinor expect him already?"

"I have never mentioned it to her, but of course she must."

"I rather think you are mistaken, for when I was talking to her yesterday of getting a new, tightly meshed grate for the guest bedchamber, she observed that there was no immediate hurry for it, as it was not likely that this room would be wanted for some time."

"How strange it is! What can be the meaning of it! But the whole of their behaviour to each other has been unaccountable! How cold, how composed were their last adieus! How languid their conversation the last evening of their being together! In Edward's farewell there was no distinction between Elinor and me: It was the good wishes of an affectionate brother to both. Twice did I leave them purposely together in the course of the last morning, and each time did he most unaccountably follow me out of the room. And Elinor, in quitting Norland and Edward, cried not as I did. Even now her self-command is invariable. When is she dejected or melancholy? When does she try to avoid society or appear restless and dissatisfied in it?"

Margaret at that moment returned from a long morning of exploring the coastline and rough interiors of Pestilent Isle, and stood in the doorway in uncharacteristic silence, contemplating a fresh mystery she had encountered as she made her way around their habitation.

"Mother?" Margaret began tremulously. "There is something I must—"

She was interrupted by a rumble of thunder loud enough to shake the little cottage like a child's toy. Mrs. Dashwood and Marianne rose and stared out the front window, where in the cove below the cottage the waves were rushing up against the rocks; and a low, ominous fog could be seen, miles out to sea but drawing nearer with the tide.

Margaret, for her part, stood staring out the *southerly* vantage, which took in the whole unwholesome geography of Pestilent Isle: the rutted swamps and sloping flats and jagged promontories—and that rock-pocked, ugly hill she had dubbed Mount Margaret.

"We are not alone here," she whispered. "We are not alone."

CHAPTER 9

THE DASHWOODS WERE NOW SETTLED at Barton Cottage with tolerable comfort to themselves. The shanty upon its jutting ridge, the fetid, wind-tossed tidewaters below, the muddy beaches dotted by clumps of brackish algae, were all now become familiar. They had strung the encircling fence with garlands of dried kelp and lamb's blood, which Sir John Middleton had proscribed as the surest method to ward off the attentions of whatever hydrophilic malevolencies might prowl the coast.

There was no other families on the island; no village; no human habitation but for themselves. Fortunately, the whole of Pestilent Isle abounded in intriguing walks. Black and rugged hills, overrun with marsh vegetation, challenged them from almost every window of the cottage to seek the enjoyment of air on their summits; towards one of these hills did Marianne and Margaret one memorable morning direct their steps, attracted by the rare appearance of sunshine in the claustrophobic gloom of their surroundings. Margaret was insistent on trekking to the centre of the island to ascend Mount Margaret and find the source of the column of steam she still swore she had seen, and Marianne was pleased to oblige. This opportunity, however, was not tempting enough to draw the others from their pencil and their book; Mrs. Dashwood sat composing short verses about sailors dying of influenza, whilst Elinor drew again and again a cryptic five-pointed symbol that had appeared to her in a fever dream on the night they first arrived in the islands.

Marianne gaily ascended the downs, trying to keep up with Margaret as she plunged forward, using the bent branch of a kapok tree for a walking stick. Together they traced the upward journey of a sprightly brook—which Margaret suspected had its headwaters at the apex of the little mountain—rejoicing in every glimpse of blue sky, and catching in their faces the animating gales of a high southwesterly wind, despite the keen odor of rot and decay it curiously bore. Marianne took little notice of the peculiar chill in the air, and the fact that the wind only increased as they rambled, seeming indeed to moan, as it swept through the trees, with the restless voices of the damned.

"Is there a felicity in the world superior to this?" asked Marianne with a grin. "Margaret, we will walk here at least two hours, and if we are set upon by any sort of man-beast with giant lobster claws, I shall swiftly butcher it with this pickaxe I brought for that purpose."

Margaret gave no reply to her sister's flight of fancy, remaining keen and alert as they tromped. She jumped, as they turned one sharp corner of the path, when suddenly she heard muted voices, mumbling in a kind of ragged chorus, a menacing, polysyllabic chant: *K'yaloh D'argesh F'ah. K'yaloh D'argesh F'ah. K'yaloh D'argesh F'ah.*

"Do you hear that?" Margaret asked her sister.

Marianne, busily composing romantic couplets dedicated to their new island home, responded with an airy, "Hear what?"

Indeed, the chanting had abruptly stopped; Margaret jerked her head, peering into the trees beside the brook for the source of this puzzling refrain. For a fleeting moment she glimpsed a pair of gleaming eyes, and then another—before they disappeared in the dark heart of the underbrush.

She shook her head and pressed on.

The sisters pursued their way against the wind, resisting it for about twenty minutes longer, when suddenly the fog that hugged the coast lifted and united into a sudden cloud cover, and a driving rain set full in their face, every drop noxious to smell and sulfurous upon the skin. Chagrined and panic-stricken as they imagined what fresh peril this sudden, acrid downpour must portend, they were obliged to turn back, for no shelter was nearer than their own house. Their hearts pounding with horror, they ran desperately down the steep side of the craggy hill which led immediately to their garden gate.

Marianne had at first the advantage, but a false step brought her splashingly into the brook, newly swollen and rushing with rainwater, where she was suddenly submerged from head to toe in the icy cold water. Margaret was involuntarily hurried along by the steepness of the hill; her face was a rictus of fear as she heard the chilling splash of her sister entering the water, and words appeared in her mind unbidden: *It's them.* The people she had spotted for those brief moments in the underbrush. *They will not let us ascend. They protect the geyser. . . . Them . . .*

Marianne, meanwhile, lay face down in the brook, her pickaxe thrown from her grip. Freezing, waterlogged, and pummeled by stones carried by the swift current, she drew her face from under and sputtered for breath—only to find her head pulled back towards the surface by the strong, ropy tentacle which had snaked itself around her neck, and which wound itself over her mouth before she could scream. As she was dragged below the surface, she saw that the tentacle was attached to an enormous, purple-black giant octopus with the long, sharp beak of a bird, and that upon the very tip of the rubbery limb now constraining her was a single, baleful eye.

Thwack! A harpoon pierced the giant octopus's bulbous head, and it burst, raining blood and ooze into the brook and all over Marianne, who managed to lift her face from the water as the tentacle released its grip. As she lay gasping on the bank, soaked by the fetid water and the foul juices of the monster, spitting small bits of brain and gore from the corners of her mouth, a gentlemen clad in a diving costume and helmet, and carrying a harpoon gun, ran to her assistance. The gentleman, opening the circular, hinged portcullis on the front of his helmet, offered his services; and perceiving that her modesty declined what her situation rendered necessary, took her up in his arms without further delay and carried her down the hill. Then passing through the garden, he bore her directly into the house, and quitted not his hold till he had seated her in a chair in the parlour.

Elinor and Mrs. Dashwood rose up in astonishment; their eyes were fixed on the gentleman with an evident wonder, and in Mrs. Dashwood's case, concern about the brackish water dripping from his diving costume onto the parlour carpet. He apologised for his intrusion by relating its cause, in a manner so frank and so graceful that his person, which was uncommonly handsome, received additional charms from his voice and expression. Had he been even old, ugly, and vulgar, the gratitude and kindness of Mrs. Dashwood would have been secured by the act of saving her child from the gruesome attentions of the beast; but the influence of youth, beauty, and elegance, gave an interest to the action which came home to her feelings.

She thanked him again and again; and, with a sweetness of address which always attended her, invited him to be seated. But this he declined, as he was covered with mud and giant octopus effluvia. Mrs. Dashwood then begged to know to whom she was obliged. His name, he replied, was Willoughby, and his present home was on Allenham Isle, from whence he hoped she would allow him the honour of calling to-morrow to enquire after Miss Dashwood. The honour was readily granted, and he then departed; from the parlour window, they watched as he leapt dolphin-like back into the brook and swam readily away upstream.

His manly beauty and abilities as a swimmer and monster slayer were instantly the theme of general admiration; and the laugh which his gallantry raised against Marianne received particular spirit from his exterior attractions. Marianne herself had seen less of his person than the rest, for the confusion which crimsoned over her face, on his lifting her up, had robbed her of the power of regarding him after their entering the house. But she had seen enough of him to join in all the admiration of the others, and with an energy which always adorned her praise. So effectively harpooning the giant octopus and carrying her into the house showed an admirable rapidity of thought. Every circumstance belonging to him was interesting. His name was good, his residence was on a neighbouring island, and she soon found out that of all manly dresses a wet-suit and flipper feet were the most becoming. Her imagination was busy, her reflections were pleasant, so much so that she could nearly disregard the pain as Mrs. Dashwood burnt off the giant octopus tentacle, still clinging demonically to her neck, with a hot poker seized from the fireplace.

Margaret sat meanwhile in a corner of the room, ignored in the general commotion; already her wild story had been dismissed as the preposterous imaginings of a child. "Margaret was beset by a malevolent cephalopod," said Elinor, "Not by any sort of muttering man-trolls meandering through the treeline."

So the youngest Dashwood simply stared out the back window, repeating to herself again and again those strange words, if words they were: *K'yaloh D'argesh F'ah. K'yaloh D'argesh F'ah.*

Sir John called on them as soon as the next interval of fair weather that morning allowed him to get out of doors; and Marianne's near-drowning and near-mauling being related to him, he was eagerly asked whether he knew any gentleman of the name of Willoughby at Allenham Isle. "Willoughby!" cried Sir John; "what, is he in the country? That is good news! I will ride over to-morrow, and ask him to come to Deadwind Island for dinner on Thursday."

"You know him, then," said Mrs. Dashwood.

"Know him? To be sure I do. Why, he is down here every year."

"And what sort of a young man is he?"

"As good a kind of fellow as ever lived, I assure you. A treasure hunter, by trade; a remarkable shot with a harpoon gun, and there is not a faster swimmer in England, in water fresh or briny."

"And is that all you can say for him?" cried Marianne, indignantly. "But what are his manners on more intimate acquaintance? What his pursuits, his talents, and genius?"

Sir John was rather puzzled.

"Upon my soul," said he, "I do not know much about him as to all that. But he is a pleasant, good-humoured fellow, and he has at his home a remarkable collection of deadman's maps, a team of handsome treasure-dogs, and for amusement a tank full of captured man-eating tropical fish, which he keeps sated with small rodents."

"But who is he?" said Elinor. "Where does he come from? Has he a house on Allenham Isle?"

On this point Sir John could give more certain intelligence; and he told them that Mr. Willoughby had no island property of his own; his estate is Combe Magna, in Somersetshire; he resided on the archipelago only while he was visiting Mrs. Smith, an old lady who lived in a stately seaside manor on Allenham Isle, to whom he was related, and whose possessions he was to inherit; adding, "Yes, yes, he is very well worth catching I can tell you, Miss Dashwood; he has a pretty little estate of his own, in Somersetshire besides, and a thirty-foot skiff outfitted with carronades for shooting at predatory serpents; and if I were you, I would not give him up to my younger sister, in spite of all this tumbling into the lairs of octopi. Miss Marianne must not expect to have all the men to herself. Brandon will be jealous, and his jealousy may cause the evil spirits that inhabit his bile ducts to erupt, with the usual consequences," he added with a shudder.

"I do not believe," said Mrs. Dashwood, with a good-humoured smile, "that Mr. Willoughby will be incommoded by the attempts of either of my daughters, towards what you call catching him. It is not an employment to which they have been brought up, and they have enough to concern themselves with. Men are very safe with us, let them be ever so rich. I am glad to find, however, from what you say, that he is a respectable young man, and one whose acquaintance will not be ineligible."

"He is as good a sort of fellow, I believe, as ever lived," repeated Sir John. "I remember last Christmas, at a little hop on the Deadwind Island, he danced from eight o'clock till four without once sitting down."

"Did he, indeed?" cried Marianne, with sparkling eyes; "and with elegance, with spirit?"

"Yes; and he was up again at eight to muck for clams off the southern coast."

"That is what I like; that is what a young man ought to be," sighed Marianne. "Whatever be his pursuits, his eagerness in them should know no moderation, and leave him no sense of fatigue. Because it is when you are tired that the monsters get you." To which concluding point the Dashwoods all nodded solemnly.

"Aye, aye, I see how it will be," said Sir John, "I see how it will be. You will be setting your cap at him now, and never think of poor, malformed Brandon."

"That is an expression, Sir John," said Marianne, warmly, "which I particularly dislike."

"Malformed?"

"No—'setting your cap.' I abhor every common-place phrase by which wit is intended; and 'setting one's cap at a man,' or 'making a conquest,' are the most odious of all. Their tendency is gross and illiberal; and if their construction could ever be deemed clever, time has long ago destroyed all its ingenuity."

Sir John laughed heartily at this, smoothed his great white beard with his massive hands, and then replied, "Aye, you will make conquests enough, I dare say, one way or other. Poor Brandon! he is quite smitten already; you should see him when your name is mentioned, gibbering and moaning and tugging at his feelers. He is well worth setting your cap at, in spite of all this tussling with giant octopi."

CHAPTER 10

WILLOUGHBY CALLED AT THE COTTAGE early the next morning to make his personal inquiries. He was received by Mrs. Dashwood with a kindness which Sir John's description of him and her own gratitude prompted; and everything that passed during the visit tended to assure him of the sense, elegance, mutual affection, and domestic comfort of the family to whom yesterday's entanglement with the octopus had now introduced him. He had not required a second interview to be convinced of the family's charms.

Elinor had a delicate complexion, regular features, and a remarkably pretty figure. Marianne was still handsomer. Her face was so lovely, that when in the common cant of praise, she was called a beautiful girl, truth was less violently outraged than usually happens. Her complexion was uncommonly brilliant; her features were all good; she looked to Willoughby's admiring gaze to have lungs of a remarkable capacity; her smile was sweet and attractive; and in her eyes, which were very dark, there was a spirit of eagerness which could hardly be seen without delight. From Willoughby their expression was at first held back, by the embarrassment and lingering disquiet which the remembrance of the monster assault created. But when this passed away she saw that to the perfect good-breeding of the gentleman, he united frankness and vivacity. He wore his diving costume, even when not planning a dive, though today it was coupled not with his flippers and helmet, but thigh-high leather boots and a hat of sleekest otter skin. Further, he was accompanied by a pet orangutan called Monsieur Pierre, who crouched obediently by his side and made amusing facial expressions. When, finally, Marianne heard Willoughby declare that he was passionately fond of singing shanties and dancing jigs, she gave him such a look of approbation as secured the largest share of his attention to herself for the rest of his stay.

It was only necessary to mention any favourite amusement to engage her to talk. She could not be silent when such points were introduced, and she had neither shyness nor reserve in their discussion. They speedily discovered that their enjoyment of dancing and music was mutual, and they shared a general conformity of judgment in all that related to either. She proceeded to question him on the subject of books; she adored tales of pirates and piracy, but her favourites were the recovered diaries of shipwrecked sailors, and she discussed these with so rapturous a delight, that any young man of five and twenty must have been insensible indeed, not to become an immediate convert to the excellence of the works in question. Their taste was strikingly alike. The same books, the same passages were idolized by each—especially the section in *Being the True Account of the Wreck of the HMS* Inopportune, *by Seamen Meriwether Chalmers, Its Sole Survivor*, where the desperate midshipman scrambles up a tree to catch a rock dove, and when it is revealed to be merely a clump of leaves, eats his belt.

Long before his visit concluded, Marianne and Willoughby conversed with the familiarity of a long-established acquaintance.

"Well, Marianne," said Elinor, busily tailing and deveining a pile of shrimp, while the fire pit was prepared to roast them, "for *one* morning I think you have done pretty well. You have already ascertained Mr. Willoughby's opinion in almost every matter of importance. But how is your acquaintance to be long supported? You will soon have exhausted each favourite topic. Another meeting will suffice to explain his sentiments on picturesque beauty, second marriages, and the virtues of breaststroke versus the Australian crawl, and then you can have nothing further to ask."

"Elinor," cried Marianne, playfully flicking raw shrimp juice at her sister's face with three fingers, "Is this fair? Is this just? Are my ideas so scanty? But I see what you mean. I have been too much at my ease, too happy, too frank. I have erred against every common-place notion of decorum; I have been open and sincere where I ought to have been reserved, spiritless, dull, and deceitful—I should have talked in dull tones of hydrology and tidal science, and spoken only once in ten minutes."

"My love," said Mrs. Dashwood to Marianne, dabbing shrimp from Elinor's cheeks with a sponge, "you must not be offended with Elinor—she was only in jest. I should scold her myself, if she were truly capable of wishing to check your delight." Marianne was softened in a moment, and soon they were all busily employed in piercing the shrimp with spits, and listening happily as they crackled over the fire pit.

Willoughby, on his side, gave every proof of his pleasure in their acquaintance. He came to them every day. Marianne was confined for some days to the house, as she recovered from the octopus attack, with Sir John monitoring the wound and applying to it a bewildering array of tinctures and extracts—in his experience such a gash, once infected, could cause the sufferer themselves to transform into an octopus; but never had any confinement been less irksome. Willoughby was a young man possessed of good abilities, quick imagination, a charming simian companion, and affectionate manners. He was, in short, exactly formed to engage Marianne's heart, and his society became gradually her most exquisite enjoyment. They read, they talked, they sang; they sat in the bay window and amusedly discerned patterns in the ever-present low-hanging fog—here a cat of fog, here a sailboat of fog, here a fog frog. His shanty-singing and composing talents were considerable; and he read her beloved journals of nautical ruin with all the sensibility which Edward had unfortunately wanted.

In Mrs. Dashwood's estimation he was as faultless as in Marianne's. Elinor saw nothing to censure in him but a propensity to say too much of what he thought on any occasion, a propensity underscored by the weirdly humanish laughter of Monsieur Pierre, which his ribaldry invariably elicited. In hastily forming and giving his opinion of other people, a habit in which he strongly resembled and peculiarly delighted her sister, he displayed a want of caution which Elinor could not approve.

Marianne began now to perceive that the desperation which had seized her at sixteen and a half, of ever seeing a man who could satisfy her ideas of perfection, had been rash and unjustifiable. Willoughby was all that her fancy had delineated in that unhappy hour, and in every brighter period. He was the sun shining on smooth rocks; he was a clear blue sky after monsoon season's end; he was perfection in a wet-suit.

Her mother too, in whose mind not one speculative thought of their marriage had been raised (by his prospect of one day becoming rich from a discovery of buried treasure) was led before the end of a week to hope and expect it; and secretly to congratulate herself on having gained two such sons-in-law as Edward and Willoughby.

The repellant Colonel Brandon's partiality for Marianne, which had so early been discovered by his friends, now became perceptible to Elinor. She was obliged to believe that the sentiments which Mrs. Jennings had assigned him for her own amusement were now real; and that however a general resemblance of disposition between the parties might forward the affection of Mr. Willoughby, an equally striking opposition of character was no hindrance to the regard of Colonel Brandon. She saw it with concern; for what was a silent man of five and thirty, bearing an awful affliction upon his face, when opposed to a very lively man of five and twenty, dripping with charisma and the sea-water streaming from his physique-accentuating diving costume? And as she could not wish Brandon successful, she heartily wished him indifferent. She liked him— in spite of his gravity and reserve and the raft of unsettling physical sensations occasioned by looking upon him directly, she beheld in him an object of interest. His manners, though serious, were mild; and his reserve appeared rather the result of embarrassment as to his peculiar condition, than of any natural gloominess of temper. Sir John in his gnomic way had dropped obscure hints of past injuries and disappointments, which justified her belief of Brandon's being an unfortunate man, having suffered disappointments even beyond the seminal misfortune written, quite literally, all over his face.

Perhaps she pitied and esteemed him the more because he was slighted by Willoughby and Marianne, who, prejudiced against him for being neither lively nor young nor entirely human, seemed resolved to undervalue his merits.

"Brandon is just the kind of man, if man he truly be," said Willoughby one day, when they were talking of him together, "whom everybody speaks well of, and nobody cares about; whom all are delighted to see, and everybody is sort of mildly afraid to look at directly."

"That is exactly what I think of him," cried Marianne.

"Do not boast of it, however," said Elinor, "for it is injustice in both of you. He is highly esteemed by all the family on Deadwind Island, and I never see him myself without taking pains to converse with him, although sometimes I shield my eyes with my hands, like this."

"That he is patronized by *you*," replied Willoughby, "is certainly in his favour; but as for the esteem of the others, it is a reproach in itself. Who would submit to the indignity of being approved by such a woman as Lady Middleton and Mrs. Jennings, that could command the indifference of anybody else?"

"Oo-oo-oo!" agreed Monsieur Pierre, leaping upon an armoire and pounding his chest with his fists.

"But perhaps the abuse of such people as yourself and Marianne will make amends for the regard of Lady Middleton and her mother. If their praise is censure, your censure may be praise, for they are not more undiscerning than you are prejudiced and unjust."

"In defense of your protégé you can even be saucy."

"My protégé, as you call him, is a sensible man; and sense will always have attractions for me. Yes, Marianne, even in a man between thirty and forty. He has seen a great deal of the world; has been abroad, has read, and has a thinking mind. I have found him capable of giving me much information on various subjects. It's true! Though I stand a few feet away, so his animation on topics of interest does not cause his tentacles to accidentally brush against me. He has always answered my inquiries with readiness of good breeding and good nature."

Through this tribute, Willoughby executed a mocking gesture with his hands, holding the flat of his palm below his nose and wiggling his fingers in comical imitation of Brandon's deformity.

Elinor rolled her eyes. "Why should you dislike him so?"

"I do not dislike him. I consider him, on the contrary, as a very respectable man, who has everybody's good word, and nobody's notice; who has more money than he can spend, more time than he knows how to employ, and two new coats every year. Who, though he may have a thinking mind, has also a fish's face, and should perhaps be more comfortable out of his gentlemen's coats and submerged in the tank in my parlour."

"Add to which," cried Marianne, "that he has neither genius, taste, nor spirit. That his understanding has no brilliancy, his feelings no ardour, and his voice makes that low gurgling noise that really turns one's stomach, does it not?"

"You decide on his imperfections so much in the mass," replied Elinor, "and so much on the strength of your own imagination—except, I grant you, your observation on the tone of his voice, which is indeed quite unsettlingly aqueous—that the commendation I am able to give of him is comparatively cold and insipid. I can only pronounce him to be a sensible man, well-bred, well-informed, of gentle address, and, I believe, possessing an amiable heart."

"Miss Dashwood," cried Willoughby, "You are endeavouring to disarm me by reason, and to convince me against my will. But it will not do. You shall find me as stubborn as you can be artful." Pleased with his point, he patted Monsieur Pierre, who was defecating. "I have three unanswerable reasons for disliking Colonel Brandon; he threatened me with rain when I wanted it to be fine; he has found fault with my harpooning grip; and I cannot persuade him to buy my fine antique canoe, carved by hand of sturdiest balsam. If it will be any satisfaction to you, however, to be told, that I believe his character to be in other respects ir-reproachable, I am ready to confess it. And in return for an acknowl-edgment, which must give me some pain, you cannot deny me the privilege of disliking him as much as ever, and referring to him privately as Ole Fishy Face."

CHAPTER 11

LITTLE HAD MRS. DASHWOOD or her daughters imagined when first they sailed into the choppy waters of the Devonshire coast, that so many engagements would arise to occupy their time, or that they should have such frequent invitations and such constant visitors. Yet such was the case. When Marianne was recovered from her assault, and the wound closed to Sir John's satisfaction, the schemes of amusement at home and abroad, which Sir John had been previously forming, were put into execution. Sir John was particularly fond of organizing events on the beach at Deadwind Island, such as tiki dances, crawfish fries, and bonfires, on which he would roast a mucilaginous sweetmeat extracted from the marsh-mallow plant; he took upon himself the responsibility both for each evening's entertainment and for taking the elaborate precautions necessary for the safety of his guests. These included both superstitious means, such as drawing a large quadrangle upon the beach in an admix-ture of squid ink and whale blood, beyond which his guests were firmly instructed never to stray; and the more practical measures represented by the stern-faced stewards, armed with tridents and torches, who stood at intervals of twelve paces, eyes fixed upon the water, while the evening's amusements were undertaken.

In every entertainment Willoughby was included; they afforded him opportunity of witnessing the excellencies of Marianne and of receiving, in her behaviour to himself, the most pointed assurance of her affection.

Elinor could not be surprised at their attachment. She only wished that it were less openly shown; and once or twice did venture to suggest the propriety of some self-command to Marianne. "For Heaven's sake, dear sister," she scolded. "You cling to him like a barnacle." But Marianne abhorred all concealment; and to aim at the restraint of sentiments which were not in themselves illaudable, appeared to her not merely an unnecessary effort, but a disgraceful subjection of reason to common-place and mistaken notions. Willoughby thought the same, and their behaviour at all times was an illustration of their opinions.

When he was present, she had no eyes for anyone else. Everything he did was right. Everything he said was clever. Every lobster he drew from the tank was the biggest and plumpest of lobsters. If battledore and shuttlecock formed the evening's sport, his was the cleverest racket-hand. If reels and jigs formed the amusement, they were partners for half the time; and when obliged to separate for a couple of dances, were careful to stand together and scarcely spoke a word to anybody else. Such conduct made them of course most exceedingly laughed at; but ridicule could not shame, and seemed hardly to provoke them.

Mrs. Dashwood entered into all their feelings with warmth; to her it was but the natural consequence of a strong affection in a young and ardent mind.

This was the season of happiness to Marianne. The fond attachment to her former life at Norland was much softened by the charms which Willoughby's society bestowed on her present island home.

Elinor's happiness was not so great. Her heart was not so much at ease, nor her satisfaction in their amusements so pure; they afforded her no companion that could make amends for what she had left behind. Neither Lady Middleton nor Mrs. Jennings could supply to her the conversation she missed; Lady Middleton was in especially dismal humour after attempting to escape back to her home country in a raft she had painstakingly constructed out of broom-straw and clamshells—and being recaptured two miles off the coast. As for Mrs. Jennings, she was an everlasting talker, and had already repeated her own history to Elinor three or four times; had Elinor been paying the scantest attention, she might have known very early in their acquaintance all the particulars of Mr. Jennings's last moments, just before his head was sliced off by an enthusiastic subaltern of Sir John's, and what he said to his wife a few minutes before he died ("Kill yourself! Kill yourself rather than suffer life with the foreign devils!").

In Colonel Brandon alone, of all her new acquaintance, did Elinor find a person who could in any degree claim the respect of abilities, excite the interest of friendship, or give pleasure as a companion. Willoughby was out of the question. He was a lover; his attentions were wholly Marianne's, and a far less agreeable man might have been more generally pleasing. Colonel Brandon, unfortunately for himself, had no such encouragement to think only of Marianne. In conversing with Elinor he found the greatest consolation for the indifference, shading into revulsion, of her sister.

Elinor's compassion for him increased, as she had reason to suspect that the misery of disappointed love had already been known to him. This suspicion was given by some words which accidently dropped from him one evening, when they were sitting together before the bonfire, staring into its guttural embers, while the others were dancing; the dancing was more spirited than usual, attributable to a punch Sir John was serving that he called Black Devil, made from a rum so dark that no light could pass through it.

Brandon's eyes were fixed on Marianne, and, after a silence of some minutes, he said, with a faint smile, "Your sister, I understand, does not approve of second attachments."

"No," replied Elinor, "her opinions are all romantic."

"Or rather, as I believe, she considers them impossible to exist."

"I believe she does."

"Well, some people believe sea witches don't exist. Or that they don't curse people. But they do. They really do," remarked Colonel Brandon bitterly.

"A few years will settle Marianne's opinions on second marriages on the reasonable basis of common sense and observation," Elinor said, politely passing over Brandon's pained comment regarding his own lamentable condition. "And then they may be more easy to define and to justify than they now are, by anybody but herself."

"This will probably be the case," he replied; "and yet there is something so amiable in the prejudices of a young mind, that one is sorry to see them give way to the reception of more general opinions." He breathed wetly through the slimy hanging forest of his face. In the pause before he resumed speaking, Elinor glanced to sea and noticed with a shiver that the fog seemed especially thick and ominous; she then discovered that with the toe of her shoe she was absently tracing a pattern— the same five-pointed symbol which she had found herself sketching in the notebook, the afternoon that Marianne was assaulted by the octopus.

She was about to remark on this when Brandon resumed the conversation by saying, "Does your sister make no distinction in her objections against a second attachment? Or is it equally criminal in everybody? Are those who have been disappointed in their first choice, whether from the inconstancy of its object, or the perverseness of circumstances, to be equally indifferent during the rest of their lives?"

"Upon my word, I am not acquainted with the minutiae of her principles. I only know that I never yet heard her admit any instance of a second attachment's being pardonable."

"This cannot hold," said he, and his fishy face fingers grew rigid, as they sometimes did when he became animated. "No, no, do not desire it; for when the romantic refinements of a young mind are obliged to give way, how frequently are they succeeded by such opinions as are but too common, and too dangerous! I speak from experience." Elinor, though engrossed in her friend's confession, noted with a start that the tide was rushing in with a fierceness wholly unsuited to the hour of evening; the armed stewards snapped to attention and redoubled their attentions to the sea. The other party-goers, their senses dulled by Sir John's concoction, continued dancing.

"I once knew a lady who in temper and mind greatly resembled your sister," Brandon continued, lost in remembrance, "who thought and judged like her, but who from an enforced change—from a series of unfortunate circumstances—"

"What in the—" shouted Sir John, rushing from the dunes, where he had been helping himself to more Black Devil, towards the tide where it now crashed furiously upon the beach. Elinor, surprised and afraid, instinctively huddled into Brandon's arms, and then instantly pulled away, wiping tentacle-snot from her shoulder. "Sir John?" Brandon cried. "What transpires?"

The attention of the party was now fully caught; their alarm was severe, and well-warranted. The water rushed yet farther up the beach and was suddenly gathered around their ankles, and from it rose a great scrabbling thing, a jellyfish twice the size of the largest man present, which presently dragged itself puckering and groaning from the tide. The stewards succumbed to fear; Elinor, observing tremulously from her position at the bonfire, saw one of the guards literally quaking at the knees, another sprinting full-bore inland. Only Sir John had the decisiveness and fortitude equal to the danger at hand; his advanced years seeming to melt away, he leapt in a swift movement to the bonfire, seized a burning ember, and proceeded to the water's edge to confront the fiend.

The gibbering sea-beast was meanwhile demonstrating itself to be faster than any creature lacking legs or other apparent means of locomotion ought naturally to be; indeed, unnatural was but the mildest appellation this massive man-o'-war might justifiably bear. Before Sir John could reach it with his torch, it threw itself in three great wet, slavering motions across the beach and launched its sickening bulk across an unfortunate girl named Marissa Bellwether.

As the party watched in stunned horror, Miss Bellwether was wrapped inside the quavering blanket-shape of the beast and consumed; the stomach acids of the enormous jellyfish dissolved her flesh, emitting a sickening sizzling noise, followed by a sort of unholy belch. And then, as quickly as it had come, the creature dragged itself back into the sea; the tide withdrew; and all that was left of Miss Bellwether was a pile of corroded bones, a clump of hair, and a whalebone corset.

Elinor turned to Brandon, only to find that he had hastened to Marianne's side. Instead she approached Sir John, who clutching his improvised torch was crouched beside the poor girl's remains; this evidence he examined carefully, producing a monocle from an inside pocket and peering at the scene of the violence. It was not the bone and hair which seemed to draw his attention, however, but a small slick of blue-green slime glimmering in the moonlight, a few paces down the beach.

"What might that be, Sir John?" Elinor inquired. "Some noxious spray emitted by the malefic cnidaria as it murdered poor Marissa?"

"Worse still," he said. And then, shaking his wizened head, repeated it. "Worse still. If I am right—the Fang-Beast . . . the dreaded Devonshire Fang-Beast . . ."

"I am sorry," inquired Elinor, smoothing her skirts. "What did you say?"

"Nothing," responded Sir John. "Nothing at all. Have some punch, dear."

AS THE PARTY WATCHED IN STUNNED HORROR, MISS BELLWETHER WAS
WRAPPED INSIDE THE QUAVERING BLANKET-SHAPE OF THE BEAST
AND CONSUMED.

CHAPTER 12

T HE NEXT MORNING, Elinor and Marianne were walking home from the sad seaside ceremony, at which the remains of Miss Bellwether were gathered in a sachet bag and solemnly tossed into the ocean. Marianne took the occasion to communicate a piece of news to her sister, which surprised Elinor by its extravagant testimony of her sister's imprudence and want of thought. Marianne told her with the greatest delight, that Willoughby had given her a domesticated sea horse—one that he himself had bred all man-hating instincts from, in his own aquatic experimentation tank in Somersetshire, among the few such tanks to be found outside Sub-Marine Station Beta—and which sea horse, with its iridescent multi-hued scaling, was exactly calculated to please a woman's sensibilities. Marianne had accepted the present without hesitation—without considering that it was not her mother's plan to keep any sea horse, and that its maintenance would require an appropriate aquarium, specially-designed exercise equipment, and a well-trained servant to tend it.

"He intends to dispatch his ship's boy into Somersetshire immediately for it," she added, "and when it arrives we will gaze at it and feed it algae every day. You shall share its use with me. Imagine to yourself, my dear Elinor, the delight of watching it describe little circles in its tank."

Most unwilling was she to comprehend all the unhappy truths which attended the affair; and for some time she refused to submit to them. Elinor then ventured to doubt the propriety of her receiving such a present from a man so little, or at least so lately known to her. This was too much.

"You are mistaken, Elinor," said Marianne warmly, "in supposing I know very little of Willoughby. I have not known him long indeed, but

I am much better acquainted with him, than I am with any other creature in the world, except yourself and Mama. It is not time or opportunity that is to determine intimacy; it is disposition alone. Seven years
would be insufficient to make some people acquainted with each other,
and seven days are more than enough for others. I should hold myself
guilty of greater impropriety in accepting a sea horse from my brother,
than from Willoughby. Of John I know very little, though we have lived
together for years; but of Willoughby my judgment was formed the moment when first he hacked off the impossibly strong tentacle that had en-
circled me."

Elinor thought it wisest to touch that point no more. She knew her
sister's temper. Opposition on so tender a subject would only attach her
the more to her own opinion. But by representing the inconveniences
which the tending of the sea horse would represent to their mother,
Marianne was shortly subdued; and she promised not to tempt her
mother to such imprudent kindness by mentioning the offer, and to tell
Willoughby that it must be declined.

She was faithful to her word; and when Willoughby arrived in his
swift, dashing one-man kayak later the same day, Elinor heard her express
her disappointment to him in a low voice, on being obliged to forego
the acceptance of the sea horse; he said, "What about a sea monkey? Or
a starfish?" and she declined those as well. He replied, in the same low
voice, "But, Marianne, the sea horse is still yours, though you cannot use
it now. I shall keep it only till you can claim it. When you leave this desolate cove to form your own establishment in a more lasting home, King
James the Sea Horse shall receive you."

This was all overheard by Elinor, and in the whole of the sentence,
and in his addressing her sister by her Christian name alone, she instantly
saw a meaning so direct as marked a perfect agreement between them.
From that moment she doubted not of their being engaged to each other;
and was surprised that neither she, nor any of their friends, should be told
of the fact directly.

Margaret related something to her the next day, which placed this matter in a still clearer light. Willoughby had spent the preceding evening with them, and Margaret, who had been sitting by herself in a corner of the parlour, sketching a rough map of Pestilent Isle as she now understood its dimensions, had had opportunity for observations, which, with a most important face, she communicated to her eldest sister, when they were next by themselves.

"Oh, Elinor!" she cried, "I have two secrets to tell you. The first relates to Marianne. I am sure she will be married to Mr. Willoughby very soon. For he has got a lock of her hair."

"Take care, Margaret," said Elinor. "It may be only the hair of some great uncle of *his*."

"But, indeed, Elinor, it is Marianne's. I am almost sure it is, for I saw him cut it off. Last night after tea, when you and Mama went out of the room, they were whispering and talking together as fast as could be, and he seemed to be begging something of her, and presently he took up her scissors and cut off a long lock of her hair, for it was all tumbled down her back; and he kissed it, and folded it up in a piece of white paper; and put it into his pocketbook."

For such particulars, stated on such authority, Elinor could not withhold her credit, but to Margaret's *second* secret, though it pressed heavier on the child's breast than the first, Elinor gave no credit at all—some complicated tomfoolery about a system of caves supposedly to be found on the island's southern face, and a tribal race that dwelt therein. . . . Elinor, her mind caught up in Marianne's engagement, chided Margaret for telling tall tales and sent her early and protesting, to bed.

Margaret's sagacity as related to her sisters' affections was not always displayed in a way so satisfactory to Elinor. One evening on Deadwind Island, Mrs. Jennings asked Margaret to supply the name of the young man who was Elinor's particular favourite. Margaret answered by looking at her sister, and saying, "I must not tell, may I, Elinor?"

This of course made everybody laugh; and Elinor tried to laugh too.

But the effort was painful. She was convinced that Margaret had fixed on a person whose name she could not bear to become a standing joke with Mrs. Jennings.

Marianne felt for her most sincerely; but she did more harm than good to the cause, by turning very red and saying in an angry manner to Margaret, "Remember that whatever your conjectures may be, you have no right to repeat them."

"I never had any conjectures about it," replied Margaret; "it was you who told me of it yourself."

This increased the mirth of the company, and Mrs. Jennings pressed the young girl to say something more. "Oh! Pray, Miss Margaret, let us know all about it. I will help you get him, Elinor, by my troth—I know an incantation, which if said at the proper pace on a properly moonlit night, will win any man! Margaret, what is the gentleman's name?"

"Margaret," interrupted Marianne with great warmth, "you know that all this is an invention of your own, and that there is no such person in existence."

"Well, then, he is lately dead, Marianne, for I am sure there was such a man once, and his name begins with an F. But I beg you all to dispense with such trivialities, given the dark truths that lie on this island, just beneath the surface of—"

But the assembled company, led by Mrs. Jennings, had degenerated into further raillery, and no one heard. Most grateful did Elinor feel to Lady Middleton for observing, as the laughter reached its apex, "that the odor of the rainfall is particularly sulfurous today," though she believed this innocuous interruption to proceed less from any attention to her, than from her ladyship's great dislike of all such inelegant subjects of raillery as delighted her husband and mother. The idea however started by her, was immediately pursued by Colonel Brandon, who was on every occasion mindful of the feelings of others; and much was said on the subject of rain, its persistence, and insufferable redolence by both of them. Willoughby took out his ukulele, and asked Marianne to perform a

highland fling; and thus amidst the various endeavours of different people to quit the topic, it fell to the ground. But not so easily did Elinor recover from the alarm into which it had thrown her.

A party was formed this evening for sailing on the following day on
Sir John's old three-master, the *Shell-Cracker*, to the sunken wreck of the
HMS *Mary*, a grand battleship of the English armada that had been sunk
in a fierce fight with a kraken some decades ago, and which sat mouldering
on the sea floor a quarter-mile out from Skull Island, in the farthest
reaches of the archipelago. The deserted ship, with coral and madrepore
growing along its bulwarks, and the salt-corroded skeletons of its crew
still tragically manning their battle stations, was declared to be a thing of
wonder, and Sir John, who was particularly warm in its praise, might be
allowed to be a tolerable judge, for he had formed parties to visit it at
least twice every summer for the last ten years.

Colonel Brandon was designated the co-host of the expedition, for,
as Sir John delicately explained to the Dashwoods, his *condition* allowed
him to breathe underwater, and thus to lead the others of the party, one
by one, in and out of the sunken hull, and swiftly swim them back to the
surface when their lungs were depleted. This feat of sustained immersion,
Sir John noted, was one Brandon did not undertake often, wishing not to
remind his acquaintance of his peculiarity—as if anyone, Mrs. Jennings
added impishly, could long forget it.

Cold provisions were to be taken, along with playing cards, har-
poons, and many yards of mosquito netting; everything conducted in the
usual style of a complete party of pleasure.

To some few of the company it appeared rather a bold undertaking,
considering the time of year, and that it had rained that thick, sulfurous
rain every day for the last fortnight; and Mrs. Dashwood, who had already a cold, was persuaded by Elinor to stay at home.

CHAPTER 13

T HEIR INTENDED EXCURSION to the sunken ship turned out very different from what Elinor had expected. She was prepared to be wet through, fatigued, frightened, and possibly attacked, bitten, or maimed; but the event was still more unfortunate, for they did not go at all.

By ten o'clock the whole party was assembled at Sir John's fortified establishment on Deadwind Island, where they were to breakfast. The morning was rather favourable, though it had rained all night, as the clouds were then dispersing across the sky, and the sun waged valiant battle against the low-hanging fog. They were all in high spirits and good humour, eager to be happy, and determined to submit to the greatest inconveniences and hardships rather than be otherwise.

While they were at breakfast the letters were brought in. Among the rest there was one for Colonel Brandon; he took it, looked at the return address, and changed colour. As they watched him read, his droopy facial appendages appeared to tie themselves into knots of emotion, and then he left the room.

"What is the matter with Brandon?" said Sir John.

Nobody could tell.

"I hope he has had no bad news," said Lady Middleton. "It must be something extraordinary that could make Colonel Brandon leave my breakfast table so suddenly."

In about five minutes, he returned.

"No bad news, Colonel, I hope," said Mrs. Jennings, as soon as he entered the room.

"None at all, ma'am, I thank you. It came from Sub-Marine Station Beta, and is merely a letter of business."

"But how came the hand to discompose you so much, if it was only a letter of business? Come, come, this won't do, Colonel; so let us hear the truth of it."

"My dear madam," said Lady Middleton, "recollect what you are saying."

"Perhaps it is to tell you that your cousin is married?" said Mrs. Jennings, without attending to her daughter's reproof.

"No, indeed, it is not."

"Well, then, I know who it is from, Colonel. And I hope she is well."

"Whom do you mean, ma'am?" said he, his tentacles fluttering wetly with embarrassment.

"Oh! You know who I mean."

"I am particularly sorry, ma'am," said he, addressing Lady Middleton, "that I should receive this letter today, for it is on business which requires my immediate attendance at Sub-Station Beta."

"Nonsense!" cried Mrs. Jennings. "What can you have to do on the Sub-Marine Station at this time of year?"

"My own loss is great," he continued, "in being obliged to leave so agreeable a party; but I am the more concerned, as I fear my presence is necessary to enable your exploration of the sunken battleship."

What a blow upon them all was this!

"We must go," said Sir John. "It shall not be put off when we are so near it. You cannot go to the Station till to-morrow, Brandon, that is all."

"I wish it could be so easily settled. But it is not in my power to delay my journey for one day!"

"Oh, do not allow your tentacles to become twisted! You would not be six hours later," said Willoughby, "if you were to defer your journey till our return." He wore his full diving costume and helmet for the expedition, and had left Monsieur Pierre, who was not a strong swimmer, at home.

"I cannot afford to lose *one* hour."

Willoughby felt the disappointment all the more keenly than the others of the party, as he had heard rumours that a chest of treasure still sat in the captain's cabin of the *Mary*, and it was his firm intention to find and crack it. Elinor heard him say, in a low voice to Marianne, "There are some people who cannot bear a party of pleasure. Brandon is one of them. He was afraid of catching cold, or being mistaken for a mating partner by a she-squid; and he invented this trick for getting out of the trip. I would lay fifty guineas the letter was of his own writing."

"I have no doubt of it," replied Marianne.

"There is no persuading you to change your mind, Brandon, I know of old," said Sir John, "when once you are determined on anything. I can tell your resolution even now, by the way your appendages point towards the door. But, however, I hope you will think better of it.

Colonel Brandon again repeated his sorrow at being the cause of disappointing the party—but at the same time declared it to be unavoidable.

"Well, then, when will you come back again?"

"I hope we shall see you at Deadwind Island," added her ladyship, "as soon as you can conveniently return to us from Sub-Marine Station Beta; and we must put off the party to the shipwreck till you return."

"You are very obliging. But it is so uncertain, when I may have it in my power to return, that I dare not engage for it at all."

"Oh! He must and shall come back," cried Sir John. "If he is not here by the end of the week, I shall go after him."

"Aye, so do, Sir John," cried Mrs. Jennings, "and then perhaps you may find out what his business is."

"I do not want to pry into other men's concerns. I suppose it is something he is ashamed of."

Colonel Brandon's vessel was announced.

"Well, as you are resolved to go, I wish you a good journey," said Sir John. "But you had better change your mind."

"I assure you it is not in my power."

He then took leave of the whole party.

"Is there no chance of my seeing you and your sisters at Sub-Marine Station Beta this winter, Miss Dashwood?"

"I am afraid, none at all. We have no business there or docking station of our own."

"Then I must bid you farewell for a longer time than I should wish to do."

To Marianne, he merely bowed, gave a polite tip of the tentacles, and said nothing. "Come Colonel," said Mrs. Jennings, "before you go, do let us know what you are going about."

He wished her a good morning, and attended by Sir John, left the room.

The complaints and lamentations which politeness had hitherto restrained, now burst forth universally; and they all agreed again and again how provoking it was to be so disappointed. Then Mrs. Jennings animatedly relayed what she suspected to be the reason of Colonel Brandon's hasty departure.

"It is about Miss Williams, I am sure."

"And who is Miss Williams?" asked Marianne.

"What! Do not you know who Miss Williams is? I am sure you must have heard of her before. She is a relation of the colonel's, my dear; a very near relation. We will not say how near, for fear of shocking the young ladies." Mrs. Jennings paused to make a leering, insinuating expression, and then said to Elinor, "She is his natural daughter."

"Indeed!"

"Oh, yes; and as like him as she can stare."

"Like him?" said Marianne. "You mean . . ."

"She's even got the . . ." echoed Elinor, trailing off and making a vague gesture towards her face.

"Oh yes," Sir John confirmed. "I dare say the colonel will leave her all his fortune."

Sir John then changed the subject to the predicament of the cancelled journey, observing that they must do something by way of being happy; and after some consultation it was agreed that they might procure a tolerable composure of mind by embarking on a brief pleasure tour of some of the tiniest specks of land that composed the outer ring of the archipelago. The yachts were then ordered; Willoughby's was first, bearing proudly on its hull his distinctive monogram, a handsome *W* shaped from four treasure-digging shovels; and Marianne never looked happier than when she got into it. They were sailed by its expert crew through the inlet very fast, and they were soon out of sight; and nothing more of them was seen till their return, which did not happen till after the return of all the rest.

Some more came to dinner, and they had the pleasure of sitting down nearly twenty to table, which Sir John observed with great contentment. For this occasion, Lady Middleton took great pleasure in slow-roasting the bile ducts of a whole family of sloths. Willoughby took his usual place between the two elder Miss Dashwoods. Mrs. Jennings sat on Elinor's right hand; and they had not been long seated, before she leant behind her and Willoughby, and said to Marianne, loud enough for them both to hear, "I have found you out in spite of all your tricks. I know where you spent the morning."

Marianne coloured, and replied very hastily, "Where, pray?"

"Did not you know," said Willoughby, "that we had been out touring the islands, like the others of the company?"

"Yes, yes, Mr. Impudence, I know that very well, and I was determined to find out *where* you had been to. I hope you like your house, Miss Marianne. It is a very large one, and well fortified!" She gave a satisfied wink and happily slurped a mouthful of her sloth bile.

Marianne turned away in great confusion. Mrs. Jennings laughed heartily and explained that in her resolution to know where they had been, she had actually made her own woman enquire of Mr. Willoughby's yachtsman; by that method she had been informed that they had gone to the manor belonging to Willoughby's aunt, on Allenham Isle, and spent a considerable time there in admiring the hanging caverns and going all over the house.

Elinor could hardly believe this to be true, as it seemed very un-likely that Willoughby should propose, or Marianne consent, to enter the house while Mrs. Smith was in it, with whom Marianne had not the smallest acquaintance. As soon as they left the dining-room, Elinor en-quired of her about it; and great was her surprise when she found that every circumstance suggested by Mrs. Jennings was perfectly true. Marianne was quite angry with her for doubting it.

"Why should you imagine, Elinor, that we did not go beach Willoughby's yacht there or that we did not see the house? Is not it what you have often wished to do yourself?"

"Yes, Marianne, but I would not go while Mrs. Smith was there, and with no other companion than Mr. Willoughby and his French orangutan."

"Mr. Willoughby is the only person who can show that house. I never spent a pleasanter morning in my life."

"I am afraid," replied Elinor, "that the pleasantness of an employ-ment does not always evince its propriety."

"On the contrary, nothing can be a stronger proof of it. If there had been any real impropriety in what I did, I should have been sensible of it at the time, for we always know when we are acting wrong, and with such a conviction I could have had no pleasure."

"But, my dear Marianne, as it has already exposed you to some very impertinent remarks, do you not now doubt the discretion of your own conduct?"

"If the impertinent remarks of Mrs. Jennings are to be the proof of impropriety in conduct, we are all offending every moment of our lives. I am not sensible of having done anything wrong in seeing Mrs. Smith's house. It will one day be Mr. Willoughby's, and—"

"If it were one day to be your own, Marianne, you would not be justified in what you have done."

Marianne blushed at this hint, and after a ten minutes' interval of earnest thought, she came to her sister again, and said with great good humour, "Perhaps, Elinor, it was rather ill-judged in me to go to Allenham Isle and enter the home there; but Mr. Willoughby wanted particularly to show me the place; and it is a charming house, I assure you. I did not see it to advantage, for nothing could be more forlorn than the furniture, unless it was the moss that clings to the exterior staircases of the manor—but if it were newly fitted up—a couple of hundred pounds, Willoughby says, would make it one of the pleasantest island redoubts off the English coast."

CHAPTER 14

THE SUDDEN AND MYSTERIOUS termination of Colonel Brandon's visit to the archipelago raised the wonder of Mrs. Jennings for two or three days, and she babbled and chattered about it constantly. She was a great wonderer, as everyone must be who takes a lively interest in the comings and goings of all their acquaintance. She wondered, with little intermission, what could be the reason of it; was sure there must be some bad news, and thought over every kind of distress that could have befallen him; and she even acted out her favourites, which were "his grandfather was seized by pirates" and "his prized post-chaise was accidentally driven into a tar pit."

"Whatever the cause, something very melancholy must be the matter, I am sure," was her conclusion. "I could see it in his face."

The rest wondered aloud how Mrs. Jennings could see anything in Colonel Brandon's face, besides a living reproach never to displease a sea witch. But all agreed they would give anything to know the truth of it.

Lady Middleton put an end to the wondering talk by declaring with an air of finality, "Well, I wish him out of all his trouble with all my heart,

and a good wife into the bargain. And"—with a meaningful glance towards her husband—"not one smuggled from her ancestral homeland in
an enormous burlap sack." At this sidelong reproach, Sir John merely
chuckled into his beard.

While Elinor felt interested in the welfare of Colonel Brandon, she
could not bestow so much wonder on his going so suddenly away; she was
more intrigued by the extraordinary silence of her sister and Willoughby
on the subject of their engagement. As this silence continued, every day
made it appear more strange and more incompatible with the disposition
of both. Elinor could not imagine why they should not openly acknowledge to her mother and herself, what their constant behaviour to
each other declared to have taken place.

She could easily conceive that marriage might not be immediately
in their power; for though Willoughby was independent, there was no
reason to believe him rich. His estate had been rated by Sir John at about
six or seven hundred a year; but he lived at an expense to which that income could hardly be equal—between maintaining a small pack of
treasure-seeking dogs, and the care and feeding of his collection of aquatic
exotica. Willoughby lived in the constant anticipation and sure expectation of one day finding a buried treasure that would render him independent, but in the meantime he had himself often complained of his
poverty. But Elinor could not account for this strange kind of secrecy relative to their engagement, which in fact concealed nothing at all; and it
was so wholly contradictory to their general opinions and practice, that
a doubt sometimes entered her mind of their being really engaged.

Nothing could be more expressive of attachment to them all than
Willoughby's behaviour. To Marianne it had all the distinguishing tenderness which a lover's heart could give, and to the rest of the family it
was the affectionate attention of a son and a brother. Their little rickety
shanty perched on the rocks above the cove seemed to be considered and
loved by him as his home; many more of his hours were spent there than
at his aunt's manor on Allenham Isle; and if no general engagement

collected them on Deadwind Island, his morning treasure hunt was al-most certain of ending there. The rest of the day was spent at Marianne's side, with Monsieur Pierre hanging familiarly from her midsection.

Though his attention was most firmly focused on Marianne, Willoughby was genial to Mrs. Dashwood and to Elinor, and he was even teasingly tolerant of young Margaret, how she was always underfoot, wan-dering about the house, muttering darkly about "Them" and "It"—and staring for hours at a time out the southerly window, her eyes locked on the desolate summit of Mount Margaret.

On one occasion did this fascination turn perilous, and Willoughby had his second opportunity of saving a Dashwood from imminent peril. The family was assembled in the second-floor parlour, listening to Mar-ianne play upon the pianoforte, when they heard Margaret screaming from below.

"*K'yaloh D'argesh F'ah!*" she shouted. "*K'yaloh D'argesh F'ah!*"

"What can those words signify?" wondered Elinor.

"And to whom is she screaming?" added Mrs. Dashwood. "There is not a soul on this island but us."

They then heard the front door slam closed; rushing to the front door, Elinor, Willoughby, and Mrs. Dashwood saw Margaret running feverishly down the rain-slicked wooden stairs that connected the cliff-side to the shore. "Mind your step, Margaret!" Mrs. Dashwood shouted.

"I must find them! I must find them!" And then, calling out deliri-ously over the island's echoing hills, "*K'yaloh D'argesh F'ah!*"

Marianne heard all this clamour from without, but did not move from where she had risen from the pianoforte—for, in rising, she had happened to look out the southerly window, and saw it: A column of steam, pouring forth with great force from the hill that sat at the centre of the island. "Elinor . . ." she said in a tremulous whisper. "Elinor?"

But Elinor did not hear—she was at that moment frozen at the top of the stairs, gasping in horror, as Margaret in her delirium lost her footing and pitched head over heels into the bay. In the next moment,

Willoughby shot out the door and plunged into the murky depths. And just in time, for a school of bluefish had instantly surrounded the hysterical Margaret, like pigeons upon a scrap of bread, sinking their knife-edged teeth into her torso and legs, roiling the water with their forked tails in their enthusiasm for this sudden gift of human flesh.

"Don't thrash," Willoughby warned Margaret sternly—and then drew a six-inch cutlass from a pocket of his wet-suit, took a deep breath, and disappeared beneath the surface. As the others watched in stunned silence, bluefish corpses bobbed to the surface one by one in a grim ring around Margaret's head, each one bearing but a single pierce wound, as Willoughby did his quick and deadly work below the surface. And then, in a matter of moments, the man himself resurfaced, a single fish impaled and wriggling on the end of his blade like a prisoner of war. As the elder Dashwoods cheered, he bit off the bluefish's head—before slinging Margaret over his shoulder and swimming her gracefully to shore.

Elinor and Mrs. Dashwood were appropriately appreciative, Marianne all the more so, given her habitual fascination with the Alteration-spawn, coupled with her excitement at seeing Willoughby again spring to the rescue. That evening, Willoughby's heart seemed more than usually open to every feeling of attachment to the objects around him. On Mrs. Dashwood's happening to mention her design of improving the shanty's monster-proofing in the spring, he warmly opposed every alteration of a place which affection had established as perfect with him.

"What!" he exclaimed, his eyes widening shock beneath his jaunty otter-skin cap. "Improve this dear old cottage! No. *That* I will never consent to. Not a plank must be added to its walls, not a single nine-gun to its charming rampart, not another layer of lead lining to its reservoir, if my feelings are regarded."

"Do not be alarmed," said Miss Dashwood, "nothing of the kind will be done, for my mother will never have money enough to attempt it."

"To me this place is faultless," he went on. "I consider it as the only form of building in which happiness is attainable, and were I rich enough

I would instantly pull down my own ancestral home at Combe Magna, in Somersetshire, and build it up again in the exact plan of this charming shanty."

"With dark narrow stairs and a kitchen that smokes, I suppose," said Elinor.

"Yes," cried he in the same eager tone. "With all and every thing belonging to it. Then, and then only, under such a roof, I might perhaps be as happy back home at Combe as I have been at Barton Cottage. This place will always have one claim of my affection, which no other can possibly share."

Mrs. Dashwood looked with pleasure at Marianne, whose fine eyes were fixed so expressively on Willoughby, as plainly denoted how well she understood him. Monsieur Pierre also looked with pleasure on the happy couple, and Elinor thought it possible he winked at her.

"Shall we see you to-morrow to dinner?" said Mrs. Dashwood, when he was leaving them. "It's prawns dipped in butter buckets." He engaged to be with them by four o'clock, and to bring his own bib. Margaret heard nothing of this entire exchange; wrapped in blankets, bandaged at her wounds, she was back at the window, staring grimly into the distance as another thick fog rolled in.

CHAPTER 15

MRS. DASHWOOD WAS ROWED over to Deadwind Island to visit Lady Middleton the next day, and two of her daughters went with her; Margaret, still recovering from her recent traumas, barely spoke on the short journey; Marianne, meanwhile, excused herself from being of the party, under some trifling pretext of employment. Her mother concluded that a promise had been made by Willoughby the night before, of calling on her while they were absent.

On their return they found Willoughby's yacht, with its distinctive shovel-formed *W* at the hull, tied up at the dockside, and Mrs. Dashwood was convinced that her conjecture had been just. But on entering the house she beheld what no foresight had taught her to expect. They were no sooner in the passage than Marianne came hastily out of the parlour apparently in violent affliction, with her handkerchief at her eyes; and without noticing them ran upstairs. Surprised and alarmed they proceeded directly into the room she had just quitted, where they found only Willoughby, in his full diving costume and helmet, leaning against the mantelpiece with his back towards them. He turned round on their coming in, and when he flipped open the portcullis they saw in his countenance the same emotion which overpowered Marianne.

"Is anything the matter?" cried Mrs. Dashwood as she entered. "Is it the octopus?"

"I'll get the fireplace poker!" cried Elinor.

"I hope not," he replied, trying to look cheerful; Elinor, with a small twinge of disappointment, lowered the poker. With a forced smile, Willoughby explained: "It is I who may rather expect to be ill—for I am now suffering under a heavy disappointment!"

"Disappointment?"

"Yes, for I am unable to keep my engagement with you. Mrs. Smith has this morning exercised the privilege of riches upon a poor dependent cousin, by sending me on business to the Sub-Marine Station. I have just received my dispatches, and taken my farewell of Allenham; and I am now come to take my farewell of you."

"To the Station! And are you going this morning?"

"Almost this moment. And I have no idea of returning to the Devonshire coast immediately. My visits to Mrs. Smith are never repeated within the twelvemonth."

"And is Mrs. Smith your only friend? Is Allenham the only isle in the archipelago to which you will be welcome? For shame, Willoughby! Can you wait for an invitation here?"

His colour increased; in embarrassment, he snapped closed his portcullis and lowered his gaze to the ground and replied, "You are too good."

Mrs. Dashwood looked at Elinor with surprise. Elinor felt equal amazement. For a few moments everyone was silent. Mrs. Dashwood first spoke.

"I have only to add, my dear Willoughby, that at Barton Cottage on Pestilent Isle, you will always be welcome."

"My engagements at present," replied Willoughby, his voice emerging tinny and muffled from within the diving helmet, "are of such a nature—that—I dare not flatter myself—"

He stopped. Mrs. Dashwood was too much astonished to speak, and another pause succeeded. This was broken by Willoughby. "It is folly to linger in this manner. I will not torment myself any longer by remaining among friends whose society it is impossible for me now to enjoy."

He then took his leave of them, his flipper feet *fwap fwap fwapping* as he hastened from the room. They saw him step into his yacht; as the yachtsman adjusted the boom and they tacked gently forward, an alligator lifted its long snout from the water and tried to attach his jaws to the hull; the yachtsman whacked the beast once with a bargepole; then again; with the third whack the gator glumly ceded its grip and sank beneath the surface of the water.

Willoughby waved sadly from the foredeck, and was gone.

Mrs. Dashwood felt too much for speech, and instantly quitted the parlour to give way in solitude to her concern and alarm.

Elinor's uneasiness was at least equal to her mother's. She sat in the kitchen plucking the eyeballs from prawns, the ritual action of which calmed her mind and cleared her head. Willoughby's embarrassment and affectation of cheerfulness in taking leave of them, and his unwillingness to accept her mother's invitation—a backwardness so unlike a lover—greatly disturbed her. One moment she feared that no serious design had ever been formed on his side; and the next that some unfortunate quarrel had taken place between him and her sister. But whatever might be the particulars of their separation, her sister's affliction was indubitable; and she thought with the tenderest compassion of that violent sorrow which Marianne was in all probability not merely giving way to as a relief, but feeding and encouraging as a duty. Her hands were now sticky with prawn goo; she washed them thoroughly until only the smallest traces remained stubbornly beneath her nails.

In about half an hour her mother returned, and though her eyes were red, her countenance was not uncheerful.

"Our dear Willoughby is now many nautical miles from Pestilent Isle, Elinor," said she, as she sat down to work, "and with how heavy a heart does he travel!"

"It is all very strange. So suddenly to be gone! It seems but the work of a moment. And last night he was with us so happy, so cheerful, so affectionate? And now, after only ten minutes notice, gone without intending to return! Something must have happened. What can it be? Can they have quarreled? Why else should he have shown such unwillingness to accept your invitation here?"

"It was not inclination that he wanted, Elinor; I could plainly see *that*. He had not the power of accepting it. I have thought it over, and I can account for everything that first seemed strange to me as well as to you."

"Can you, indeed!"

"Yes. I have explained it to myself in the most satisfactory way—but you, Elinor, who love to doubt where you can—it will not satisfy *you*, I know; but you shall not talk *me* out of my trust in it. I am persuaded that Mrs. Smith suspects his regard for Marianne, disapproves of it, and on that account is eager to get him away. Or, alternatively, he has in his quest for treasure disturbed the burial site of a pirate captain, and incurred the wrath of the pirate captain's ghost, who has thusly cursed him to wander the seven seas until fate should claim him. It's one of those two."

"But, mother—"

"You will tell me, I know, that this may or may *not* have happened;

but I will listen to no cavil, unless you can point out any other method of understanding the affair as satisfactory as one of the two options I have presented. And now, Elinor, what have you to say?"

"Nothing, for you have anticipated my answer. I cannot presume to know Mrs. Smith's motives; and as for pirate curses, my education and understanding leads me to cast a wary eye on such superstitions, as I would hope would be the same for you."

"Oh, Elinor, how incomprehensible are your feelings! You had rather take evil upon credit than good. You had rather look out for misery for Marianne, and guilt for poor Willoughby, than an apology for the latter. You are resolved to think him blamable, because he took leave of us with less affection than his usual behaviour has shown. You refuse to imagine that he has labours under the jealousy of a relative, or the Sisyphean curse of a pirate-ghost! And is no allowance to be made for inadvertence, or for spirits depressed by recent disappointment? Is nothing due to the man whom we have all such reason to love, and no reason in the world to think ill of? After all, what is it you suspect him of?"

"I can hardly tell myself. But suspicion of something unpleasant is the inevitable consequence of such an alteration as we just witnessed in him. There is great truth, however, in the allowances for him you have urged, and it is my wish to be candid in my judgment of everybody. Willoughby may undoubtedly have very sufficient reasons for his conduct, or it may be there really is such a thing as a pirate-ghost, and I will hope that he has, or there is. But it would have been more like Willoughby to acknowledge them at once. Secrecy may be advisable; but still I cannot help wondering at its being practiced by him."

"Ah," said Mrs. Dashwood, handing Elinor a file with which to remove the prawn residue clinging 'neath her nails. "I am happy—and he is acquitted."

"Not entirely. It may be proper to conceal their engagement (if they *are* engaged) from Mrs. Smith—and if that is the case, it must be highly expedient for Willoughby to be but little among us on these islands at present. But this is no excuse for their concealing it from us."

"Concealing it from us! My dear child, do you accuse Willoughby and Marianne of concealment? This is strange indeed, when your eyes have been reproaching them every day for incautiousness."

"I lack no proof of their affection," said Elinor; "but of their engagement I do."

"I am perfectly satisfied of both."

"Yet not a syllable has been said to you on the subject, by either of them."

"I have not wanted syllables where actions have spoken so plainly. Has not his behaviour to Marianne and to all of us, for at least the last fortnight, declared that he loved and considered her as his future wife? Have we not perfectly understood each other? Has not my consent been daily asked by his looks, his manner, his attentive and affectionate respect? My Elinor, is it possible to doubt their engagement?"

"I confess," replied Elinor, "that every circumstance except *one* is in favour of their engagement; but that *one* is the total silence of both on the subject, and with me it almost outweighs every other."

"How strange this is! You must think wretchedly indeed of Willoughby! Has he been acting a part in his behaviour to your sister all this time? And what is that five-pointed shape you are tracing in prawn guts on the table linen? "

"Oh! It is merely a—a sort of—a shape that has—that keeps occurring to me somehow."

"How odd. Well, do you suppose Willoughby really indifferent to her?"

"You must remember, my dear mother, that I have never considered this matter as certain. I have had my doubts, I confess; but they are fainter than they were, and they may soon be entirely done away. If we find they write to one another, every fear of mine will be removed."

"A mighty concession indeed! But what if the iron sides of the correspondence ship are pierced and sunk by the tusks of some demonic walrus, as you know happens with distressing frequency! I require no such proof. Nothing in my opinion has ever passed to justify doubt; no secrecy has been attempted; all has been uniformly open and unreserved. You cannot doubt your sister's wishes. It must be Willoughby therefore whom you suspect. But why? Is he not a man of honour and feeling? Has there been any inconsistency on his side to create alarm? Can he be deceitful?"

"I hope not, I believe not," cried Elinor, her finger now obsessively tracing the five-pointed star pattern, independent of her control. "I sincerely love Willoughby; and suspicion of his integrity cannot be more painful to yourself than to me. I confess I was startled by his manners this morning. He did not speak like himself, and did not return your kindness with any cordiality. But all this may be explained by such a situation of his affairs as you have supposed: either 'twas Mrs. Smith's displeasure, or a pirate captain's vengeful incarnation, that drove him hence."

"You speak very properly. Willoughby certainly does not deserve to be suspected. He has saved Marianne from the giant octopus, and Margaret from the toothsome bluefish! Though *we* have not known him long, he is no stranger in this part of the world; and who has ever spoken to his disadvantage?"

They saw nothing of Marianne till dinner-time, when she entered the room and took her place at the table without saying a word. The butter buckets were warmed, the prawns were served in their prawn-boats, but the conversation was strained. Margaret was lost in her own contemplations; Marianne's eyes were red and swollen, and it seemed as if her tears were even then restrained with difficulty. She avoided the looks of them all, could neither eat nor speak, and after some time, on her mother's silently pressing her hand with tender compassion, she burst into tears, tore off her butter-bib, and fled the room.

CHAPTER 16

MARIANNE WOULD HAVE THOUGHT herself very inexcusable had she been able to sleep the first night after Willoughby's departure for Sub-Marine Station Beta. She would have been ashamed to look her family in the face the next morning, had she not risen from her bed in more need of repose than when she lay down in it. She was awake the whole night, and she wept the greatest part of it. She got up with a headache, was unable to talk, and unwilling to take even a spoonful of the light breakfast of cold bass-belly soup that Mrs. Dashwood had prepared. Her sensibility was potent enough!

When breakfast was over she walked out by herself, and wandered in hip-high galoshes through the miry bottomlands to the cottage's southeast, machete idly chopping at the tangled marsh reeds, indulging the recollection of past enjoyment and crying over the present reverse.

The evening passed off in the equal indulgence of feeling. She played over every favourite shanty that she had used to play to Willoughby, every air in which their voices had been oftenest joined, and sat at the instrument gazing on every line of music that he had written out for her. She spent whole hours at the pianoforte alternately singing and crying; her voice often totally suspended by her tears. She read nothing but what they had been used to read together, paging for hours on end through the dog-eared tales of deserted islands, revisiting the madness, wolf attacks, and cannibalism which had been the amusement of their idle hours together.

Such violence of affliction indeed could not be supported for ever; like a tide loses force with the waning moon, it sunk within a few days into a calmer melancholy; but her solitary walks and silent meditations still produced occasional effusions of sorrow as lively as ever.

No letter from Willoughby came; and none seemed expected by Marianne. Her mother was surprised, and Elinor again became uneasy. But Mrs. Dashwood could find explanations whenever she wanted them.

"Remember, Elinor," said she, "how Sir John often rows out to the post-ship by dinghy, and carries our letters back from it. We have already agreed that secrecy may be necessary, and we must acknowledge that it could not be maintained if their correspondence were to pass through Sir John's hands."

Elinor could not deny the truth of this, and she tried to find in it a motive sufficient for their silence. But there was one method so direct, so simple, and in her opinion so eligible of knowing the real state of the affair, and of instantly removing all mystery, that she could not help suggesting it to her mother.

"Why do you not ask Marianne," said she, "whether or not she is engaged to Willoughby? From you, her kind and indulgent mother, the question could not give offence."

"I would not ask such a question for the world. Supposing it possible that they are not engaged, what distress would such an enquiry inflict! It would be most ungenerous. I would not attempt to force the confidence of anyone, and of my child much less." Elinor thought this generosity overstrained, considering her sister's youth, and urged the matter further, but in vain; common sense, common care, common prudence, were all sunk like capsized frigates in the ocean of Mrs. Dashwood's romantic delicacy.

One morning, about a week after his leaving the country, Marianne was prevailed on to join her sisters in their usual walk, instead of wandering away by herself. Hitherto she had carefully avoided every companion in her rambles. When Elinor intended to tromp through the quaggy mudflats, she directly stole away towards the beaches; Margaret pleaded for her aid in exploring the island's southern, cave-pocked face, to discover the truth about the creatures she still swore resided therein, or again ascending Mt. Margaret—but Marianne had chased the memory of the column of curious steam from her mind, too subsumed in her own melancholy contemplations to partake in Margaret's mounting anxieties. But at length she was secured for a walk by the exertions of Elinor, who greatly disapproved such continual seclusion.

They walked along the bramble-strewn path that followed the rushing brook—the very same brook into which Marianne had once tumbled, precipitating her first encounter with the lamented Willoughby. Their journey was undertaken in silence, for Marianne's *mind* could not be controlled, and Elinor, satisfied with gaining one point, would not then attempt more. A long stretch of the road lay before them; and on reaching that point, they stopped to look around them.

Amongst the objects in the scene, they soon discovered an animated one; it was a man riding upstream on the back of a porpoise, a mode of transportation exceedingly rare outside the cosmopolitan districts of Sub-Marine Station Beta. Travelling upon a domesticated sea-beast for a mount marked him certain as a gentleman; and in a moment afterwards Marianne rapturously exclaimed, "It is he! It is indeed! I know it is!" and hastened to meet him.

Elinor cried out, "Indeed, Marianne, I think you are mistaken. It is not Willoughby. The person is not tall enough for him, and has not his air. And look, too, how he rides unsteady on the back of the porpoise—surely Willoughby would have a surer hand at the fish-rein."

"He has, he has," cried Marianne, "I am sure he has. His air, his coat, his horse, his otter-skin cap. I knew how soon he would come."

She walked eagerly on as she spoke, and Elinor quickened her pace to keep up with her. They were soon within thirty yards of the gentleman. Marianne looked again; her heart sunk within her; and abruptly turning round, she was hurrying back when a voice called out, begging her to stop. She turned round with surprise to see and welcome Edward Ferrars.

He was the only person in the world who could at that moment be forgiven for not being Willoughby; the only one who could have gained a smile from her; but she dispersed her tears to smile on *him*, and in her sister's happiness forgot for a time her own disappointment.

He called an uneasy "Whoa!" to the porpoise, slipped carefully from its back onto the shore, and watched as it swam rapidly back towards the inlet. Edward greeted the girls warmly, and together they walked back to the house on Barton Cove.

He was welcomed by them all with great cordiality, but especially by Marianne, who showed more warmth of regard in her reception of him than even Elinor herself. To Marianne, indeed, the meeting between Edward and her sister was but a continuation of that unaccountable coldness which she had often observed at Norland in their mutual behaviour. On Edward's side she found a deficiency of all that a lover ought to look and say on such an occasion. He was confused, seemed scarcely sensible of pleasure in seeing them, looked neither rapturous nor gay, said little but what was forced from him by questions—"Was your ship beset by the sea-fiends on its way in?" "Indeed"; "Where any crewmen killed?" "Some"—and distinguished Elinor by no mark of affection. Marianne saw and listened with increasing surprise. She began almost to feel a dislike of Edward; and it ended by carrying back her thoughts to Willoughby, whose manners formed a striking contrast.

After a short silence, Marianne asked Edward about their old estate. "How does dear, dear Norland look?"

"Dear, dear Norland," said Elinor, "probably looks much as it always does at this time of the year. The woods covered with dead leaves, the beaches strewn with matted heaps of dried seaweed."

"Oh," cried Marianne, "with what transporting sensation have I formerly seen them wash up on the shore in their brackish clumps! How have I delighted, as I walked, to see them surround my feet, pulled playfully about by the undertow! Now there is no one to regard them. They are seen only as a nuisance, swept hastily off, and driven as much as possible from the sight."

"It is not every one," said Elinor, "who has your passion for sargassum."

"No; my feelings are not often shared, not often understood. But *sometimes* they are." As she said this, she sunk into a reverie for a few moments.

"Have you an agreeable habitation here?" Edward inquired. "Are the Middletons pleasant people?"

"No, not at all," answered Marianne. "We could not be more unfortunately situated."

"Marianne," cried her sister, "how can you say so? How can you be so unjust? They are a very respectable family, Mr. Ferrars, and towards us have behaved in the friendliest manner. Have you forgot, Marianne, how many pleasant days we have owed to them?"

"No," said Marianne, in a low voice, "nor how many painful moments."

Elinor took no notice of this; and directing her attention to their visitor, endeavoured to support something like discourse with him, by talking of their present residence, its conveniences, and Sir John's ingenious and ancient methods for guarding the shores, notwithstanding the more-than-man-sized jellyfish that had invaded the dance at the beach. These tales extorted from Edward only the occasional questions and remarks. His coldness and reserve mortified her severely: she was vexed and half angry; but resolving to regulate her behaviour to him by the past rather than the present, she avoided every appearance of resentment or displeasure, and treated him as she thought he ought to be treated from the family connection.

CHAPTER 17

MRS. DASHWOOD WAS SURPRISED only for a moment at seeing Edward. He received the kindest welcome from her; and shyness, coldness, reserve could not stand against such a reception.

They had begun to fail him before he entered the house, and they were quite overcome by the captivating manners of Mrs. Dashwood. Indeed a man could not very well be in love with either of her daughters, without extending the passion to her; and Elinor had the satisfaction of seeing him soon become more like himself. More than likely, she reflected, he was still recovering from sea-sickness, after a long and uneasy journey by water from Sussex; indeed, she thought she detected flecks of vomit on the collar of his tailcoat.

Now his affections seemed to reanimate towards them all, and his interest in their welfare again became perceptible. And yet, though he was attentive and kind, still he was not in spirits. The whole family perceived it, and Mrs. Dashwood, attributing it to some want of liberality in his mother, sat at the dinner table indignant against all selfish parents.

"What are Mrs. Ferrars's views for you at present, Edward?" said she, when dinner was over and they had drawn round the fire; the night was queerly cold, and the fog seemed to gather around the very windows of their shanty, and seep in under the door. "Are you still to be a great politician, in spite of yourself?"

"No. I hope my mother is now convinced that I have no more talents than inclination for a public life!"

"But how is your fame to be established? For famous you must be to satisfy all your family; and with no inclination for expense, no affection for strangers, no profession, and no assurance, you may find it a difficult matter."

"I shall not attempt it. I have no wish to be distinguished; and have every reason to hope I never shall. Thank Heaven!"

"You have no ambition, I well know. Your wishes are all moderate."

"As moderate as those of the rest of the world. I wish as well as everybody else to be perfectly happy; but, like everybody else it must be in my own way. Greatness will not make me so."

"Strange that it would!" cried Marianne. "What have wealth or grandeur to do with happiness?"

"Grandeur has but little," said Elinor, "but wealth has much to do with it."

"Elinor, for shame!" said Marianne. "Money can only give happiness where there is nothing else to give it. Beyond a competence, it can afford no real satisfaction, as far as mere self is concerned."

"Perhaps," said Elinor, pulling another blanket on top of the two in which she was already wrapped, "we may come to the same point. *Your* competence and *my* wealth are very much alike, I dare say; without them, every kind of external comfort must be wanting. Your ideas are only more noble than mine. Come, what is your competence?"

"About eighteen hundred or two thousand a year; not more than *that.*"

Elinor laughed. "*Two* thousand a year! *One* thousand I call wealth! I guessed how it would end."

"And yet two thousand a year is a very moderate income," said Marianne. "A family cannot well be maintained on a smaller. A proper establishment of torchmen, a canoe or two, and treasure dogs, cannot be supported on less. Lead bars on all seaward windows cost at least five hundred alone. I am sure I am not extravagant in my demands."

Elinor smiled again, to hear her sister describing so accurately their future expenses at Combe Magna.

"Treasure dogs!" repeated Edward. "But why must you have treasure dogs? Everybody does not treasure hunt."

Marianne coloured as she replied, "But most people do."

"I wish," said Margaret, turning for the first time in many hours from where she sat staring out the fog-crowded southerly window and the mysterious prospect without. "That somebody would give us all a large fortune a-piece."

"Oh that they would!" cried Marianne, her cheeks glowing at the delight of such imaginary happiness.

"I wish also," Margaret added in a quiet and trembling voice, though the conversation had already moved forward. "That we were far, far from this queer and terrifying place, and that its secrets, whatever they may be, would remain buried here forever."

"We are all unanimous in the wish for fortune, I suppose," said Elinor, "in spite of the insufficiency of wealth. Only I wonder what one would do with it!"

Marianne looked as if she had no doubt on that point.

"What magnificent orders would travel from this family to London," said Edward, "in such an event! What a happy day for booksellers, music-sellers, and driftwood collectors! You, Miss Dashwood, would give a general commission for every new chunk of wood to be sent you, so you might whittle them with your singular expertise—and as for Marianne, I know her greatness of soul, there would not be music enough in London to content her. And books!—*The Encyclopedia of Accidental Drownings, The True Account of Roger Smithson's Journey through the Bowel of a Whale*—she would buy them all: She would buy up every copy, I believe, to prevent their falling into unworthy hands! Should not you, Marianne? Forgive me, if I am very saucy. I think this beverage is rather potent."

"It comes to us from Sir John," noted Mrs. Dashwood. "I would not recommend more than one cup."

Turning again to Marianne, Edward concluded, "I was willing to show you that I had not forgot our old disputes."

"I love to be reminded of the past, Edward—whether it be melancholy or gay, I love to recall it—and you will never offend me by talking of former times. You are very right in supposing how my money would be spent—some of it, at least. My loose cash would certainly be employed in filling my shelves with disaster journals."

"And the bulk of your fortune, perhaps, would be bestowed as a reward on that person who wrote the ablest defense of your favourite maxim—that no one can ever be in love more than once in their life. Your opinion on that point is unchanged, I presume?"

"Undoubtedly. At my time of life opinions are tolerably fixed. It is not likely that I should now see or hear anything to change them."

"Marianne is as steadfast as ever, you see," said Elinor, sipping slowly at her own cup of the strong rum puncheon. "She is not at all different."

"She is only grown a little more grave than she was."

"Nay, Edward," said Marianne, "you need not reproach me. You are not very gay yourself."

"Why should you think so!" replied he, with a sigh. "But gaiety never was a part of *my* character."

"Nor do I think it a part of Marianne's," said Elinor; "I should hardly call her a lively girl—she is very earnest, very eager in all she does—sometimes talks a great deal and always with animation—but she is not often really merry."

"I believe you are right," he replied, "and yet I have always set her down as a lively girl."

"I have frequently detected myself in such kind of mistakes," said Elinor. "Sometimes one is guided by what they say of themselves, and very frequently by what other people say of them, without giving oneself time to deliberate and judge. Like flying fish, you know, don't really fly; they merely leap extremely high."

"Excellent point," agreed Mrs. Dashwood.

"But I thought it was right, Elinor," said Marianne, "to be guided wholly by the opinion of other people."

"No, Marianne. My doctrine has never aimed at the subjection of the understanding. All I have ever attempted to influence has been the behaviour. You must not confound my meaning. I have often wished you to treat people with greater attention; but when have I advised you to conform to their judgment in serious matters?"

"You have not been able to bring your sister over to your plan of general civility," said Edward to Elinor. "Do you gain no ground?"

"Quite the contrary," replied Elinor, looking expressively at Marianne.

"My judgment," he returned, "is all on your side of the question; but I am afraid my practice is much more on your sister's. I never wish to offend, but my shyness often seems to others as negligence, when I am only kept back by my natural awkwardness. I have frequently thought that I must have been intended by nature to be fond of low company, I am so little at my ease among strangers of gentility!"

"Marianne has no shyness to excuse her inattention," said Elinor. "Excuse me—"

Elinor, though engaged in the direction of conversation, and eager to make herself understood, was distracted by a mysterious darkness at the corners of her vision.

"She knows her own worth too well for false shame," replied Edward. "Shyness is only the effect of a sense of inferiority in some way or other; or sometimes the result of a tapeworm causing such discomfort that proper attention to others becomes impossible. If I could persuade myself that my manners were perfectly easy and graceful, I should not be shy."

"But you would still be reserved," said Marianne, "and that is worse."

Elinor, while this conversation proceeded, rubbed at her eyes in an effort to dispel the darkness that clouded her sight. The room heaved, as if she were aboard a ship; her legs trembled; the conversation of the others dimmed into a dull background hum. Dark pinpoints of light now appeared in the swimming blackness and formed into a constellation: It was the same pattern again, the exact five-pointed star that had haunted her since their arrival at the island.

"Reserved!" Edward responded meanwhile. "Am I reserved, Marianne?"

"Yes, very."

"I do not understand you," replied he. "Reserved! How? In what manner?"

Elinor blinked as her proper vision suddenly restored itself, and she was flooded with relief—though for that the night still felt intolerably cold, and the fog that huddled around the bay windows of an ominous thickness. She drew her blankets up around her, and, trying to laugh off the clammy and damp fear that clutched at her, said to Edward, "Do not you know my sister well enough to understand what she means? She calls every one reserved who does not talk as fast, and admire what she admires as rapturously as herself!"

Edward made no answer. His gravity and thoughtfulness returned on him in their fullest extent—and he sat for some time silent and dull. Elinor shivered and wished for the night to end, and the sun to rise.

CHAPTER 18

ELINOR SAW WITH GREAT UNEASINESS the low spirits of her friend. Edward's visit afforded her but a very partial satisfaction, because his own enjoyment in it appeared so imperfect. The only thing that seemed to raise his spirits was a visit to Deadwind Island, where strolling the seashore she showed him the spot where Miss Bellwether had met her grisly doom in the stomach of the beast. Still, his unhappiness was evident; she wished it were equally evident that he still felt the same affection for her which once she had felt no doubt of inspiring, but his preference seemed very uncertain.

Edward joined her and Marianne in the kitchen the next morning before the others were down to aid in their stirring of the gigantic pot of stew, thickened with shark cartilage, which would serve as that day's breakfast, and the next day's, and the next's; and Marianne, who was always eager to promote their happiness as far as she could, soon left them to themselves, which was considerate on the one hand, but most inconvenient as stirring cartilage stew properly is, as is well known, an effort requiring three people at the very least. And before Marianne was half way upstairs she heard the kitchen door open, and, turning round, was astonished to see Edward himself come out.

"As you are not yet ready for breakfast; I will go for a walk and be back again presently." And from the kitchen Marianne heard the unmistakable grunts of exertion, as her sister thickened the stew alone.

*   *   *

Edward returned to them with fresh admiration of the surrounding country, and a note of caution.

"As I paused on a charming table of land to admire the prospect, about a mile southwesterly from the cottage, and in the shadow of that craggy hill in the island's centre, I noticed with concern that the ground had become rather less steady than one might wish a patch of ground to be. In the moment it took me to understand that this was not a charming expanse of ground, but a pit of quicksand, my feet and ankles were already well immersed in the shifting terrain. With disorienting rapidity I found myself submerged, to the knees, and then to the waist, and then to the very torso."

"Oh dear!" interjected Elinor.

"I found, moreover, that the more I struggled to free myself from its deadly embrace, the more the sands drew tighter around me. It was only as the suffocating sands rose to my neck, and threatened soon to cover my mouth and nose, and thusly steal my life, that I noticed a vine dangling just overhead; it is fortuitous, indeed, for whatever my life may be worth, that I had thought to raise my hands above my head before the sand covered my midsection, and could grasp the dangling limb and laboriously tug myself to freedom."

"Fortuitous indeed," Elinor agreed. "We are mightily grateful for your survival."

"While I appreciate the sentiment, I mention the incident not to earn your compliments, but only to explain why I am wearing this tattered sail instead of pants; mine were thoroughly soiled by the muddy quicksand, and so I discarded them rather than sully your parlour."

The subject ensured Marianne's attention, though it was Edward's passing mention of the admirable prospect, more so than the deadly ground which had nearly consumed him, that she found of greater interest, and she pressed him for more detail.

"You must not enquire too far, Marianne—remember I have no knowledge in the picturesque, and I shall offend you by my ignorance and want of taste if we come to particulars. And it was impossible to pay the appropriate attention to the peculiar beauty of the surroundings, so concerned was I with keeping my mouth above the point where oxygen would no longer be accessible to me. You must be satisfied with such admiration as I can honestly give. I call this a very fine island—the hills are steep, what trees one finds are full of shrieking, unfamiliar birds; the small caverns lined with handsome bats that hang like so many black, red-eyed stalactites; and none of the frogs I encountered bore claws nor attempted to leap at my throat. No—in fact—one did. Only the one, though. The island exactly answers my idea of a fine place, because it unites strange beauty with utility—I can easily believe it to be full of rocks and promontories, grey moss and brush wood, but these are all lost on me. I know nothing of the picturesque."

"I am afraid it is but too true," said Marianne; "but why should you boast of it?"

"I suspect," said Elinor, "that to avoid one kind of affectation, Edward here falls into another. Because he believes many people pretend to more admiration of the beauties of nature than they really feel, he affects greater indifference in viewing them himself than he possesses. He is fastidious and will have an affectation of his own."

"It is very true," said Marianne, "that admiration of landscape scenery is become a mere jargon. I detest jargon of every kind, except for sailor's argot and pirate slang. I have kept my feelings to myself when I could find no fresh language to describe them.

The subject was continued no further; and Marianne remained thoughtfully silent until a new object suddenly engaged her attention. She was sitting by Edward, and in taking his tea from Mrs. Dashwood, he unknowingly revealed a decorative compass, with a plait of hair in the centre, hanging from a watch chain on the inside of his tailcoat.

"I never saw you wear a compass before, Edward," she cried. "Is that Fanny's hair?"

When Marianne saw how much she had pained Edward, she was vexed at her want of thought. He coloured very deeply, and giving a momentary glance at Elinor, replied, "Yes, it is my sister's hair. The glass of the compass-case always casts a different shade on it, you know."

Elinor had met his eye, and felt vexed as well. That the hair was her own, she instantaneously felt as well satisfied as Marianne; what Marianne considered as a free gift from her sister, Elinor was conscious must have been procured by some theft or contrivance unknown to herself.

Edward's embarrassment lasted some time, and it ended in an absence of mind still more settled. He was particularly grave the whole morning; he had only one bite of shark cartilage stew. Before the middle of the day, they were visited by Sir John and Mrs. Jennings, who, having heard of the arrival of a gentleman at the cottage, came to take a survey of the guest. With the assistance of his mother-in-law, Sir John was not long in discovering that the name of Ferrars began with an *F*, and this prepared a future mine of raillery against the devoted Elinor. But the mirth was rapidly dispelled when Sir John recalled the weathered old Tahitian fortune-teller who long ago had warned him of an intruder bearing that initial, who would appear at first to be a friend, and then murder him in his sleep. Sir John, with a celerity belying his advanced age, leapt upon Edward, yanked up his shirtfront, and drew his scaling knife to disembowel his adversary. But then Mrs. Jenkins fortuitously recalled that the murderous stranger would have the *F* beginning his *Christian* name, not his surname, and so the incident was ended satisfactorily. Apologies and laughter naturally followed, and Mrs. Dashwood brought out more punch for all.

Sir John never came to the Dashwoods without either inviting them to dine at Deadwind Island the next day, or to come by for a talismanic salamander bloodletting ceremony that evening. On the present occasion, for the better entertainment of their visitor, he wished to engage them for both.

"You *must* drink salamander blood with us tonight," said he, "for we shall be quite alone—and to-morrow you must absolutely dine with us, for we shall be a large party."

Mrs. Jennings enforced the necessity. "And who knows but you may raise a dance," said she. "And that will tempt *you*, Miss Marianne."

"A dance!" cried Marianne. "Impossible! Who is to dance?"

"Who! Why yourselves, and the Careys, and Whitakers to be sure. What! You thought nobody could dance because a certain person that shall be nameless is gone!"

"I wish with all my soul," cried Sir John, "that Willoughby were among us again."

This, and Marianne's blushing, gave new suspicions to Edward. "And who is Willoughby?" said he, in a low voice, to Miss Dashwood, by whom he was sitting.

She gave him a brief reply. Marianne's countenance was more communicative. Edward saw enough to comprehend, not only the meaning of others, but such of Marianne's expressions as had puzzled him before; and when their visitors left them, he went immediately round her, and said, in a whisper, "I have been guessing. Shall I tell you my guess?"

"What do you mean?"

"Shall I tell you?"

"Certainly."

"Well then; I guess that Mr. Willoughby is a treasure hunter."

Marianne was surprised and confused, yet she could not help smiling at the quiet archness of his manner, and after a moment's silence, said, "Oh, Edward! I am sure you will like him."

"I do not doubt it," replied he.

CHAPTER 19

EDWARD REMAINED ONLY A WEEK at the rickety shanty perched high above Barton Cove; as if he were bent only on self-mortification, he seemed resolved to be gone when his enjoyment among his friends was at the height. His spirits, during the last two or three days, were greatly improved—he grew more and more partial to the house and environs—never spoke of going away without a sigh—declared his time to be wholly disengaged—spoke of his fear of climbing back aboard a sailing ship and trusting his fate to the tides—but still, go he must. Never had any week passed so quickly—he could hardly believe it to be gone. He said so repeatedly; other things he said too, which marked the turn of his feelings and gave the lie to his actions. He had no pleasure at Norland; he detested being in-Station; but either to Norland or Sub-Marine Station Beta, he must go. He valued their kindness beyond anything, and his greatest happiness was in being with them. Yet, he must leave them at the end of a week, in spite of their wishes and his own, and without any restraint on his time.

Elinor placed all that was astonishing in this way of acting to his mother's account; she rejected all suggestion from her mother that a pirate-ghost was again responsible for the ambiguities in their guest's behaviour. His want of spirits, openness, and consistency, were attributed to his want of independence, and his better knowledge of Mrs. Ferrars's disposition and designs. The shortness of his visit, the steadiness of his purpose in leaving them, originated in the same fettered inclination, the same inevitable necessity of temporizing with his mother. The old well-established grievance of duty against will, parent against child, was the cause of all.

"I think, Edward," said Mrs. Dashwood, as they stood upon the rick-ety dock the last morning, where she, desirous of an opportunity for in-timate conversation, had enticed him to join her in her habitual morning quarter-hour of spear fishing. "You would be a happier man if you had any profession to engage your time. Some inconvenience to your friends might result from it—you would not be able to give them so much of your time. But you would know where to go when you left them."

"I do assure you," he replied, heaving his pike into the water and—since it was attached to his wrist by a long length of cable—bracing him-self so he was not tugged in after it, "that I have long thought on this point, as you think now. It has been, and probably will always be a heavy misfortune to me, that I have no necessary business to engage me or af-ford me anything like independence. But unfortunately my own nicety, and the nicety of my friends, have made me what I am: an idle, helpless being; isolated with my scholarly tomes and my theory of the Alteration. We never could agree in our choice of a profession. I always imagined myself a lighthouse keeper, as I still do. A quiet room atop an observation post, shining my beacon light when required, otherwise satisfied in the company of my books and my thoughts. But that was not smart enough for my family." With a sigh he reeled back in his spear with no pierced specimen caught upon it, and a wry chuckle escaped him. "I suppose we may add fish-slayer to the list of professions to which I am unsuited."

"Come, come; this is all an effusion of immediate want of spirits, Edward. You are in a melancholy humour, and fancy that anyone unlike yourself must be happy. Oof!" With a grunt, Mrs. Dashwood retrieved her own pike, upon which was impaled a perfect specimen of tuna. "But remember that the pain of parting from friends will be felt by everybody at times, whatever be their education or state. Know your own happi-ness. You want nothing but patience. Your mother will secure to you, in time, that independence you are so anxious for. How much may not a few months do?"

"I think," replied Edward, "that I may defy many months to produce any good to me." He tossed his spear idly from hand to hand, as if considering whether to plunge it into his breast rather than back into the blue-black depths where it could not hope to find its target.

But before any such drastic measure could be undertaken, a tuna the size of a man slammed its broadside against the leg of the dock. The waterlogged wood gave way with a muffled splintering *crack*, plunging both Mrs. Dashwood and Edward into the churning water.

Gasping, Edward gallantly sought to interpose himself between his hostess and the six-foot-long, broad-flanked tuna, but to no avail; it nosed Edward aside with a mighty shove, and bore down on Mrs. Dashwood, who was finding it hard to stay afloat in her empire dress and girdle. Apart from its sheer girth, their foe bore an unmistakable glimmer in its eyes, impossible to mistake for mere fish-hunger—Mrs. Dashwood had murdered his companion, and this tuna was intent upon revenge. Edward sought to grapple with the rear quarters of the great fish but its tail slipped from his grasp, whilst it opened his massive wet maw around Mrs. Dashwood's head, hoping, it seemed, to dispense with biting and swallow her whole.

Mrs. Dashwood, not ready to join her husband in Heaven, nor in the stomach of an ocean-dwelling monstrosity, managed to recover from her décolletage a long sewing needle, razor sharp, which she had secreted there after sewing a replacement stitch in Marianne's party gown that morning. Just as the tuna's sickening mouth was about to close around her forehead, she withdrew the needle and drove it into the palate of the beast.

With surprise and indignation the tuna thrashed, trying to untwist itself from the sewing needle, while Mrs. Dashwood let go and doggy-paddled her way towards the dock-pillar that remained standing. Edward, seeing his chance to aid in the overcoming of their attacker, took a deep breath and swam *under* the body of the beast; emerging suddenly above the water line directly in front of it. In a paroxysm of fury and pain from the sewing needle impaled in its mouth, the tuna now drove its giant

EDWARD SOUGHT TO GRAPPLE WITH THE REAR QUARTERS OF THE GREAT FISH
WHILST IT OPENED ITS MASSIVE WET MAW AROUND MRS. DASHWOOD'S HEAD.

head crashing into Edward's chest, knocking him backwards and sending the breath sputtering from his body. Disappearing beneath the surface, his mouth filling with salty water, Edward was suddenly faced with the prospect that his melancholy, death-embracing spirits might find their consummation sooner than he had wished.

As Edward sank, the tuna slammed the broad side of its long, flat head against his skull; he spun in the water, noting with the numb, half-seeing eyes of a drowning man where the piles were submerged in the sea floor. The fish battered away at him, intent (or so it seemed) on beating him to death before consuming him. Edward thought of Elinor. He had no hope left, no means of counter-attack—no weapon but his own hands.

With a burst of vigor, Edward kicked his feet and sent himself hurtling upwards at the tuna; he knew from his conversations with the wise Elinor that there was but one perfect place to assault a sea-breathing creature from below: the gills. Grasping the surprised fish on either side of its broad face, Edward tore at its fleshy slitted openings, clawing and scraping, plunging in his fingers mercilessly and gouging out great ooz-ing hunks of fish flesh. He pulled himself face to face with the beast, his eyes bulging from oxygen loss, staring into the cold eyes of the fish—which also bulged from the shock and pain of Edward's assault. He dug deeper, his fingernails crawling inside the face of the tuna, until its wild thrashing suddenly ceased; its eyes turned from cruel and cold to glassy and dead.

A moment later Edward emerged, gasping, and slowly swam to shore.

Meanwhile, Elinor was in her room on the second floor of Barton Cottage, midway through getting dressed, bent over double and clutch-ing her temples; it was again the five-pointed figure which had engen-dered her agony. What she did not know—nor how could she?—was that the moment it appeared again in her mind, crowding out all thought and filling her body with the most exquisite, searing pain, was the very instant of Edward's most extreme peril.

* * *

Shortly after delivering a wet and discomfited Mrs. Dashwood back to the house, Edward departed, still very much in a desponding turn of mind. This despondence gave additional pain to all in the parting and left an uncomfortable impression on Elinor's feelings especially, which required some trouble and time to subdue. But as it was her determination to prevent herself from appearing to suffer more than the rest of her family on his going away, she did not adopt the method of embracing solitude so judiciously employed by Marianne, on a similar occasion. She did not shut herself in her room with tales of hunger-maddened sailors, nor moan the verses of ancient shanties and shake and sigh. Their means of despondence were as different as their objects, and equally suited to the advancement of each.

Elinor sat down to her driftwood-whittling table as soon as he was out of the house and busily employed herself the whole day, steadily transforming a fresh bucket of wood into a parade of winged cherubs. She neither sought nor avoided the mention of his name and appeared to interest herself almost as much as ever in the general concerns of the family. Inside, her mind was alive with questions—as to Edward's conduct, as to her own affection, and as to the curious and discomfiting hallucination, if such it was, that continued to plague her. But such considerations were alive only in her own mind, and never in conversation; if, by this conduct, she did not lessen her own grief, it was at least prevented from unnecessary increase, and her mother and sisters were spared much solicitude on her account.

Without shutting herself up from her family, or leaving the house in determined solitude to avoid them, or lying awake the whole night to indulge meditation, Elinor found every day afforded her leisure enough to think of Edward, and of Edward's behaviour, in a variety of lights—with tenderness, pity, approbation, censure, and doubt.

When she was roused one morning, by the arrival of company, Elinor happened to be quite alone. The creak of the rickety wooden staircase drew her eyes to the window, and she saw a large party walking up to the door. Amongst them were Sir John and Lady Middleton and Mrs. Jennings, but there were two others, a gentleman and lady, who were quite unknown to her. She was sitting near the window, and as soon as Sir John perceived her, he left the rest of the party to the ceremony of knocking at the door and, vaulting over his cane in a fluid motion onto the porch, obliged her to speak to him.

"Well," said he, "we have brought you some strangers. How do you like them?"

"Hush! They will hear you."

"Never mind if they do. It is only the Palmers. Charlotte is very pretty, I can tell you. You may see her if you look this way."

As Elinor was certain of seeing her in a couple of minutes, without taking that liberty, she begged to be excused.

"Where is Marianne? Has she run away because we are come?"

"She is walking the beach, I believe."

"I do hope she is careful. I noticed a distinct trail of slime along the cove as we rowed in; very likely further evidence of the Fang-Beast."

"Pardon me?"

But they were now joined by Mrs. Jennings, who had not patience enough to wait till the door was opened before she told her story. She came hallooing to the window, "How do you do, my dear? How does Mrs. Dashwood do? And where are your sisters? What! All alone! You will be glad of a little company to sit with you. I have brought my daughter and her husband to see you. Only think of their coming so suddenly! I thought I heard a canoe or a clipper ship last night, while we were drinking our tea, but it never entered my head that it could be them. I thought of nothing but whether it might not be Colonel Brandon come back again; so I said to Sir John, I do think I hear a canoe being tied up against the dock. Perhaps it is Colonel Brandon come back again—"

Elinor was obliged to turn from her, in the middle of her prattling, to receive the rest of the party; Lady Middleton introduced the two strangers; Mrs. Dashwood and Margaret came down stairs at the same time, and they all sat down to look at one another.

Mrs. Palmer was Lady Middleton's younger sister; she, too, been abducted at machete-point by Sir John and his hunting party; short and plump, she had gone as prize to Mr. Palmer, Sir John's right-hand man on that particular expedition. Several years younger than Lady Middleton, she was totally unlike her in every respect; she had a very pretty face, and the finest expression of good humour. Her attitude had none of the simmering resentment of her sister's, and one never received the impression from her, as one did on occasion from Lady Middleton, that given the right opportunity she would slit the throats of all present and decamp to her native country. She came in with a smile, and smiled all the time of her visit, except when she laughed. Her husband was grave-looking, with an air of more fashion and sense than his wife, but of less willingness to please or be pleased. Clad in the hunting boots and battered hunting cap of the ex-adventurer he was, he entered the room with a look of self-consequence, slightly bowed to the ladies, without speaking a word, and, after briefly surveying them and their apartments, took up a newspaper from the table, and continued to read it as long as he stayed.

"Mr. Palmer," said Sir John quietly to Elinor, by way of explanation, "has a certain unwholesome frame of mind. There are men, such as myself, who set off to see the world and return with an animated spirit, pleased with the things they have known and seen. Others—there are others who return with the darkness upon them."

Mrs. Palmer, on the contrary, was strongly endowed by nature with a turn for being uniformly civil and happy. "Well! What a delightful room this is! I never saw anything so charming! How I should like such a place for myself! Should not you, Mr. Palmer?"

Mr. Palmer made her no answer, and did not even raise his eyes from the newspaper.

"Mr. Palmer does not hear me," said she, laughing. "He never does sometimes. It is so ridiculous!"

This was quite a new idea to Mrs. Dashwood; she had never found wit in the inattention of anyone, and could not help looking with surprise at them both.

Mrs. Jennings, in the meantime, talked on as loud as she could and continued her account of their surprise the evening before on seeing their family, without ceasing till everything was told. Mrs. Palmer laughed heartily at the recollection of their astonishment, and everybody agreed, two or three times over, that it had been quite an agreeable surprise.

"You may believe how glad we all were to see them," added Mrs. Jennings, leaning forward towards Elinor, and speaking in a low voice as if she meant to be heard by no one else, though they were seated on different sides of the room; "but I can't help wishing they had not travelled quite so fast, nor made such a long journey of it, for they came all round by Sub-Marine Station Beta upon account of some business, for you know (nodding significantly and pointing to her daughter) it was wrong in her situation. I wanted her to stay at home and rest this morning, but she would come with us; she longed so much to see you all!"

Mrs. Palmer laughed, and said it would not do her any harm.

"She expects to be confined in February," continued Mrs. Jennings.

Lady Middleton could no longer endure such a conversation, and therefore exerted herself to ask Mr. Palmer if there was any news in the paper.

"Whaler eaten by whale. Crew all dead," he replied curtly, and read on.

"Here comes Marianne," cried Sir John. "Now, Palmer, you shall see a monstrous pretty girl." Mr. Palmer did not look up, but rather turned the page of his newspaper slowly, communicating thereby that the very idea of prettiness in a girl was trivial in the extreme, when set against the great masses of un-prettiness of which the world was in essence comprised.

Sir John grabbed his cane and went into the passage, opened the front door, and ushered her in himself. Mrs. Jennings asked her, as soon as she appeared, if she had not been to Allenham Isle; and Mrs. Palmer laughed so heartily at the question, as to show she understood it. Mrs. Palmer's eye was now caught by the driftwood sculpture of Buckingham Palace which decorated the sideboard. She got up to examine it.

"Oh! How well carved that is! Do but look, Mama, how sweet! I declare it is quite charming; I could look at it for ever." And then sitting down again, she very soon forgot that there was any such thing in the room, even though the driftwood palace smelled unpleasantly of the algae that still clung to it.

When Lady Middleton rose to go away, Mr. Palmer rose also, laid down the newspaper, stretched himself and looked at them all around.

"My love, have you been asleep?" said his wife, laughing.

He made her no answer; and only observed, after again examining the room, that it was very low pitched, and that the ceiling was crooked. He then made his bow, sighed heavily, and departed with the rest.

Sir John had been very urgent with them all to spend the next day on Deadwind Island. Mrs. Dashwood, who did not choose to dine with them oftener than they dined at the cottage, absolutely refused on her own account; her daughters might do as they pleased. But they had no curiosity to see how Mr. and Mrs. Palmer ate their dinner, and no expectation of pleasure from them in any other way. They attempted therefore to excuse themselves also; the weather was uncertain, the fog so thick as to be virtually impassable. But Sir John would not be satisfied—his yacht, with fog-cutters attached, should be sent for them and they must come. Mrs. Jennings and Mrs. Palmer joined their entreaties, and the young ladies were obliged to yield.

"Why should they ask us?" said Marianne, as soon as they were gone. "The rent of this shanty is low; but we have it on very hard terms, if we are to dine on Deadwind Island whenever anyone is staying either with them, or with us."

"They mean no less to be civil and kind to us now," said Elinor, hands busy once more with a new hunk of driftwood, which she intended to shape into Henry VIII. "The difference is not in them, if their parties are grown tedious and dull. We must look for the change elsewhere."

CHAPTER 20

A S THEY ENTERED the drawing-room of the Middleton's at one door, Mrs. Palmer came running in at the other, looking as good humoured and merry as before. She took them all most affectionately by the hand, and expressed great delight in seeing them again.

"I am so glad to see you!" said she, seating herself between Elinor and Marianne, "for the fog is so thick today, and bears such an ominous aspect, that I was afraid you might be lost at sea, or crash up against the rocks, or otherwise meet your watery doom, which would be a shame, as we go away again to-morrow. We must go, for the Westons come to us next week you know. It was quite a sudden thing our coming at all, and I knew nothing of it till the clipper was chained at the dock, and then Mr. Palmer asked me if I would go with him. He is so droll! He never tells me anything! I am so sorry we cannot stay longer; however, we shall meet again in-Station very soon, I hope."

Elinor was obliged to put an end to such an expectation.

"Not go to Sub-Marine Station Beta!" cried Mrs. Palmer, with a laugh, "I shall be quite disappointed if you do not. I could get the nicest docking in the world for you, next door to ours. You must come, indeed!"

They thanked her, but were obliged to resist all her entreaties.

"Oh, my love," cried Mrs. Palmer to her husband, who just then entered the room. "You must help me to persuade the Miss Dashwoods to sail to Station Beta this winter."

Her love made no answer. After slightly bowing to the ladies, he began complaining of the weather.

"How horrid is this smothering fog!" said he. "It is like death itself—insatiable, unavoidable, all-consuming. What the devil does Sir John mean by not having a billiard room in his house? How few people know what comfort is!"

The rest of the company soon dropped in. When all were seated in the dining-room, the table was set, the roasted armadillo was served, and the sconces were lit, Sir John observed with regret that they were only eight all together.

"My dear," said he to his Lady Middleton, "it is very provoking that we should be so few. Why did not you ask the Gilberts to come to us today?"

"Did not I tell you, Sir John, when you spoke to me about it before, that it could not be done? Mrs. Gilbert is averse to dining upon armadillo, as she fears its armored plates will cleave her intestines."

"Nonsense," said Mrs. Jennings, and earning an approving laugh from Sir John but a glare of disapproval from Mr. Palmer.

"Your comment reveals you very ill-bred," said he to his mother-in-law.

"My love, you contradict everybody," said his wife with her usual laugh. "Do you know that you are quite rude?"

"I did not know I contradicted anybody in calling your mother ill-bred."

"Aye, you may abuse me as you please," said the good-natured old lady, "you have taken Charlotte off my hands, dragged her off in a net, in fact, and cannot give her back again. So there I have the whip hand of you."

Charlotte laughed heartily to think that her husband could not get rid of her; she exultingly said, she did not care how cross he was to her, as they must live together. It was impossible for anyone to be more thoroughly good-natured, or more determined to be happy than Mrs. Palmer. The studied indifference, insolence, and discontent of her husband gave her no pain; and when he scolded or abused her, she was highly diverted.

"Mr. Palmer is so droll!" said she, in a whisper, to Elinor, as Mr. Palmer shook his head at the abject meaningless of all around him. "He is always out of humour."

Elinor was not inclined, despite Sir John's explanation for Mr. Palmer's world-weariness, to give him credit for being so genuinely and unaffectedly ill-natured as he wished to appear. His temper might perhaps be a little soured by finding, like many others of his sex that he was the husband of a very silly woman, though one he himself had chosen to abduct, out of many possible concubines, from her native village.

"Oh, my dear Miss Dashwood," said Mrs. Palmer soon afterwards, "I have got such a favour to ask of you and your sister. Will you come to us this Christmas? Now, pray do—and come while the Westons are with us. My love," applying to her husband, "don't you long to have the Miss Dashwoods visit?"

"Certainly," he replied, with a sneer. "I came into Devonshire with no other view."

"There now," said his lady. "You see Mr. Palmer expects you; so you cannot refuse to come."

They both eagerly and resolutely declined her invitation.

"But indeed you must and shall come. I am sure you will like it of all things. The Westons will be with us, and it will be quite delightful."

Elinor was again obliged to decline her invitation; and by changing the subject to the giant tuna that had lately tried to consume her mother, put a stop to her entreaties. She thought it probable that as they lived in the same county, Mrs. Palmer might be able to give some account of Willoughby's general character. She began by inquiring if they were intimately acquainted with him.

"Oh dear, yes; I know him extremely well," replied Mrs. Palmer. "Not that I ever spoke to him, indeed; but I have seen him forever in town. Somehow or other I never happened to be staying on the Devonshire coast while he was on Allenham Isle. However, I dare say we

should have seen a great deal of him in Somersetshire, if it had not happened very unluckily that we should never have been in the country together. He is very little at Combe, I believe; but if he were ever so much
there, I do not think Mr. Palmer would visit him, for it such a way off, and
Mr. Palmer despises all of humanity. I know why you inquire about him,
very well; your sister is to marry him."

"Upon my word," replied Elinor, "you know much more of the
matter than I do, if you have any reason to expect such a match."

"Don't pretend to deny it, because you know it is what everybody
talks of. I assure you I heard of it in my way here."

"My dear Mrs. Palmer!"

"Upon my honour I did. I met Colonel Brandon Monday morning on Bond Causeway, just before we left the Sub-Station, and he told
me of it directly."

"You surprise me very much. Colonel Brandon tell you of it! Surely
you must be mistaken. To give such intelligence, even if it were true, is not
what I should expect Colonel Brandon to do."

"But I do assure you it was so. When we met him, we began talking of my brother and sister, and one thing and another, and I said to him,
'So, Colonel, there is a new family come to Barton Cottage, I hear, and
Mama sends me word they are very pretty, and that one of them is going
to be married to Mr. Willoughby of Combe Magna. Is it true, pray?'"

"And what did the colonel say?"

"Oh, he did not say much. He just sort of gibbered and moaned, as
he does sometimes helplessly, as you know. But he looked as if he knew
it to be true, so from that moment I set it down as certain."

"Colonel Brandon was very well, I hope?"

"Yes, quite well, and so full of your praises. He did nothing but say
fine things of you, the pitiable creature."

"I am flattered by his commendation. He seems an excellent man;
and I think him uncommonly pleasing, at least so far as his manner, his
physical nature being another matter entirely."

"So do I. It is quite a shame he should be so afflicted by the sea witch's curse. Mama says *he* was in love with your sister too. I assure you it was a great compliment if he was, for he hardly ever falls in love with anybody."

"Is Mr. Willoughby much known in your part of Somersetshire?" said Elinor.

"I do not believe many people are acquainted with him, because Combe Magna is so far off, but they all think him extremely agreeable I assure you. He cuts quite a figure, as you know, with his otter-skin hat and flipper feet and orangutan valet. Nobody is more liked than Mr. Willoughby wherever he goes, and so you may tell your sister. She is a monstrous lucky girl to get him, upon my honour, and he in getting her, because she is so very handsome and agreeable." Mrs. Palmer's information respecting Willoughby was not very material; but any testimony in his favour, however small, was pleasing to her.

"You have been long acquainted with Colonel Brandon, have you not?" asked Elinor.

"Yes, a great while. He is a dear friend of Sir John's." She added in a low voice, "I believe Colonel Brandon would have been very glad to have had me, if he could. The very thought of becoming his wife fills me with nausea, and a sort of queer nameless dread. In sooth, I am much happier as I am. Mr. Palmer is the kind of man I like."

As if invoked by the pronunciation of his name, Mr. Palmer at that moment entered the room, and paused before Elinor, ignoring entirely the presence of his wife.

"How long have you resided on Pestilent Isle?" he enquired roughly, gesturing out the window to where the island sat in the distance, crowned by the craggy flat top of Mount Margaret. Elinor explained their situation, but Mr. Palmer seemed barely to listen. He only stared, his eyes hooded and empty—as if seeing something in that desolate spit of land he did not want to see, and understanding something he wished not to understand.

CHAPTER 21

T HE PALMERS SET OFF the next day to return to their customary habitation, a houseboat called *The Cleveland*, moored off the shore of Somersetshire. Elinor had hardly got their last visitors out of her head before Sir John procured new acquaintances to see and observe.

In a morning's crossing to Plymouth for supplies, Sir John met with two amiable young ladies and invited them directly to Deadwind. Lady Middleton was thrown into no little alarm by hearing that she would soon be visited by two girls whom she had never seen in her life, and of whose elegance—whose tolerable gentility even, she could have no proof. The alarm was compounded by the information, let out offhandedly by Sir John, that a panfish the size of a coach-and-four, with two rows of lion's teeth, had nearly sunk the clipper. Charles the Oarsman, a great favourite of Lady Middleton, had valiantly fought it off, rolling up his sleeves and plunging his bare hands into the churning tide to snap the spine of the monster; but he had been too vigorous and tumbled over the side and into the sea, where his foe proved the fiercer fighter. Sir John's detailed description of the incident, particularly the sound of the panfish's teeth crunching into dear Charles's skull, disquieted her nearly as much as the information regarding their new houseguests-to-be.

As it was impossible, however, to prevent the arrival of the visitors, Lady Middleton resigned herself to the idea of it, with all the regal bearing of the island princess that she was—or had been before her unwilling matrimony—contenting herself with merely giving her husband a gentle reprimand on the subject five or six times every day.

The mysterious young ladies arrived: Their appearance was by no means ungenteel or unfashionable. Their dress was very smart, their manners very civil, they were delighted with the house, and in raptures with the furniture, and they happened to be so dotingly fond of children that Lady Middleton's good opinion was engaged in their favour before they had been an hour on Deadwind Island. She declared them to be very agreeable girls indeed, which for her ladyship was enthusiastic admiration. Sir John's confidence in his own judgment rose with this animated praise, and he rowed directly to Barton Cottage to tell the Miss Dashwoods of the Miss Steeles' arrival, and to assure them of their being the sweetest girls in the world. From such commendation as this, however, there was not much to be learned; Elinor well knew that the sweetest girls in the world were to be met with in every part of England, under every possible variation of form, face, temper, and understanding. Sir John wanted the whole family to row to Deadwind Island directly and look at his guests. Benevolent, philanthropic, old adventurer! It was painful to him even to keep a pair of kind strangers to himself.

"Do come now," said he. "Pray come! You must come! Lucy is monstrous pretty, and so good humoured and agreeable! She is helping Lady Middleton in the kitchen, plucking the wings from dragonflies so they can be ground into paste! And both sisters long to see you of all things, for they have heard at Plymouth that you are the most beautiful creatures in the world; and I have told them it is all very true. You will be delighted with them I am sure. How can you be so cross as not to come?" His old eyes bugged out from his head as he exhorted them, and he tugged earnestly on his beard for emphasis.

But Sir John could not prevail. He could only obtain a promise of their calling at Deadwind within a day or two, and then left in amazement at their indifference, to row home and boast anew of their attractions to the Miss Steeles, as he had been already boasting of the Miss Steeles to them. He broke into the rum early, and the more he drank, the more he boasted; drinking, boasting, drinking, and boasting, until he fell asleep on the hammock, a coconut half-filled with punch dangling from his ropy hands.

When their introduction to these young ladies finally took place, the Miss Dashwoods found nothing to admire in the appearance of the eldest, Anne, who was nearly thirty and had a very plain and not a sensible face; but in Lucy, who was not more than three and twenty, they acknowledged considerable beauty; her features were pretty, and she had a sharp quick eye, and a smartness of air which gave distinction to her person. Their manners were particularly civil, and Elinor soon allowed them credit for sense, when she saw with what constant and judicious attention they were making themselves agreeable to Lady Middleton. They put to her polite questions about her former life as ruler of an island race, and with her children they were in continual raptures, extolling their beauty, courting their notice, and humouring their whims. A fond mother, in pursuit of praise for her children, is the most rapacious of human beings and likewise the most credulous.

"What a sweet woman Lady Middleton is!" said Lucy Steele, when that lady had returned to the kitchen to attend to her dessert: a lightly glazed pastry with a single maggot baked inside, and served in slices, so the person served the piece with the maggot earns a prize.

Marianne was silent; it was impossible for her to say what she did not feel, however trivial the occasion; and to Elinor the task of telling polite lies always fell. She did her best when thus called on, by speaking of Lady Middleton with more warmth than she felt, though with far less than Miss Lucy.

"And Sir John too," cried the elder sister, "what a charming man he is!"

Here too, Miss Dashwood's commendation, being only simple and just, came in without any éclat. She merely observed that he was perfectly good humoured and friendly, and had once survived three months in the Amazon navigating by the stars and drinking filtered rainwater.

"And what a charming little family they have! I never saw such fine children in my life. I declare I quite dote upon them already, and indeed I am always distractedly fond of children."

"I should guess so," said Elinor, with a smile, "from what I have witnessed this morning."

"I have a notion," said Lucy, "you think the little Middletons rather too much indulged; perhaps they may be the outside of enough; but it is so natural in Lady Middleton; and for my part, I love to see children full of life and spirits; I cannot bear them if they are tame and quiet."

"I confess," replied Elinor, "that while I am on Deadwind Island, I never think of tame and quiet children with any abhorrence."

A short pause succeeded this speech. The waves lashed the beach, and the wind moaned in the sky. Then Miss Steele, who seemed very much disposed for conversation, and said rather abruptly, "And how do you like Devonshire, Miss Dashwood? I suppose you were very sorry to leave Sussex."

In some surprise at the familiarity of this question, Elinor replied that she was.

"Norland is a prodigious beautiful place, is not it?" added Miss Steele, leaning forward slightly and offering an insinuating glance.

"I think everyone *must* admire it," replied Elinor, "though few can estimate its beauties as we do."

"And had you many smart beaux there? I suppose you have not so many in this part of the world."

"But why should you think," said Lucy, looking ashamed of her sister, "that there are not as many genteel young men in Devonshire as Sussex?"

"Nay, my dear, I'm sure I don't pretend to say that there ain't. I'm sure there's a vast many smart beaux in Plymouth; it is a coastal city, drawing its share of adventurous young men interested in murdering sea swine. But you know, how could I tell what smart beaux there might be about the islands off the coast; and I was only afraid the Miss Dashwoods might find it dull, if they had not so many as they used to have. But perhaps you young ladies may not care about the beaux. For my part, I think they are vastly agreeable, provided they dress smart and keep their monster-slaying swords sheathed on the dance floor. But I can't bear to see them dirty and nasty, dripping with sea-water and reeking of fish guts.

I suppose your brother was quite a beau, Miss Dashwood, before he married, as he was so rich?"

"Upon my word," replied Elinor, "I cannot tell you, for I do not perfectly comprehend the meaning of the word. But this I can say, that if he ever was a beau before he married, he is one still for there is not the smallest alteration in him."

"Oh! One never thinks of married men's being beaux—they have something else to do."

This specimen of the Miss Steeles was enough. The vulgar freedom and folly of the eldest left her no recommendation, and Elinor was not blinded by the beauty or the shrewd look of the youngest, to her want of real elegance and artlessness. She left the house without any wish of knowing them better.

Not so the Miss Steeles. They came from Exeter, well provided with admiration for the use of Sir John Middleton and his family, and no small proportion was now dealt out to his fair cousins. To be better acquainted, therefore, Elinor soon found was their inevitable lot; that kind of intimacy must be submitted to, which consists of sitting an hour or two together in the same room almost every day.

Elinor had not seen them more than twice, before the elder of them wished her joy on her sister's having been so lucky as to make a conquest of a very smart beau since she came to the islands.

"'Twill be a fine thing to have her married so young," said she, "and I hear he is quite a swift swimmer, dashing in his flipper feet, and prodigious handsome. And I hope you may have as good luck yourself soon—but perhaps you already have a crab in the net, as they say."

Elinor supposed that Sir John had proclaimed his suspicions of her regard for Edward; indeed it was rather his favourite joke. Since Edward's visit, they had never dined together without his drinking, and drinking, and drinking, to her best affections with so many nods and winks, as to excite general attention.

The Miss Steeles now had all the benefit of these jokes, which the eldest of them raised a curiosity to know the name of the gentleman alluded to. But Sir John did not sport long with the curiosity. One night, they sat as a group before the dinner table, where a broiled rattlesnake had been laid out upon the table by Lady Middleton, cut into individual slices as if it were a long, flat cake.

"His name is Ferrars," said Sir John, in a very audible whisper; "but pray do not tell it, for it's a great secret."

"Ferrars!" repeated Miss Steele, chewing with her back teeth on a tough bite of snake. "Mr. Ferrars is the happy man, is he? What! Your sister-in-law's brother, Miss Dashwood? A very agreeable young man to be sure; I know him very well."

"How can you say so, Anne?" cried Lucy, who generally made an amendment to all her sister's assertions. "Though we have seen him once or twice at my uncle's, it is rather too much to pretend to know him very well."

Elinor heard all this with attention and surprise. "And who was this uncle? Where did he live? How came they acquainted?" She wished very much to have the subject continued, though she did not join in it herself; she wished also that dinner would end, so she could stop pretending to eat the rattlesnake, which she was collecting in her lap to dispose of later. Nothing more of the Ferrars was said, and for the first time in her life, she thought Mrs. Jennings deficient either in curiosity after petty information, or in a disposition to communicate it. The manner in which Miss Steele had spoken of Edward, increased her curiosity; for it struck her as being rather ill-natured, and suggested the suspicion of that lady's knowing something to his disadvantage. But her curiosity was unavailing, for no further notice was taken of Mr. Ferrars's name by Miss Steele when alluded to, or even openly mentioned by Sir John.

At last the dinner was concluded, and they were rowed home in silence, the oarsmen navigating skillfully, relying greatly upon the fog-cutters. The Dashwood sisters travelled home in silence, except for the small splashes as they all cast the remains of their dinner into the sea.

CHAPTER 22

MARIANNE, WHO HAD NEVER much toleration for anything like impertinence, vulgarity, or even difference of taste from herself, was at this time particularly ill-disposed to be pleased with the Miss Steeles. She was cold towards them and checked every endeavour at intimacy on their side.

Lucy was naturally clever; her remarks were often just and amusing; and as a companion for half an hour Elinor frequently found her agreeable; she was even quick with a blade; one night in the Middleton's kitchen Elinor watched her decapitate a not-quite-dead flounder in one smooth chop. But her powers had received no aid from education: She was illiterate of even the most basic knowledge of fish species, navigation, and grades of net meshing; and her deficiency of all mental improvement, her want of information in the most common particulars, could not be concealed from Miss Dashwood. Elinor pitied her for it; but she saw, with less tenderness of feeling, the thorough want of delicacy, of rectitude, and integrity of mind, which her attentions and flatteries at Deadwind Island betrayed; and she could have no lasting satisfaction in the company of a person who joined insincerity with ignorance.

"You will think my question an odd one," said Lucy to her one day, as they were co-rowing a two-person kayak from Deadwind Island back to Barton Cottage, "but are you acquainted with your sister-in-law's mother, Mrs. Ferrars?"

Elinor did think the question a very odd one, and in her surprise she stopped rowing for three beats; the boat described a small semi-circle in the water before she answered that she had never seen Mrs. Ferrars.

"Indeed!" replied Lucy. "I thought you must have seen her at Norland. Then, perhaps, you cannot tell me what sort of a woman she is?"

"No," returned Elinor. "I know nothing of her."

"I am sure you think me very strange, for enquiring about her in such a way," said Lucy, eyeing Elinor attentively as she spoke, "but perhaps there may be reasons—"

"Watch out!" called Elinor, for Lucy had taken her gaze off the sea-lane and now they were rowing directly into a flat rock, grey and slick, which jutted up from the deep water ahead. "Row! Row!"

Together the girls endeavoured to maneuver the boat around the partially submerged promontory, and Lucy took up her apology once more. "I hope you will do me the justice of believing that I do not mean to be impertinent."

Elinor made a civil reply and they rowed on for a few minutes in silence. It was broken by Lucy, who renewed the subject again by saying, "I cannot bear to have you think me impertinently curious."

"For Heaven's sake, be careful!" called Elinor again. Something very bizarre—the rock formation, or was it a patch of coral, somehow elevated above the surface?—which they had seemed to row around was again ahead. Examining it more closely, Elinor realised with a pang of unease that the rock was rippling slightly as the water coursed over it; this was not a thing of rock or coral at all, but the flexing grey back of a living creature. Lucy took no note of this vexing phenomenon and continued to speak:

"I am sure I would do anything in the world than be thought impertinent by a person whose good opinion is so well worth having as yours."

"Lucy—" Elinor began, removing her oar from the water and holding it high above her head, prepared to crack it down on the back of the beast, at the instant it should raise its head to strike.

"And I am sure I should not have the smallest fear of trusting *you*," the other girl continued, noticing neither Elinor's defensive crouch, nor that the "rock" was now rising slowly from the water, revealing more of its slimy, silvery bulk—and here were two red eyes, deep-set and glowering, set above a pair of nostrils breathing hot steam.

"Lucy!" Elinor shouted.

"Indeed, I should be very glad of your advice how to manage in such an uncomfortable situation as I am; but, however, there is no occasion to trouble *you*."

The Thing had now drawn itself so far up from beneath the surface that its whole frontal portion was fully visible, and facing them directly. It bore a long, flat head, the red eyes glimmering with preternatural intelligence. The body was long and twisted, dripping with slime; a cloud of thick water-borne slime oozed from its body, muddying the waters around the creature. As the tiny boat came ever closer, the Thing opened its mouth, revealing fangs. Elinor turned cold. The Devonshire Fang-Beast!

"I am sorry you do not happen to know Mrs. Ferrars."

"I am sorry I do *not*," said Elinor, in great astonishment, "But for now the subject must be dropped, and we must focus our attentions—"

But Lucy was lost in her reverie. Even as Elinor snapped her oar over her knee with the intention of repeating her mother's trick of dispatching the vast beast that had attacked their boat on the way to Barton Cottage, the other girl continued her peroration. "Mrs. Ferrars is certainly nothing to me at present—but the time *may* come—how soon it will come must depend upon herself—when we may be very intimately connected."

Lucy looked down as she said this, amiably bashful, with only one side glance at her companion to observe its effect on her.

"Good heavens!" cried Elinor, swinging her oar towards the flat head of the Fang-Beast, as astonished by the sheer size of the creature she faced, as by her dawning understanding of Lucy Steele's meaning. "What do you mean? Are you acquainted with Mr. Robert Ferrars? Can you be?" The Fang-Beast, meanwhile, easily avoided the strike of the oar, which splashed uselessly on the surface of the water.

"No," replied Lucy, "not to Mr. *Robert* Ferrars. I never saw him in my life; but to his elder brother."

Elinor turned towards Lucy in silent amazement, and it was in that moment that a *second* great head reared out of the surface of the water, compounding Elinor's shock. While the first of the Fang-Beast's monstrous faces hissed fiercely, this second long head slid up onto their boat and caught Elinor at the knees in a coil of its slimy neck. She went into the water, and landed with a gasp, her mouth filling with the thick mucous cloud that emanated from the Beast.

"You may well be surprised," continued Lucy, and then stopped short, at last noticing that something was amiss, and she stood alone in the vessel. "Elinor?"

Elinor, suffocating in the cloud of slime, caught in the hideous rubbery embrace of the Fang-Beast, was struggling to keep her head above the surface of the water. She recalled as she struggled for breath the lore she had learned from Sir John when in his cups: There is a certain strain of overgrown monster-fish that takes its sustenance from fog like infants from their mother's milk. Thus the lately suffocating weather pattern could be no coincidence—this fearsome, two-headed beast had been thriving in this dank weather, expanding its bulk, awaiting its chance to strike.

This knowledge was useless to Elinor now—all she could do was earnestly hope for assistance from Lucy, who at last was through unburdening herself of her secret and attentive to their unenviable circumstance. To Elinor's considerable surprise, the younger Miss Steele proved equal to the task. Tucked into the calf of her stylish travelling boot was a long serrated fish-knife; without the slightest hesitation, she wrapped her fist around its handle and plunged the business end into the churning cove-water to slash violently at the neck coil that was wrapped python-like around Elinor's waist.

But while the coil tightened around Elinor, the Fang-Beast's first head slunk along the floor of the boat to within striking distance of

THIS FEARSOME, TWO-HEADED BEAST HAD BEEN THRIVING IN THIS DANK
WEATHER, EXPANDING ITS BULK, AWAITING ITS CHANCE TO STRIKE.

Lucy Steele; she deftly stomped on its flat snout with the heel of her boot, bringing forth an eruption of slime and blood from its nostril and causing the thing to withdraw in pain. Thus emboldened, Lucy redoubled her assault on the first head, and soon she had hacked Elinor free; with each strike, more slime poured from the neck of the Beast, until both girls were covered with the noxious emanation. At last, the Fang-Beast, maimed but not, evidently, unto death, sunk back beneath the water's surface and away.

In a few moments more, the little craft bumped against the shore below Barton Cottage, and the two girls lay flopping and heaving for breath, like fish plucked from a stream and tossed on the riverbank. But before Elinor could begin to recover herself, Lucy picked up the thread of her engagement story.

"I dare say Edward never dropped the smallest hint of our engagement to you because it was always meant to be a great secret. Not a soul of all my relations know of it but Anne, and I never should have mentioned it to you, if I had not felt the greatest dependence in the world upon your secrecy; and I really thought my behaviour in asking so many questions about Mrs. Ferrars must seem so odd, that it ought to be explained. And I do not think Mr. Ferrars can be displeased, when he knows I have trusted you, because I know he has the highest opinion in the world of all your family, and looks upon yourself and the other Miss Dashwoods quite as his own sisters."

Elinor for a few moments remained silent; her frame was still quivering from muscular exertion and sheer fright, and her soul was shaken even more by the information Lucy had imparted. At length forcing herself to speak, and to speak cautiously, she said, with calmness of manner, "May I ask if your engagement is of long standing?"

"We have been engaged these four years."

"Four years!" A pain in Elinor's spine, where the Fang-Beast had tightened its grasp around her, throbbed with the shock of this revelation.

"Our acquaintance is of many years. He was under my uncle's care for a considerable while."

"Your uncle!"

"Yes, Mr. Pratt. Did you never hear him talk of Mr. Pratt?"

"I think I have," replied Elinor, with an exertion of spirits, her body pulsing with discomfort and dismay.

"He was four years with my uncle, and it was there our acquaintance begun, for my sister and me were often staying with my uncle, and it was there our engagement was formed, though not till a year after he had quitted as a pupil; but he was almost always with us afterwards. I was too young, and loved him too well, to be so prudent as I ought to have been. Though you do not know him so well as me, Miss Dashwood, you must have seen enough of him to be sensible he is very capable of making a woman sincerely attached to him."

"Certainly," answered Elinor, without knowing what she said; but after a moment's reflection, she added, with revived security of Edward's honour and love, "Engaged to Mr. Edward Ferrars! I confess myself so totally surprised at what you tell me. Surely there must be some mistake of person or name. We cannot mean the same Mr. Ferrars."

"We can mean no other," cried Lucy, smiling. "Mr. Edward Ferrars, the eldest son of Mrs. Ferrars, of Park Street, and brother of your sister-in-law, Mrs. John Dashwood, is the person I mean; you must allow that I am not likely to be deceived as to the name of the man on who all my happiness depends."

"It is strange," replied Elinor, "that I should never have heard him even mention your name."

"Considering our situation, it was not strange. Our first care has been to keep the matter secret. You knew nothing of me, or my family, and, therefore, there could be no *occasion* for ever mentioning my name to you; and, as he was always particularly afraid of his sister's suspecting anything, *that* was reason for his not mentioning it."

She was silent. Elinor's security sunk; but her self-command did not sink with it.

"Four years you have been engaged," said she with a firm voice.

"Yes; and heaven knows how much longer we may have to wait. Poor Edward! It puts him quite out of heart." Then taking a small miniature from her pocket, she added, "To prevent the possibility of mistake, be so good as to look at this face. It does not do him justice, to be sure, but yet I think you cannot be deceived as to the person it was drew for. I have had it above these three years."

She put it into her hands as she spoke; Elinor returned it almost instantly, acknowledging the likeness.

"I have never been able," continued Lucy, "to give him my picture in return, which I am very much vexed at, for he has been always so anxious to get it! But I am determined to set for it the very first opportunity."

"You are quite in the right," replied Elinor calmly. They struggled to their feet now, and began the walk on unsteady legs, up the stairs to the door of the shanty.

"I am sure," said Lucy, "I have no doubt of your faithfully keeping this secret, because you must know of what importance it is to us, not to have it reach his mother; for she would never approve of it, I dare say. I shall have no fortune, and I fancy she is an exceeding proud woman."

"Your secret is safe with me," assured Elinor.

As she said this, she looked earnestly at Lucy, hoping to discover something in her countenance; perhaps the falsehood of the greatest part of what she had been saying; but Lucy's countenance suffered no change. For a fleeting moment, Elinor wished that the Fang-Beast had succeeded in eating her or, better yet, in eating Lucy; such was her distress and anxiety over what she had heard.

"I was afraid you would think I was taking a great liberty with you," Lucy continued, "As soon as I saw you, I felt almost as if you were an old acquaintance. And I am so unfortunate, that I have not a creature whose advice I can ask. I only wonder that I am alive after what I have suffered for Edward's sake these last four years. Everything in such suspense and uncertainty; and seeing him so seldom—we can hardly meet above twice a-year. I wonder my heart is not quite broke."

Here she took out her handkerchief, but Elinor did not feel very compassionate.

"Sometimes," continued Lucy, after wiping her eyes, "I think whether it would not be better for us both to break off the matter entirely. What would you advise me to do in such a case, Miss Dashwood? What would you do yourself?"

"Pardon me," replied Elinor, startled by the question; "but I can give you no advice under such circumstances. Your own judgment must direct you."

They had by now ascended the stairs and reached the door of the shanty, and agreed it was wise to sponge their bodies of all traces of the foul spew that had emanated from the Fang-Beast. They stood at a modest distance from one another as they removed their sodden clothing and undergarments. Meanwhile, Lucy continued her self-pitying tale. "To be sure, his mother must provide for him sometime or other; but poor Edward is so cast down by it! Did not you think him sadly out of spirits when he was here?"

"We did, indeed, particularly so when he first arrived."

"I begged him to exert himself for fear you should suspect what was the matter; but it made him so melancholy, not being able to stay more than a fortnight with us, and seeing me so much affected. Poor fellow! I gave him a lock of hair set in a ship's compass when he was at Longstaple last, and that was some comfort to him. Perhaps you might have noticed it when you saw him?"

"I did," said Elinor, with a composure of voice, under which was concealed an emotion and distress beyond anything she had ever felt before. Glancing up in her shock, she was confronted with the strangest sight of all: Miss Steele was lacing up her whale-bone corset and there, on the small of her back, was etched a tattoo in scarlet ink; it was the cryptic five-pointed pattern, exactly as had appeared to Elinor so many times, in such darkly portentous fashion, since her arrival on Pestilent Isle.

CHAPTER 23

WHAT LUCY HAD ASSERTED to be true Elinor dared not doubt, supported as it was on every side by such probabilities and proofs, and contradicted by nothing but her own wishes. Their opportunity of acquaintance in the house of Mr. Pratt was a foundation for the rest, and Edward's uncertain behaviour towards herself overcame every fear of condemning him unfairly, and established as a fact his ill-treatment of herself. Her resentment of such behaviour, her indignation at having been its dupe, for a short time made her feel only for herself; but other ideas, other considerations, soon arose. Had Edward been intentionally deceiving her? Had he feigned a regard for her which he did not feel? Was his engagement to Lucy an engagement of the heart?

Such thoughts swirled about in Elinor's mind as, standing before her bedroom mirror, she slowly worked a rough patch of red alder bark over her entire body, a salutary measure dictated by Sir John to remove any lingering traces of the Fang-Beast's viscous emissions from her skin.

"It stings," she cried, reacting to both the pain of Lucy's revelation and the infinite small abrasions of the tree bark upon her flesh—though somewhat more to the latter. "O, it stings."

And yet, whatever might once have been, Elinor could not believe Edward loved Lucy at present. His affection was all her own. She could not be deceived in that. Her mother, sisters, Fanny, all had been conscious of his regard for her at Norland; it was not an illusion of her own vanity. He certainly loved her. Elinor proceeded to the second step of Sir John's cleansing protocol, wringing a bolt of worsted in warm, fresh water and pressing it delicately against every inch of her abraded skin.

Could Edward ever be tolerably happy with Lucy Steele? Could he, with his integrity, his delicacy, and well-informed mind, be satisfied with a wife like her—illiterate, artful, too selfish to notice even when her own kayak was about to be bit to splinters by a two-headed, forty-foot-long sea serpent exuding a cloud of malodorous sludge? Elinor did not have the answer. The youthful infatuation of nineteen would naturally blind Edward to everything but Lucy's beauty and good nature; but the four succeeding years must have opened his eyes to her defects of education, while the same period of time had perhaps robbed her of that simplicity which might once have leant interesting character to her beauty.

Then there was the matter of the tattoo—that strange shape that had called to Elinor from her nightmares, only to appear, writ in the very flesh of her rival's lower back. The thought of it pained Elinor's mind as much as did the rough scratch of the worsted wool upon her arms.

As these considerations occurred to her in painful succession, she wept for Edward more than for herself, and only stopped weeping when the salt of her tears burned like acid on her tenderized cheeks. Consoled by the belief that Edward had done nothing to forfeit her esteem, she thought she could command herself to guard every suspicion of the truth from her mother and sisters. When she joined them at dinner only two hours after she had first suffered the extinction of all her dearest hopes, no one would have supposed from the appearance of herself, that Elinor was mourning in secret over obstacles; her face glowed red from neither embarrassment nor grief, but only from the punctilious removal of a dermal layer.

The necessity of concealing from her mother and Marianne, what Lucy had entrusted in confidence to herself was no aggravation of Elinor's distress. She knew she could receive no assistance from them. So she gave out to them only the details of the Fang-Beast's attack and the nearness of their escape; this adventuresome anecdote led to a warm discussion of whether the girls should sew balloons into their bustles, to keep them buoyed if occasion should knock them from their vessels; thusly did the conversation drift forward through the dessert course, which was taffy.

Much as she had suffered from her first conversation with Lucy on the subject, Elinor soon felt an earnest wish of renewing it. She wanted to hear many particulars of their engagement repeated again; she wanted more clearly to understand what Lucy really felt for Edward; and she particularly wanted to convince Lucy, by her readiness to enter on the matter again, that she was no otherwise interested in it than as a friend. And also, then, from some dim part of her mind came a dark, insistent voice, demanding she find some means of again inspecting the mysterious tattoo on Lucy's back, and discovering its origins.

But there was no immediate opportunity of doing either. The weather was growing ever more dreadful, with winds whipping strong enough in recent days to tear off the roof of an abandoned shed on Deadwind Island and down upon one of the servants, who was knocked off his feet and then decapitated by the weather vane. A walk, where they might most easily separate themselves from the others, was therefore ill-advised; and though they met at least every other evening either at the Middleton's estate or at Barton Cottage, they could not be supposed to meet for the sake of conversation. Such a thought would never enter either Sir John or Lady Middleton's head; and therefore, very little leisure was ever given for particular discourse. They met for the sake of eating, drinking, oyster-shucking, laughing together, or playing any game that was sufficiently noisy.

Then one morning Sir John rowed up to the rebuilt dockside to beg, in the name of charity, that they would all dine with Lady Middleton that day, as he was obliged to help re-bury the poor unfortunate who had been decapitated by the weather vane; the other servants had done so inadequately, and so the corpse had been dug up by hyenas and now lay rotting on the beach. Elinor immediately accepted the invitation; Marianne agreed more grudgingly. Margaret asked and received enthusiastic permission from her mother to join the party as well, and all were glad to see that the girl had regained some of her childish spirit.

Weeks had passed since Margaret had last mentioned her skittering cave-people or the geyser of mysterious steam; they'd succeeded, Mrs. Dashwood hoped, in persuading the girl that it was all a matter of her imagination.

The insipidity of the evening at the Middletons was exactly as Elinor had expected; it produced not one novelty of thought or expression, and nothing could be less interesting than the whole of their discourse both in the dining parlour and drawing-room. They quitted it only with the removal of the tea-things. The card-table was then moved to pursue an amusement called Karankrolla, native to Lady Middleton's homeland, and Elinor began to wonder at herself for having ever entertained a hope of finding time for conversation with Miss Steele.

"I am glad," said Lady Middleton to Lucy, as she opened an ivory chest and produced a bewildering array of multi-coloured game pieces, "that you are not going to finish poor little Annamaria's ship-in-a-bottle this evening, for I am sure it must hurt your eyes to work the miniatures by candlelight."

This hint was enough. Lucy replied, "Indeed you are very much mistaken, Lady Middleton. I am only waiting to know whether you have enough participants for your amusement without me, or I should have had out my miniature sail-trimming equipment already. I would not disappoint the little angel for all the world."

"You are very good, I hope it won't hurt your eyes—will you ring the bell for some working candles?"

Lucy directly drew her work table near her and reseated herself with an alacrity and cheerfulness which seemed to imply that she could taste no greater delight than in building a diminutive clipper ship within the confines of an emptied-out glass beer bottle for a spoilt child.

Lady Middleton explained the rules of Karankrolla, which no one present could comprehend except for Mrs. Jennings, who offered no assistance in elucidating them to the rest of the company. As best Elinor could understand, each participant had to win fourteen Ghahalas to make a Hephalon; earning a Ghahala was a simple matter of turning one's Ja'ja'va shell three times round the Pifflestick; unless the wind was blowing from the northeast, in which case alternate rules were applied. All of this was detailed very rapidly by Lady Middleton, who concluded finally that if Karankrolla is not played for money, the gods are angered.

Out of politeness, no one made any objection but Marianne, who with her usual inattention to the forms of general civility, exclaimed, "Your Ladyship will have the goodness to excuse *me*—I shall go to the pianoforte; I have not touched it since it was tuned." And without further ceremony, she turned away and walked to the instrument.

Lady Middleton looked as if she thanked heaven that *she* had never made so rude a speech, she did not bother to be offended by Margaret, who joined Marianne at the pianoforte, since the youngest Dashwood sister obviously had no money to wager. With no further warning, she shook the Flakala ball, pronounced herself the winner of the first Ghahala, and collected three sovereigns from the elder Miss Steele.

"Oh!" cried Miss Steele. "I shall hope for better luck next time."

"Perhaps," said Elinor apologetically, as shells were distributed for the next round, "if I should happen to cut out, I may be of some use to Miss Lucy Steele, in laying the planks of the ship-in-a-bottle."

"I shall be obliged to you for your help," cried Lucy, "for I find there is more to be done to it than I thought there was; and it would be a shocking thing to disappoint dear Annamaria after all."

Their effusive efforts to hide the true nature of their desire to be together was unnecessary; all eyes were focused on the Karankrolla game, where Lady Middleton was collecting another three sovereigns from the elder Miss Steele.

The two fair rivals were thus seated side by side at the same table, and, with the utmost harmony, engaged in forwarding the same work. The pianoforte, where Marianne was wrapped up in her own music and her own thoughts, was so near them that Miss Dashwood now judged she might safely, under the shelter of its noise, introduce the interesting subject, without any risk of being heard at the Karankrolla table.

CHAPTER 24

IN A FIRM, THOUGH CAUTIOUS tone, Elinor began. "I should be undeserving of the confidence you have honoured me with, if I felt no further curiosity on its subject. Therefore I will not apologise for bringing it forward again."

"Thank you for breaking the ice," cried Lucy. "You have set my heart at ease. I was afraid I had offended you by what I told you Monday."

"Offended me! How could you suppose so? Believe me," and Elinor spoke it with the truest sincerity, "nothing could be further from my intention than to give you such an idea. Could you have a motive for the trust that was not honourable and flattering to me?"

"And yet I do assure you," replied Lucy, her pupils dancing in her little sharp eyes like carp in two ponds, "there seemed to me to be a coldness and displeasure in your manner that made me quite uncomfortable."

"Recall, dear Lucy, that at the time of your revelation, we were fending off the attentions of the massive, dicephalic, multitudinously-teethed Fang-Beast," replied Elinor, grateful to have the monster attack as an excuse for her reticence. "It may have lessened my sympathy to your tale beyond what was appropriate."

"Of course. And yet, I felt sure that you were angry with me."

"If I may be so impertinent as to re-enumerate: Fang-Beast; ooze-cloud; spinal column. My mind was elsewhere."

"Of course," said Lucy once more, carefully lashing together three toothpicks to serve for the flying jib of the *Infinitesimal*. "I am very glad to find it was only my own fancy. If you only knew what a consolation it was to me to relieve my heart speaking to you of what I am always thinking of every moment of my life."

From the gaming table came a noise of happy surprise from Miss Steele. "O! I am beginning to comprehend! If I turn my Ja'ja'va *thusly*—"

"Oops," said Mrs. Jennings suddenly. "I believe the wind just shifted."

"Alternate rules!" cried Lady Middleton.

"Indeed," Elinor continued to her friend and rival, "I can easily believe that it was a very great relief to you, to acknowledge your situation to me. Your case is a very unfortunate one; you seem to me to be surrounded with difficulties. Mr. Ferrars, I believe, is entirely dependent on his mother."

"He has only two thousand pounds of his own; it would be madness to marry upon that, though for my own part, I could give up every prospect of more without a sigh. I have been always used to a very small income; as girls we lived for a time in a turned-over rowboat, and wove our own clothes out of sea moss. I could struggle with any poverty for him; but I love him too well to be the selfish means of robbing him, perhaps, of all that his mother might give him if he married to please her. We must wait, it may be for many years. With almost every other man in the world, it would be an alarming prospect; but Edward's affection and constancy nothing can deprive me of, I know."

Unsure how to respond, Elinor toyed uncomfortably with the beer bottle, soon to house the tiny clipper ship.

"That conviction must be everything to you; and he is undoubtedly supported by the same trust in yours."

"Edward's love for me," said Lucy, "has been pretty well put to the test, by our long, very long absence since we were first engaged, and it has stood the trial so well, that I should be unpardonable to doubt it now. He has never given me one moment's alarm on that account."

Elinor, in her silent distress, so increased her grip on the beerbottle that it burst into a thousand pieces, burying shards of glass in her hand.

Lucy smiled forgivingly at this accident, took up a new bottle, and went on. "I have a jealous temper by nature, and from our continual separation, I was enough inclined for suspicion, to have found out the truth in an instant, if there had been the slightest alteration in his behaviour to me."

"All this," thought Elinor, as she went about the floor on hands and knees, gathering up stray pieces of glass, "is very pretty, but it can impose upon neither of us." She looked away from Lucy, whose attention was focused on rigging the tiny mainsail with miniature tweezers.

"But what," Elinor said after a short silence, "are your views? Or have you none but that of waiting for Mrs. Ferrars's death? Is Edward determined to submit to this, and to the many years of suspense, rather than run the risk of her displeasure for a while by owning the truth?"

"Mrs. Ferrars is a very headstrong proud woman. In her first fit of anger, she would very likely secure everything to his brother Robert!"

"Do you know Mr. Robert Ferrars?" asked Elinor.

"Not at all—I never saw him; but I fancy he is very unlike his brother—silly and a great coxcomb."

"A great coxcomb!" repeated the elder Miss Steele, looking up from the card-table, where she was writing out a promissory note to Lady Middleton, the decisive winner of seven straight rounds. "Oh, they are talking of their favourite beaux!"

"No sister," cried Lucy, "you are mistaken there, our favourite beaux are *not* great coxcombs."

"I can answer for it that Miss Dashwood's is not," said Mrs. Jennings, "for he is one of the modestest, prettiest-behaved young men I ever saw; but as for Lucy, she is such a sly little creature, there is no finding out who *she* likes."

"Oh," cried Miss Steele, looking significantly round at them, "I dare say Lucy's beau is quite as modest and pretty-behaved as Miss Dashwood's."

Elinor blushed in spite of herself. Lucy bit her lip, and looked angrily at her sister. A mutual silence took place for some time.

Lucy resumed their conversation only once Marianne and Margaret were giving them the powerful protection of performing a very lively dockside polka on the pianoforte.

"I will honestly tell you of one scheme which has lately come into my head. I dare say you have seen enough of Edward to know that he would prefer to be a lighthouse keeper to every other profession. Now my plan is that he should find such a position as soon as he can, and then through your interest, which I am sure you would be kind enough to use out of friendship for him, and I hope out of some regard to me, your brother might be persuaded to give him the Norland Tower; which I understand is a very good one, and the present incumbent has been targeted as insolent by a pirate crew and is thus not likely to live a great while. That would be enough for us to marry upon, and we might trust to time and chance for the rest."

"I should always be happy," replied Elinor, "to show any mark of my esteem and friendship for Mr. Ferrars, but do you not perceive that my involvement would be perfectly unnecessary? Edward is brother to Mrs. John Dashwood—*that* must be recommendation enough to her husband."

"But Mrs. John Dashwood would not much approve of Edward's becoming a lighthouse keeper. The family still hopes for him to be a great politician or Sub-Station engineer."

"Then I rather suspect that my involvement would do very little."

They were again silent for many minutes. At length Lucy exclaimed with a deep sigh, "I believe it would be wisest to end the business by dissolving the engagement. We seem so beset with difficulties on every side, that though it would make us miserable for a time, we should be happier perhaps in the end. But you will not give me your advice, Miss Dashwood?"

"No," answered Elinor, with a smile; her feelings were evident only in her fingers, which twirled the tiny ship's flag in an agitated fashion, as if the wee clipper ship was sailing steadily against an ill wind. "On such a subject I certainly will not. You know very well that my opinion would have no weight with you, unless it were on the side of your wishes."

"Indeed you wrong me," replied Lucy, with great solemnity; "I know nobody of whose judgment I think so highly as I do of yours; and I do really believe, that if you was to say to me, 'I advise you by all means to put an end to your engagement with Edward Ferrars, it will be more for the happiness of both of you,' I should resolve upon doing it immediately."

Elinor, vexed, said nothing. At the card-table, a new round of Karankrolla was beginning, and the elder Miss Steele removed her earrings and locket to offer as collateral.

"'Tis because you are an indifferent person," Lucy continued, "that your judgment might justly have such weight. If you were biased in any respect by your own feelings, your opinion would not be worth having."

Elinor thought it wisest to make no answer to this, lest they might provoke each other to an unsuitable increase of ease and unreserve. Another pause therefore of many minutes' duration succeeded this speech before Lucy ended their silence.

"Shall you be docking in Sub-Marine Station Beta this winter, Miss Dashwood?" said she with all her customary complacency.

"Certainly not."

"I am sorry for that," returned the other. "It would have gave me such pleasure to meet you there! To be sure, your brother and sister will ask you to come to them."

"It will not be in my power to accept their invitation if they do."

"How unlucky that is! I had quite depended upon meeting you there. My sister and I will be meeting some relations who have been wanting us to visit them for several years! And though I have some curiosity about the most recent alterations to the Sub-Station, and have heard of marvelous new displays at the Aqua-Museo-Quarium, I go mainly for the sake of seeing Edward. He will be there in February, otherwise the Station would have few charms for me."

Elinor sat down at the Karankrolla table with the melancholy persuasion that Edward was not only without affection for the person who was to be his wife; but that he had not even the chance of being tolerably happy in marriage. Her mood was not improved by the rounds of play that followed, in which Mrs. Jennings took her for three Ghahalas before Elinor had even got to shake her Pifflestick.

The visit of the Miss Steeles at Deadwind Island was lengthened far beyond what the first invitation implied. But the subject of Lucy and Edward's engagement was never revived by Elinor; when entered on by Lucy, who seldom missed an opportunity of introducing it, she treated it with calmness and caution, and dismissed it as soon as civility would allow; she felt such conversations to be an indulgence which Lucy did not deserve, and which were dangerous to herself. Nearly as dangerous, in fact, as playing Karankrolla, which Elinor was fastidious in avoiding in future.

CHAPTER 25

THOUGH MRS. JENNINGS WAS IN THE HABIT of spending a large portion of the year at the houses of her children and friends, her settled habitation was at Sub-Marine Station Beta, where she spent every winter in a docking station along one of the canals near Portman Grotto. Towards this undersea habitation, she began on the approach of January to turn her thoughts, and thither she one day abruptly asked the elder Misses Dashwood to accompany her. Elinor immediately gave a grateful but absolute denial for both. The reason alleged was their determined resolution of not leaving their mother. Mrs. Jennings received the refusal with some surprise, and repeated her invitation immediately.

"Oh, *pngllgpg!*" she emitted, a phrase from her native tongue translating, roughly, to "don't be a foolish pile of elephant excrement."

"I am sure your mother can spare you very well, and I *do* beg you will favour me with your company. Don't fancy that you will be any inconvenience to me, for I shan't put myself at all out of my way for you. We three shall be able to go in my personal submarine; and when we arrive at the Station, there will be so much to do. The Aqua-Museo-Quarium is said to have added a wealth of new creatures this season, and Kensington Undersea Gardens is expanded and more splendid than ever! I am sure your mother will not object to the journey; and if I don't get at least one of you married before I have done with you, it shall not be my fault. I shall speak a good word for you to all the young men, you may depend upon it."

"I thank you, ma'am," said Marianne, with warmth. "Your invitation has insured my gratitude for ever, and it would give me such happiness to accept it. But my mother, my dearest, kindest mother—nothing should tempt me to leave her!"

Elinor understood that her sister's eagerness to be with Willoughby was creating a total indifference to almost everything else. She therefore ventured no further direct opposition to the plan, and merely referred it to her mother's decision. On being informed of the invitation, Mrs. Dashwood was persuaded that such an excursion would be productive of much amusement to both her daughters. She would not hear of their declining the offer upon *her* account; insisted on their both accepting it directly.

"I am delighted with the plan," she cried, "it is exactly what I could wish. Margaret and I shall be as much benefited by it as yourselves. When you and the Middletons are gone, we shall go on so quietly and happily together with our books and our music."

At that very moment, they heard a terrible, full-throated scream, loud and long, from the second floor.

"No!! Noooo!"

"My goodness!" said Miss Dashwood. "What—"

"Again!" cried Margaret, as she hurtled down the stairs and into the parlour. "It begins again!"

"I thought we had finished with this nonsense, dear Margaret!" cried Mrs. Dashwood.

"Mother! Mother, you must—" began the girl, her eyes rolling wildly in her head, her chest heaving.

"I said *enough!* You soon will be a child no longer, Margaret, but a woman, and these flights of fancy are no longer to be tolerated."

"Mother," interjected Elinor cautiously, for something in her youngest sister's pale-white appearance and trembling shoulders led her to wonder whether there was more to Margaret's troubled state than mere fancy.

"No, Elinor," replied Mrs. Dashwood. "I can countenance no more such behaviour."

Marianne meanwhile drifted towards the pianoforte, closing her mind against any further consideration of what she knew—somewhere in some dark corner of her heart—that she had seen on the day of the blue-fish attack, seen blossoming foully from the peak of Mount Margaret.

"Upstairs, child," Mrs. Dashwood commanded, "and return to your needlepoint."

Margaret regretfully relented; she returned with heavy tread to her bedroom, to stare out the window at the same sight that had so terrified her moments ago: Mount Margaret, again issuing forth its strange geyser of steam—whilst came crawling up the hillside towards it, in uneven rows like so many black ants, hundreds and hundreds of . . . of *what* they were she knew not. The same uncanny, subhuman figures she had spotted on her rambles, crawling about the woods and darting in and out of the caves.

From the window, she could hear them chanting in unison, their words echoing across the island as they ascended the hill towards the grey-white jet of water: *K'yaloh D'argesh F'ah! K'yaloh D'argesh F'ah! K'yaloh D'argesh F'ah!*

★   ★   ★

Downstairs, Mrs. Dashwood continued as if no interruption had taken place. "It is very right that you *should* Descend to the Station; I would have every young woman of your condition in life acquainted with the sights and phenomena of life in-Station. You will be under the care of Mrs. Jennings, a motherly good sort of woman, of whose kindness I can have no doubt. And in all probability you will see your brother, and whatever may be his faults, or the faults of his wife, I cannot bear to have you wholly estranged from each other."

"There is still one objection," said Elinor, "which cannot be so easily removed."

Marianne's countenance sunk.

"And what," said Mrs. Dashwood, "is my dear prudent Elinor going to suggest? What formidable obstacle is she now to bring forward? What iceberg raises she to breach the hull of our collective happiness?"

"My objection is this: Though I think very well of Mrs. Jennings's heart, and very much admire the collection of shrunken heads she keeps in a drawer of her vanity, she is not a woman whose society can afford us pleasure, or whose protection will give us consequence."

"That is very true," replied her mother, "but of her society, separately from that of other people, you will scarcely have anything at all, and you will almost always appear in public with Lady Middleton."

"If Elinor is frightened away by her dislike of Mrs. Jennings," said Marianne, "at least it need not prevent *my* accepting her invitation. I have no such scruples, and I am sure I could put up with every unpleasantness of that kind with very little effort."

Elinor could not help smiling at this display of indifference towards the manners of a person, to whom she had often had difficulty in persuading Marianne to behave with tolerable politeness. She resolved within herself that if her sister persisted in going, she would go likewise. To this determination she was the more easily reconciled, by recollecting that Edward Ferrars, by Lucy's account, was not to be docked at Sub-Marine Station Beta before February; and that they would likely have Ascended already by then.

"I will have you *both* go," said Mrs. Dashwood. "These objections are nonsensical. You will have much pleasure in the journey by personal submarine, and in being at the Station, and especially in being together; and if Elinor would ever condescend to anticipate enjoyment, she would foresee it there from a variety of sources; she would, perhaps, expect some from improving her acquaintance with her sister-in-law's family."

Elinor welcomed this knowing comment as an opportunity of weakening her mother's dependence on the attachment of Edward and herself, that the shock might be less when the whole truth were revealed. She now said, as calmly as she could, "I like Edward Ferrars very much, and shall be glad to see him whether below surface or above; but as to the rest of the family, it is a matter of perfect indifference to me, whether I am ever known to them or not."

Mrs. Dashwood smiled, and said nothing. Marianne lifted up her eyes in astonishment, and Elinor conjectured that she might as well have held her tongue.

It was settled that the invitation should be fully accepted. Mrs. Jennings received the information with a great deal of joy. Sir John was delighted; for to a man, whose prevailing anxiety was the dread of being alone, and who had developed during his years of island roving a lingering terror of angry tribal gods demanding virgin sacrifice, the acquisition of two, to the number of inhabitants in Sub-Marine Station Beta, was something. Even Lady Middleton took the trouble of being delighted, which was putting herself rather out of her way; and as for the Miss Steeles, especially Lucy, they had never been so happy in their lives. Marianne's joy was almost a degree beyond happiness, so great was the perturbation of her spirits and her impatience to be gone.

Their launching took place in the first week in January, in Mrs. Jennings' personal submarine, a charming, thirty-six-foot cigar-shaped vessel with a periscope detailed in the latest fashionable colours. They pulled away from the dock, and as the submarine began its slow descent under the surface of the cove, Elinor glimpsed her sister Margaret in the upstairs window, looking steadily back at her, grim-faced and piteous.

"Please," Margaret mouthed helplessly, as the submarine disappeared beneath the surface of the water. "Please don't leave me here alone."

CHAPTER 26

THE DASHWOOD SISTERS had never been to Sub-Marine Station Beta, but of course they had known all their lives about the city of wonders planted upon the ocean's floor, England's greatest achievement in its ongoing defense against the forces unleashed by the Alteration. The Station was a fully functioning human habitation, with all of its many residences, churches, offices, and famous shopping esplanades securely contained within a massive Dome of reinforced glass, seven miles long by three miles high.

The Dome itself, the greatest engineering triumph of human history since the Roman aqueducts, had been constructed over a decade and a half at the shipyards in Blackwall and Deptford, and transported in pieces down the Thames and out to sea, to a carefully selected spot some miles off the Welsh coast, just beyond the Cardigan Bay. There, upon the decks of vast battleships, the Dome had been assembled; and then down, down, she was lowered by teams of expertly trained British marines in float-suits and breathing apparatuses; down, guided by the first minds in British engineering; down and down and down, pushing all water out of the way as it went—until the Dome was landed gently into place, triple-anchored to the floor of the sea. When all was made ready, the Beta-Station Turbines were switched on—and they had sat humming away ever since, the crown jewels of His Majesty's Corps of Aquatic Engineers, constantly sucking in the ocean water that surrounds the Station and churning it out as pure freshwater—which, once pumped inside, was channeled into a series of interlocking canals and sluices that form the "roadways" of Sub-Marine Station Beta, by which its residents

THE DOME ITSELF, THE GREATEST ENGINEERING TRIUMPH OF HUMAN HISTORY
SINCE THE ROMAN AQUEDUCTS, HAD BEEN CONSTRUCTED OVER A DECADE
AND A HALF.

travelled from docking station to docking station as they went about their business.

And thusly was implanted, four miles below the ocean's surface, a thriving city of some five and seventy thousand souls. Here were the living laboratories, where teams of hydro-zoologists worked to perfect new techniques of marine animal domestication and control; here were munitions experts and shipwrights, designing more effective vessels and armaments to wage war against the sea-beasts; and here, for those having the means, was a place to live and work and be diverted by numerous undersea pleasure gardens and aquatic exhibition halls. All in the total safety provided by a fortress in the very heart, as it were, of the enemy camp.

Mrs. Jennings and her charges were three days on their journey, their anticipation building with each passing hour. They plowed the dark undersea currents, plotting a rough southwesterly course along the Devonshire coast, and then bearing starboard, up around the Cornwall peninsula, then due north, parallel to the western coast and towards Sub-Marine Station Beta.

Their passing was unremarkable, except for two terrifying hours during which the ship was piloted through a school of lantern-fish. These were slow-moving, lurking creatures, as big as houses, each with a single gigantic, glowing eye affixed to the end of a tentacle springing out from above its mouth.

"Ach, these are but like minnows, in'they?" growled the submariner at the helm of the craft, an old accomplice of Sir John's with a bushy black beard and a steely expression. "Less'n you should plant ya right in their peeper-grasp, in'it?"

Mrs. Jennings cheerily translated his mariner's argot to Marianne, who eagerly attended to every detail relating to these fascinating monsters. One was safe from the lantern-fish if one avoided crossing their field of vision, which trick the submariner and his crew performed by weaving slowly, for two terrifying hours, through the vast herd.

They reached Sub-Marine Station Beta at three o'clock; the sturdy leaden hull of the submarine drew up against the Pipe, as it was known—this was the steel tunnel, a half mile in circumference, that jutted up from the lip of the Dome like an enormous stovepipe. At half-mile intervals the Pipe was dotted with circular entrances, which swung open by a system of winches, to allow submarines to be piloted inside and discharge their passengers for Descencion into the Station.

One by one, beginning with Mrs. Jennings, the three passengers emerged from the submarine and stepped into a spotless, glass-walled welcome chamber, where they were politely searched for outside organic material; none-such being found, the travellers were lowered together on a hydraulic lift down, down, and farther down—the shift in atmospheric pressure offset by the calibrated speed of their Descent, and the handfuls of guar beans they were given to chew on—until at last they landed with a gentle *pfffft* onto the sea floor, in the vast welcome garden of Sub-Marine Station Beta.

The Dashwood sisters were happy to arrive in-Station, and were glad to be released, after such a journey, from the confines of the personal submarine, and ready to enjoy all the luxury of a good fire—though in this particular they were swiftly disappointed, as open flame was strictly limited within the carefully controlled atmosphere of the Dome. They travelled by gondola through a series of freshwater canals to Mrs. Jennings's docking station, enjoying brief glimpses of some of the more adventure-some modes of transport available in-Station; dandies in bowler hats whizzed past riding on dolphins, whilst elderly women were ferried regally on the backs of dim-eyed sea turtles. Both sisters expressed delight at having arrived in a world where—thanks to hydro-zoology science, chemical desalination, and other scientific wonders passing common un-derstanding—the water, and the beasts within it, had been so thoroughly brought to heel.

Mrs. Jennings's docking in Berkeley Causeway was handsome, and handsomely fitted up. It had no back wall; or, rather, because it was an outer-ring docking, the back wall was composed of the curving surface of the Dome itself. In essence, then, when standing in the rear rooms of Mrs. Jennings's docking, one stood in a giant aquarium, looking out on the sea-life, treacherous and beautiful by turns, that went past the protected world of the Sub-Station. And so, once Elinor and Marianne were put in possession of their very comfortable apartment, they could gaze at their leisure from within the undersea paradise of the Sub-Station, and out into the inky depths of the ocean; there they saw magnificent formations of deepwater coral and floating varietals of which Elinor had read but never seen. As they stared, openmouthed, there came in view also a school of fearsome barracuda, prowling slowly past the glass, a reminder of the vast array of deadly creatures that lurked just on the other side of the divide, whose murderous intentions were thwarted only by the miracle of engineering in which all residents of Station Beta were cosseted.

The Dashwoods swiftly refreshed their wardrobes, making sure to don their Float-Suits over their new ensembles. The Float-Suits were composed firstly of arm-bands, one worn around each bicep, and a kind of waist-sash, all of which could be swiftly inflated by tugging on a cord tucked up one's sleeve; and secondly of a reed worn under the nose, connected by a long snaking hose to a tiny tank at the small of the back, containing enough oxygen for four minute's worth of respiration. The suits were cumbersome, to be sure, but they were required by law at all times in Sub-Marine Station Beta—most wisely, considering what happened to Sub-Marine Station Alpha.

Elinor determined to write immediately to their mother, and sat down for that purpose. In a few moments Marianne did the same. "I am writing home, Marianne," said Elinor; "had not you better defer your letter for a day or two?"

"I am *not* going to write to my mother," replied Marianne, hastily, as if wishing to avoid any further inquiry. Elinor said no more; it immediately struck her that she must then be writing to Willoughby; and the conclusion which as instantly followed was that they must be engaged.

This conviction, though not entirely satisfactory, gave her pleasure, and she continued her letter with greater alacrity, looking up only when one of the barracuda returned and rammed its snout against the glass. Marianne's letter was finished in a very few minutes; in length it could be no more than a note; it was then folded up, sealed, and directed with eager rapidity. Elinor thought she could distinguish a large *W* in the direction; and no sooner was it complete than Marianne, ringing the bell, requested the gondolier who answered to get that letter conveyed for her at once.

Marianne's spirits still continued very high; but there was a flutter in them which prevented their giving much pleasure to her sister, and this agitation increased as the evening drew on.

Dinner was a quick affair, as were all meals in-Station, fresh food and drink being nearly impossible to obtain for even the wealthiest of its residents. This dispiriting fact was due to the carefully regulated and pressurized atmosphere within the Dome, which did not allow for fires larger than those required for candlelight; and further to the Station's remote location below the surface of the sea, which made the importation of fresh vegetation and livestock extravagantly expensive. Dining options were, therefore, largely limited to jerkies, gelatinous food-flavoured loaves, and packets of powder that—when mixed with imagination and chemically desalinated water—could approximate one's favourite libation.

When the Dashwoods and their hostess returned to the drawing-room, Marianne seemed to be anxiously listening for the oar splash of every passing gondola.

It was a great satisfaction to Elinor that Mrs. Jennings, by being much engaged in her own room, could see little of what was passing. Already had Marianne been disappointed more than once by a rap at a neighbouring door, when a loud one was suddenly heard which could not be mistaken for one at any other docking, Elinor felt secure of its announcing Willoughby's approach. Marianne smoothed her hair, adjusted her bodice, and even removed the unsightly nasal-reed of her Float-Suit, but

Elinor insisted she return it to its required position under her nose.

Marianne advanced a few steps towards the stairs, and after listening half a minute, returned into the room in all the agitation which a conviction of having heard him would naturally produce; in the ecstasy of her feelings at that instant she could not help exclaiming, "Oh, Elinor, it is Willoughby, indeed it is!" and seemed almost ready to throw herself into his arms, when Colonel Brandon appeared.

It was too great a shock to be borne with calmness, and she immediately left the room. Elinor was disappointed too, and all the more so to find that the months of separation had not eased her instinctive nausea and dread at the sight of him. At the same time her regard for Colonel Brandon ensured his welcome with her; and she felt particularly hurt that a man so partial to her sister should perceive that she experienced nothing but grief and disappointment and queasiness in seeing him. She instantly saw that it was not unnoticed by him, that he observed Marianne as she quitted the room, with such astonishment and concern, as hardly left him the recollection of what civility demanded towards herself. She also noticed that Brandon wore no Float-Suit; she was about to inquire, when she realised with a start that his quasi-fishiness, and in particular his ability to breathe underwater, had likely earned him a dispensation.

"Is your sister ill?" said he, his flagellum wavering worriedly beneath his nose.

Elinor answered in some distress that she was, and then talked of head-aches, low spirits, and a mild case of diver's disease stemming from their Descent that morning.

He said no more on the subject, and began directly to speak of his pleasure at seeing them in-Station, making the usual inquiries about the peril of their journey, and the friends they had left behind. Elinor told him of the lantern-beasts; he recalled a similar anecdote from his service in the East Indies, except it was not lantern-beasts that threatened the boat, but piranhas; and rather than carefully weave their way through the swarm of creatures, the crew had satiated them by throwing overboard a shackled would-be deserter.

In this calm kind of way, with very little interest on either side, they continued to talk, both of them out of spirits, and the thoughts of both engaged elsewhere. Elinor wished very much to ask whether Willoughby were in town, but she was afraid of giving Brandon pain by any enquiry after his rival; and at length, by way of saying something, she asked if he had been at Sub-Marine Station Beta ever since she had seen him last. "Yes," he replied, with some embarrassment, "almost ever since; I have been once or twice at Delaford for a few days, but it has never been in my power to return to the Devonshire coast."

This, and the manner in which it was said, immediately brought back to her remembrance all the circumstances of his quitting that place. She was fearful that her question had implied much more curiosity on the subject than she had ever felt.

Mrs. Jennings soon came in. "Oh! Colonel," said she, with her usual noisy cheerfulness, "I am monstrous glad to see you—"

Elinor gasped audibly at this inauspicious word choice, Brandon looked at his hands, and even the usually imperturbable Mrs. Jennings blanched at her poor choice of words.

"Ah yes, sorry, I am *very* glad to see you—I didn't mean *monstrous* glad, as in—not to imply that you are—sorry—beg your pardon, but I have been forced to look about me a little, and settle my matters; for it is a long while since I have been at home. But pray, Colonel, how came you to conjure out that I should be in the Sub-Station today?"

"I had the pleasure of hearing it at Mr. Palmer's, where I have been dining."

"You did! How does Charlotte do? I warrant you she is swollen as a puffer-fish by this time."

"Mrs. Palmer appeared quite well, and I am commissioned to tell you, that you will certainly see her to-morrow."

"Ay, to be sure, I thought as much. Well, Colonel, I have brought two young ladies with me. You see but one of them now, but there is another somewhere. Your friend, Miss Marianne, too—which you will not be sorry to hear. I do not know what you and Mr. Willoughby will do between you about her. Aye, it is a fine thing to be young and handsome—" Mrs. Jennings blanched again. "Or, well—young, anyway. But Colonel, where have you been to since we parted? And how does your business go on? Do my eyes deceive me, or do you have slightly fewer of those things on your face than previously? No? Ah, well. Come, come, let's have no secrets among friends!"

He replied with his customary mildness to all her inquiries, but without satisfying her in any. Elinor now began to slice off chunks of gelatinous scone loaf to be eaten with their tea, and Marianne was obliged to appear again.

After her entrance, Colonel Brandon became more thoughtful and silent than he had been before, absentmindedly stroking his squigglers and looking blankly about the room; Mrs. Jennings could not prevail on him to stay long. No other visitor appeared that evening, and the ladies were unanimous in agreeing to go early to bed. For some time, however, a school of clownfish organized themselves to batter against the glass of the Dome for an hour and a half, between midnight and one thirty, making sleep impossible; once they ceased in their efforts, all slept pleasantly.

Marianne rose the next morning with recovered spirits and happy looks. The disappointment of the evening before seemed forgotten in the expectation of what was to happen that day. They had not long finished their toast-and-beans-flavoured gelatin cubes before Mrs. Palmer's gondola was glimpsed being tied up at the dock, and in a few minutes she came laughing into the room, so delighted to see them all.

"Mr. Palmer will be so happy to see you," said she; "What do you think he said when he heard of your coming with Mamma? I forget what it was now, but it was something so droll—touching, I think, upon the uselessness of social visits when one considers the ultimate darkness that awaits us all, or something of that nature. Droll indeed!"

After an hour or two spent in what her mother called comfortable chat, it was proposed by Mrs. Palmer that they should all accompany her to the Retail Embankment, to which Mrs. Jennings and Elinor readily consented, the latter having heard of the dazzling array of specialty items on offer in-Station, from embossed fans made from dorsal fins to crystallized serpent eyes fashioned into earrings; and Marianne, though declining it at first, was induced to go likewise.

It was late in the morning before they returned home; and no sooner had they entered the docking than Marianne flew eagerly upstairs, and when Elinor followed, she found her turning from the table with a sorrowful countenance, which declared that no Willoughby had been there.

"Has no letter been left here since we went out?" said she to the footman who then entered with the parcels. She was answered in the negative. "Are you quite sure of it?" she replied. "No one has swum up and left something? No bottle has floated to the door, a note carefully folded within? Are you certain that no servant, no porter has left any letter or note?"

The man replied that none had.

"How very odd!" said she, in a low and disappointed voice, as she turned away to the observation glass.

"How odd, indeed!" repeated Elinor within herself, regarding her sister with uneasiness. "If she had not known him to be at the Sub-Marine Station she would not have written to him, as she did; she would have written to Combe Magna; and if he is docked here, how odd that he should neither come nor write!" Elinor recalled rumours of ultra-secret government laboratories in-Station; supposedly men were experimented upon in various chilling ways, with the goal of creating improvements in human anatomy that would allow our bedeviled species decisive advantage over the chordate races. She wondered whether it were possible that Willoughby had submitted to such an experiment, and had his brain exchanged with that of a tortoise or was similarly indisposed? And yet to make such a sacrifice seemed unlike Willoughby—but what did they truly know of him!

Marianne passed that evening restlessly; she sometimes endeavoured for a few minutes to read, having acquired at a fashionable Retail Embankment book shop a new volume titled *The Near-Drowning, Near-Starvation, and Subsequent Rescue of the Spanish Seaman Alphonso James*; but the book was soon thrown aside, and she returned to the more interesting employment of walking backwards and forwards across the room, pausing for a moment whenever she came to the window, in hopes of distinguishing the long-expected rap. Instead all she saw was the passing gondolas of strangers; or, if looking out the room's glass rear wall, the teeming hordes of slithering and swimming things, all as desperate to get into the Station as was Marianne to meet again with her lamented friend.

CHAPTER 27

"REPORTS FROM THE SURFACE-LANDS are of sunny skies," said Mrs. Jennings, employing the phrase common in-Station to refer to the world outside, "If the open weather continues, Sir John will not like setting off from the archipelago next week. On fine days, he likes to prowl his grounds, trolling the freshwater ponds for serpents and strangling them barehanded. He will not want to lose a day's pleasure."

"That is true," cried Marianne with happy surprise. Walking to the back glass as she spoke, she watched with cheerful fascination as a cutlassfish speared a carp and swallowed it whole. "I had not thought of that. This weather will keep many monster hunters in the country, and treasure hunters, too."

It was a lucky recollection, all her good spirits were restored by it. "It sounds like they are having charming weather, indeed," she continued, as she sat down at the table to stir a packet of tea flavouring into a glass of water. "How much they must enjoy it! But it cannot be expected to last long. Frosts will soon set in, and in all probability with severity—nay, perhaps it may freeze tonight!"

"At any rate," said Elinor, wishing to prevent Mrs. Jennings from seeing her sister's thoughts as clearly as she did, "I dare say we shall have Sir John and Lady Middleton in-Station by the end of next week."

"Aye, my dear, I'll warrant you we do. My daughter always has her own way; except, of course, when it comes to achieving what she most desires: to flee Sir John's household, never to see him or this country, again."

The morning was chiefly spent in leaving decorated hermit-crab shells—used as calling cards by fashionable Sub-Station residents—at the houses of Mrs. Jennings's acquaintance to inform them of her being in Station; and Marianne was all the time busy imagining that, through the slightest shifts in atmospheric pressure in the great encased Dome of the Sub-Station, she could divine the temperature in the Surface-Lands. Time and again, Elinor gently reminded Marianne that the weather in Sub-Marine Station Beta was created by the workings of cloud-engines and temperature-stabilizers, all powered by Newcomen steam-devices, and bearing no relation to the warmth or cold of the Surface-Lands. But Marianne would not be deterred from her amateur aerology.

"Don't you find it more pressurized than it was in the morning, Elinor? There seems to me a very decided difference in pressure; my ear drums are continually popping, such that I have to go like this with my face to unclog them."

Elinor was alternately diverted and pained; but Marianne persevered, and saw every night in the shadows of submarines passing overhead, and every morning in the subtlest alterations in her inner ear, the certain symptoms of approaching frost in the country.

The Miss Dashwoods had no reason to be dissatisfied with Mrs. Jennings's style of living, and her behaviour to themselves was invariably kind. Colonel Brandon, who had a general invitation to the docking station, was with them almost every day. He came to look at Marianne and talk to Elinor, who often derived more satisfaction from conversing with him than from any other daily occurrence. At the same time she saw with much concern his continued regard for her sister. She noted that his appendages at times seemed to stiffen a bit when he chanced to glance upon Marianne, as if excess blood were flowing into them. It grieved her to see the earnestness with which he often watched Marianne, and discomfited her to see the aforementioned tentacle-stiffness; his spirits were certainly worse than when at Deadwind.

About a week after their arrival, it became certain that Willoughby was also arrived. His hermit-crab shell calling card, marked with the distinctive *W* formed from crossed treasure shovels, was on the table when they came in after a brief pleasure cruise of the canals one morning.

"Good God!" cried Marianne. "He has been here while we were out!" Elinor, rejoiced to be assured of his being at Sub-Marine Station Beta, now ventured to say, "Depend upon it, he will call again to-morrow." But Marianne seemed hardly to hear her, and on Mrs. Jennings's entrance, escaped with the precious shell.

This event, while it raised the spirits of Elinor, restored to Marianne all her former agitation. From this moment her mind was never quiet; the expectation of seeing him every hour of the day, made her unfit for anything. Nor could she be persuaded to accompany them, the next morning, on their planned excursion to Mr. Pennywhistle's Aqua-Museo-Quarium, a petting zoo and showplace designed for the diversion of children and unmarried women. There some of the gentler and more thoroughly domesticated sea-beasts, such as snails, dolphins, and pollywogs, could be marveled at and even ridden upon.

Elinor's thoughts were full of what might be passing in Berkeley Causeway during their absence, so much so that out of inattention she let her hand slip off the reins and was nipped by a pony-sized sea snail upon which she had been riding; the beast's white-jacketed handler apologised profusely, and was heard to mutter darkly to the errant gastropod that "butter could be warmed for you yet."

A moment's glance at her sister when they returned from the Aqua-Museo-Quarium was enough to inform Elinor that Willoughby had paid no second visit there. A note was just then brought in, and laid on the table.

"For me!" cried Marianne, stepping hastily forward.

"No, ma'am, for my mistress."

But Marianne, not convinced, took it instantly up.

"It is indeed for Mrs. Jennings! How provoking! I cannot read a word of it!" (Which was precisely true—the note was written in Mrs. Jennings's native tongue, which used neither vowels nor spaces between the words.)

"You are expecting a letter, then?" said Elinor.

"Yes, a little—not much."

Mrs. Jennings soon appeared, and the note being given her, she read it aloud.

"*Hghgljtxlxthrhralkxvjlklklqrdl*," she read quickly, and then, after clearing her throat, explained. The letter was from Lady Middleton, announcing their Descension into the Station the night before, and requesting the company of her mother and cousins the following evening. The invitation was accepted; but when the hour of appointment drew near, Elinor had some difficulty in persuading her sister to go, for still she had seen nothing of Willoughby; and she was unwilling to run the risk of his calling again in her absence.

Elinor found, when the evening was over, that disposition is not materially altered by a change of abode, for although scarcely settled in town, Sir John had contrived to collect around him, nearly twenty young people, and to amuse them with a pirate-themed ball, gentlemen of fortune being very much in vogue that season. This was an affair, however, of which Lady Middleton did not approve. In the country, an unpremeditated thematic dance was very allowable; but in the Sub-Station, where the reputation of elegance was more important and less easily attained, it was risking too much for the gratification of a few girls, to have it known that Lady Middleton had given a small dance of eight or nine couples, with two fiddlers and a small assortment of appe-tizer-flavoured paste cakes.

Mr. and Mrs. Palmer were of the party; the former, they knew from Sir John, had been a buccaneer in his youth, and so his general darkness of spirit was compounded on this occasion by a scorn for the inauthen-ticity of the theme dance. He looked at Elinor and Marianne slightly, shook his head gloomily, and merely nodded to Mrs. Jennings from the other side of the room. Marianne gave one glance round the apartment as she entered, lifting up the eye patch she had affected for the evening to assure herself that *he* was not there—and sat down, equally ill-disposed to receive or communicate pleasure, despite her warm affection for pirate slang and custom. After they had been assembled about an hour, Mr. Palmer sauntered towards the Miss Dashwoods to express his surprise on seeing them in town.

"The Island. Pestilent Isle," said he curtly. "You are shut of it, then?"

"We are indeed, though our mother and youngest sister remain," replied Elinor.

"Then pray for them," he said darkly. "Pray for them." And, provid-ing no chance for Elinor to divine his meaning, Palmer turned on his boot heel and stalked away.

Never had Marianne been so unwilling to dance a jig in her life, as she was that evening, and never so much fatigued by the exercise. She complained of it as they returned to Berkeley Causeway.

"Aye, aye," said Mrs. Jennings, "we know the reason of all that very well. If a certain person who shall be nameless, had been at the theme dance, you would have been a most sprightly pirate lass indeed. To say the truth, it was not very pretty of him not to give you the meeting when he was invited."

"Invited!" cried Marianne.

"So my daughter Middleton told me, for it seems Sir John met him somewhere this morning." Marianne said no more, but looked exceed-ingly hurt. Impatient in this situation to be doing something that might lead to her sister's relief, Elinor resolved to write the next morning to her mother.

About the middle of the day, Mrs. Jennings went out by herself on business, and Elinor began her letter directly, while Marianne, too restless for employment, too anxious for conversation, walked from the front window to the back glass, listlessly tapping on the glass at a school of clusterfish—clustered, characteristically, outside. Elinor was very earnest in her application to her mother, relating all that had passed, her suspicions of Willoughby's inconstancy, urging her by every plea of duty and affection to demand from Marianne an account of her real situation with respect to him.

Her letter was scarcely finished, when a rap foretold a visitor, and Colonel Brandon was announced. Marianne, who had seen him from the window, left the room before he entered it. He looked more than usually grave; his dark eyes were downcast, and his weird, squiddish protrusions lay like a dark, quivering cloud over his jowls. Though he expressed satisfaction at finding Miss Dashwood alone, as if he had something urgent to tell her, he sat for some time without saying a word. After a pause of several minutes, during which her impatience and the deep, mucousy workings of Brandon's respiration conspired to drive Elinor to the point of distraction, their silence was broken—by his asking when he was to congratulate her on the acquisition of a brother. Elinor was not prepared for such a question, and was obliged to adopt the simple and common expedient of asking what he meant. All the tentacles in the world could not have hidden the insincerity of his smile as he replied, "Your sister's engagement to Mr. Willoughby is very generally known?"

"It cannot be generally known," returned Elinor, "for her own family do not know it."

He looked surprised and said, "I beg your pardon, I am afraid my inquiry has been impertinent; but I had not supposed any secrecy intended, as they openly correspond, and their marriage is universally talked of."

"How can that be? By whom can you have heard it mentioned?"

"By many—by some of whom you know nothing, by others with whom you are most intimate, Mrs. Jennings, Mrs. Palmer, and the Middletons. But still I might not have believed it, for where the mind is perhaps rather unwilling to be convinced, it will always find something to support its doubts. But when the servant let me in today, and stepped past onto the gangplank to tie up the porpoise on which I arrived, I accidentally saw a letter in his hand, directed to Mr. Willoughby in your sister's writing. Is everything finally settled? Is it impossible to—"

He stopped himself, and his fleshy face fingers twisted themselves into knots of awkwardness.

"Excuse me, Miss Dashwood. I believe I have been wrong in saying so much, but I hardly know what to do. Tell me that it is all absolutely resolved on, that any attempt, that in short concealment, if concealment be possible, is all that remains."

These words, which conveyed to Elinor a direct avowal of his love for her sister, affected her very much. She was not immediately able to say anything, and even when her spirits were recovered, she debated for a short time, on the answer it would be most proper to give. The real state of things between Willoughby and her sister was so little known to herself, that in endeavouring to explain it, she might be as liable to say too much as too little. Yet she thought it most prudent and kind to say more than she really knew or believed.

She acknowledged, therefore, that though she had never been informed by themselves of the terms on which they stood with each other, of their mutual affection she had no doubt, and of their correspondence she was not astonished to hear.

He listened to her with silent attention, nodding sadly so as to cause his tentacle-mass to shake limply. On her ceasing to speak, Brandon rose directly from his seat, and said in a voice of emotion, "to your sister I wish all imaginable happiness; to Willoughby that he may endeavour to deserve her." Then he took leave and went away.

Elinor derived no comfortable feelings from this conversation; she

was left, on the contrary, with a melancholy impression of Colonel
Brandon's unhappiness. From the window she saw him pause and stare for
several long seconds into the canal; it seemed to Elinor that Brandon contemplated abandoning his steed and simply diving in and swimming
away—as if in the moment of his heart's defeat he had become more fish
than man.

CHAPTER 28

NOTHING OCCURRED during the next three or four days to
make Elinor regret applying to her mother; for Willoughby neither came nor wrote. They were engaged about the end of that time to attend with Lady Middleton an event at Hydra-Z, more properly known as
the Hydro-Zoological Laboratory and Exhibition Arcade. Admission to the
spectacle was an enormous honour, one the Dashwoods could only enjoy
through their connection with Sir and Lady Middleton. Hydra-Z was the
very heart of the Station's scientific facilities, where captured monsters
were submitted to the most rigorous re-training and biological modifi-
cation programs—and, when the results were satisfactory, brought before
paying audiences to demonstrate how completely they had been made to
do the will of man.

As Elinor understood the intention of tonight's amusement, they
would be seated with the rest of the guests in an amphitheatre, arrayed
semi-circularly before a vast pool, and be treated to a command performance by a dozen giant, super-intelligent, domesticated lobsters.

For this spectacle, Marianne prepared wholly dispirited, careless of
her appearance, and seeming equally indifferent whether she went or
stayed; she listlessly adjusted her Float-Suit and selected a pair of opera
glasses from Mrs. Jennings collection. She sat in the drawing-room till the

moment of Lady Middleton's arrival, without once stirring from her seat, or altering her attitude, lost in her own thoughts, and insensible of her sister's presence; and when at last they were told that Lady Middleton waited for them at the door, she started as if she had forgotten that any-one was expected.

They arrived in due time at Hydra-Z and were ushered to Amphithe-atre Seven, where the spectacle was to unfold; they heard their names an-nounced from one landing-place to another in an audible voice, and entered to find the whole pool, with surrounding seating area, splendidly lit up. They began to mingle in the crowd—the lobsters had not yet been led in, leaving time for other amusement until the performance began. Lady Middleton was able to organize a handful of strangers for a game of Karankrolla, by the sure method of not telling them exactly what it was; as Marianne was not in spirits for moving about, she and Elinor succeeded to the raked seating area, placing themselves at no great distance from the pool.

They had not remained in this manner long, before it was an-nounced that the lobsters were to be brought in. Enthusiastic applause welling up from the crowd, all eyes turned to the pool, into which the twelve magnificent, genetically enhanced Nephropidae were swimming from a small side stream. Trotting parallel to them at the water's edge was a handsome trainer in a bathing costume and cap, holding an elongated lobster-crop in one hand and waving with the other to the crowd.

It was then that Elinor perceived Willoughby, standing by the water's edge within a few yards of them, in earnest conversation with a very fash-ionable looking young woman; startled, Elinor wondered at first if it was truly he, until she saw Monsieur Pierre, hopping gaily from one foot to another at Willoughby's side. She soon caught his eye—Willoughby's, not Monsieur Pierre's—and he immediately bowed, but without attempting to speak to her or to approach Marianne, though he could not but see her; and then continued his discourse with the same lady. Elinor turned in-voluntarily to Marianne, to see whether it could be unobserved by her.

At that moment she first perceived him, and her whole countenance glowing with sudden delight, she would have moved towards him instantly, had not her sister caught hold of her.

The lobsters had now all swum into the pool, each one half again as big as a cow. Elinor recoiled instinctually from the creatures, but then watched with fascination as, under the trainer's command, they began to swim slow, precise figure eights in the pool. Still holding Marianne by the shoulder, she raised her opera glasses. Their enormous size magnified the disturbing appearance of the crustaceans—the twin antennae extending from beneath the beady eyes; the ribbed, mottled-brown exoskeletons; the army of skittering pereiopod lining the torso; and of course the claws, each pair like a gigantic brown-black nutcracker, except razor-sharp where it clacked together. Like privates being drilled by a sergeant, these hideous creatures dipped in and out of the water as they swam, bobbing up and down, snapping their oversized claws in the air each time they surfaced.

Marianne could not be distracted, even by the elegant athletic turns of the lobsters. "Good heavens!" she exclaimed. "Why does he not look at me? Why cannot I speak to him?"

"Pray be composed," cried Elinor, "and do not betray what you feel to everybody present. Perhaps he has not observed you yet."

This, however, was more than she could believe herself; and to be composed at such a moment was not only beyond the reach of Marianne, it was beyond her wish. She sat in an agony of impatience which affected every feature. In the pool, the trainer shouted a rough command, and the lobsters were in an instant up on their caudal furca in the shallow water, claws extended upwards in a comically servile posture like so many hunting dogs begging for scrap. The lobsters waited at bay for their next command, their antennae wavering tremulously in the air, as the trainer produced from a small valise a croquet ball and hurled it up towards them. The first of the lobsters in the line reached out a claw and deftly crushed the croquet ball to powder. The crowd cheered its approval.

Next the trainer produced a billiard ball, and tossed it before the next lobster in the line, who dispatched it with similar ease. Elinor saw that Willoughby applauded heartily along with his fellow spectators; could he be so at ease?

Now from the valise came the skull of some animal—Elinor thought it was a sheep. After this grim object had been tossed, and destroyed with a swift claw-snap from another of the monster lobsters, Willoughby at last turned round, and regarded the sisters; Marianne started up, and pronouncing his name in a tone of affection, held out her hand to him. He approached, and addressing himself rather to Elinor than Marianne, as if wishing to avoid her eye, and determined not to observe her attitude, inquired in a hurried manner after Mrs. Dashwood, and asked how long they had been in-Station. Elinor was robbed of all presence of mind by such an address, and was unable to say a word. As her mind tried in vain to alight on an appropriate response, she saw over Willoughby's shoulder that one of the lobsters had, for some reason, broken the neat line and resumed its natural position, belly in the water.

Marianne was too focused on Willoughby's strange behaviour to note this aberration in the program; her feelings were instantly expressed. Her face was crimsoned over, and she exclaimed, in a voice of the greatest emotion, "Good God! Willoughby, what is the meaning of this? Have you not received my letters? Will you not shake hands with me?"

Poolside, the scowling trainer set down the enormous ripe casaba melon he was about to throw to the lobsters and jumped in to corral his errant charge.

Willoughby, meanwhile, could not now avoid the insisted-upon handshake, but Marianne's touch seemed painful to him, and he held her hand only for a moment. During all this time he was evidently struggling for composure. Elinor watched his countenance and saw its expression becoming more tranquil. After a moment's pause, he spoke with calmness.

"I did myself the honour of calling in Berkeley Causeway last Tuesday, and very much regretted that I was not fortunate enough to find yourselves and Mrs. Jennings at home. My hermit-crab card was not lost, I hope: It's the one with the shovels formed into a *W*."

"But have you not received my notes?" cried Marianne in the wildest anxiety. "Here is some mistake I am sure—some dreadful mistake. What can be the meaning of it? Tell me, Willoughby; for heaven's sake tell me, what is the matter?"

Before her tormentor could proffer an answer, all conversation was stilled by a most terrible and unnatural sound emerging from the direction of the pool, and echoing through the vast room. It was a sound, thought Elinor as she clutched her ears against it, like the squeal of a rat amplified a thousandfold and merged with the screams of a frightened child.

It was the lobsters—all had now broken formation and converged on the unfortunate trainer. In an instant, every exposed inch of his flesh came under assault by a dozen pairs of gigantic claws; huge chunks of meat were ripped from his arms and from his legs, the very scalp torn from his head. "Help! For God's sake, help!!—" he managed to choke out, his crop flailing helplessly against the water, before the largest of the lobsters, in fluid motions no doubt learned from this very trainer, clawed himself up onto the man's chest, wrapped its long, whip-like antennae around his neck, and cleanly garroted off his head. As the guests looked at each other, horrified and uncertain, the decapitated trainer's arms thrashed, thrashed again, and then went still, as streams of blood gushed into the pool water from the stump of his neck.

Now, with a redoubling of their ungodly screech of a war cry, the lobsters climbed out of the water and advanced on the guests in a perfect, soldierly *V* formation.

"Willoughby!" cried Marianne in terror of the advancing wedge of warlike crustaceans.

"Willoughby!" cried the fashionable lady to whom he had been speaking a moment ago. The lobsters screeched louder and clacked their claws together like nightmarish rust-brown castanets.

Willoughby backpedaled from the water's edge, as his complexion changed and all his embarrassment returned; he contemplated the two ladies, both desperate for his protection and the affection it would imply. At last he turned on his heel and ran to the unknown young lady, where she had scampered up onto the closest row of seats. Marianne, now looking dreadfully white, and unable to stand, sunk into her chair. Elinor slapped her hard, three times, to get her moving; this was no time for a swoon. The lobsters grew closer by the instant, each one scuttling rapidly forward on five pairs of monstrous legs. One stopped abruptly in its forward march and clamped its terrible claws around the exposed neck of a young woman; a river of blood launched from her throat and poured down the bodice of her elegant swimming costume.

The guests, Elinor and Marianne among them, began a screaming stampede for the exit, shoving and fighting past one another to get out of the path of the death-lobsters; only Lady Middleton, who in her former life as an island princess had defended her people from such threats, was vigorously engaged in battle against the monsters. She grabbed one of the lobsters and snapped its bulging fore claw off at the joint, then used the limb to batter at the beast's hideous cephalothorax. The lobster screeched in pain and rage, snapping in vain at the dexterous Lady Middleton with its remaining claw.

"Go to him, Elinor," Marianne pleaded, insensible of the immediate peril, even as a lobster corralled the Careys, a handsome couple of Sir John's acquaintance; with one claw the beast mauled Mr. Carey, carving large gashes from his torso, while simultaneously, with the other claw, it snapped off Mrs. Carey's feet and hands with four snaps. "Force him to come to me. Tell him I must see him again—must speak to him instantly. I cannot rest—I shall not have a moment's peace till this is explained— some dreadful misapprehension or other. Oh, go to him this moment!"

"This is not the place for explanations. Wait only till to-morrow. We must go! We must go!" As a lobster scuttled menacingly towards them, Elinor drove the pointed heel of her fashionable boot into that vulnerable spot, a quarter of the way down the back of a crustacean, where the

THE GUESTS BEGAN A SCREAMING STAMPEDE FOR THE EXIT, SHOVING AND
FIGHTING PAST ONE ANOTHER TO GET OUT OF THE PATH OF
THE DEATH-LOBSTERS.

head meets the thorax. She felt the satisfying crunch of her boot heel driving past exoskeleton and into pure vulnerable meat—the beast was stopped in its scuttling tracks.

With relief Elinor saw Willoughby quit the room by the door towards the staircase, dragging the terrified young lady with him; and telling Marianne that he was gone, urged the impossibility of speaking to him again that evening as a fresh argument for her to be calm and join her in evacuating the premises immediately. The urgency of the situation was paramount; it seemed as if wherever she looked in Hydra-Z, lobsters were furiously clawing and snapping at the maimed and bloodied unfortunates who remained.

Elinor begged her sister to entreat Lady Middleton to rescue them and take them home, although that estimable lady seemed rather to be enjoying herself, picking up lobsters wholly and dashing them to the ground. But Elinor persisted and at last Lady Middleton acceded—the three reached the exit just as a joint command of hydro-zoologists and British marines, wearing thrice-reinforced danger suits, poured into the amphitheatre.

Scarcely a word was spoken by the Dashwoods during their return to Berkeley Causeway. Elinor was still quivering with the exertion of their near escape; Marianne was in a silent agony, too much oppressed even for tears; and Lady Middleton was happily gnawing lobster meat from the giant claw she had earlier torn free from its bearer.

Mrs. Jennings was luckily not come home, so they could go directly to their own room, where water mixed with the contents of two wine powder packets restored Marianne a little to herself. She was soon undressed and in bed, and as she seemed desirous of being alone, her sister then left her, and while she waited the return of Mrs. Jennings, had leisure enough for thinking over what had happened.

That some kind of engagement had subsisted between Willoughby and Marianne she could not doubt, and that Willoughby was weary of it, seemed equally clear; for however Marianne might still feed her own wishes, *she* could not attribute such behaviour to mistake or misapprehension of any kind. Nothing but a thorough change of sentiment could account for it. Absence might have weakened his regard, and convenience might have determined him to overcome it—but there was no doubt that such a regard had formerly existed.

As for Marianne, on the pangs which so unhappy a meeting must already have given her, and on those still more severe which might await her in its probable consequence, she could not reflect without the deepest concern. Her own situation gained in the comparison; for while she could *esteem* Edward as much as ever, however they might be divided in future, her mind might be always supported. But every circumstance that could embitter such an evil seemed uniting to heighten the misery of Marianne in a final separation from Willoughby—in an immediate and irreconcilable rupture with him.

There was something else troubling about the night's events: those lobsters, as best Elinor could tell, hadn't even attempted to feast on their victims, only to savage them and then move on to the next. They were, in other words, mauling and killing human beings for pleasure—the foremost trait that was supposed to have been trained from them in the laboratories of Hydra-Z.

This disturbing fact competed with her contemplations of Marianne's misfortune, until at last she fell into an exhausted, fitful sleep.

CHAPTER 29

ELINOR WOKE THE NEXT MORNING with visions of rust-coloured claws still snapping menacingly in her head; her sister, contrastingly, seemed to have little remembrance of the homicidal lobsters and remained mired in her former preoccupation. Only half dressed, Marianne was kneeling against one of the window-seats for the sake of all the dim sea-green light that poured in from the swirling ocean outside the glass, and writing as fast as a continual flow of tears would permit her. She ignored the squid that sat slavering just outside the glass, watching her with its giant popeyes and dragging its tentacles against the Dome-glass. After observing her for a few moments with silent anxiety, Elinor asked in a tone of the most considerate gentleness:

"Marianne, may I ask—"

"No, Elinor," she replied. "Ask nothing; you will soon know all."

The sort of desperate calmness with which this was said, lasted no longer than while she spoke, and was immediately followed by a return of the same excessive affliction. It was some minutes before she could go on with her letter, and the frequent bursts of grief which still obliged her, at intervals, to withhold her pen, were proof enough that she was writing for the last time to Willoughby.

Elinor paid her every quiet and unobtrusive attention in her power, She would have tried to soothe and tranquilize her still more, had not Marianne eagerly entreated her not to speak. In such circumstances, it was better for both that they should not be long together; and the restless state of Marianne's mind not only prevented her from remaining in the room a moment after she was dressed, but requiring at once solitude and continual change of place, made her wander about the house, avoiding the sight of everybody.

At breakfast Marianne neither ate nor attempted to eat anything; her packets of tea powder and scone-and-jam-flavoured food loaf sat unopened on the table before her. They were just setting themselves in, after breakfast, round the common working table, when a letter was delivered to Marianne, which she eagerly caught from the servant, and, turning of a death-like paleness, instantly ran out of the room. Elinor knew that it must come from Willoughby, and she felt immediately such a sickness at heart as made her hardly able to hold up her head, and sat in such a general tremor as made her fear it impossible to escape Mrs. Jennings's notice. But that good lady, much distracted by Elinor's detailed description of the mutant lobsters who had set upon them at Hydra-Z, saw only that Marianne had received a letter from Willoughby, which appeared to her a very good joke, and which she treated accordingly, by hoping, with a laugh, that she would find it to her liking.

"Upon my word, I never saw a young woman so desperately in love in my life! *My* girls were foolish enough, running after this or that young princeling or shaman, until the day when Sir John's adventuring party dragged us all away in sacks." Here she laughed and then sighed with amused nostalgia before picking up the thread of her comment. "But as for Miss Marianne, she is quite an altered creature. I hope, from the bottom of my heart, he won't keep her waiting much longer, for it is quite grievous to see her look so ill and forlorn. Pray, when are they to be married?"

Elinor, though never less disposed to speak than at that moment, obliged herself to answer. "And have you really, Ma'am, talked yourself into a persuasion of my sister's being engaged to Mr. Willoughby? I thought it had been only a joke, but so serious a question seems to imply more. I do assure you that nothing would surprise me more than to hear of their going to be married. If you had told me yesterday that monster-lobsters would rise from their pool and attempt to slay everyone present, I could not have found the notion more surprising—though obviously today I know differently."

"For shame, for shame, Miss Dashwood! How can you talk so? Don't we all know that it must be a match, that they were in love with each other from the first moment they met? Did not I see them together in Devonshire every day, and all day long, dancing jigs and singing shanties and carrying on? And did not I know that your sister came to the Sub-Station with me on purpose to buy wedding clothes at the Retail Embankment's most fashionable shops? Come, come, this won't do. Because you are so sly about it yourself, you think nobody else has any senses; but it is no such thing, I can tell you, for it has been known all over the Station ever so long. I tell every body of it and so does Charlotte."

"Indeed, Ma'am," said Elinor, very seriously, "you are mistaken. Indeed, you are doing a very unkind thing in spreading the report."

Mrs. Jennings laughed again, but Elinor had not spirits to say more, and eager at all events to know what Willoughby had written, hurried away to their room, where, on opening the door, she saw Marianne stretched on the bed, almost choked by grief, one letter in her hand, and two or three others laying by her. Elinor drew near, but without saying a word; and seating herself on the bed, took her hand, kissed her affectionately several times, and then gave way to a burst of tears, which at first was scarcely less violent than Marianne's. The latter, though unable to speak, put all the letters into Elinor's hands; and then covering her face with her handkerchief, almost screamed with agony. A school of minnows observed her pitilessly from the other side of the glass. Elinor watched by her till this excess of suffering had somewhat spent itself, and then turning eagerly to Willoughby's letter, read as follows:

Bond Causeway, *January*.

MY DEAR MADAM,

I have just had the honour of receiving your letter, for which I beg to return my sincere acknowledgments. I trust that you and your sister survived the crustaceous uprising unharmed, and are safely returned to your docking. I am much concerned to find there was anything in my behaviour last night that did not meet your approbation; if I should have offered you some measure of protection from the clawing onslaught, I regret that in the panic I was unable to do so. I shall never reflect on my former acquaintance with your family off the coast of Devonshire without the most grateful pleasure. My esteem for your whole family is very sincere; but if I have been so unfortunate as to give rise to a belief of more than I felt, or meant to express, I shall reproach myself for not having been more guarded in my professions of that esteem. That I should ever have meant more you will allow to be impossible, when you understand that my affections have been long engaged elsewhere, and it will not be many weeks, I believe, before this engagement is fulfilled. This treasure hunter has found that treasure which is most sought, and soon I am to dig it up. It is with great regret that I obey your commands in returning the letters with which I have been honoured from you, and the lock of hair, which you so obligingly bestowed on me.

I am, dear Madam,

Your most obedient

humble servant,

JOHN WILLOUGHBY.

It may be imagined with what indignation this letter was read by Miss Dashwood. Though aware, before she began it, that it must confirm their separation forever, she was not aware that such language could be suffered to announce it; nor could she have supposed Willoughby capable of departing so far from the appearance of every honourable and delicate feeling—so far from the common decorum of a gentleman, as to send a letter so impudently cruel: a letter which acknowledged no breach of faith, denied all peculiar affection whatever—a letter of which every line was an insult, and which proclaimed its writer to be deep in hardened villainy.

She paused over it for some time with indignant astonishment; then read it again and again; but every perusal only served to increase her abhorrence of the man. She dared not trust herself to speak, lest she might wound Marianne still deeper by treating their disengagement, not as a loss to her of any possible good but as an escape from the worst and most irremediable of all evils. To have been engaged to such a man was like falling under a curse more grave even than the one afflicting Colonel Brandon; to have the engagement broken was to see the curse lifted in a stroke.

On hearing the splash of oars outside, Elinor went to the front window to see who could be coming so unreasonably early. She was astonished to perceive Mrs. Jennings's regal, swan-drawn gondola being made ready, though she knew it had not been ordered till one. Determined not to quit Marianne, though hopeless of contributing to her ease, she hurried away to excuse herself from attending Mrs. Jennings, on account of her sister being indisposed; she explained that Marianne had an aeroembolism, as the excuse most likely to be believed. Mrs. Jennings, with a thoroughly good-humoured disbelief in the origin of Marianne's indisposition, admitted the excuse most readily; and Elinor, after seeing her safe off, returned to Marianne, whom she found attempting to rise from the bed, and whom she reached just in time to prevent her from falling on the floor, faint and giddy from a long want of proper rest and food. A glass of lukewarm water, mixed with a wine flavouring packet, which Elinor procured for her directly, made her more comfortable, and she was at last able to express some sense of her kindness.

"Poor Elinor!" she said. "How unhappy I make you!"

"I only wish," replied her sister, "there were anything I *could* do, which might be of comfort to you."

Marianne could only exclaim, "Oh! Elinor, I am miserable, indeed," before her voice was entirely lost in sobs.

Just then the minnows which had been silently observing Marianne's grief from outside the glass were consumed in one gulp by a passing marlin.

"Exert yourself, dear Marianne," Elinor cried. "Think of your mother; think of her misery while *you* suffer. For her sake you must exert yourself."

"I cannot, I cannot!" cried Marianne. "Leave me, leave me, if I distress you; leave me, hate me, forget me! Drown me in the all-consuming sea! Let my bones calcify with the passing centuries and be turned to coral! But do not torture me so. Happy, happy Elinor, *you* cannot have an idea of what I suffer."

"Have you no comforts? No friends? Is your loss such as leaves no opening for consolation? Much as you suffer now, think of what you would have suffered if the discovery of his character had been delayed to a later period—if your engagement had been carried on for months and months, as it might have been, before he chose to put an end to it. Every additional day of unhappy confidence, on your side, would have made the blow more dreadful."

"Engagement!" cried Marianne. "There has been no engagement."

"No engagement!"

"No, he is not so unworthy as you believe him. He has broken no faith with me."

"But he told you that he loved you."

"Yes—no—never. It was every day implied, but never professedly declared. Sometimes I thought it had been—but it never was."

"Yet you wrote to him?"

"Yes—could that be wrong after all that had passed?"

Elinor turned again to the three letters and directly ran over the contents of all. The first, which was what her sister had sent him on their arrival in town, was to this effect:

> Berkeley Causeway, *January*.
>
> How surprised you will be, Willoughby, on receiving this; and I think you will feel something more than surprise, when you know that I have Descended into the Station. An opportunity of coming hither, though with Mrs. Jennings, was a temptation we could not resist. I wish you may receive this in time to come here to-night, but I will not depend on it. At any rate I shall expect you to-morrow. For the present, adieu.
>
> M. D.

Her second note, which had been written on the morning after the pirate-themed amusement at the Middletons', was in these words:

I cannot express my disappointment in having missed you the day before yesterday, nor my astonishment at not having received any answer to a note which I sent you above a week ago. I have been expecting to hear from you, and still more to see you, every hour of the day. Pray call again as soon as possible, and explain the reason of my having expected this in vain. Such is the behaviour not of a gentleman, but of a rank scallywag. I have been told that you were asked to be of the pirate party, and Sir John even would have lent you a cutlass and pegleg for adornment. But could it be so? You must be very much altered indeed since we parted, if that could be the case, and you not there. But I will not suppose this possible, and I hope very soon to receive your personal assurance of its being otherwise.

M. D.

The contents of her last note to him were these:

What am I to imagine, Willoughby, by your behaviour last night? Again I demand an explanation of it, and I will not accept the lobster attack as an excuse. I was prepared to meet you with the pleasure which our separation naturally produced, with the familiarity which our intimacy at Barton Cottage appeared to me to justify. I was repulsed indeed! I have passed a wretched night in endeavouring to excuse a conduct which can scarcely be called less than insulting; but though I have not yet been able to form any reasonable apology for your behaviour, I am perfectly ready to hear your justification of it. It would grieve me indeed to think ill of you; but if I am to do it, if I am to learn that your behaviour to me was intended only to deceive, let it be told as soon as possible. I wish to acquit you, but certainty on either side will be ease to what I now suffer. If your sentiments are no longer what they were, you will return my notes, and the lock of my hair which is in your possession.

M. D.

Elinor lowered the letter and reflected on its contents, whilst a swordfish began to tap softly against the Dome-glass. She would have been unwilling to believe that such letters, so full of affection and confidence, could have been answered as Willoughby had done.

"I felt myself," Marianne said, "to be solemnly engaged to him, as if the strictest legal covenant had bound us to each other."

"I can believe it," said Elinor, "but unfortunately he did not feel the same."

"He *did* feel the same, Elinor—for weeks and weeks he felt it. I know he did!" The swordfish rapped ardently, punctuating the passion of Marianne's outburst. "Have you forgotten the last evening of our being together at Barton Cottage? The morning that we parted too! When he told me that it might be many weeks before we met again—his distress—can I ever forget his distress? The shocked and saddened expression behind the portcullis of his diving helmet!"

For a moment or two Marianne could say no more; but when this emotion had passed away, she added, in a firmer tone, "I have been cruelly used, but not by Willoughby."

"Dearest Marianne, who but himself? By whom can he have been instigated?"

"By all the world! I would rather believe every creature of my acquaintance leagued together to ruin me in his opinion, than believe his nature capable of such cruelty. This woman of whom he writes—whoever she be—must have somehow ensorcelled him—to alter his inclinations and turn his affection from me."

Again they were both silent. Elinor paced back and forth, watching idly as a cod gobbled up a mass of cockles, and then was consumed in its turn by an orca; all the while, the swordfish tapped continually against the glass. For some reason, its persistent presence connected itself in Elinor's mind with the rampaging lobsters—but, before she could ponder what association there might be, Marianne again took up Willoughby's letter and exclaimed, "I must go home. I must go and comfort Mama. Can we not Ascend to-morrow and hire some convenient submersible or submarine to take us home?"

"To-morrow, Marianne!"

"Why should I stay here? I came only for Willoughby's sake—and now who cares for me? Who regards me?"

"It would be impossible to go to-morrow. Civility of the commonest kind must prevent such a hasty removal as that."

"Well then, another day or two, perhaps; but I cannot stay here long, I cannot stay to endure the questions and remarks of all these people. The Middletons and Palmers—how am I to bear their pity?"

Elinor advised Marianne to lie down again, and for a moment she did so; but no attitude could give her ease; and in restless pain of mind and body she moved from one posture to another, till growing more and more hysterical, her sister could with difficulty keep her on the bed at all. Neither, absorbed in Marianne's grief, noticed the tiny crack in the glass that had been the fruit of the swordfish's relentless exertions, nor the tiny cartilaginous grin it wore as it swam away.

CHAPTER 30

MRS. JENNINGS CAME IMMEDIATELY to their room on her return.

"How do you do, my dear?" said she in a voice of great compassion to Marianne, who turned away her face without answering. "Rashes? Joint pain? Itching?" she inquired, naming some of the symptoms often attending to aeroembolism—though she knew well that Marianne's trouble was one of the heart, not one caused by the precipitation of dissolved bubbles within the body accompanying rapid compression or decompression.

"Poor thing!" Mrs. Jennings continued. "She looks very bad. No wonder. Aye, it is but too true. He is to be married very soon—a good-for-nothing scoundrel! I have no patience with him. Mrs. Taylor told me of it half an hour ago, and she was told it by a particular friend of Miss Grey herself, else I am sure I should not have believed it. I wish with all my soul his wife may be like a tapeworm to him: May she dwell symbiotically in the digestive tract of his existence, consuming all joy, causing him writhing pain at odd intervals, until she is finally defecated out. And so I shall always say, my dear, you may depend on it; I love to repeat a parasite metaphor, once I first have invented it. But there is one comfort, my dear Miss Marianne; he is not the only young man in the world; and with your pretty face, strong back, and noticeable lung capacity, you will never want admirers."

She then went away, walking on tiptoe out of the room, as if she supposed her young friend's affliction could be increased by noise.

Marianne, to the surprise of her sister, determined on dining that night with Mrs. Jennings and her guests. When there, though looking most wretchedly, she managed to choke down several cubes of rack-of-lamb paste, and was calmer than Elinor had expected. Mrs. Jennings saw that Marianne was unhappy, and felt that everything was due to her which might make her less so. She treated her with all the indulgent fondness of a parent towards a favourite child on the last day of its holidays. Marianne was to have the best seat, looking right out at the Dome-glass, and to be amused by the relation of all the news of the day. There had been news of a particularly dramatic shipwreck, in which a fully outfitted French frigate was beset by a tempest and capsized in the shark-infested waters off eastern Tasmania; Mrs. Jennings relayed the tale to Marianne with particular zest, acting out the terrified "*mon dieu!*"s and "*aidez-moi!*"s of the sailors as they were surrounded by the befinned man-consumers. But soon Marianne could stay no longer. With a sign to her sister not to follow her, she directly got up and hurried out of the room.

"Poor soul!" cried Mrs. Jennings, as soon as she was gone, "Never have I known of spirits so low they could not be raised by hearing of a Frenchman eaten by a shark! I am sure if I knew of anything she would like, I would send all over the Sub-Marine Station for it. And this weekend brings new exhibits at the Aqua-Museo-Quarium: Harbour seals that have been made to grow sideburns! Clownfish dancing the tarantella! But it seems nothing will cheer her! Well, it is the oddest thing to me, that a man should use such a pretty girl so ill! But when there is plenty of money on one side, and next to none on the other, Lord bless you! They care no more about such things!"

"The lady, then," Elinor interposed. "Miss Grey, I think you called her—is she very rich?"

"Fifty thousand pounds, my dear."

"Is she said to be amiable?"

"I never heard any harm of her; indeed I hardly ever heard her mentioned. But now your poor sister has gone to her room. Is there nothing one can get to amuse her? What shall we play at? You two are not fond of Karankrolla, but is there no game she cares for?"

"Dear ma'am, this kindness is quite unnecessary. I shall persuade Marianne to go early to bed, for I am sure she wants rest."

"Aye, that will be best. Lord! No wonder she has been looking so green about the gills this last week or two, for this matter has been hanging over her head. And so the letter that came today finished it! Poor soul!"

"I must do *this* justice to Mr. Willoughby—he has broken no positive engagement with my sister."

"Don't pretend to defend him. No positive engagement indeed! After taking her all over Allenham Isle, and making her a gift of that sea horse, King John—"

"James."

"Yes, King James, and fixing on the very rooms they were to live in hereafter!" After a short silence on both sides, Mrs. Jennings, with all her natural hilarity, burst forth again. "Well, my dear, this will be all the better for poor, fish-faced Colonel Brandon. He will have her within the reach of those tentacles that so unpleasantly decorate his maw. Mind me, now, if they ain't married by Midsummer. Lord! How he'll chuckle a gurgling, unsettling chuckle over this news! I hope he will come tonight. It will be a much better match for your sister. Two thousand a year without debt or drawback. Delaford is a nice place, I can tell you; exactly what I call a nice old-fashioned place, full of comforts and conveniences; he has a long practice of privacy, owing to his condition, and so the estate is quite shut in with great garden walls! I shall spirit up the colonel as soon as I can. If we *can* but put Willoughby out of her head!"

"Ay, if we can do *that*, Ma'am," said Elinor, "we shall do very well with or without Colonel Brandon." And then rising, she went away to join Marianne, whom she found, as she expected, in her own room, pressing her face up against the Dome-glass, and signing to a passing suckerfish an ardent desire to switch places.

"You had better leave me," was all the notice that her sister received from her, and even that pale utterance was difficult to comprehend, since her mouth was very much smashed against the glass.

In the drawing room, whither she then repaired, Elinor was joined again by Mrs. Jenning—and much to the surprise of both, Colonel Brandon arrived soon after. By his manner of looking round the room for Marianne, Elinor immediately fancied that he neither expected nor wished to see her there. Mrs. Jennings walked across the room to the tea-table where Elinor presided and whispered, "The colonel looks as grave as ever. See how his face-feelers stand at grim attention? He knows nothing of it. Do tell him, my dear."

Shortly afterwards, Colonel Brandon drew a chair close to Elinor's and inquired after her sister.

"Marianne is not well," said she. "She has been indisposed all day, and we have persuaded her to go to bed."

"Itching?"

"No."

"Rashes?"

"No."

"Joint pain?"

Elinor only shook her head. "It is not an aeroembolism that afflicts her. Ah, if only it were."

"Perhaps, then," he hesitatingly replied, "what I heard this morning may be—there may be more truth in it than I could believe possible."

"What did you hear?"

"If you know it already, as surely you must, I may be spared."

"You mean," answered Elinor, with forced calmness, "Mr. Willoughby's marriage with Miss Grey. Yes, we *do* know it all. Where did you hear it?"

"In the Retail Embankment, where I had business. Two ladies were waiting for their decorated tortoise shell, and one of them was giving the other an account of the intended match, in a voice so little attempting concealment, that it was impossible for me not to hear all. The name of John Willoughby, frequently repeated, first caught my attention; and what followed was a positive assertion that everything was now finally settled respecting his marriage with Miss Grey, daughter of Sterling Grey."

"But have you likewise heard that Miss Grey has fifty thousand pounds? In that, if in any thing, we may find an explanation."

"It may be so; the man proves a treasure hunter to the last!" He stopped a moment, gurgled softly, then added in a voice which seemed to distrust itself, "And your sister? How did she—"

"Her sufferings have been very severe. I have only to hope that they may be proportionately short. It is a most cruel affliction. Till yesterday, I believe, she never doubted his regard; and even now, perhaps—but I am almost convinced that he never was really attached to her."

"Ah!" said Colonel Brandon, his tentacles dancing with animation below his chin. "But your sister does not—I think you said so—she does not consider quite as you do?"

"You know her disposition, and may believe how eagerly she would still justify him if she could."

He made no answer; and soon afterwards, the subject was dropped. Mrs. Jennings expected to see the effect of Miss Dashwood's communication as an instantaneous gaiety on Colonel Brandon's side; instead she saw him remain the whole evening more serious and thoughtful than usual.

CHAPTER 31

FROM A NIGHT of more sleep than she had expected, Marianne awoke the next morning to the same consciousness of misery in which she had closed her eyes.

Elinor encouraged her to talk of what she felt; and before the breakfast-loaf was sliced on the table, they had gone through the subject again and again. Marianne expressed her wish for the very lid of Sub-Station Beta to open and all the world to be drowned—which earned the stern condemnation of Elinor, who reminded her that such a possibility was not to be taken lightly, considering the tragic fate of Sub-Station Alpha!

With a letter in her outstretched hand, and countenance gaily smiling, Mrs. Jennings entered their room, saying, "Now, my dear, I bring you something that I am sure will do you good."

Marianne heard enough. In one moment her imagination placed before her a letter from Willoughby, full of tenderness and contrition, explanatory of all that had passed; and instantly followed by Willoughby himself, rushing eagerly into the room costumed in his dashing diving suit and flipper feet, streaming with sea-water as he had been on the day they met. The work of one moment was destroyed by the next. The hand writing of her mother, never till then unwelcome, was before her.

The letter, when she was calm enough to read it, brought little comfort. Its opening sections, written with an unusually shaky hand, related their mother's fresh concerns regarding Margaret.

> Since your departure for the Station, your sister's peculiar behaviour has not, I fear, been remedied—to the contrary, I grow increasingly worried about her. The girl is dreadfully quiet at mealtimes, all the youthful exuberance with which she once attacked a plate of crawfish all but sapped from her. Many a night of late have I been awakened from a restless, worried sleep by the slam of the door, followed by the rapid clatter of Margaret's footfalls down the front steps, as she heads off to . . . Heaven only knows where. At breakfast next morning, she denies ever having left the house, but never eats nor converses, only mutters strangely to herself, her head half-bowed, as if offering prayers to some unknown deity. There are unwholesome changes in her physical being, as well: her once-rosy cheeks have grown pale, her hair limpid and ashen; and her teeth, dear daughters, her teeth are filed to sharp points, like those of an animal.

Here Elinor and Marianne, reading the letter together, exchanged a troubled glance, and then continued:

> What she sees and does out in the reaches of this Island under the baleful light of the moon, I dare not imagine; but my fervent hope is that all of this wandering, and the bizarre habits with which she returns, represent nothing but youth in its va-

garies, and by the time we are reunited, she will be once again the old, joyful Margaret you have loved.

As Elinor tried to make sense of such an unwelcome transfiguration, a second scrap of paper tumbled forth from the envelope, this piece not of the customary eel-grass parchment on which Mrs. Dashwood's missive was composed, but a tissue-thin sheath that Elinor instantly recognized as torn from the Dashwood family Bible. It was, Elinor found as she bent to examine the scrap, a page from the book Isaiah, with one passage—circled in what she knew at once, with dread certainty, was Margaret's blood:

In that day the LORD with his sore and great and strong sword shall punish LEVIATHAN the piercing serpent, even LEVIATHAN that crooked serpent; and he shall slay the dragon that is in the sea.

Elinor swiftly folded the page in half and tucked it away in her bodice. The rest of Mrs. Dashwood's letter brought still less comfort; Willoughby filled every page. Marianne's impatience to be at home again now returned; her mother was dearer to her than ever; dearer through the very excess of her mistaken confidence in Willoughby, and she was wildly urgent to Ascend from Sub-Marine Station Beta. Elinor, unable herself to determine whether it were better for Marianne to be in-Station or on Pestilent Isle, offered no counsel of her own except of patience till their mother's wishes could be known.

Mrs. Jennings left them earlier than usual; for she could not be easy till the Middletons and Palmers were able to grieve as much as herself. Elinor, with a very heavy heart, aware of the pain she was going to communicate, sat down to write her mother an account of what had passed, and to inquire further as to Margaret's unsettled condition; Marianne remained fixed at the table where Elinor wrote, watching the advancement of her pen, grieving over her for the hardship of such a task, and grieving still more fondly over its effect on her mother.

In this manner they had continued about a quarter of an hour, when Marianne, whose nerves could not then bear any sudden noise, was startled by a rap at the door.

"Who can this be?" cried Elinor. "So early too! I thought we *had* been safe."

Marianne moved to the window.

"It is Colonel Brandon! Blech!" said she, with vexation. "We are never safe from *him*."

"He will not come in, as Mrs. Jennings is from home."

"I will not trust to *that*," Marianne said, retreating to her own room. "A fish-man who has nothing to do with his own time has no conscience in his intrusion on that of others."

The event proved her conjecture right, for Colonel Brandon *did* come in; and Elinor, who was convinced that solicitude for Marianne brought him thither, and who saw *that* solicitude in the woeful and melancholy hang of his tentacles, could not forgive her sister for esteeming him so lightly.

"I met Mrs. Jennings in Bond Causeway," said he, after the first salutation, "and she encouraged me to come on; and I thought it probable that I might find you alone. My object—my wish—glurb—hurble—is to be a means of giving comfort and gurble—" He stopped, and with a genteel motion of his handkerchief dabbed away a greenish mixture of spittle and mucus that had accumulated on his chin.

"I think I understand you," said Elinor. "You have something to tell me of Mr. Willoughby that will open his character further. Your telling it will be the greatest act of friendship that can be shown Marianne. My gratitude will be insured immediately by any information tending to that end. Pray, pray let me hear it."

"You will find me a very awkward narrator, Miss Dashwood; I hardly know where to begin. A short account of myself, I believe, will be necessary, and it shall be a short one. On such a subject," he said, sighing wetly, "I have little temptation to be diffuse."

He stopped a moment for recollection, and then, with another wet sigh, continued:

"You have probably forgotten a conversation between us one evening at Deadwind Island—it was the evening of a beach-side bonfire—a girl was consumed by a jellyfish—in which I alluded to a lady I had once known, as resembling your sister Marianne."

"Indeed," answered Elinor, "I have *not* forgotten it." He looked pleased by this remembrance; she smiled at him, and then lurched and looked away immediately. He added:

"There is a very strong resemblance between them. The same warmth of heart, the same eagerness of fancy and spirits. This lady Eliza was one of my nearest relations, an orphan from her infancy, and under the guardianship of my father. Our ages were nearly the same, and from our earliest years we were playfellows, friends, and constant companions. She was, as you might have guessed, as blind as a cave bat. I cannot remember the time when I did not love Eliza, but at seventeen she was lost to me forever. She was married against her inclination to my brother, who is like me in many respects but suffers not from that prominent misfortune which has marked my fate as much as my face. Her fortune was large, and our family estate much encumbered.

My brother did not deserve her; he did not even love her. The blow was severe—but had her marriage been happy, a few months might have reconciled me to it. But my brother had no regard for her; he played tricks on her blindness, such as telling her she was wearing a red spencer jacket when really it was lemon-coloured. The consequence of this, upon a mind so young, so lively, so inexperienced, was but too natural. Eliza, now Mrs. Brandon, resigned herself to all the misery of her situation. I meant to promote the happiness of both by removing from her for years, and so requested posting with a unit of the British marines, assaulting serpent grottos in the West Indies. The shock which her marriage had given me," he continued, his voice gurgling and warbling along with his agitation, "was nothing compared to what I felt when I heard, about two years afterwards, of her divorce."

He could say no more, and rising hastily walked for a few minutes about the room. He stared mournfully out the observation glass as a black barbed dragonfish came upon a bigfin squid unawares, and devoured it in four ghastly bites. Elinor, affected by Brandon's distress, could not speak. He saw her concern, and coming to her, took her hand, pressed it, and kissed it with grateful respect; she waited till he looked away and wiped her hand on the hem of her dress. A few minutes more of snuffling, gurglingly heavy breathing and he was able to proceed with composure.

"My first care, when I returned to England after three years, was of course to seek her, but the search was fruitless. I presumed a blind woman of middle-age, in mismatched clothing, travelling alone, would be easy to track, but I could not trace her beyond her first seducer, and there was every reason to fear that she had removed from him only to sink deeper in a life of sin. Her legal allowance was not adequate to her fortune, and I learnt from my brother that the power of receiving it had been made over some months before to another person. He imagined, and calmly could he imagine it, that her extravagance, and consequent distress, had obliged her to dispose of it for some immediate relief. He laughed cruelly to imagine her blindly wandering the beaches. At last, however, after I had been six months in England, I *did* find her. Regard for a former servant of my own, who had since fallen into misfortune, carried me to visit him in a sponging-house, where he was confined for debt—forced by his creditors to make sponges until he had worked off his obligations; and there, under a similar confinement, was my unfortunate sister-in-law. What I endured in so beholding her—'twas the worst I have ever suffered, far worse even than the daily portion of suffering that is mine when I regard myself in the mirror. That she was in the last stage of a consumption was my greatest comfort. Life could do nothing for her, beyond giving time for a better preparation for death. I saw her placed in comfortable lodgings, and under proper attendants; I visited her every day during the rest of her short life; I was with her in her last moments. She reached out before all strength left her hands, and stroked my face, and I can only pray that its writhing, spaghetti-like texture was not disgusting to her, at such a moment, but comforting in its familiarity."

Again he stopped to recover himself; tears rolled down his cheeks and mingled freely with the effluvia of his tentacles. Elinor spoke her feelings in an exclamation of tender concern, at the fate of his unfortunate friend.

"Your sister, I hope, cannot be offended," said he, "by the resemblance I have fancied between her and my poor disgraced relation. Their fates, their fortunes, cannot be the same. But to what does all this lead? I seem to have been distressing you for nothing. Ah! Miss Dashwood—a subject such as this—untouched for fourteen years—it is dangerous to handle it at all! I *will* be more collected—more concise. Eliza left to my care her only child, a little girl, the offspring of her first guilty connection, which had been with a hirsute seaman who peddled fried cakes on the Dover boardwalk. The girl was then about three years old. My little Eliza was placed at school, and I saw her there whenever I could. I called her a distant relation; but I am well aware of rumours that she has my same unfortunate facial misfortune. Nothing could be further from the truth; she has only an unwomanly tendency to sprout hair 'pon her lip, an inheritance from the crinite cake-vendor who was her natural parent.

"Last February she suddenly disappeared. I had allowed her, at her earnest desire, to go to Bath with one of her young friends. I knew the girl's father to be a very good sort of man, and I thought well of his daughter—better than she deserved, for she would tell nothing, would give no clue, though she certainly knew all. I could learn nothing but that she was gone; all the rest, for eight long months, was left to conjecture. What I thought, what I feared, may be imagined; and what I suffered too."

"Good heavens!" cried Elinor, "Could it be—Willoughby!"

"The first news that reached me," he continued, "came in a letter from herself, last October. It was forwarded to me from Delaford, and

I received it on the very morning of our intended party to explore the sunken husk of the *Mary*; and this was the reason of my leaving the archipelago so suddenly, which I am sure must at the time have appeared strange to everybody. Little did Mr. Willoughby imagine, I suppose, when his looks censured me for incivility in breaking up the party, that I was called away to the relief of one whom he had made poor and miserable. At Bath, he had met young Eliza, had saved her from the attack of a giant octopus—"

"No!"

"Yes! 'Tis one startling coincidence among several. And then he had left the girl whose youth and innocence he had seduced, in a situation of the utmost distress, with no creditable home, no help, no friends, ignorant of his address! He had buried her in the sand in a playful fashion, as lovers do when sporting; and then, without digging her up, he had gone off, he said, to buy them lemonades; he never returned. She had been found and dug up three days later by a travelling party from Switzerland, who were in search of charming seaside English vistas and instead found a ruined girl with a faint moustache, buried in the sand."

"This is beyond everything!" exclaimed Elinor.

"His character is now before you: expensive, dissipated, and worse than both. Knowing all this, as I have known it many weeks, guess what I must have felt on seeing your sister as fond of him as ever? On being assured that she was to marry him? But what could I do? I had no hope of interfering; and sometimes I thought your sister's influence might yet reclaim him. But now, after such dishonourable usage, who can tell what were his designs on her! Use your own discretion, however, in communicating to her what I have told you. You must know best what will be its effect; but had I not seriously believed it might be of service, might lessen her regrets, I would not have suffered myself to trouble you with this account of my family afflictions."

Elinor's thanks followed this speech with grateful earnestness; attended too with the assurance of her expecting material advantage to

Marianne, from the communication of what had passed. "Have you seen Mr. Willoughby since you left him on Deadwind Island?"

"Yes," he replied gravely, "once I have. One meeting was unavoidable."

Elinor, startled by his manner, looked at him anxiously, saying,

"What? Have you met him to—"

"I could meet him no other way. Eliza had confessed to me, though most reluctantly, the name of her lover; and when he returned to Sub-Marine Station Beta, which was within a fortnight after myself, we were to meet by appointment, he to defend, I to punish his conduct. We returned unwounded, and the meeting, therefore, never got abroad.

Elinor sighed over the fancied necessity of this, but to a man and a soldier she presumed not to censure it.

"Such," said Colonel Brandon, after a pause, "has been the unhappy resemblance between the fate of mother and daughter! And so imperfectly have I discharged my trust!"

Recollecting, soon afterwards, that he was probably dividing Elinor from her sister, he put an end to his visit, receiving from her again the same grateful acknowledgments, and leaving her full of compassion and esteem for him, and entirely absent the gastric discomfort that usually attended his presence.

CHAPTER 32

WHEN THE PARTICULARS of this conversation were repeated by Miss Dashwood to her sister, as they very soon
were, the effect was not entirely such as the former had hoped to see.
Marianne did not appear to distrust the truth of any part of it, for she
listened with steady and submissive attention, attempted no vindication
of Willoughby, and seemed to show by her tears that she felt such vindication to be impossible—especially when Elinor arrived at the dé-
nouement, in which poor seduced and lightly mustachioed Eliza was
left buried to her neck in summer sand, and abandoned to the whims
of the tide.

But though Marianne's reaction assured Elinor that the conviction
of this guilt *was* carried home, she did not see her less wretched. Her
mind did become settled, but it was settled in a gloomy dejection. She still
sang no shanties, and turned no happy reels, as Elinor was accustomed to
see her undertake at odd intervals; still she sat sighing for hours out the
Dome-glass, her head held in the crook of her arm, occasionally letting
slip an admiring murmur regarding the midnight blues and emerald
greens of the deep-sea flora.

To give the feelings or the language of Mrs. Dashwood on receiving and answering Elinor's letter would be only to give a repetition of
what her daughters had already felt and said, and would furthermore require a tremendous variety of words ill-suited for public consumption,
such as those shouted by sailors off their decks while trying to keep their
ship righted in a maddening gale. Suffice it to report in her a disappointment hardly less painful than Marianne's, and an indignation even greater

than Elinor's, and a wide vocabulary of uncharactaristic profanity. Long letters from her, quickly succeeding each other, arrived to tell all that she suffered and thought; to express her anxious solicitude for Marianne, and entreat she would bear up with fortitude under this misfortune.

Against the interest of her own individual comfort, Mrs. Dashwood had determined that it would be better for Marianne to be anywhere, at that time, than the little rickety shanty on Pestilent Isle, where everything within her view would be bringing back the past in the strongest and most afflicting manner, by constantly placing Willoughby before her, such as she had always seen him there. She recommended it to her daughters, therefore, by all means not to shorten their visit to Mrs. Jennings at Sub-Marine Station Beta. A variety of occupations and company which could not be procured at Barton Cottage, would be inevitable there, along with the wide menu of hydrophilial amusements on offer in-Station; these might yet, she hoped, cheat Marianne into some interest beyond herself.

From all danger of seeing Willoughby again, her mother considered her to be at least equally safe at the Station as back on the islands, since his acquaintance must now be dropped by all who called themselves her friends. Design could never bring them in each other's way: negligence could never leave them exposed to a surprise; and chance had less in its favour in the crowd of the Station than even in the retirement of Barton Cottage, where it might force him before her while paying that visit at Allenham Isle on his marriage.

She had yet another reason for wishing her children to remain where they were; a letter from her son had told her that he and his wife were to Descend before the middle of February, and she judged it right that they should sometimes see their brother.

Mrs. Dashwood closed the letter by noting that, without wanting to increase the burden of what was clearly a difficult time, there was further news of their sister's condition. Margaret had returned from her latest midnight ramble with no hair on her body. In answer to Mrs. Dashwood's frantic enquiries, Margaret had refused to utter a word—and, indeed, had not spoken so much as a syllable since.

As Elinor considered what psychic ailment or indisposition might have caused this further alteration in their sister, Marianne's attention remained focused upon their mother's suggestion that they continue in-Station. She had promised to be guided by her mother's opinion, but it proved perfectly different from what she expected. By requiring her longer continuance at Sub-Marine Station Beta, her mother deprived her of the only possible alleviation of her wretchedness—the personal sympathy of her mother.

Elinor took great care in guarding her sister from ever hearing Willoughby's name mentioned; neither Mrs. Jennings, nor Sir John, nor even Mrs. Palmer herself, ever spoke of him before her. Elinor wished that the same forbearance could have extended towards herself, but that was impossible, and she was obliged to listen day after day to the indignation of them all.

Sir John could not have thought it possible. "I wish him at the devil with all my heart!" he cried, gesticulating angrily with his huge, bear-paw-like hands. Mrs. Palmer, in her way, was equally angry. She was determined to drop his acquaintance immediately. She hated him so much that she was resolved never to mention his name again, and she should tell everybody she saw, how good-for-nothing he was.

What appeared to be calm and polite unconcern of Lady Middleton towards the entire affair arose in fact from her preoccupation with her latest scheme to escape and return to her home country. Some weeks ago she had discovered, in a deserted warehouse in the Dome's northwesterly quadrant, an ancient but still operable single-hull, one-person submarine. She had laboriously dragged this hunk of ancient metal back to her docking, where it lay hidden behind cartons of unused drink packets; every night, after Sir John retired to their bedchamber, Lady Middleton climbed inside the ancient submarine's cockpit and studied the dashboard, attempting to decipher its instruments, dreaming of the day when she would find her moment to pilot the thing out of the Station and all the way home to her native isle.

Thus, whilst the others were assailing Elinor with their tiresome indignation, Lady Middleton was lost in thought, contemplating the details of her propulsion system or plotting her coordinates. Her apparent disregard for the situation was a happy relief to Elinor's spirits, oppressed as they were by the clamorous kindness of the others. It was a great comfort to her to be sure of exciting no interest in *one* person at least among their circle of friends: a great comfort to know that there was *one* who would meet her without feeling any curiosity after particulars or any anxiety for her sister's health. "Dive depth . . ." Lady Middleton once muttered, when the two happened to be alone. "There is still the question of dive depth . . ." And when Elinor said, "Pardon me?" Lady Middleton only gave a haughty, enigmatic smile and wandered away.

Early in February, within a fortnight from the receipt of Willoughby's letter, Elinor had the painful office of informing her sister that he had been married in a great gala at Station Beta's most eloquent catering hall before departing in an elegant forty-five-foot skiff—and, most cuttingly of all, the theme of the reception had been Shipwrecked Sailors. Marianne received the news with resolute composure; at first she shed no tears, but after a short time they would burst out, and for the rest of the day, she was in a state hardly less pitiable than when she first learnt to expect the event.

 The Willoughbys left town as soon as they were married; and Elinor now hoped to prevail on her sister to go out again, to enjoy the undersea amazements of the Sub-Station and stroll the canalside shops of the Retail Embankment.

About this time the two Miss Steeles, lately arrived in-Station, were welcomed by them all with great cordiality. Elinor only was sorry to see them—not least because, the moment her eyes met those of Lucy Steele, she experienced a sensation like a dagger's sharp edge slashing at the edges of her mind, and felt a rising darkness in her thoughts that she struggled with difficulty to suppress.

"I suppose you will go and stay with your brother and sister, Miss Dashwood, when they Descend to the Sub-Station," said Lucy.

"No, I do not think we shall," Elinor replied.

"Oh, yes, I dare say you will. What a charming thing it is that Mrs. Dashwood can spare you both for so long a time together!"

"Long a time, indeed!" interposed Mrs. Jennings. "Why, their visit is but just begun!"

Lucy was silenced. Elinor, closing her eyes to gather her thoughts, experienced a resurgence of the slashing pain, along with a sudden flash—a symbol—*the* symbol—the five-pointed symbol—forcing itself before her mind's eye.

What could it mean, Elinor wondered, her head throbbing in agony as the exchange of trivialities continued about her. Why had this misery recurred? Why did the presence of the Miss Steeles engender in her this vision, coupled with such agonizing discomfort? Elinor resolved to put the question to Colonel Brandon, who was so wise in so many ways; before recalling in the next moment the sad tale that he had lately related and determining that the misfortunate colonel had enough to worry him.

"I am sorry we cannot see your sister, Miss Dashwood," said Miss Steele, for Marianne had left the room on their arrival.

"You are very good," Elinor responded, glad for the interruption that had drawn her attention back to her immediate reality, and away from the mystifying five-pointed polyhedron that danced menacingly in her mind's eye. "My sister will be equally sorry to miss the pleasure of seeing you; but she has been very much plagued lately with nervous headaches, which make her unfit for company or conversation."

"Oh, dear, that is a great pity! But such old friends as Lucy and me! I think she might see *us*; and I am sure we would be as quiet as a bucket of clams."

"But less malodorous," added Lucy hastily.

Elinor, with great civility, declined the proposal. Her sister was perhaps laid down upon the bed, or in her dressing gown, and therefore not able to come to them.

CHAPTER 33

THAT NIGHT, Marianne slept but restlessly, her mind wracked by terrifying dreams. The Dashwoods were somehow installed again at Norwood, and Willoughby was there with them. She strolled with him along the beach, Monsieur Pierre hopping happily alongside them. They stopped, gazed into each other's eyes, and Willoughby extended an affectionate hand—he was *himself* again, he whom she had so loved at Barton Cottage. But when Marianne reached for that hand, grasped it lovingly and pressed it against her cheek, it transmogrified from a hand to an octopus's tentacle, purple and writhing, closing its powerful sucker over her mouth. Choking, desperate for breath, Marianne awoke with tears streaming down her face.

Elinor, too, was plagued by nightmares. In her dreamscape, the five-pointed figure came yet more vividly to life, dancing cruelly about in her mind, pulsating and quivering in a nightmare pallet of purple-blacks and blood-scarlets.

Sometime after midnight she woke with a start and rose from her bed, her body atremble, her brow slick with sweat, and sat till morning staring out into the inky depths of the sea beyond the observation glass. Her terrifying visions, she felt, were doing more than scaring her—it was warning her—but of what? Of Willoughby's treachery? Too late, surely, for that alarm!

In the dim bioluminescence of a passing gulper eel, Elinor spied a tiny crack in the Dome-glass, at the very spot where she had seen the little swordfish tapping away at the glass; her mind still troubled by the

MARIANNE STROLLED WITH WILLOUGHBY ALONG THE BEACH, AND MONSIEUR
PIERRE HOPPED HAPPILY ALONGSIDE THEM.

dream's ill-imagery, her body by the exertion of suffering through same, she hardly marked the small spider web of cracks before the gulper eel swam off in pursuit of a hapless school of copepods, and the sea was plunged again in darkness.

Just as the dawn's light reached its long fingers from the Surface-Lands into the depths of Sub-Station, a fog-horn bleated noisily through the Dome. The sounding of the horn meant that a merman had been reported, and the accused would soon be brought to the Justice Embankment for testing and—if veracity were found in the accusation—execution by gutting knife.

After some opposition, Marianne yielded to her sister's entreaties, and consented to go out with her and Mrs. Jennings to watch the solemnities.

Sir John, as a respected elder who knew much of the watery part of the world, was in charge of the proceedings. As a crowd gathered, many training opera glasses on the proceedings, Sir John lined seven suspected mermen along the water's edge, where they stood quivering in fear. Narrowing his piercing grey eyes, the old man leveled an accusing finger at the first suspect, who was quickly wrapped by three Station attendants in secure netting, as if he were naught but an oversized marlin—which, in a sense, he may indeed have been. Sir John then bodily lifted the net-wrapped man, and with a grunt of determined exertion, tossed him screaming into the canal.

"What—?" began Elinor.

"It's simple," said Mrs. Jennings, clapping delightedly along with the rest of the crowd as the suspected merman thrashed helplessly within the net. "If he is truly a merman, he will reveal his tail rather than drown, at which point Sir John will fish him from the water and slice him from crotch to throat. If no tail appears, and he is proved thereby to be human through and through, your uncle will fish him from the water and slice him from his crotch to his throat, as a warning to the others."

"Pardon me?" said Elinor. "It strikes me that—"

"Best not to ask questions, dear," cautioned Mrs. Jennings.

After the gruesome exhibition—at which three of the suspected proved indeed to be mermen, and the other four innocent, and all were duly executed by Sir John—even Marianne agreed that a calming walk would do well to clear their minds of the grim ritual they had just witnessed. All proceeded to the Retail Embankment, where Elinor was carrying on a negotiation for the exchange of a few old-fashioned pearl-strings of her mother's.

When they stopped at the door of the shop, Mrs. Jennings recollected that there was a lady at the far end of the Causeway on whom she ought to call; and she got back in the gondola, announcing that she would pay her visit and return for them.

The Miss Dashwoods found so many people before them in the room, that there was not a person at liberty to tend to their orders; and they were obliged to wait. All that could be done was to sit down at that end of the counter; only one gentleman was standing there. He was giving orders for a customised Float-Suit for himself; the design of the suits were strictly regulated under Station law, but it was common practice for those with means to have theirs customised and inlaid with all manner of fashionable modifications. Till its size, shape, and ornaments were determined, the clerk had no leisure to bestow any other attention on the two ladies, but at last the affair was decided. The ivory, gold, and pearls would spell out *Hail* on one inflatable arm-band, and *Britannia* on the other. Then the gentleman left with a happy air of real conceit and affected indifference.

Elinor lost no time in bringing her business forward, and she had nearly concluded it when another gentleman presented himself at her side. She found him with some surprise to be her brother.

Their affection and pleasure in meeting was just enough to make a very creditable appearance in the shop. Elinor found that he and Fanny had been in town two days.

"I wished to call upon you yesterday," said he, "but it was impossible, for we were obliged to take Harry to see the otter fights at Exeter

Exchange; it's really quite remarkable; they've trained the slippery little fellows to go after each other with straight razors. But to-morrow I think I shall certainly be able to call, and be introduced to your friend, Mrs. Jennings. I understand she is a woman of very good fortune, except for the unfortunate circumstance of her extended husband and sons being slaughtered, and her two daughters dragged off into marital servitude. And the Middletons too, you must introduce me to *them*. They are excellent neighbours to you on the islands, I understand."

"Excellent indeed. Their attention to our comfort, their friendliness in every particular, is more than I can express. Sir John's knowledge of sea-monster habit and vulnerability has kept us safe many times over."

The next day, Mr. Dashwood's visit was duly paid. His manners to *them*, though calm, were perfectly kind; to Mrs. Jennings, most attentively civil; and on Colonel Brandon's coming in soon after himself, he started and grabbed a kitchen knife, but laid it down promptly when it was explained that this was a human being, facial features notwithstanding.

After staying with them half an hour, he asked Elinor to take him to be introduced to Sir John and Lady Middleton. The weather was remarkably fine, and she readily consented. As soon as they were out of the house, his enquiries began.

"Who is Colonel Brandon? Is he a man of fortune? What in the name of the Father and the Son is wrong with his face?"

"He has very good property in Dorsetshire. And, it is reported, a sea-witch curse."

"Well, he seems a most gentlemanlike man; and I think, Elinor, I may congratulate you on the prospect of a very respectable establishment in life."

"Me, brother! What do you mean?"

"He likes you. I am convinced of it."

"I am very sure that Colonel Brandon has not the smallest wish of marrying *me*."

"You are mistaken, Elinor; you are very much mistaken. Perhaps just at present he may be undecided; the smallness of your fortune may make him hang back; his friends may all advise him against it. But some of those little attentions and encouragements which ladies can so easily give will fix him, in spite of himself. Brush those tentacles of his as if by accident with the back of your hand; adjust his cravat, wipe the excretions from his chin. It is a match that must give universal satisfaction. Your friends are all truly anxious to see you well settled; Fanny particularly, for she has your interest very much at heart, I assure you. And her mother too, Mrs. Ferrars, a very good-natured woman, I am sure it would give her great pleasure; she said as much the other day."

Elinor would not vouchsafe any answer.

"It would be something remarkable, now," he continued, "if Fanny should have a brother and I a sister settling at the same time."

At this surprising declaration from her brother, the five-pointed star flashed in Elinor's mind with the suddenness and violence of a pistol shot; and then was gone again.

"Is Mr. Edward Ferrars," said Elinor, with resolution, "going to be married?"

"It is not actually settled, but there is such a thing in agitation. His mother will come forward and settle on him a thousand a year, if the match takes place. The lady is the Honourable Miss Morton, only daughter of the late Lord Morton, the very engineer and public hero who oversaw the creation of Sub-Marine Station Alpha. It is a very desirable connection on both sides, and I have not a doubt of its taking place in time. A thousand a year is a great deal for a mother to give away, but Mrs. Ferrars has a noble spirit. On occasion, I tell you confidentially, she puts bank-notes into Fanny's hands; I find this extremely acceptable, for we must live at a great expense while we are here. But I am also finding ways to earn a bit extra."

"Oh?"

"Indeed. I am—*participating*."

Elinor, having lived in the Station now for a period of weeks, knew the meaning of the expression; her brother was submitting himself to the attentions of the Station's government scientists, in their ongoing efforts to enhance human beings, to provide us advantages over the sea-borne beasts determined to bedevil our race. John was giving his sister to understand, in short, that he was allowing his body to be experimented upon, in exchange for financial recompense. Having now said enough to make his poverty clear, and to do away the necessity of buying a pair of ear-rings for each of his sisters, John inquired after Marianne. "She looks very unwell," he said.

"She has had a nervous complaint on her for several weeks."

"I am sorry for that. At her time of life, anything of an illness destroys the bloom forever! She was as handsome a girl last September, as I ever saw; and as likely to attract the man. I question whether Marianne *now*, will marry a man worth more than five or six hundred a year, at the utmost, and I am very much deceived if you will not do better."

Elinor tried very seriously to convince him that there was no likelihood of her marrying Colonel Brandon; but he was really resolved on seeking an intimacy with that gentleman, and promoting the marriage by every possible attention, before at last he put on his Float-Suit and departed.

CHAPTER 34

MRS. JOHN DASHWOOD had so much confidence in her husband's judgment, despite his chemically altered perceptions, that she waited the very next day on Mrs. Jennings and her daughter. Her confidence was rewarded by finding the woman with whom her sisters were staying most worthy of her notice; and as for Lady Middleton, she found her one of the most charming women in the world, even if she had been married, as the saying has it, out of a bag!

Lady Middleton was equally pleased with Mrs. Dashwood. There was a kind of cold-hearted selfishness on both sides, a desire to escape, on the one hand, from pecuniary anxiety, and on the other, from civilization as a whole, which mutually attracted them.

To Mrs. Jennings, however, Mrs. Dashwood was a mere *pxtypyp*; that is, a little proud-looking woman of uncordial address. She met her husband's sisters without any affection, and almost without having anything to say to them; for of the quarter of an hour bestowed on Berkeley Causeway, she sat at least seven minutes and a half in silence.

Elinor wanted very much to know, though she did not choose to ask, whether Edward was in town; but nothing would have induced Fanny voluntarily to mention his name before her. The intelligence she would not give, however, soon flowed from another quarter. Lucy came very shortly to claim Elinor's compassion on being unable to see Edward, though he had arrived in-Station with Mr. and Mrs. Dashwood. Despite their mutual impatience to meet, they could do nothing at present but write.

Edward assured them himself of his being in town, within a very short time, by twice calling in Berkeley Causeway. His hermit-crab shell calling card was found on the table when they returned from a diverting morning at Mr. Pennywhistle's Aqua-Museo-Quarium, where they had spent an hour and a quarter mesmerised by the antics of a troupe of flying fish who had been trained in sub-aqueous acrobatics. Elinor was pleased that Edward had called; and still more pleased that she had missed him.

The Dashwoods were so prodigiously delighted with the Middletons that they determined to give them a dinner; soon after their acquaintance began, they invited them to dine in Harley Piscina, where they had taken a very good docking for three months. Their sisters and Mrs. Jennings were invited likewise, and John Dashwood was careful to secure Colonel Brandon. Always glad to be where the Miss Dashwoods were, he received his civilities with some surprise, but much more pleasure. He prepared his best dress uniform and neatly combed his tentacles.

They were to meet Mrs. Ferrars; but Elinor could not learn whether her sons were to be of the party. The expectation of seeing *her*, however, was enough to make her interested in the engagement.

The evening promised other amusements as well. Given the minimal time required for the preparation and consumption of foodstuffs, the custom of dinner parties in Sub-Marine Station Beta placed a large emphasis on the after-dinner entertainment. As taken as was Fanny Dashwood with the Middletons, it came as no surprise to Elinor that she intended to present for them the most rarified of amusements—namely of arranging for their domestic servants to compete in various contests of skill and strength against enhanced sea creatures.

The important Tuesday arrived, and Elinor found Lucy professing a state of extreme anxiety as they disembarked from their gondola at the home of the Dashwoods.

"Pity me, dear Miss Dashwood!" said Lucy. "There is nobody here but you that can feel for me. I declare I can hardly stand. Good gracious! In a moment I shall see the person that all my happiness depends on—that is to be my mother!"

Mrs. Ferrars was a little, thin woman, upright in her figure, and serious in her aspect. Her complexion was sallow; and her features small, without beauty, and naturally without expression. As Fanny presented her with that evening's main course, an elegantly presented large loaf of beef-steak–flavoured gelatin paste, she felt it unnecessary to present a peroration on the deficiencies of Station cuisine; she simply wrinkled her sour nose and said "Ick." Of the few syllables that did escape her that evening, not one fell to the share of Miss Dashwood, whom she eyed with the spirited determination of disliking her at all events.

Elinor could not *now* be made unhappy by this behaviour. A few months ago, it would have hurt her exceedingly; but it was not in Mrs. Ferrars's power to distress her by it now; and the difference of her manners to the Miss Steeles, a difference which seemed purposely made to humble her more, only amused her. She could not but smile to see the graciousness of both mother and daughter towards Lucy, the very person whom of all others (had they known as much as she did) they would have been most anxious to mortify.

She herself, who had comparatively no power to wound them, sat pointedly slighted by both. But while she smiled at a graciousness so mis-applied, she could not reflect on the mean-spirited folly from which it sprung without thoroughly despising them all four, and idly trying to re-call a method of swiftly murdering a person with two fingers pressed to the throat, which she had once been taught by a drunken Sir John.

The dinner was a grand one, the servants were numerous, and every-thing bespoke the Mistress's inclination for show, and the Master's ability to support it. The after-dinner entertainment was truly remarkable; first came a display in which a household servant played three hands of *Jeu d'enfer* against a sea horse; and then one in which their housemaid was caged in-side a giant razor-clam from which she had to fight her way out. Mrs. Fer-rars, not to be satisfied, pronounced the clamshell a weak one, its razors dull, and averred that, were she a younger woman, she might have bro-ken free much quicker.

Before departing Norland, Elinor had whittled out of flotsam a very pretty pair of parakeets for her sister-in-law; and these birds, catch-ing the eye of John Dashwood on his following the other gentlemen into the room, were officiously handed by him to Colonel Brandon for his admiration.

"These are done by my eldest sister," said he, "and you, as a man of taste, will, I dare say, be pleased with them. I do not know whether you have seen any of her Elinor's work before, but she is reckoned to whittle extremely well."

The colonel, though disclaiming all pretensions to connoisseurship, warmly admired the driftwood budgies, as he would have done anything created by Miss Dashwood, and they were handed round for general in-spection. Mrs. Ferrars, not aware of their being Elinor's work, particu-larly requested to look at them; and after they had received gratifying testimony of Lady Middleton's approbation, Fanny presented them to her mother, considerately informing her, at the same time, that they were done by Miss Dashwood.

"Hum," said Mrs. Ferrars, "very pretty," and dropped them on the ground, causing one of the parakeet's tailfeathers to snap off.

Perhaps Fanny thought for a moment that her mother had been quite rude enough, for, colouring a little, she immediately said, "They are very pretty, ma'am—ain't they?" But then again, the dread of having been too civil, too encouraging herself, probably came over her, for she dropped the other parakeet (causing *its* tail to fall off) and presently added, "Do you not think they are something in Miss Morton's style of whittling, Ma'am? She *does* sculpt most delightfully! How masterfully her diorama of the late, lamented Sub-Marine Station Alpha was done! One nearly felt that one was there!"

"Beautifully indeed! But *she* does every thing well. Have you seen her peel a banana? It is like listening to a symphony."

Marianne could not bear this. She was already greatly displeased with Mrs. Ferrars, and such ill-timed praise of another, at Elinor's expense, though she had not any notion of what was principally meant by it, provoked her immediately to say with warmth, "This is admiration of a very particular kind! What is Miss Morton to us?" And so saying, she took the parakeets out of her sister-in-law's hands, and reattached their dismembered tailfeathers with bandages she removed for the purpose from the still-bleeding, shell-sliced housemaid.

"It is Elinor of whom *we* think and speak," Marianne continued angrily. "Who knows, or who cares, for this Miss Morton!"

Mrs. Ferrars looked exceedingly angry, and drawing herself up more stiffly than ever, pronounced in retort this bitter philippic, "Miss Morton is Lord Morton's daughter. *The* Lord Morton! He, the great hydraulic engineer of his or any age; he who was so dreadfully betrayed!"

It was not necessary for Mrs. Ferrars to relate the details; all present were familiar with the tragic story of Lord Morton and Sub-Marine

Station Alpha. The great man had been commissioned by the Crown to create the original underwater fortress, and his plans for the Station had been flawless, his execution exemplary. How could Lord Morton have known that Sir Bradley, his faithful amanuensis and chief engineer, was a merman in disguise, an ally to the sea creatures bent on the destruction of all mankind? This Bradley, cursed be the name, had waited patiently, tail disguised, for the entire Station to be constructed and inhabited by a city's worth of good English souls, before he triggered the gate-failure that flooded Morton's masterwork in an instant, and took the lives of so many brave undersea pioneers, Lord Morton included. The fortunate ones had been drowned, while the rest were shortly feasted upon by the swimming army of deep-sea murder-beasts that poured into the breached gate.

For Marianne to sully the name of Lord Morton in such company was a grave *faux pas*; Fanny looked very angry, and her husband was all in a fright at his sister's audacity. Elinor was much more hurt by Marianne's warmth than by what produced it; but Colonel Brandon's eyes, as they were fixed on Marianne, declared that he noticed only what was amiable in it, the affectionate heart which could not bear to see a sister slighted in the smallest point. His tentacles performed a sort of gentle, romantic sway as he gazed upon her.

Marianne's feelings did not stop here. She moved to her sister's chair, and putting one arm round her neck, and one cheek close to hers, said in a low, but eager, voice, "Dear, dear Elinor, don't mind them. Don't let them make *you* unhappy."

She could say no more; her spirits were quite overcome, and hiding her face on Elinor's shoulder, she burst into tears. Mrs. Jennings, with a very intelligent "Ah! poor dear," immediately gave her her salts, and Sir John instantly changed his seat to one close by Lucy Steele, and gave her, in a whisper, a brief account of the whole shocking Willoughby affair.

And then the bell was rung for the next act of the floor show, in which a man was to play badminton against a fur seal.

CHAPTER 35

E LINOR'S CURIOSITY TO SEE Mrs. Ferrars was satisfied, as
was her curiosity to know how a fur seal might wield a badminton
racquet. She had found in Mrs. Ferrars everything that could make a further connection between the families undesirable. She had seen enough
of her pride, her meanness, and her determined prejudice, to comprehend all the difficulties that must have perplexed the engagement of
Edward and herself, had he been otherwise free.

"My dear friend," cried Lucy, as soon as they met the next day, "I
come to talk to you of my happiness. Could anything be so flattering as
Mrs. Ferrars's way of treating me yesterday? So exceeding affable as she
was! Arranging me a seat up front, where I could best view the floorshow,
but draping me considerately with a poncho. You know how I dreaded
the thoughts of seeing her; but the very moment I was introduced, there
was such an affability in her behaviour. She had quite took a fancy to me.
Now was not it so? You saw it all; and was not you quite struck with it?"

"She was certainly very civil to you."

"Civil! Did you see nothing but civility? I saw a vast deal more. Such
kindness as fell to the share of nobody but me!"

Elinor wished to talk of something else; rifling through her mind for
other topics of interest, she recalled the subject of the swordfish and the
tiny cracks she had noticed in the Dome, and enquired whether Lucy
had ever seen such a crack before, during her time in-Station—but Lucy
would not allow the subject to be changed; she still pressed her to admit
she had reason for her happiness, and Elinor was obliged to go on.

"If they had known your engagement," said she, "nothing could be more flattering than their treatment of you; but as that was not the case—"

"I guessed you would say so," replied Lucy quickly, "but there was no reason in the world why Mrs. Ferrars should seem to like me, if she did not. Mrs. Ferrars is a charming woman, and so is your sister-in-law. They are both delightful women, indeed! I wonder I should never hear you say how agreeable Mrs. Dashwood was!"

To this Elinor had no answer to make, and did not attempt any.

"Are you ill, Miss Dashwood? You seem low. You don't speak. Sure you ain't well?"

"I never was in better health." In truth, as the conversation on the hated topic continued, Elinor felt the familiar terrifying darkness swimming about her eyes, saw the familiar star pattern begin to form itself in her mind. She took a series of deep breaths, in desperate hope that she could keep the eerie vision at bay. What was this torment? Why would it not leave her be?

"I am glad of it with all my heart," Lucy continued. "But I cannot help notice you are squeezing your eyes shut and holding your head between your legs. I should be sorry to have *you* ill. Heaven knows what I should have done without your friendship."

Elinor was prevented from making any response by the door's being thrown open, the servant's announcing Mr. Ferrars, and Edward immediately walking in.

It was a very awkward moment; and the countenance of each showed that it was so. They all looked exceedingly foolish; and Edward seemed to have as great an inclination to walk out of the room again, as to advance farther into it. The very circumstance, which they would each have been most anxious to avoid, had fallen on them. They were not only all three together, but were together without the relief of any other person. There they were, like three fish, caught unexpectedly together in the same net—all wishing they could be eaten straightaway, rather than continue together in their current company.

The ladies recovered themselves first. It was not Lucy's business to put herself forward; the appearance of secrecy must still be kept up. After slightly addressing him, she said no more. For Elinor's part, she was only glad that Edward's familiar, comforting presence had for now dispelled the five-pointed design, and the weird, suffocating darkness, from her mind.

Elinor resolved that she would not allow the presence of Lucy, nor the consciousness of some injustice towards herself, deter her from saying that she was happy to see him. She would not be frightened by Lucy from paying him those attentions which, as a friend and almost a relation, were his due.

Her manners gave some reassurance to Edward, and he had courage enough to sit down; but his embarrassment still exceeded that of the ladies in a proportion; for his heart had not the indifference of Lucy's, nor could his conscience have quite the ease of Elinor's.

It only contributed to the awkwardness when a loud bang was heard against the glass back wall of the docking; turning their heads, they saw that a servant, who had been changing the water filtration tank and come detached from the breathing hose of his special Ex-Domic Float-Suit, was clamouring for their attention. The operations of the Station's various life-sustaining apparatuses were meant to be entirely invisible to the inhabitants, and the man's noisy exhibition was a rather embarrassing violation of decorum; Elinor and her guests studiously ignored him, and his increasingly insistent thrashing became the background to the ensuing uncomfortable exchange.

Almost everything that *was* said proceeded from Elinor, who was obliged to volunteer all the information about her mother's health, their coming to town, etc.—all things Edward ought to have inquired about, but never did. In the resulting silence, the drowning servant pounded violently against the Dome, forming his mouth into the words *HELP ME* and clawing at the glass.

Elinor then determined, under pretence of fetching Marianne, to leave the others by themselves; and she really did it, and *that* in the handsomest manner, for she loitered away several minutes on the landing-place before she went to her sister. When that was once done, however, it was time for the raptures of Edward to cease; for Marianne's joy hurried her into the drawing-room immediately. Her pleasure in seeing him was like every other of her feelings, strong in itself, and strongly spoken. She met him with a hand that would be taken, and a voice that expressed the affection of a sister. "Dear Edward!" she cried. "This is a moment of great happiness! This would almost make amends for everything! Oh my God, there is a man out there—a drowning man!" Elinor leveled her sister with a corrective expression, to warn her from excessive enthusiasm regarding the presence of Edward, or as to the fate of the filtration-unit attendant. A gigantic and grotesquely toothsome anglerfish was swimming rapidly towards the latter, it's photophore angled upwards like a spotlight; seeing the fish, the man turned back to the glass wall, eyes bulging, pleading wordlessly for rescue.

Edward tried to return Marianne's kindness as it deserved, but before such witnesses he dared not say half what he really felt. Again they all sat down, and for a moment or two all were silent; while Marianne was looking with the most speaking tenderness, sometimes at Edward and sometimes at Elinor, regretting only that their delight in each other should be checked by Lucy's unwelcome presence.

The anglerfish closed its hundreds of razor-like teeth on the man's lower half, splitting him messily in two.

Edward was the first to speak, and it was to notice Marianne's altered looks, and express his fear of her not finding the Sub-Station agreeable.

"Oh, don't think of me!" she replied with spirited earnestness. The filtration-man's upper body floated upwards, as his legs disappeared in ragged hunks into the gullet of the anglerfish. "Elinor is well, you see. That must be enough for us both."

This remark was not calculated to make Edward or Elinor more easy, nor to conciliate the good will of Lucy, who looked up at Marianne with no very benignant expression.

"Do you like the Sub-Station?" said Edward, willing to say anything that might introduce another subject.

"Not at all. I expected much pleasure in it, but I have found none. The sight of you, Edward, is the only comfort it has afforded; and thank Heaven! You are what you always were!"

Outside the Dome, enough blood was left in the man's upper portion for him to remain conscious, and he watched in horror as his lower portion was chewed to pieces by the great beast. Marianne paused—and no one spoke. The anglerfish finished the legs and began its assault on the remaining portion of the filtration attendant. The ocean fogged with blood.

"I think, Elinor," she presently added, "we must employ Edward to take care of us in our return to Barton Cottage. In a week or two, I suppose, we shall be going; and, I trust, Edward will not be very unwilling to accept the charge."

Poor Edward muttered something, but what it was, nobody knew—it may have been to the effect of, "Anglerfish certainly have a lot of teeth." But Marianne, who saw his agitation, was perfectly satisfied, and soon talked of something else. "We spent such a day, Edward, in Harley Piscina yesterday! So dull, so wretchedly dull! But I have much to say to you on that head, which cannot be said now."

And with this admirable discretion did she defer the assurance of her finding their mutual relatives more disagreeable than ever, and of her being particularly disgusted with his mother, till they were more in private.

"But why were you not there, Edward? Why did you not come?"

"I was engaged elsewhere."

"Engaged! What was that, when such friends were to be met?"

"Perhaps, Miss Marianne," cried Lucy, eager to take some revenge on her, "you think young men never stand upon engagements, if they have no mind to keep them, little as well as great."

Elinor was very angry, but Marianne seemed entirely insensible of the sting. The water-tank servant was all the more insensible, and would remain so forever, as the anglerfish swallowed his head in two great gulps. At this, Edward gasped and hid his eyes behind his hand.

"I am very sure that only conscience kept Edward from Harley Piscina," Marianne calmly replied to Lucy's slight. "And I really believe he *has* the most delicate conscience in the world; the most scrupulous in performing every engagement, however minute, and however it may make against his interest or pleasure. He is the most fearful of giving pain, of wounding expectation, and the most incapable of being selfish, of anybody I ever saw. Edward, it is so, and I will say it." Winding up her speech, she turned and looked at the observation glass. "My God! That will need cleaning!"

CHAPTER 36

WITHIN A FEW DAYS after this meeting, the newspapers announced to the world that the lady of Thomas Palmer, Esq. was safely delivered of a son and heir. This event, highly important to Mrs. Jennings's happiness, produced a temporary alteration in the disposal of her time, and influenced the engagements of her young friends; for as she wished to be as much as possible with Charlotte, she went thither every morning as soon as she was up, and did not return till late in the evening; and the Miss Dashwoods found their hours made over to Lady Middleton and the two Miss Steeles—by whom their company, in fact was as little valued, as it was professedly sought.

The presence of more guests was particularly undesirable to Lady Middleton, who of late had much to hide; at night she was clandestinely repairing the submarine that sat hidden in her pantry, teaching herself the secrets of the shipwright's art as were necessary to weld the hull and repair the battered old propellers; by day she continued to quiz herself on intricacies of navigation and underwater piloting, preparatory to her long-dreamed-of escape. As for Lucy, she considered Elinor and Marianne with a jealous eye, as intruding on *her* ground, and sharing the kindness which she wanted to monopolize.

Elsewhere in-Station, the pirate vogue that had been in evidence at Sir John's theme ball had become, by this point in the season, the very height of fashionability; well-heeled gentlemen increasingly affected the air of gentlemen of fortune. A cutlass was suddenly a required accessory, and one could not stroll the Retail Embankment nor row down Marleybone High Causeway without hearing the squawk of parrots chattering on the shoulders of kerchiefed *beaux*. Games of chance and aquatic amusements such as the sea-lion rodeo were less and less in favour, replaced by sword fights, in which the men of the Station tested their mettle—though to come into combat with actual pirates would be the furthest thing from anyone's imagining.

Elinor found these styles distasteful, especially since they coincided with a very real increase in the number of pirate attacks in the Surface-Lands; various buccaneers, including the fearsome Pirate Dreadbeard, were making the seas even more dangerous than usual, boarding any ship short of a four-master, rampaging the stores and throwing anyone aboard to the mercy of the sea monsters.

Yet more distressing was that the piratical colouring to their social round did little to elevate Marianne's spirits. She prepared quietly and mechanically for every evening's engagement, donning her galoshes, though without expecting the smallest amusement from any, and very often without knowing, till the last moment, where it was to take her.

One evening they travelled to the house of an acquaintance of her sister-in-law, where they were to witness a series of fights, performed with cutlass and dirk, of the sort that it was imagined brave gallants would engage in with pirates. The events of this evening were not very remarkable. The party, like other sword-fighting parties, comprehended a great many people who had real taste for the sport, and a great many more who had none at all; and the performers themselves were, as usual, in their own estimation and that of their immediate friends, the best private duelists in England.

As Elinor was not martial, nor affecting to be so, she made no scruple of turning her eyes from the "gangplank," which had been carefully constructed to resemble the foredeck of a schooner, such as that where an actual pirate fight might occur. In one of these excursive glances, she perceived among a group of young men, one who wore two customised arm-bands, one reading *Hail*, the other *Britannia*. She perceived him soon afterwards looking at herself, and speaking familiarly to her brother; when they both came towards her, Mr. Dashwood introduced him to her as Mr. Robert Ferrars.

He addressed her with easy civility, and twisted his head into a bow which assured her as plainly as words could have done, that he was exactly the coxcomb she had heard him described to be by Lucy. Happy had it been for her, if her regard for Edward had depended less on his own merit, than on the merit of his nearest relations! But while she wondered at the difference of the two young men, she did not find that the emptiness of conceit of the one, put her out of all charity with the modesty and worth of the other. Why they *were* different, Robert exclaimed to her himself in the course of a quarter of an hour's conversation, as the clang of metal on metal rang out from the artificial foredeck behind them; for, talking of his brother, and lamenting the extreme *gaucherie* which he believed kept him from mixing in proper society, he candidly and generously attributed it to the misfortune of a private education; while he himself, merely from the advantage of a public school, was as well-fitted to mix in the world as any other man.

"Upon my soul," he added, "I believe it is nothing more; and so I often tell my mother, when she is grieving about it. 'My dear Madam,' I always say to her, 'you must make yourself easy. The evil is now irremediable, and it has been entirely your own doing. Why would you place

Edward under private tuition at the most critical time of his life? There to mingle with wharf rats, and become obsessed with tedious scholarly trivialities and myths of the Alteration! If you had only sent him to Westminster as well as myself, all this would have been prevented.'This is the way in which I always consider the matter, and my mother is perfectly convinced of her error."

As John Dashwood had no more pleasure in swordplay than his eldest sister, his mind was equally at liberty to fix on anything else; he spent most of the evening trying to recall if he had yet been paid in full for a recent experiment, in which he had eaten nothing but paddlefish roe for three days. This led to a most agreeable thought, which he communicated to his wife, for her approbation, when they got home. He would be most monstrously sick for the following week, recovering from an operation that would line his lungs with thin filaments and lamellae, such as those found in gills—surely Fanny would like to have company during his period of recovery. It would only be sensible and polite, therefore, to invite his sisters to be their guests.The expense would be nothing and the inconvenience not more, but Fanny was startled at the proposal.

"They are Lady Middleton's visitors. How can I ask them away from her?"

Her husband did not see the force of her objection. "They had already spent a week with her, and Lady Middleton could not be displeased at their giving the same number of days to such near relations."

"My love, I had just settled within myself to ask the Miss Steeles to spend a few days with us.They are very well behaved, good kind of girls, and I am told by Lady Middleton the younger one makes a devilish clever ship-in-a-bottle.We can ask your sisters some other year, you know; but the Miss Steeles may not be in-Station anymore!"

And so Mr. Dashwood was convinced. He saw the necessity of inviting the Miss Steeles immediately, and his conscience was pacified by the resolution of inviting his sisters another year; at the same time, however, slyly suspecting that another year would make the invitation needless, by bringing Elinor in-Station as Colonel Brandon's wife, and Marianne as *their* visitor.

Fanny, rejoicing in her escape, wrote the next morning to Lucy, to request her company and her sister's, as soon as Lady Middleton could spare them. This was enough to make Lucy really and reasonably happy. Such an opportunity of being with Edward and his family was the most material to her interest, and such an invitation the most gratifying to her feelings! It was an advantage that could not be too gratefully acknowledged, nor too speedily made use of; and the visit to Lady Middleton, which had not before had any precise limits, was instantly discovered to have been always meant to end in two days' time. Lady Middleton, for her part, was supremely pleased, as now she could focus her full attention on finalizing her rebuilt submarine.

When the note was shown to Elinor, as it was within ten minutes after its arrival, it gave her, for the first time, some share in the expectations of Lucy; for such a mark of uncommon kindness seemed to declare that the good-will towards her arose from something more than merely malice against herself; and might be brought, by time and address, to do everything that Lucy wished. Lucy possessed a remarkable, even a supernatural skill at flattery, Elinor thought, which had already subdued the pride of Lady Middleton, and made an entry into the close heart of Mrs. John Dashwood.

Thus the Miss Steeles removed to the residence of John and Fanny Dashwood, and all that reached Elinor of their influence there, strengthened her expectation of the event. Sir John, who called on them more than once, brought home such accounts of the favour they were in, as must be universally striking. Mrs. Dashwood had never been so much pleased with any young women in her life, as she was with them; she called Lucy by her Christian name; utilised her help in keeping John's lung-gills moistened with fresh rounds of sea-water; and did not know whether she should ever be able to part with them.

CHAPTER 37

MRS. PALMER WAS SO WELL at the end of a fortnight that her mother felt it no longer necessary to give up the whole of her time to her. Content with visiting her once or twice a day, she returned to her own docking station, in which she found the Miss Dashwoods very ready to resume their former share.

About the third or fourth morning after their being thus resettled, Mrs. Jennings, on returning from her ordinary visit to Mrs. Palmer, entered the drawing-room, where Elinor was sitting by herself, tearing into a package of thrice-exsiccated crumpets.

"My dear Miss Dashwood! Have you heard the news?"

"No, ma'am. What is it?"

"Something so strange!"

"Has another infant been sucked up into a filtration duct?"

"No, thank heavens! When I got to Mr. Palmer's, I found Charlotte quite in a fuss about the child. She was sure it was very ill—it cried, and fretted, and was all over pimples. So I looked at it directly, and, 'Lord! my dear,' says I, 'it is nothing in the world, but a tapeworm bedeviling the poor child's small intestine—fetch me a tweezers and a box of wooden matches!' and nurse said just the same. But Charlotte, she would not be satisfied, so Mr. Donavan was sent for; and as soon as ever he saw the child, he said just as we did, that it was nothing in the world but a tapeworm, and he forced the child's jaw open, lowered a fishing line in there, and got the bugger out; I burnt it thoroughly in the ash-heap, and then Charlotte was easy. And so, just as he was going away again, it came into my head, I am sure I do not know how I happened to think of it, but it came into my head to ask him if there was any news. So upon that, he smirked, and simpered, and looked grave, and says I, "Did another infant get sucked up into a filtration duct?" and he says, "no," and then—at last— he said in a whisper, 'For fear any unpleasant report should reach the young ladies under your care, I must say I believe there is no great reason for alarm. I hope Mrs. Dashwood will do very well.'"

"What!" cried Elinor. "Is Fanny ill?"

"That is exactly what I said, my dear. 'Lord!' says I, 'is Mrs. Dashwood ill? Did *she* get sucked up into the filtration duct?' And the doctor replied no, and begged me to stop asking that, and from frustration with my single-mindedness on it, I believe, revealed the whole story. The long and the short of the matter seems to be this: Mr. Edward Ferrars, the very young man I used to joke with you about, has been engaged above this twelvemonth to Lucy Steele!"

Upon the utterance of that name, and this public revelation of the news she had privately held for so long, Elinor found herself at once in a kind of debilitated, feverish state, combined with a headache of unutterable agony; she doubled over, her head clutched between her legs. As she exhaled deep, heaving breaths, the five-pointed star danced malevolently in the dark space between her eyes.

Mrs. Jennings, from an excess of either politeness or self-regard, gave no notice to this extraordinary reaction.

"There's for you, my dear!" she continued, heedless. "And not a creature knowing a syllable of the matter, except Anne! Could you have believed such a thing possible? That matters should be brought so forward between them, and nobody suspect it! I never happened to see them together, or I am sure I should have found it out directly. Well, and so this was kept a great secret, for fear of Mrs. Ferrars, and neither she nor your brother or sister suspected a word of the matter; till this very morning, poor Lucy, her sister Anne, you know, is a well-meaning creature, but a few sails short of a schooner, popped it all out. And so, away she went to your sister, who was sitting all alone at her carpet-work, little suspecting what was to come—you may think what a blow it was to all her vanity and pride. She fell into violent hysterics immediately, with such screams as reached your brother's ears, as he was sitting in his own dressing-room downstairs, writing a letter. The screams were of displeasure, amplified tenfold by surprise, and tenfold again, at least as far as your brother was concerned, by his having been implanted last Thursday with the hyper-sensitive eardrums of a pinecone soldierfish.

"So up he flew directly, hands covering his poor ears to muffle the *shriek-shriek-shriek*, and a terrible scene took place, for Lucy was come to them by that time, little dreaming what was going on. Poor soul! I pity *her*. And I must say, I think she was used very hardly; for your sister scolded like any fury, and soon drove her into a fainting fit. Anne, she fell upon her knees, and cried bitterly; and your brother, he walked about the room, disoriented, ears still ringing, blundering into the walls, and said he did not know what to do. Mrs. Dashwood declared they should not stay a minute longer in the house, and your brother was forced to go down upon *his* knees too, to persuade her to let them stay till they had packed up their clothes."

"My goodness," interposed Elinor.

"The gondola was moored dockside, ready to take the poor Miss Steeles away, and they were just stepping in as Mr. Donavan came off; poor Lucy in such a condition, he says, she could hardly walk; and Anne, she was almost as bad. Lord! What a taking poor Mr. Edward will be in when he hears of it! To have his love used so scornfully! The whole af-fair is simply . . ." Mrs. Jennings then lapsed into her native tongue, indeci-pherable to Elinor, who tried to collect her thoughts.

But a slight rapping at the glass of the Station Dome distracted her from her course of reflection. Glancing up, she saw that the source of the sound was a small swordfish, tapping on the glass. Even as she was buffeted by the waves of inner turmoil caused by Edward's undoing, the appear-ance of the small fish, with its slight, small, but determined tapping, sent a queer chill down Elinor's spine. The chill intensified when she observed that this swordfish had a gleaming patch of silver iridescence under its horn; it was not, therefore, the same swordfish that had rapped 'pon the glass previously. It was a *different* fish.

As Mrs. Jennings could talk on no subject but Edward's engagement, Elinor soon saw the necessity of preparing Marianne for its discussion. No time was to be lost in undeceiving her, in making her acquainted with the real truth, and in endeavouring to bring her to hear it talked of by others, without betraying that she felt any uneasiness for her sister, or any resentment against Edward.

Elinor's office was a painful one. She was going to remove what she really believed to be her sister's chief consolation, to give such particulars of Edward as she feared would ruin him forever in her good opinion, and to make Marianne, by a seeming resemblance in their situations, which to *her* fancy would seem strong, feel all her own disappointment over again. But unwelcome as such a task must be, like the scraping of barnacles off a long-neglected hull, it was necessary to be done.

She was very far from wishing to dwell on her own feelings; she told the tale of Edward's engagement to Lucy in a manner calm and clear, endeavouring to ignore both her own feelings on the matter and the persistent tap-a-tap of the swordfish on the glass. Her narration was not accompanied by violent agitation, nor impetuous grief. *That* belonged rather to the hearer, for Marianne listened with horror, and cried excessively.

"How long has this been known to you, Elinor? Has he written to you?"

"I have known it these four months. When Lucy first came to Pestilent Isle last November, on the day we were nearly drowned and mauled by the hideous two-headed Fang-Beast, she told me in confidence of her engagement."

At these words, Marianne's eyes expressed the astonishment which her lips could not utter. After a pause of wonder, she exclaimed—

"Four months! Have you known of this four months? Since the Fang-Beast?"

Elinor confirmed it.

"What! While attending me in all my misery, this has been on your heart? And I have reproached you for being happy!"

"It was not fit that you should then know how much I was the reverse!"

"Four months!" cried Marianne again. "So calm! So cheerful! How have you been supported?"

"By feeling that I was doing my duty. My promise to Lucy obliged me to be secret. I owed it to her, therefore, to avoid giving any hint of the truth."

Marianne seemed much struck. Behind her, on the glass, a second swordfish joined the first, and the two tapped together, labouring diligently, their glassy eyes staring straight ahead. Had Elinor not been distracted by the emotional intensity of the subject matter at hand, she might have reflected that the presence of the two swordfish, side by side, confirmed a certain sense of grim and unholy purpose about their labours.

"I have very often wished to undeceive yourself and my mother," said Elinor; "and once or twice I have attempted it; but without betraying my trust, I never could have convinced you."

"Four months! And yet you loved him!"

"Yes. But I did not love only him; and while the comfort of others was dear to me, I was glad to spare them from knowing how much I felt. I would not have you suffer on my account."

"Oh, Elinor!" she cried. "You have made me hate myself for ever. My behaviour has been more barbarous to you, my own sister, than the most rapacious of pirates—worse than Dreadbeard himself! You, who have been my only comfort, who have borne with me in all my misery, who have seemed to be only suffering for me!"

The tenderest caresses followed this confession. In such a frame of mind as she was now in, Elinor had no difficulty in obtaining from her whatever promise she required; and at her request, Marianne engaged never to speak of the affair to anyone with the least appearance of bitterness; to meet Lucy without betraying the smallest increase of dislike to her;

and even to see Edward himself without any diminution of her usual cordiality. As the sisters consoled one another, a spider web of tiny cracks appeared in the glass. The two swordfish swam away, making little playful patterns as they disappeared into the dark of the deep ocean.

Marianne performed her promise of being discreet to admiration. She attended to all that Mrs. Jennings had to say upon the subject with an unchanging complexion. When Mrs. Jennings talked of Edward's affection, it cost her only a spasm in her throat, easily attributed to the effort of swallowing so much desiccated food paste. Such advances towards heroism in her sister, made Elinor feel equal to anything herself.

The next morning brought a further trial of it, in a visit from their brother, who came with a most serious aspect to talk over the dreadful affair, and bring them news of his wife.

"You have heard, I suppose," said he with great solemnity, in a wheelchair because his feet were recovering from the surgery necessary to make his toes webbed, to increase (or so hoped his physicians) his speed and agility in the water. "Of the very shocking discovery that took place under our roof yesterday.

They all looked their assent; it seemed too awful a moment for speech.

"Your sister," he continued, "has suffered dreadfully. Mrs. Ferrars too—in short it has been a scene of such complicated distress—but I will hope that the storm may be weathered without our being any of us quite overcome." Here he paused and let out a most inhuman shrieking noise; besides the toe webbing, John Dashwood had submitted (for four pounds sterling) to have implanted in his throat a complex biological mechanism for echolocation, such as that used by toothed whales and other *odontoceti* to navigate unseeing through the ocean's depths. Thus far Mr. Dashwood did not have the system under his control, and so periodically he gave off a chilling shriek, which his sisters attempted to politely ignore.

"Poor Fanny! She was in hysterics all yesterday. But I would not alarm you too much. The doctor says there is nothing materially to be apprehended; her constitution is a good one, and her resolution equal to anything." John paused, and let out another of the strange loud shrieks. "She has borne it all, with the fortitude of an angel! She says she never shall think well of anybody again; and one cannot wonder at it, after being so deceived! It was quite out of the benevolence of her heart, that she had asked these young women to her docking station; merely because she thought they deserved some attention. Otherwise we both wished very much to have invited you and Marianne to be with us! And now to be so rewarded! 'I wish, with all my heart,' says poor Fanny in her affectionate way, 'that we had asked your sisters instead of them.'"

Here he stopped and darted his head violently around the room, as his bat-like hearing informed him of some minute motion past his field of vision.

"What poor Mrs. Ferrars suffered, when first Fanny broke it to her, is not to be described. While she with the truest affection had been planning a most eligible connection for Edward, was it to be supposed that he could be all the time secretly engaged to another person! Such a suspicion could never have entered her head! If she suspected *any* prepossession elsewhere, it could not be in *that* quarter. 'There, to be sure,' said she, 'I might have thought myself safe.' She was quite in an awful humour. A servant coughed, interrupting her loud denunciation of Ms. Steele, and she had the unfortunate man shot out of her docking with the water cannon, and shouted 'huzzah' when he landed in the canal. At last she determined to send for Edward. He came. But I am sorry to relate what ensued. All that Mrs. Ferrars could say to make him put an end to the engagement was of no avail. She filled up a tank with sea-water and forced him to stand in it, and then added vicious biting snapfish, one by one. 'Foreswear your engagement!' she cried, adding the second of the snapfish even as the first nipped eagerly at Edward's toes, but he remained solid. Duty, affection, everything was disregarded. 'Foreswear it!' and added a third snapfish. 'But no; I never thought Edward so stubborn, so unfeeling before. And indeed, the soles of his feet must be fashioned of pure lead.'

"His mother explained to him her liberal designs, in case of his marrying Miss Morton; told him she would settle on him the Norfolk estate, which, clear of land-tax, brings in a good thousand a-year; she threw in another dozen vicious biting snapfish, which went to work on his feet most mercilessly; she offered even, when still he refused, to make it twelve hundred. She vowed to never see him again; she swore to do all in her power to prevent him from advancing in any profession. At last he was allowed to emerge from the tank, his feet bleeding and gouged."

Here Marianne, in an ecstasy of indignation, clapped her hands together, and cried, "Gracious God! Can this be possible!"

"Well may you wonder, Marianne," replied her brother, "at the obstinacy which could resist such arguments, combined with such physical tortures, as these. Your exclamation is very natural."

Marianne was going to retort, but she remembered her promises, and forbore.

"All this, however," he continued, "was urged in vain. Edward said very little; but what he did say, was in the most determined manner. Nothing should prevail on him to give up his engagement."

"Then he has acted like an honest man!" cried Mrs. Jennings with blunt sincerity, no longer able to be silent, "I beg your pardon, Mr. Dashwood, but if he had done otherwise, I should have thought him a rascal. I believe there is not a better kind of girl in the world than Lucy, nor one who more deserves a good husband." This sentiment was especially offensive to Elinor, and its utterance for some reason caused a recurrence of the flashing five-pointed star and the attendant pain; she clutched her hands to her temples and willed it away.

John Dashwood replied, without any resentment, "Miss Lucy Steele is, I dare say, a very deserving young woman, but in the present case, you know, the connection must be impossible." Here again he paused in his speech to shriek vividly and rush to the far side of the room in search of the source of some peripheral movement. Recovering himself, he continued: "We all wish her extremely happy; and Mrs. Ferrars's conduct throughout the whole, has been dignified and liberal. Edward has drawn his own lot, and I fear it will be a bad one."

Marianne sighed out her similar apprehension; and Elinor's heart wrung for the feelings of Edward, while braving his mother's threats and collection of tiny biting fish, for a woman who could not reward him.

"Well, sir," said Mrs. Jennings, "how did it end?"

"I am sorry to say, ma'am, in a most unhappy rupture. Edward is dismissed for ever from his mother's notice. His feet were so afflicted that he is, for the time being, to wear shoes made of soft leather. He left her house yesterday, but where he is gone, or whether he is still in town, I do not know; for *we* of course can make no inquiry."

"Poor young man! And what is to become of him?"

"What, indeed, ma'am! It is a melancholy consideration. Born to the prospect of such affluence! I cannot conceive a situation more deplorable. The interest of two thousand pounds—how can a man live on it? And when to that is added the recollection, that he might, but for his own folly, within three months have been in the receipt of two thousand, five hundred a year (for Miss Morton has thirty thousand pounds, the legacy of her father, who perished along with his most splendid creation) I cannot picture to myself a more wretched condition. We must all feel for him; and the more so, because it is totally out of our power to assist him."

"Poor young man!" cried Mrs. Jennings, "I am sure he should be very welcome to bed and board at my house; and so I would tell him if I could see him."

"If he would only have done as well by himself," said John Dashwood, "as all his friends were disposed to do by him, he might now have been in his proper situation. But as it is, it must be out of anybody's power to assist him. And there is one thing more preparing against him, which must be worse than all—his mother has determined, with a very natural kind of spirit, to settle *that* estate upon Robert immediately, which might have been Edward's, on proper conditions."

"Well!" said Mrs. Jennings, "that is *her* revenge. Everybody has a way of their own. But I don't think mine would be, to make one son independent, because another had plagued me. Of course, all my sons were murdered and their corpses mutilated by a group of adventurers, so that may colour my feelings on that particular hypothetical."

Shortly thereafter Mr. Dashwood departed, leaving the three ladies unanimous in their sentiments on the present occasion, as far at least as it regarded Mrs. Ferrars's conduct, the Dashwoods', and Edward's. Marianne's indignation burst forth as soon as he quitted the room; and as her vehemence made reserve impossible in Elinor, and unnecessary in Mrs. Jennings, they all joined in a very spirited critique upon the party.

CHAPTER 38

MRS. JENNINGS WAS VERY WARM in her praise of Edward's conduct, but only Elinor and Marianne understood its true merit. Elinor gloried in his integrity; and Marianne forgave all his offences in compassion for his punishment. But though confidence between them was, by this public discovery, restored to its proper state, it was not a subject on which either of them were fond of dwelling when alone.

On the third day succeeding their knowledge of the particulars, they decided to make an excursion to Kensington Undersea Gardens, among the most remarked upon of Sub-Marine Station Beta's recently added pleasure-places. Mrs. Jennings and Elinor were of the number; but Marianne, who knew that the Willoughbys were again in-Station, and had a constant dread of meeting them, chose not to venture into so public a place. It was also rumoured that a coral sculpture in the shape of a giant octopus was among the wonders on display at Kensington, and the sentimental associations with such an artwork might prove, she imagined, too much to bear.

The Undersea Gardens had been created through a singular feat of hydraulic engineering, by which a single, non-load–bearing panel of the Dome's reinforced glass sidewall had been opened, allowing visitors, for a considerable fee, to venture outside the glass wall of the Sub-Station. There, they could roam for several minutes directly on a patch of ocean's floor, four acres square, that had been specially treated with an experimental chemical process to destroy all traces of marine life—but which allowed the awe-inspiring undersea fauna, such as no human could ever hope to lay eyes upon elsewhere, to thrive.

To venture into the Gardens, one was required first to don an elaborate sea-floor navigation costume, more extensive in its particulars but similar in basic outline to a diving suit. Aided by a courteous attendant, Elinor changed from her full-skirted dress to a seamless orange rubber suit. Then the large glass helmet was carefully lowered over her head. Next were added the supple gloves and the lead-lined galoshes which would ensure that her feet remained firmly upon the ocean's floor during her ex-Domic perambulation; lastly came the heavy air tank, strapped to her back, that would keep a vital supply of oxygen flowing into Elinor's helmet.

Once Mrs. Jennings was similarly attired, she and her friend were led by guides into a small ante-chamber, where the door of the Dome was sealed shut behind them with an audible *whoosh*; after a few moments they heard a loud whistle, and saw water begin to pour in to the chamber. After a moment, a second door opened on the far side of the chamber—the water had been let in, Elinor now understood, only to allow the atmospheric pressures to even out; now they were free to exit the ante-chamber and stroll the floor of the ocean itself.

All this extraordinary preparation, Elinor instantly concluded, was entirely justified by the miraculous sights that greeted her. Her eyes widened to see the endless varieties of multi-coloured undersea plants; the deep scarlet ceramiaceae, the wavy tendrils of the nereocystis barely swaying in the light undersea currents; her fingertips brushed against the thick stems of the acetabula.

As she tromped in her thick boots, through this marvelous undersea universe, isolated in the confines of her suit, Elinor was lost to quiet reflection; all her inner torment and confusion, all the drama that had attended Edward's engagement, it was all the merest triviality when compared to the vastness of what she could now comprehend through the glass front-piece of her navigation suit: acres of coral, staghorn, sea whips, delicate and marvelous in their infinite variety. She tromped about the ocean floor, marveling at every blue-green tendril, curving her hands along every stalk; and, most of all, enjoying the isolation of her private world within her navigation suit. She was alone; she saw nothing of the Willoughbys, nothing of Edward, and for some time nothing of anybody who could be interesting to her.

But at last she found herself with some surprise, accosted by Anne Steele, looking rather shy as she approached her within her own navigation suit and glass helmet. Communication of course was impossible, which was some relief for Elinor, who had nothing to say to Miss Steele and desired to hear nothing from her. But the latter personage, from within her own suit, waved vigorously to Elinor, expressing by a series of delighted facial expressions and fervent gesticulations her great satisfaction in meeting her, and, by pointing back to the antechamber, that she wished to return to where communication was possible, and converse.

Elinor was shaking her head and forming her lips into an exaggerated *No*, turning on her heel to hide in a bower of *alariae*, when Miss Steele's expression changed entirely. Her eyes, which had been pleased and imploring, turned first distressed and then terrified; at that moment Elinor felt a sharp, painful sting directly at the base of her neck. The source was a sea scorpion, not less than five inches long; how it had survived the chemical process that had cleansed this patch of ocean and breached the walls of her rubber suit, were questions that must be answered later. At present her only concern was the crablike stinging horror that had crawled inside her helmet and attached one of its fearsome chelicerae directly into her neck. Terrified, and in the most excruciating pain, Elinor spun in a furious circle, trying to dislodge the loathsome eurypterid, but to no avail; as she spun, the thing spun too, clinging to her throat, its armored body whipping in circles and smacking against the glass of the helmet.

In desperation, Elinor raised her hands in their protective gloves to pluck the creature off her, but her hands only slapped in vain against the reinforced helmet; her head was enclosed in glass, and the same glass barrier which allowed her continued respiration kept her hands out, and her attacker in. The sea scorpion dug its claws deeper into the flesh of her neck. The blood ran down Elinor's chest, and she saw blood coat her like a bright red apron.

Mrs. Jennings had appeared beside her, and was mouthing to her, "OPEN THE SUIT! OPEN THE SUIT!" Elinor took a deep breath, drawing as much oxygen as possible into her lungs, and with a burst of pain-driven strength, pried open the face plate against the pressure of the water.

The icy temperature of the undersea depths hit her like a slap in the face. Without time to contemplate the bitter coldness now swiftly stealing over her body, or how far she had ventured from the antechamber that led back into the Sub-Station and precious oxygen, or to note the horrified expressions on the faces of both Mrs. Jennings and Miss Steele, Elinor grasped the sea scorpion with both hands, crushing its carapace between her protective gloves, tugging mightily to dislodge it. Still the thing clung, its claws firmly embedded in her neck. The harder she pulled, the worse the pain became, and with every passing second she felt her breath growing shorter. Still she pulled, and at last the devilish persistence of the eurypterid was overcome, and the claws came loose and the beast was torn free—taking with it a sizable chunk of flesh from her throat. Blood spurted forth in a wild gush, the sight of which—combined with the bitter cold of the water and her nearly extinguished air supply—caused her vision to swim black.

AT PRESENT HER ONLY CONCERN WAS THE CRABLIKE STINGING HORROR THAT
HAD CRAWLED INSIDE HER HELMET AND ATTACHED ONE OF ITS FEARSOME
CHELICERAE DIRECTLY INTO HER NECK.

*   *   *

Elinor awoke in a chair of the plushest otter skin, in the richly appointed Visitor Centre of the Kensington Undersea Gardens, her hands and feet submerged in small dishes of lukewarm water to ward off hypothermia. Anne Steele was on the other side of the room, brushing her hair to restore its former shape after an afternoon spent within the diving helmet.

Mrs. Jennings, seated beside her, immediately whispered to Elinor, "Thank God! You have survived."

And after inquiring with her customary enthusiasm of affection for the state of Elinor's health, and reassuring her that her neck would certainly heal given time, Mrs. Jennings nodded her head towards Miss Steele and remarked, "Get it all out of her, my dear. You have suffered most grievously and nearly died; she is bound to be sympathetic and therefore talkative; she will tell you anything if you ask!"

In her uneasy state, it took a moment for Elinor to realise that Mrs. Jennings was desirous that she pry out of Miss Steele more details regarding Lucy's engagement to Edward. It was lucky, however, for Mrs. Jennings's curiosity and Elinor's too, that she would tell anything *without* being asked; for nothing would otherwise have been learnt. Elinor rose and walked unsteadily across the room, gingerly touching her bandaged throat.

"I am so glad to meet you; and that you managed to tear that hideous thing from your neck, and that Mrs. Jennings and I were able to drag you back into the Sub-Station before you died," said Miss Steele, taking her familiarly by the arm, "for I wanted to see you of all things in the world." And then lowering her voice, "I suppose Mrs. Jennings has heard all about it. Is she angry?"

"Not at all, I believe, with you."

"That is a good thing. And Lady Middleton, is *she* angry?"

"I cannot suppose it possible that she should be."

"I am monstrous glad of it. Good gracious! I have had such a time of it! I never saw Lucy in such a rage in my life. Oh, dear—are you quite well? I would leave it alone, dear."

The last remark was in response to Elinor's wince of pain; she had ventured to lift off one of her bandages, and found in doing so that the pain of her neck was as sharp as when the sea scorpion had originally connected itself to her.

"Well, but Miss Dashwood," Miss Steele continued triumphantly, "people may say what they choose about Mr. Ferrars declaring he would not have Lucy, for it is no such thing I can tell you; and it is quite a shame for such ill-natured reports to be spread abroad. Whatever Lucy might think about it herself, you know, it was no business of other people to set it down for certain."

"I never heard anything of the kind hinted at before, I assure you," said Elinor.

"Oh, did not you? But it *was* said, I know, and by more than one! At the man versus giant catfish event on Thursday evening, in Hydra-Z, Miss Godby told Miss Sparks, that nobody in their senses could expect Mr. Ferrars to give up a woman like Miss Morton, with thirty thousand pounds to her fortune, and heir to the Sub-Station Alpha Family besides, for Lucy Steele that had nothing at all."

"I believe in my heart Lucy gave it up all for lost; for we came away from your brother's docking Wednesday, and we saw nothing of Mr. Ferrars not all Thursday, Friday, and Saturday, and did not know what was become of him. Once Lucy thought to write to him, but then her spirits rose against that. However this morning he came and it all came out, how he had been sent for Wednesday to Harley Piscina, and been talked to by his mother and all of them, and how he had declared before them all that he loved nobody but Lucy, and nobody but Lucy would he have.

"As soon as he had went away from his mother's house, and Ascended the Station entirely and taken off in his own personal submarine, he stayed at an inn all Thursday and Friday just to get the better of it. And after thinking it all over and over again, he said that it would be quite unkind to keep her on to the engagement. If he was to become a poor light-house keeper, how were they to live upon that? Edward could not bear to think of her doing no better, and so he begged, if she had the least mind for it, to put an end to the matter directly, and leave him shift for himself. I heard him say all this as plain as could possibly be. And it was entirely for *her* sake, and upon *her* account, that he said a word about being off, and not upon his own. I will take my oath he never dropped a sylla-ble of being tired of her, or of wishing to marry Miss Morton, or anything like it. But Lucy would not give ear to such kind of talking. She told him directly (with a great deal about sweet and love, you know, and all that— one can't repeat such kind of things), she had not the least mind in the world to be off, for she could live with him upon a trifle, and how little so ever he might have, she should be very glad to have it all. So then he was monstrous happy, and talked on some time about what they should do, and they agreed he should become a lighthouse keeper directly, and they must wait to be married till he got some good, desolate monster-wracked beach in need of able lighthouse keeping. And just then I could not hear any more, for my cousin called from below to tell me Mrs. Richardson was come 'pon her tortoise, and would take one of us to the Gardens; so I was forced to go into the room and interrupt them, to ask Lucy if she would like to go."

"I do not understand what you mean by interrupting them," said Elinor. "You were all in the same room together, were not you?"

"No, indeed, not us. La! Miss Dashwood, do you think people make love when anybody else is by? You must know better than that! No, no, they were shut up in the drawing-room together, and all I heard was by holding the funnel end of a seashell up to the door and listening in the pointy end."

"How!" cried Elinor. "Have you been repeating to me what you only learnt yourself by listening at the door? I am sorry I did not know it before; for I certainly would not have suffered you to give me particulars of a conversation which you ought not to have known yourself. How could you behave so unfairly by your sister?"

"Oh, there is nothing in *that*. I only stood at the door, and heard what I could. And I am sure Lucy would have done just the same by me; for a year or two back, when Martha Sharpe and I had so many secrets together, Lucy never made any bones of hiding in a closet, or behind a chimney-board, or once even in the hollowed-out corpse of a walrus on purpose to hear what we said."

Elinor tried to talk of something else; but Miss Steele could not be kept beyond a couple of minutes from what was uppermost in her mind.

"What an ill-natured woman his mother is, ain't she? And your brother and sister were not very kind! However, I shan't say anything against them to *you*; and to be sure they did send us home in their own gondola, which was more than I looked for."

Elinor finished now unwinding the bandages, and, as Anne continued to speak she looked long at herself in the mirror—a deep gouge now marked her across the neck, exactly where her flesh had been torn free by the lobster-like claw of the scorpion. She gently drew a finger along the wound.

"Oh! Here come the Richardsons. I had a vast deal more to say to you, but I must not stay away from them not any longer." Elinor gladly assented to Anne's departure. She was left in possession of knowledge which might feed her powers of reflection for some time, though she had learnt very little more than what had been already foreseen and foreplanned in her own mind. Edward's marriage with Lucy was as firmly determined on, and the time of its taking place remained as absolutely uncertain, as she had concluded it would be.

As they made their way home by gondola, Mrs. Jennings was so eager for information, it seemed as though she had forgotten that Elinor's head had nearly been torn from her body by a demonically animated sea scorpion. As Elinor wished to spread as little as possible intelligence that had in the first place been so unfairly obtained, she confined herself to the brief repetition of such simple particulars, as she felt assured that Lucy would choose to have known. The continuance of their engagement, and the means that were able to be taken for promoting its end, was all her communication; and this produced from Mrs. Jennings the following natural remark.

"Wait for his having a good lighthouse! Aye, we all know how *that* will end. They will wait a twelvemonth, and finding no good comes of it, will set down as keeper of some sad mud-pond at fifty pounds a year. Then they will have a child every year! And Lord help 'em! How poor they will be! Dancing for fried-cakes and living beneath overturned canoes! I must see what I can give them towards furnishing their house."

The next morning's post-kayak brought Elinor a letter by the two-penny post from Lucy herself. It was as follows:

> I hope my dear Miss Dashwood will excuse the liberty I take of writing to her; I know your friendship for me will make you pleased to hear such a good account of myself and my dear Edward. Though we have suffered dreadfully, we are both quite well now, and as happy as we must always be in one another's love. We have had great trials, and great persecutions, of the heart and, in my Edward's case, of the feet also, but gratefully acknowledge many friends, yourself not the least among them. I am sure you will be glad to hear, as likewise dear Mrs. Jennings, I spent two happy hours with him yesterday afternoon, he would not hear of our parting, though earnestly did I urge him to it for prudence sake. Our prospects are not very bright, to be sure, but we must wait and hope for the best. Should it ever be in your power to recommend him to anybody that has an open lighthouse in need of keeping, I am very sure you will not forget us. I am almost out of squid ink; begging to be most

gratefully and respectfully remembered to Mrs. Jennings, and to Sir John and Lady Middleton, and the dear children, when you chance to see them, and love to Miss Marianne,

I am, etc., etc.

As soon as Elinor had finished the letter, she performed what she concluded to be its writer's real design, by placing it in the hands of Mrs. Jennings, who read it aloud with many comments of satisfaction and praise.

"Very well indeed! How prettily she writes! Aye, that was quite proper to let him be off if he would. That was just like Lucy. Poor soul! I wish I *could* get him an open lighthouse, with all my heart. She calls me *dear* Mrs. Jennings, you see. She is a good-hearted girl as ever lived. That sentence is very prettily turned. O! Elinor! There is blood dripping from your neck. Here—hold this sponge to the wound—I am sorry I keep forgetting."

CHAPTER 39

THE MISS DASHWOODS HAD NOW BEEN living in Sub-Station Beta for more than two months, and Marianne's impatience to be gone increased every day. She sighed for the air, the liberty, the noxious but comforting sea-wind of Pestilent Isle; and fancied that if any place could give her ease, rickety old Barton Cottage must do it.

Elinor was hardly less anxious for their removal, but she was conscious of the difficulties of so long a journey, which Marianne could not be brought to acknowledge. She began to turn her thoughts towards its accomplishment, and had already mentioned their wishes to their kind hostess, who resisted them with all the eloquence of her good-will, when a plan was suggested, which, though detaining them from home yet a few weeks longer, appeared to Elinor altogether much more eligible than any other. The Palmers were to remove to their houseboat, *The Cleveland* about the end of March, for the Easter holidays; and Mrs. Jennings, with both her friends, received a very warm invitation from Charlotte to go with them.

When Elinor told Marianne what she had done, however, her first reply was not very auspicious.

"*The Cleveland*!" she cried, with great agitation. "No, I cannot be moored upon *The Cleveland*."

"You forget," said Elinor gently, "that it is not in the neighbourhood of . . ."

"But it is moored off Somersetshire. I cannot go into Somersetshire! No, Elinor, you cannot expect me to go there."

Elinor would not argue upon the propriety of overcoming such feelings; she only endeavoured to counteract them by working on others; represented it, therefore, as a measure which would fix the time of her returning to that dear mother, whom she so much wished to see. As they spoke, they noticed various of the household servants rushing by in great haste—Elinor endeavoured to stop one to inquire as to its cause, but was rebuffed; whatever the cause of their hurry, it could not brook surcease, even for a moment's conversation.

Elinor returned to her entreaties. From *The Cleveland*, which was within a few miles of Bristol, the distance to the Devonshire coast was not far; and as there could be no occasion of their staying above a week aboard *The Cleveland*, they might now be at home in little more than three weeks' time. As Marianne's affection for her mother was sincere, it must triumph with little difficulty, over the imaginary evils she had started.

Mrs. Jennings was so far from being weary of her guests that she pressed them very earnestly to return with her again from *The Cleveland*. Elinor was grateful for the attention, but it could not alter her design; everything relative to their return was arranged as far as it could be; and Marianne found some relief in drawing up a statement of the hours that were yet to divide her from their beloved shanty high atop the wind-swept cliffs of Pestilent Isle.

The issue was settled, and now Elinor was allowed luxury to dis-cover the cause of agitation among the servants, who were still rushing hither and thither, and one of whom was donning his Ex-Domic Float-Suit and being outfitted with a pair of shiny gutting knives. By way of answer to Elinor's enquiries, the newly costumed servant merely ges-tured with his knives to the back wall of the Dome-glass, where a half dozen swordfish were tapping steadily, and with military precision, against the glass. As Elinor watched, a seventh joined their school, and then an eighth. Looking closer, Elinor saw the true root of the servants' distress and quick action: A clearly discernible and rapidly spreading network of tiny cracks in the Dome-glass, with its epicenter where the swordfish continued at their unending labour.

Tap, tap, tap . . . tap tap tap . . . taptaptap . . .

She gave the servant an encouraging smile, and watched as he dis-appeared down the small hallway that led to the emergency exit cham-ber. By then, Colonel Brandon had arrived, and Mrs. Jennings had apprised him of the Dashwoods' plan for Ascending the Sub-Station and returning home, via a visit to the Palmers.

"Ah! Colonel Brandon, I do not know what you and I shall do without the Miss Dashwoods," was her plaintive address to him, "for they are quite resolved upon going home from the Palmers—and how for-lorn we shall be, when I come back! Lord! We shall sit and gape at one another as dull as two cats; one old, slightly crazy cat, and one cat with a mass of writhing slimy tentacles in place of whiskers!"

Perhaps Mrs. Jennings was hoping, by this vigorous sketch of their future ennui, to provoke Colonel Brandon to make that offer which might give himself an escape from it—and if so, she had soon afterwards good reason to think her object gained; for, on Elinor's moving to the aquarium glass to watch the knife-bearing servant's efforts to dispatch the ever-multiplying number of swordfish, he followed her to it with a look of particular meaning, and conversed with her there for several minutes. But his subject was not, as Mrs. Jennings hoped, romantic affection; all over the Sub-Station, Colonel Brandon confided to Elinor, outer-ring residents were reporting similar pecking swordfish massing outside the Dome, and all were sending out their own servants to do battle with them.

Preferring not to contemplate the possible outcome of such an un-welcome event, they conversed on other topics for several minutes. And though Mrs. Jennings was too honourable to listen, and had even changed her seat, on purpose that she might *not* hear, to one close by the pianoforte on which Marianne was playing a tender, melancholy, high-octave arrange-ment of "Yo, Ho, Ho, and a Bottle of Rum," she could not keep herself from seeing that Elinor changed colour, attended with agitation, and was too intent on what he said. Still further in confirmation of her hopes, in the interval of Marianne's turning from "Rum" to "A Pirate's Life for Me," some words of the colonel's inevitably reached her ear, in which he seemed to be apologizing for the badness of his house. This set the matter beyond a doubt. She wondered, indeed, at his thinking it necessary to do so; but supposed it to be the proper etiquette. What Elinor said in reply she could not distinguish, but judged from the motion of her lips, that she did not think *that* any material objection—and Mrs. Jennings commended her in her heart for being so honest. They then talked on for a few minutes longer without her catching a syllable, when another lucky stop in Marianne's performance brought her these words in the colonel's calm voice: "I am afraid it cannot take place very soon."

Astonished and shocked at such a speech, Mrs. Jennings was almost ready to cry out, "Lord! what should hinder it?" So engrossed was she with these snippets of conversation, she did not notice that the servant outside the glass had been run through on the rapier-like horn of a swordfish; two of his fellows grasped him beneath each of his armpits and hauled him hastily upwards; the other fish, thankfully, did not offer chase; they continued instead with their steady, determined rapping upon the Dome.

On Elinor and Colonel Brandon breaking up their conference soon afterwards, and moving different ways, Mrs. Jennings very plainly heard her say, with a voice showing strong feeling, "I shall always think myself very much obliged to you."

Mrs. Jennings was delighted with her gratitude, and only wondered that after hearing such a sentence, the colonel should be able to take leave of them, as he immediately did, with the utmost sang-froid, tentacles tipping politely by way of farewell, without making her any reply! She had not thought her old friend could have made so indifferent a suitor.

What had really passed between them was to this effect:

"I have heard," said he, with great compassion, "of the injustice your friend Mr. Ferrars has suffered from his family. If I understand the matter right, he has been entirely cast off by them for persevering in his engagement with a very deserving young woman. Have I been rightly informed? Is it so?"

Elinor told him that it was.

"The cruelty, the impolitic cruelty," he replied, with great feeling, "of dividing, or attempting to divide, two young people long attached to each other, is terrible. I have seen Mr. Ferrars two or three times in Harley Piscinca, and am much pleased with him. I understand that he intends a career as a lighthouse keeper. Will you be so good as to tell him that the lighthouse at Delaford is his; as I am informed by this day's post that it is now vacant, the old keeper having been dragged off by the Pirate Dreadbeard for some trivial slight; anyway, the post is his, if he think it worth his acceptance. I only wish it were more valuable. It is a lake, merely, and a small one, with only one or two tiny monsters within it, and a couple of villages surrounding that live in mild terror of same; the late incumbent, I believe, did not make more than two hundred pounds per annum, and though it is certainly capable of improvement, I fear, not to such an amount as to afford him a very comfortable income. The lighthouse itself can hardly be deserving of the name; it is really just a tumbledown cottage, with a couple of torches kept burning in the tallest branches of a nearby sycamore tree. Such as it is, however, my pleasure in presenting it will be very great. Pray assure him of it."

Elinor's astonishment at this commission could hardly have been greater, had the colonel been really making her an offer of his hand. The preferment, which only two days before she had considered as hopeless, would enable him to marry—and *she*, of all people in the world, was fixed on to bestow it! Her emotion was such as Mrs. Jennings had attributed to a very different cause; but whatever minor feelings less pure, less pleasing, might have a share in that emotion, her esteem for the general benevolence, and her gratitude for the particular friendship, which together prompted Colonel Brandon to this act, were strongly felt, and warmly expressed. She thanked him for it with all her heart, spoke of Edward's principles and disposition with that praise which she knew them to deserve; and promised to undertake the commission with pleasure. She could undertake therefore to inform him of it, in the course of the day. After this had been settled, Colonel Brandon began to talk of his own advantage in securing so respectable and agreeable a neighbour, and *that* it was that he mentioned with regret, that the house was small and indifferent.

"I cannot imagine any inconvenience to them," said Elinor, "for it will be in proportion to their family and income."

By which the colonel was surprised to find that *she* was considering Mr. Ferrars's marriage as the certain consequence of the presentation; for he did not suppose it possible that the lighthouse at Delaford could supply such an income, as anybody in his style of life would venture to settle on—and he said so.

"A simple lake-side lighthouse can do no more than make Mr. Ferrars comfortable as a bachelor; it cannot enable him to marry. I am sorry to say that my patronage ends with this; and my interest is hardly more extensive. If, however, by an unforeseen chance it should be in my power to serve him further, I am ready to be useful to him. What I am now doing indeed, seems nothing at all, since it can advance him so little towards what must be his principal object of happiness. His marriage must still be a distant good—at least, I am afraid it cannot take place very soon."

Such was the sentence which, when misunderstood, so justly offended the delicate feelings of Mrs. Jennings.

As they all departed the room, the swordfish continued to mass; now a dozen, now two dozen, now three dozen beady-eyed beasts, some as small as cats, some big as horses, all with their cruel sharp bills clattering away against the glass. All over the Dome it was the same, and by nightfall there were a thousand pairs of deadly golden fish-eyes glowing eerily in the darkness, just outside the protective glass shell of the Sub-Station. An army of malevolent fish, mostly tapping, but some simply staring—staring, staring coldly in from without.

CHAPTER 40

"WELL, MISS DASHWOOD," said Mrs. Jennings, sagaciously smiling, at the next morning's breakfast of gelatinated oatmeal loaf and fatback powder, "I do not ask what the colonel has been saying to you; upon my honour, I *tried* to keep out of hearing. But his set of distended maxillae were leaping and fluttering most anxiously under his nose, and though his gurgly breathing was if anything more pronounced than usual, I could not help catching enough to understand his business. I assure you I never was better pleased in my life, and I wish you joy with all my heart."

"Thank you, ma'am," said Elinor. "It is a matter of great joy to me; and I feel the goodness of Colonel Brandon most sensibly. There are not many men who would act as he has done. Few people who have so compassionate a heart! I never was more astonished in my life that this opportunity should occur."

"Opportunity!" repeated Mrs. Jennings. "When a man has once made up his mind to such a thing, somehow or other he will soon find an opportunity. Well, my dear, I wish you joy of it again and again; and if ever there was a happy couple in the world, I think I shall soon know where to look for them."

"You mean to go to Delaford after them I suppose," said Elinor, with a faint smile.

"Aye, my dear, that I do, indeed! And as to the house being a bad one, I do not know what the colonel would be at, for it is as good a one as ever I saw."

"He spoke of its being out of repair."

"Well, and whose fault is that? Why don't he repair it? Who should do it but himself?"

As Elinor puzzled over Mrs. Jennings remarks, they were interrupted by a great, shuddering crash as the whole docking station absorbed an enormous blow. Their conversation ceased, and from her place at the pianoforte Marianne looked up, startled and wide-eyed.

As one, they turned their eyes to the glass, and comprehended what looked for all the world like a swordfish grown to gargantuan proportions. A moment's inspection revealed that this was not a swordfish at all, but a narwhal—a whale of some 3,500 pounds, with tiny eyes gleaming from its giant head, and a long, wicked and twisted horn upon its brow; a sea-beast, in other words, bearing the same relation to the swordfish as a snarling lion does to a Cheshire cat. And indeed, a small school of swordfish darted about the tail and torso of the narwhal in delighted little circles, as if proclaiming it their champion.

"Dear God," cried Elinor. "They've brought reinforcements."

The narwhal now commenced ramming the blunted tip of its six-foot spiraled horn against the glass, again and again, not with the persistent *tick-tock* tapping of the swordfish, but with a giant, reverberating smash;

and then a long pause as it drew back, and then a second smash.

"I think it is time to summon Sir John, and see what he may think of this," said Mrs. Jennings.

Before the older woman rushed off in pursuit of that errand, Elinor reminded her not to mention the subject of their prior conversation to anyone. "Oh, very well," said Mrs. Jennings, rather disappointed; and then, as she double- and then triple-checked that her Float-Suit was properly assembled and attached, "Then you would not have me tell it to Lucy?"

"No, ma'am, not even Lucy if you please. One day's delay will not be very material; and till I have written to Mr. Ferrars, I think it ought not to be mentioned to anybody else. I shall do *that* directly. It is of importance that no time should be lost with him, for he will, of course, have much to do relative to his new position."

This speech puzzled Mrs. Jennings exceedingly. She could not comprehend why Elinor might need to write to Mr. Ferrars in such a hurry. She was preparing to enquire further of its meaning when the loudest crash yet rattled the whole of the Dome, like it was a snow globe in the hands of a careless child. The narwhal had now turned its body lengthwise and was bringing its whole huge flank lolloping into the wall of the Station, again and again, faster and faster. From the pianoforte, her fingers frozen above the keys, Marianne swore the swordfish were cheering.

"Good-bye, my dear," said Mrs. Jennings hurriedly to Elinor. "I have not heard of any news to please me so well since Charlotte was brought to bed. I only hope our joy in it is not undone by . . . by—" Again, a great and terrifying smash against the glass; again, the whole of the Dome trembled in its moorings. "By whatever is happening."

Elinor sat considering how to begin—how she should express herself in her note to Edward? How could she summon the delicacy to compose such a missive, when her very home, her very world was under assault from a marine army, under the command of a gigantesque narwhal? She sat deliberating over her paper, with the pen in her hand, till interrupted by the entrance of Edward himself. Her astonishment and confusion were very great on his so sudden appearance. She had not seen him before since his engagement became public, and therefore, not since his knowing her to be acquainted with it. The consciousness of what she now had to tell him made her feel particularly uncomfortable. He too was much distressed; but now he had much more immediate concerns. He glanced swiftly at the Domeglass and said gravely, "Ah. They are here. So they are *here*, as well!"

"And why do you suppose they are so determined to lay this siege against Mrs. Jennings's docking?' inquired Elinor innocently, glad to have a subject of conversation other than his engagement, and the new information regarding the lighthouse at Delaford that she was bound to impart.

"Do you think they are only here?" said Edward. "This strange phenomenon has made itself known in every quarter of the Station. At Berkeley's, a great dugong slams its broad forehead upon the Dome; at Rumpole Piscina, it is a school of bass, a thousand strong, that form a mighty armada and slam against the glass in a thick barrage, time and time again. The engineers say we have nothing to worry about, that every panel is tested and re-tested a thousand times over before installation, and that the Dome is secure."

"And so we have nothing to fear," said Elinor, preparing to turn to the subject of which she needed to unburden herself.

"Indeed," replied Edward. "And yet . . ."

Outside the glass, a servant swam within a dozen yards of the narwhal, and leveled a Furci-Landy gun—a high-powered air-rifle designed to shoot a shell through the foreboding density of water at 4,000 leagues beneath—at the broad flank of the beast. He fired, missed, and turned to reload.

"Mrs. Jennings told me," said Edward, in this brief pause in the action, "that you wished to speak with me. I certainly should not have intruded on you in such a manner; though at the same time, I should have been extremely sorry to Ascend from the Station without seeing you and your sister; especially as it will most likely be some time—it is not probable that I should soon have the pleasure of meeting you again."

"You would not have gone, however," said Elinor, recovering herself, and determined to get over what she so much dreaded as soon as possible, "without receiving our good wishes, even if we had not been able to give them in person." Again the servant fired his Furci-Landy gun, and this time found his mark; the narwhal, however, reacted no more to the pellet than would a vast iron-hulled warship to a bit of gravel tossed against its broadside.

Elinor shook her head slightly and continued. "Mrs. Jennings was quite right in what she said. I have something of consequence to inform you of, which I was on the point of communicating by paper. Colonel Brandon, who was here only ten minutes ago, has desired me to say, that he has great pleasure in offering you the lighthouse at Delaford, now just vacant, and only wishes it were more valuable. Allow me to congratulate you on having so respectable and well-judging a friend."

"Colonel Brandon!"

"Yes," continued Elinor, gathering more resolution, as some of the worst was over, "Colonel Brandon means it as a testimony of his concern for what has lately passed—for the cruel situation in which the unjustifiable conduct of your family has placed you—a concern which I am sure Marianne, myself, and all your friends, must share; and likewise as a proof of his high esteem for your general character, and his particular approbation of your behaviour on the present occasion."

Another walloping crash came against the Dome; the servant fired his gun a third time, wildly, and again the shell glanced harmlessly off the vast flank of the narwhal.

"Colonel Brandon give *me* a living! Can it be possible?"

Elinor smiled in spite of herself. "It seems the unkindness of your own relations has made you astonished to find friendship anywhere."

"No," replied be, with sudden consciousness, "not to find it in *you*; for I cannot be ignorant that to you, to your goodness, I owe it all."

"You are very much mistaken. I do assure you that you owe it entirely, at least almost entirely, to your own merit, and Colonel Brandon's discernment of it. I have had no hand in it. I did not even know, till I understood his design, that the old lighthouse keeper had been dragged off by Pirate Dreadbeard, nor had it ever occurred to me that he might have had such a living in his gift."

For a short time Edward sat deep in thought, after Elinor had ceased to speak. At last, and as if it were rather an effort, he said, "Colonel Brandon seems a man of great worth and respectability. I have always heard him spoken of as such, and your brother I know esteems him highly. He is undoubtedly a sensible man, and in his manners perfectly the gentleman."

Further expression of gratitude was impossible, as their attention was drawn anew by the continued pitched battle outside the glass. After carelessly absorbing two or three more bits of buckshot from the Furci-Landy gun, the narwhal swiveled his massive head and eyed the servant up and down, as if deciding whether he was worth its trouble. Evidently it decided in the affirmative, as it then thrust forward its gigantic head and speared the man, waving his arms helplessly, like a shish kebab, upon its horn.

This easy victory served to inspire the narwhal and its cohort of swordfish attendants to ever more vigorous efforts; they all turned their attention back to the Dome-glass and resumed banging and tapping and pounding upon it at a furious pace. What had begun as a light spider web of cracks had now blossomed into a network of ominous furrows, growing deeper and longer by the instant. Edward rose rapidly and made for the door.

Elinor did not offer to detain him; and they parted, with a rapid assurance on *her* side of her unceasing good wishes for his happiness in every change of situation that might befall him; on *his* with rather an attempt to return the same good will, than the power of expressing it; and on *both* their parts that the world in which they were safely cosseted against the ravaging sea would prove as durable as the engineers claimed it to be.

"When I see him again," said Elinor to herself, as the door shut him out, "I shall see him the husband of Lucy." She paused in her reflections, and then added, with glance to the Dome-glass, "*If* I see him again."

Mrs. Jennings ran back into the docking, panting heavily, her boots dripping wet from having disembarked too hurriedly from her gondola.

"Hurry, Elinor! You must hurry! Marianne!"

"What? Mrs. Jennings you are in a panic! What can be—"

Mrs. Jennings grabbed Elinor by the collar, a gesture which sent a jolt of pain from the scar on her neck. "Pay attention, dear girl! I know you are in a state of pleasurable distraction, owing to your recent engagement to Colonel Brandon—"

"Engagement? Why no—what can you be thinking of?— Why, Colonel Brandon's only object is to be of use to Mr. Ferrars."

"Lord bless you, my dear!" she replied in confusion, somewhat lessening her grip. "Sure you do not mean to persuade me that the colonel only marries you for the sake of giving ten guineas to Mr. Ferrars!"

The deception could not continue after this, especially in these circumstances, as the glass was increasingly splintered, with fresh fissures appearing every moment, each one serving to further encourage the narwhal and her underlings. An explanation rapidly took place: Colonel Brandon wanted not to marry Elinor, but to offer Edward a living as lighthouse keeper of Delaford.

"But none of that matters now!" sputtered Mrs. Jennings. "For God's sake, can't you see that? We have to go! We cannot tarry another moment! The Dome—the whole of the Dome is going to collapse!"

"But the engineers—" cried Marianne, rushing from upstairs, a look of concern etched on her pale brows.

"Forget the engineers! We must get to the Ascension Station—now!"

CHAPTER 41

OUTSIDE, MRS. JENNINGS and the Dashwood sisters encountered a world transformed.

As their terrified retinue of remaining servants paddled Mrs. Jennings's elegant gondola furiously towards the Ascension Station, Marianne and Elinor clutched the handles of their luggage, staring upwards at the curved ceiling of the Sub-Station Dome; it was clear now that what had appeared to be a couple of rogue swordfish, perhaps a handful, engaged in a quixotic effort to crack the glass where it abutted Mrs. Jennings's docking, was in fact the smallest expression of an assault of unimaginable proportions. A thick blanket of fish coated every inch of the Station's exterior, ramming again and again, in ragged rows, against the ceiling of the world. The Dome was cracked in a million places; it trembled under the weight of the fish ceaselessly battering themselves against it.

Men and women looked at each other with chilled expressions—or stared numbly ahead as they streamed through the canals in a mad dash for the Ascension Station. The waterways were crowded with people on rafts and gondolas and tugs and kayaks and skiffs; with people riding sea horses, sea cows, tortoises, sea lions; all imaginable means of conveyance had been pressed into use; one servant swam a desperate Australian crawl with a woman and two frightened infants strapped upon his back.

No longer were servants seen swimming outside the glass, trying with gutting knives or air-rifles to do battle against the swordfish, narwhals, humpbacks, silverfish, skates, dugongs, bass, and the other legions of fish that were massed against them—the enemy by now was too numerous. To reach the Ascension Station, and escape to safety before . . . the *unspeakable* occurred, was the goal of every mind.

Except for the one lone swimmer—either mad or courageous or both—who was suddenly seen paddling determinedly outside the glass.

"By God!" cried Marianne. "It's Sir John!"

And nor was that intrepid luminary wearing a Ex-Domic Float-Suit, Sir John was stripped stark naked, but for a diving helmet and air-pack; in his right hand he clutched a glinting, foot-long silver cutlass, as with his left hand he propelled himself mightily forward, like a giant single-flippered fish, his bald head cutting through the water like a bullet, his beard tucked inside the helmet. He swam unerringly towards a gigantic green-grey walrus, which by its size and regal purple-orange crest seemed to be as the leader of the fish army.

As the thousands of terrified residents of Sub-Station Beta watched wide-eyed, Sir John raised the cutlass with a wild expression and descended furiously upon the bull walrus. Sir John cut a deep, angry gash in the thick flank of the bull, which reared back angrily and turned its tusks upon the old adventurer. They exchanged blows—One! Two! Three!—as inside the cracked Dome the citizens of the Station ooh'ed and ahh'ed, and outside it the fish legions stared at their leader with glassy eyes.

Thrust! Thrust! Parry! Sir John danced backwards in the water from the thrusting tusks of the beast. And then, with a surge of maniacal energy, he plunged his cutlass deep into the front lobe of the walrus's skull. Thick black blood gushed from the hole, like ocean-spray spurting from the devil's own blowhole.

The remaining fish seemed to hesitate—unwilling, perhaps, to resume their assault upon the Sub-Station if their champion was dead. Elinor allowed herself a sigh of relief. "Can it be?" she murmured to Marianne. "Are we saved?" Unconsciously, her eyes swept the crowds for some sign of Edward; to see confidence in his eyes would be her surest, her most encouraging sign.

But then, with one last furious, dying burst of energy, the bull walrus launched his shaggy head and protruding tusks back again towards Sir

John. The beast missed him by the slimmest of margins, and his huge, thick head instead crashed into the Dome—causing a horrible, impossibly loud crack that echoed through the Sub-Station.

Then there was silence. In that queer long stretch of silence—which could not, in truth, have lasted more than a split second—the many thousands of people crowded in the central canals of Sub-Marine Station Beta, staring wide-eyed up at their now-crumbling protective shell, understood what was about to occur; and could at last, and too late, fully comprehend what it meant that they had made their home four miles below the surface of the ocean.

And then the silence ended, and glass tumbled in great jagged chunks from the roof of the Dome, and the water rushed in.

Once it began, the Dome gave way quickly, with sheets of glass heaving end over end to the ground, followed by waves of water rushing in from all directions; by walls of water pouring in from above; by great torrents of water crashing down like the wrath of God.

"Activate!" cried Elinor to Marianne, who looked about helplessly as the water buffeted them angrily about and bore them upwards. "Activate your Float-Suit!" With the same desperate motion, the girls tugged on the cords tucked up within their sleeves, and felt their twin armbands inflate and the nasal reeds begin to pump oxygen; and not a moment too soon, for in a matter of seconds the great glass Dome was in ruins, and they were underwater. The girls kicked their legs furiously and propelled themselves upwards as swiftly as they could, as all around them the world was subsumed.

* * *

"Ten . . . ten minutes to departure . . ."

The voice was that of a servant, walking the long echoing corridors of the Ascension Station, where Marianne, Elinor, and Mrs. Jennings sat, huddled in towels, awaiting the departure of Emergency Ferry No. 12.

THE DOME GAVE WAY QUICKLY, WITH SHEETS OF GLASS TUMBLING AND SLICING
TO THE GROUND, FOLLOWED BY WAVES OF WATER RUSHING IN
FROM ALL DIRECTIONS.

Sub-Station Beta had been reclaimed by the ocean. All that remained was the Ascension Station, the gigantic plain white waiting room, at the base of the long stovepipe that had once jutted proudly from the lip of the Dome; and soon the Ascension Station, too, would be abandoned, once all surviving residents were boarded onto emergency ferries and evacuated to safety. All around Elinor, hundreds of people sat in miserable small crowds, shivering and waterlogged, wondering whether friends and loved ones had survived, largely presuming they had not. Many had been drowned as the great waves crashed in, many had been eaten by the fish who swarmed giddily in, and many had been drowned and *then* eaten, or vice versa.

Elinor stared out the glass window of the Ascension Station and watched as the crew of gigantic monster lobsters, whom she had seen wreak such havoc that night at Hydra-Z, swam happily by; they were joined in their flotilla by a flight of swordfish, and Elinor swore she saw among the group the one with a gleaming patch of silver iridescence under its horn—the very fish that had led the tapping pack on Mrs. Jennings's docking station.

This unsettling reverie was interrupted by the sudden appearance of Lucy Steele, who, alone among the miserable survivors awaiting emergency Ascension, seemed perfectly content—the destruction of the Station, after all, did not affect her newly decided prospects. Her own happiness, and her own spirits, were at least very certain; and she joined Mrs. Jennings most heartily in her expectation of their being all comfortably together in Delaford before long. She openly declared that no exertion for their good on Miss Dashwood's part, either present or future, would ever surprise her, for she believed her capable of doing anything in the world for those she really valued.

"Yes, yes," replied Elinor; this was the last topic of conversation she felt interested in discussing at such a moment.

"Nine . . . nine minutes to departure . . ."

As for Colonel Brandon, Lucy was not only ready to worship him as a saint, but was moreover truly anxious that he should be treated as one in all worldly concerns; anxious that his tithes should be raised to the utmost; and scarcely resolved to avail herself, at Delaford, as far as she possibly could, of his servants, his carriage, his cows, and his poultry.

"Yes, yes," said Mrs. Jennings, "Understood."

Lucy, finding the others less enthusiastic about pondering her happy future than she was, left to find her sister, who she had last seen desperately struggling to engage her Float-Suit. Elinor's gladness at her departure lasted until the arrival of John Dashwood, whose recent experiences in the service of the Sub-Station laboratories had served him in good stead in the catastrophe, particular the prodigious swimming ability lent to him by his webbed toes and begilled lungs.

"Eight . . . eight minutes . . ."

"I am not sorry to see you alone," he said to Elinor, "for I have a good deal to say to you."

"Do not fear, brother—I have survived the wreck of the Sub-Station, as has Marianne. Margaret and our mother, as you know, are safe at home on Pestilent Island and so were spared this ungodly calamity." Even as she said the words, Elinor recalled the distressing news of Margaret she had had in her mother's last missive, and she silently fingered the torn patch of thin paper, with its grim Biblical quotation, still tucked inside her bodice and miraculously (or was it ominously?) preserved in the flood.

"Oh, yes, yes, that," said Mr. Dashwood dismissively. As always, financial matters, for him, trumped all considerations, even the destruction of the foremost British city by an army of all-destroying fish. "This lighthouse provided by Colonel Brandon's—can it be true? Has he really given it to Edward? I was coming to you on purpose to enquire further about it when all of this began."

"It is perfectly true. Colonel Brandon has given the lighthouse at Delaford to Edward."

"Really! Well, this is very astonishing! No relationship! No connection between them! And now that lighthouse posts fetch such a price! What was the value of this?"

"About two hundred a year."

"It is truly astonishing!" he cried, after hearing what she said. "What could be the colonel's motive?"

"A very simple one—to be of use to Mr. Ferrars."

"Well, well; whatever Colonel Brandon may be, Edward is a very lucky man. You will not mention the matter to Fanny, however, for though I have broke it to her, and she bears it vastly well, she will not like to hear it much talked of. If she survived all this, of course," he added, a shadow of distress passing over his face. "You haven't seen her, have you? No? Ah, well."

"Seven. . . . Gather your belongings, if any you may still possess."

"Mrs. Ferrars," added Mr. Dashwood, lowering his voice so as not to be heard by the white-coated ferry servant counting down the minutes to the emergency ferry's Ascension, "knows nothing about it at present, and I believe it will be best to keep it entirely concealed from her as long as may be. When the marriage takes place, I fear she must hear of it all.

"My God!" Elinor replied. "Can such an elderly personage have survived this calamity?"

"Indeed," he answered. "I saw her with my own eyes; her Float-Suit engaged and she kicked with a strength quite startling in someone of her advanced age." Elinor reflected that someone who took such evident displeasure in all aspects of life should fight so stubbornly against death.

"It is doubtless, Elinor," John continued, "that when Edward's unhappy match takes place, depend upon it, his mother will feel as much as if she had never discarded him; and, therefore, every circumstance that may accelerate that dreadful event, must be concealed from her as much as possible. Mrs. Ferrars can never forget that Edward is her son."

"You surprise me. I should think it must nearly have escaped her memory by *this* time."

"Six . . ."

"You wrong her exceedingly. Mrs. Ferrars is one of the most affectionate mothers in the world."

Elinor was silent.

"We think *now*," said Mr. Dashwood, after a short pause, "of *Robert's* marrying Miss Morton. If, that is, Robert has survived, and Miss Morton has survived." For a moment, John and Elinor hung their heads in silence, as the overwhelming nature of this great tragedy struck them like a blow. So much death—so much destruction.

Elinor at last summoned the fortitude to calmly reply, "The lady, I suppose, has no choice in the affair."

"Choice!—how do you mean?"

"Five minutes," called the servant, "All aboard . . . all aboard for emergency Ascension . . ."

They continued their conversation as they climbed aboard the Emergency Ferry, a one-hundred-foot iron-hulled submarine with a vast interior cabin, wide as a cow-pasture, lined with uncomfortable, utilitarian wooden benches.

"I only mean that I suppose," Eleanor continued as they squeezed into spots, "from your manner of speaking, it must be the same to Miss Morton whether she marry Edward or Robert."

"Certainly, there can be no difference; for Robert will now to all intents and purposes be considered as the eldest son; and as to anything else, they are both very agreeable young men: I do not know that one is superior to the other."

Elinor said no more, and John was also for a short time silent; they felt the powerful engines of the submarine engage, and Elinor breathed an interior sigh of relief that the vessel hadn't been sabotaged by sea monsters, or simply waterlogged in the catastrophe.

"Of *one* thing, my dear sister," John said, kindly taking her hand, and speaking in an awful whisper, "I have good reason to think—indeed I have it from the best authority, or I should not repeat it, for otherwise it would be very wrong to say anything about it—"

"Four minutes!"

"You best summon the ability to reveal it, dear brother."

"I have it from the very best authority—not that I ever precisely heard Mrs. Ferrars say it herself—but her daughter *did*, and I have it from her—that in short, whatever objections there might be against a certain—a certain connection—you understand me—it would have been far preferable to her, it would not have given her half the vexation that *this* does. But however, all that is quite out of the question—not to be thought of or mentioned—as to any attachment you know—it never could be—all that is gone by. But I thought I would just tell you of this, because I knew how much it must please you. Not that you have any reason to regret, my dear Elinor. There is no doubt of your doing exceedingly well. Has Colonel Brandon been with you lately?"

Elinor had heard enough to agitate her nerves and fill her mind, and she was glad to be distracted by the powerful sensation of the submarine's thruster-propellers whirring to life beneath the vast hull. She was spared from the necessity of saying much in reply herself, and from the danger of hearing anything more from her brother, by the entrance of Mr. Robert Ferrars, panting and out of breath, lugging an oversized wooden trunk on his back like a mule.

"I made it!" he cheered gaily. "By God I made it, and barely nicked the good china along the way!"

"Three . . ." came the voice of the servant, and it was instantly echoed by the voice of the captain, hollering along the long cabin of the submarine. "Three minutes to Ascension."

"Three! My God!" hollered John Dashwood, and hastened away to make a last-minute search for Fanny and their child. Elinor was left to improve her acquaintance with Robert, who, by the happy self-complacency of his manner on this most desperate of occasions, was confirming her most unfavourable opinion of his head and heart.

As he buckled himself in to an adjoining ferry bench, Robert promptly began to speak of Edward; for he, too, had heard of the posting at the Delaford lighthouse, and was very inquisitive on the subject. Elinor repeated the particulars of it, as she had given them to John; and their affect on Robert, though very different, was not less striking than it had been on *him*. He laughed most immoderately. The idea of Edward's being a mere lighthouse keeper, and tracking the movements of some second-rate Loch Ness Monster, diverted him beyond measure; he could conceive nothing more ridiculous.

"Two minutes!"

Elinor, even as she gritted her teeth and prepared for the lurching motion of the great submarine's departure, could not restrain her eyes from being fixed on Robert with a look that spoke all the contempt it excited.

"We may treat it as a joke," said he, at last, recovering from the affected laugh which had considerably lengthened out the genuine gaiety of the moment—"but, upon my soul, it is a most serious business. Poor Edward! He is ruined forever. I am extremely sorry for it—for I know him to be a very good-hearted creature. You must not judge of him, Miss Dashwood, from *your* slight acquaintance. Poor Edward! His manners are certainly not the happiest in nature. But we are not all born, you know, with the same powers. Poor fellow!—to see him in a circle of strangers!—among *lake* people! But upon my soul, I believe he has as good a heart as any in the kingdom; and I declare and protest to you I never was so shocked in my life, as when it all burst forth. My mother was the first person who told me of it; and I, feeling myself called on to act with resolution, immediately said to her, 'My dear madam, I do not know what you may intend to do on the occasion, but as for myself, I must say, that if Edward does marry this young woman, I never will see him again.' Poor Edward! He has done for himself completely, shut himself out for ever from all decent society! But, as I directly said to my mother, I am not in the least surprised at it; from his style of education, it was always to be expected. My poor mother was half frantic."

Unmoved by this appeal to empathy for Mrs. Ferrars, and indeed weary of the whole line of conversation, Elinor happened to look outside the window of the Ferry, where a universe of fish now swam and darted happily through the ruins of the elaborate civilization that had been built on their turf. She happened to spy, as she looked disconsolately

at the wreck of the Sub-Station, a small, cigar-shaped one-person sub-
marine of an old-fashioned design, whooshing rapidly by in a spray of
bubbles. Behind the wheel was Lady Middleton, who—for the first time
since she had made that worthy's acquaintance—was smiling; indeed,
grinning from ear to ear, and, or so Elinor thought, whooping loudly
with pleasure.

Recovering herself from this remarkable sight, Elinor rejoined her
conversation with Robert Ferrars. "Have you ever seen Edward's intended?"
she asked.

"Yes; once, while she was staying in our house, I happened to drop
in for ten minutes; and I saw quite enough of her. The merest awkward
country girl, without style, or elegance, and almost without beauty. Just the
kind of girl I should suppose likely to captivate poor Edward. I offered immediately, as soon as my mother related the affair to me, to talk to him
myself, and dissuade him from the match; but it was too late *then*, I found,
to do anything. But had I been informed of it a few hours earlier—I think
it is most probable—that something might have been hit on. I certainly
should have represented it to Edward in a very strong light. 'My dear fellow, you are making a most disgraceful connection, and such a one as
your family are unanimous in disapproving.' But now it is all too late. He
must be starved, you know—that is certain; absolutely starved. He would
have been better off, *if* he lived through what has just occurred, to have
drowned instead."

Elinor thought she could bear no more of this, when the grave voice
of the public address reached its conclusion.

"ONE . . . be braced . . ."

And the turbines revved up to their full capacity, and the propellers
whirred faster, and the seat rumbled beneath her as the Ascension Station
discharged the emergency ferry, with all its passengers aboard; Elinor
looked around, and saw that, two benches over, Marianne was looking
out the window of the ferry with the same sentimental regard she looked
upon all places, at all times, on leaving them—no matter what level of

affection she may have bore during her time there. On this occasion, however, Elinor shared in her moist-eyed regard.

Sub-Marine Station Beta was no more.

CHAPTER 42

THERE WAS NO SENSE in further discussion; continuance on Sub-Station Beta having been rendered a tragic impossibility, every circumstance now dictated that the Dashwood sisters, in company with Mrs. Jennings, proceed to *The Cleveland*, from where they would proceed after a suitable interval back to Pestilent Isle and the comforts of Barton Cottage. The two parties who would be travelling hence, disembarked from Emergency Ferry No. 12 and met on a small atoll, three nautical miles from the former location of Sub-Marine Station Beta. For the convenience of Charlotte and her child, they were to be more than two days on their journey. Colonel Brandon, travelling separately, was to join them aboard *The Cleveland* soon after their arrival.

They would travel to *The Cleveland* aboard the *Rusted Nail*, the hearty old two-masted pirate schooner which Mr. Palmer captained in his buccaneering youth; their escort was an assortment of Palmer's former crewmen, with whom he had fortuitously been assembled on an island redoubt for a reunion holiday at the time of the Sub-Station's collapse. These gentlemen of fortune were the usual assortment of colourful characters, each with their own affable eccentricities; there was, besides Mr. Palmer, by now well known to the Dashwoods, McBurdry, the genial and foul-smelling ship's cook; One-Eyed Peter, who had two working eyes, and Two-Eyed Scotty, who had one; Billy Rafferty, the cabin boy; and the first mate, Mr. Benbow, a massively tall half-blood Irishman with feathers sewn into his beard; Benbow was as famous a curmudgeon as any man on the seas, and he looked so dourly upon the prospect of passengers that, whenever he encountered Mrs. Palmer, her child, or either Dashwood, he made the sign of the cross and spat thickly on the foredeck.

As eager as Marianne had been to quit the Station, she could not bid adieu to the now-extinct undersea paradise in which she had for the last time enjoyed her confidence in Willoughby. Elinor's only consolation was her expectation that the company of the *Nail's* crew would provide the pirate-enthusiast Marianne with a pleasurable distraction from her thorough-going melancholy.

For her part, Elinor's satisfaction, as the *Rusted Nail* navigated southeasterly from the Station to the swampy Somersetshire inlet where *The Cleveland* was moored, was entirely positive. The waters were piloted smoothly by Mr. Benbow; the sea air was fresh and clean; and the only threat of attack was swiftly dispelled. This peril was from a school of monster-fish unlike anything Elinor had ever seen: a pack of floating eyeballs, each as big as a man's head, all trailing long tentacles behind them like hideous jellyfish, and blinking terribly as they floated for several nautical miles behind the *Nail*. But a single perfectly aimed shot from Two-Eyed Scotty's blunderbuss neatly pierced one of these ocular horrors, exploding it in the water and scattering the rest.

Each day at twilight, the crewmen drank their daily allotted jigger of bumboo, roasted a pig, and scared each other with terrifying tales of Dreadbeard. At the uttering of his name, all men present, blasphemous and God-denying mercenaries to a one, crossed themselves and looked skyward; Dreadbeard, captain of the *Jolly Murderess*, was the most infamous of pirates. While most gentlemen of fortune became so for a love of plunder; and some for a love of the seas and for killing the monsters that dwelt therein; Dreadbeard's motivations (they whispered) were all for blood and the love of killing. His own piratical crewmen, pressed into service from among the crews of plundered frigates, trembled in fear of him, as they were keelhauled or dropped to dance the hempen jig at the slightest insubordination—or, Dreadbeard's favourite, thrown naked and screaming to the sharks, whom Dreadbeard purposefully kept trailing his ship by tossing bloody bits of flank steak off the stern at odd intervals. He was a madman; a murderer; and, it was whispered with particular meaning to Elinor and Marianne, he saw no distinction between fellow pirates and honest lubbers, men and women, boys and girls.

"If a creature has a coin, I'll snatch it," went the cold-eyed captain's nefarious motto, which the crew of the *Rusted Nail* could recite in whispered unison. "If a creature walks a deck, I'll kill it and eat its heart like salmagundi."

Marianne listened to these tales with wide eyes, drinking in the stories of press-ganged swabs and men murdered in their bunks with a flushed cheek, barely disguising a frank delight that such a creature as Dreadbeard could live; Elinor, for her part, retained sense enough to be feared of such stories, but to remain skeptical of the sordid details. Mr. Palmer, Elinor noted with some curious interest, never spoke on the matter, lapsing into his customary black silence as his crewmen whispered their lurid tales of Dreadbeard, passing them around with their cups of bumboo, each night as the yellow sea-sun disappeared beneath the horizon line.

The second day brought them into the coast of Somerset, and in the forenoon of the third they arrived at the Palmers' four-and-forty foot houseboat, *The Cleveland*. As they climbed aboard, the Dashwoods and their companions bade a hearty good-bye to the crew of the *Rusted Nail*; Mr. Benbow and his company hoisted anchor and set sail, top guns loaded and Jolly Roger fluttering, on hard lookout for Dreadbeard.

The Cleveland consisted (rather marvelously) of a spacious, well-built two-story cottage, in the country style, with French windows and a charming verandah—all serving as the cabin atop a wide-decked rivership; the ship was piloted, when it left its moorings, by a giant captain's wheel which sat just beyond the front, or bow-ward, door of the cottage; through a trap at the stern connected to the holds, below. Marianne climbed aboard the houseboat with a heart swelling with emotion from the consciousness of being only eighty miles from Pestilent Isle, and not thirty from Willoughby's lair at Combe Magna; and before she had been five minutes in *The Cleveland*'s gently listing parlour, while the others were busily helping Charlotte to show her child to the ship's maid, she quitted it again, went ashore and clambered atop a charming mud dune. Marianne's eye, wandering over a wide tract of country to the southeast, could fondly rest on the farthest ridge of hills in the horizon, and fancy that from their summits Combe Magna might be seen.

In such moments of precious, invaluable misery, she rejoiced in tears of agony to be on *The Cleveland*; and as she returned by a different circuit to the houseboat, feeling all the happy privilege of country liberty, she resolved to spend almost every hour of every day while she remained with the Palmers, in the indulgence of such solitary rambles.

Marianne returned just in time to join the others as they quitted the house, on an excursion through its more immediate premises, and was promptly upbraided by her sister for the lack of sensible caution shown by such a venture.

"Is it your earnest desire to be murdered by rapacious pirates?" demanded Elinor. "After such a narrow escape from the destruction of Sub-Marine Station Beta, can you be so foolish as to risk your life by wandering so directly into harm's way? Did you forget the tales of Dreadbeard whispered by the men upon the *Nail*?"

Marianne was preparing to respond, when Mrs. Palmer broke in with her happy laugh.

"In fact," said she, laughing lightly, "we are as safe here as possible, and can fear nothing in the surrounding country."

In response to Elinor's puzzled inquiries, Mr. Palmer gruffly related that, indeed, Dreadbeard was the fiercest of the pirates who plied these waters, and the one most feared as murderous and vengeful. But Palmer, or so he explained, had once served alongside him when both were but boys and sailors in His Majesty's service, on a fire-serpent hunting mission off the coast of Africa; Palmer, seeing where his shipmate had fallen into the sea, clambered out onto the bowsprit, leapt into the water, and rescued the other boy—just as he was about to be consumed bodily by a crocodile. If there was one code respected by Dreadbeard (and, as far as could be discerned, there was but the one) it was that a man who had saved his life would never fall under harm by his hands, and to the contrary would live under his protection.

And so, upon his retirement, Palmer had moored his houseboat here, off Somerset Shore, where others would be *most* afraid, but where he and Mrs. Palmer could live the most securely—safe not only from Dreadbeard but also from any other murdering freebooter, none of whom would dare to harm anyone whose safety was guaranteed by the most merciless of buccaneers.

"If I had never pulled that lunatic from the crocodile's mouth, and Dreadbeard were to discover us here, having heaved anchor in the very bosom of his territory, he would slaughter us all and cook us for stew—but only after having his unsavory way with the women and torturing every man slowly, for the sheer pleasure of it," Palmer concluded grimly.

"Ah!" laughed Mrs. Palmer. "How droll!"

"Wouldn't it be a tremendous thing, though," sighed Marianne rapturously, "To encounter such a character, if only for a moment . . ."

"Marianne!" said Elinor, aghast at her passionate-minded sister's lack of sense.

Mr. Palmer shook his head gravely—dismissing with one gesture Marianne's romantic enthusiasm for pirates and Elinor's sensible fear of them. "There are worse things in the world than pirates," he muttered cryptically, before descending down the trap. "Far worse indeed."

The rest of the morning was easily whiled away, in lounging round the kitchen, examining the astonishing varieties of meat, from venison to vulture jerky that were kept aboard for shipside mess—and in visiting the below-deck, where Mr. Palmer was persuaded to show off the variety of mushrooms he cultivated in the dank of the ship's hold.

The morning was fine and dry, and Marianne had not calculated for any change of weather during their stay at *The Cleveland*. With great surprise therefore, did she find herself prevented by a settled rain from going out again after dinner. She had depended on a twilight walk to the mud dune, and perhaps all over the grounds, and an evening merely cold or damp would not have deterred her from it; but a heavy and settled rain even *she* could not fancy dry or pleasant weather for walking.

Their party was small, and the hours passed quietly away. Mrs. Palmer had her child, and Mrs. Jennings her carpet-work, and they talked of the friends they had left behind. Elinor, however little concerned in it, joined in their discourse; and Marianne, who had the knack of finding her way in every house to the library, soon procured herself a satisfyingly gory book of shipwrecks.

Nothing was wanting on Mrs. Palmer's side that could make them feel more welcome. Her kindness, recommended by so pretty a face, was engaging; her folly, though evident was not disgusting, because it was not conceited; and Elinor could have forgiven everything but her laugh.

Elinor had seen so little of Mr. Palmer, and in that little had seen so much variety in his address to her sister and herself, that she knew not what to expect to find him in his own family, aboard his own houseboat. She found him, however, perfectly the gentleman in his behaviour to all his visitors, and only occasionally rude to his wife and her mother. His only direct interaction with Elinor, however, came a few days after they had arrived, when he suddenly came upon her on the verandah, where she stood breathing in the marshy air, and asked with abruptness: "Are your relations still on Pestilent Isle?"

"Indeed; and awaiting our return, or so we understand."

"So you *hope*."

Of Edward, she now received intelligence from Colonel Brandon, who had been to Delaford to see him installed at the lake-side lighthouse. Treating her at once as the disinterested friend of Mr. Ferrars, and the kind of confidant of himself, Colonel Brandon talked to her a great deal of the lighthouse at Delaford, described its deficiencies, and told her what he meant to do himself towards removing them. His behaviour in this, his open pleasure in meeting her after an absence of only ten days, his readiness to converse with her, and his deference for her opinion, and the way his tentacles danced gaily as they spoke, might very well justify Mrs. Jennings's persuasion of his attachment. But such a notion had scarcely entered Elinor's head. She knew the true object of the colonel's affections.

On the fourth evening on *The Cleveland*, Marianne took yet another of her delightful twilight walks to the mud flat. She paused before a babbling brook where it ambled through the swamp, suddenly struck by how greatly it resembled the very stream where she had been assaulted by the giant octopus, before being so fortuitously rescued by the dashing Willoughby. Lost in the reflections such a sight engendered, pleasant and unbearable by turns, Marianne sank down to perch upon a log—which promptly spewed forth from a crag in its side a buzzing, furious swarm of mosquitoes. This humming devilish cloud soon entirely overwhelmed the flailing Marianne, who helplessly, uselessly, threw herself to the swampy ground and batted about as the insects covered every inch of her like a blanket. Again and again they sunk their tiny mandibles into her flesh, producing dozens upon dozens of deep stinging wounds—Marianne crying out all the while—until six or seven of the devilish buzzing things swarmed into her mouth and down her throat; the pain of which, combined with a single bite received directly in her eye, drove her past the point of consciousness.

Marianne was discovered, covered in suppurating sores, by a worried Elinor some three-quarters of an hour later, and put promptly into her bed. She woke the next morning with the swelling from the bites greatly decreased, but, alas, that major discomfort had been replaced by another—a set of the most violent symptoms. Prescriptions poured in from all quarters, and as usual, were all declined. Though heavy and feverish, with a pain in her limbs, and a cough, and a sore throat, headache, sweats, and vomiting, a good night's rest was to cure her entirely; and it was with difficulty that Elinor prevailed upon her to try one or two of the simplest of the remedies.

CHAPTER 43

MARIANNE GOT UP the next morning at her usual time; to every inquiry replied that she was better, and tried to prove herself so, by engaging in her customary employments. But a day spent shivering on a hammock with a book in her hand, which she was unable to read, or in lying, weary and languid, on a sofa, did not speak much in favour of her amendment. When at last she went early to bed, more and more indisposed, Colonel Brandon was only astonished at her sister's composure, who, though attending and nursing Marianne the whole day, trusted to the certainty and efficacy of sleep, and felt no real alarm.

A very restless and feverish night, however, disappointed the expectation of both. When Marianne, after persisting in rising, confessed herself unable to sit up, and returned into the cottage and went voluntarily to her bed, Elinor was very ready to send for the Palmers' apothecary, Mr. Harris.

He came on a swift boat from inland, examined his patient, and, once having heard of the mosquitoes' bites, swiftly determined that Marianne had malaria.

Such a diagnosis gave instant alarm to Mrs. Palmer on the account of her baby. Mrs. Jennings, who was born and bred along a mosquito-plagued coast, had been inclined from the first to think Marianne's complaint more serious than Elinor thought, now looked very grave on Mr. Harris's report, and confirming Charlotte's fears and caution, urged the necessity of her immediate removal with her infant. Her departure, therefore, was fixed on; and within an hour after Mr. Harris's arrival, she set off, with her little boy and his nurse, for the house of a near relation of Mr. Palmer's, who lived a few miles on the other side of Bath; whither her husband promised, at her earnest entreaty, to join her in a day or two; and whither she was almost equally urgent with her mother to accompany her. Mrs. Jennings, however, with a kindness of heart which made Elinor really love her, declared her resolution of not stepping foot off *The Cleveland* as long as Marianne remained ill, and of endeavouring, by her own attentive care, to supply to her the place of the mother she had taken her from.

Poor Marianne, languid and low from her malaria, violently disgorging the contents of her stomach at irregular intervals in a silver chamber pot that was again and again rinsed and returned to her bedside, could no longer hope that to-morrow would find her recovered. The idea of what to-morrow would have produced, but for this unlucky illness, made every ailment severe; for on that day they were to have begun their journey home, ferried thereto by Palmer's old companions aboard the *Rusted Nail*, and to have taken their mother by surprise on the following forenoon. The little she said was all in lamentation of this inevitable delay; though Elinor tried to raise her spirits, and make her believe, as she *then* really believed herself, that it would be a very short one.

The next day produced little or no alteration in the state of the patient; she certainly was not better, and her body was covered from head to toe with deep, suppurating sores. Her right eye, which had been bitten directly by the largest of the insects, had swollen such that it was permanently shut, the eyelid layered with a crustulent glaze of pus.

Their party was now further reduced; for Mr. Palmer was preparing to follow his wife; and while he was preparing to go, Colonel Brandon himself, with a much greater exertion, began to talk of going likewise. Here, however, the kindness of Mrs. Jennings interposed most acceptably; for to send the colonel away while his love was in so much uneasiness on her sister's account, would be to deprive them both, she thought, of every comfort; and therefore, telling him at once that his stay at *The Cleveland* was necessary to herself, that she should want him to play at Karankrolla of an evening, while Miss Dashwood was above with her sister. She urged him so strongly to remain, that he, who was gratifying the first wish of his own heart by a compliance, could not long even affect to demur.

Elinor realised too late the grave implication of Mr. Palmer's departure. It was *he* who had saved the life of Dreadbeard, so many years past; it was *he*, therefore, whose presence guaranteed security against an invasion by that infamous king of the pirates. With his departure, the unfortunate circumstance of Marianne's illness was compounded a hundredfold by the evaporation of that safety. Not wanting to worry the still gravely ill Marianne, nor impede the nurturing kindness of Mrs. Jennings, Elinor shared this distressing understanding to Colonel Brandon, whose ropy face tendrils grew rigid with concern. After Mrs. Jennings retired to her bedroom on the houseboat's second floor; and Marianne, in the next room and overcome by a consuming fever, lay in her wracked, hacking quasi-sleep, murmuring hallucinatory inanities, Brandon and Elinor began the grim business of putting the vessel (as the colonel put it) on a battle footing: They gathered long curtains of moss and *Sagittaria* leaves and hung them from the gables of the houseboat to obscure their position; they draped black fabric over the French windows; and they moved along the rails, adjusting the long-guns and carronades in their quoins, and making sure each artillery piece had adequate wadding and balls at the ready.

The next day, Marianne, even in her fleeting moments of alertness, was kept in ignorance of all these arrangements. She knew not that she had been the means of sending the owners of *The Cleveland* away, in about seven days from the time of their arrival, and what fresh peril their departure had engendered. It gave her no surprise that she saw nothing of Mrs. Palmer; and as it gave her likewise no concern, she never mentioned her name.

Two days passed from the time of Mr. Palmer's departure, and Marianne's situation continued with little variation. Mr. Harris, who attended her every day, still talked boldly of a speedy recovery, but the expectation of the others was by no means so cheerful. Mrs. Jennings, having observed that the girl's moments of consciousness were increasingly rare, and more fleeting when they came, arrived at the unfortunate conclusion that she had contracted not just malaria, but yellow fever as well—and that, in short, she would never recover. Colonel Brandon, who was chiefly of use in listening to Mrs. Jennings's forebodings, was not in a state of mind to resist their influence. He tried to reason himself out of fears, and even spent hours each morning catching sardines out of the shallows with his own face, so Marianne might have sustenance readily available when her appetite returned; but the many hours of each day in which he was left entirely alone, were but too favourable for the admission of every melancholy idea, and he could not expel from his mind the persuasion that he should see Marianne no more.

All the next day, Elinor sat perched on the deck of *The Cleveland*, manning the carronade, her attention torn between thoughts of her poor suffering sister where she lay feverish within the cabin; and her ever-growing terror of the mad pirate captain she felt with grim certainty would shortly be arriving to murder the lot of them, and toss their bodies to the monsters of the sea.

The day ended even less auspiciously. For a time, Marianne seemed to recover, but in the evening she became ill again, growing more heavy, restless, and uncomfortable than before. Marianne's sleep lasted a considerable time and Elinor resolved to sit with her during the whole of it, while Colonel Brandon took the night watch at the carronades and Mrs. Jennings went early to bed.

As the night wore on, Marianne's sleep became more and more disturbed; and her sister, who watched, with unremitting attention her continual change of posture, and heard the frequent but inarticulate sounds of complaint which passed her lips, was almost wishing to rouse her from so painful a slumber, when Marianne, suddenly started up and cried out, "Is Mama coming?"

"Not yet," cried the other, concealing her terror, and assisting

Marianne to lie down again, "but she will be here, I hope, before it is long. It is a great way, you know, from hence to Barton Cottage."

"But she must not go 'round by Sub-Marine Station Beta!" cried Marianne, in the same hurried manner. "I shall never see her, if she goes by the Station."

Elinor perceived with alarm that she was not quite herself. There seemed little point in reminding her, at such a moment, that the Station had been swallowed into the sea. While calmly attempting to soothe her, Elinor felt her sister's pulse. It was lower and quicker than ever! She knew she must send instantly for Mr. Harris, and dispatch a messenger to Barton Cottage for her mother. To consult with Colonel Brandon on the best means of effecting the latter; as soon as Elinor had rung up Mrs. Jennings to take her place by her sister, she exited the cabin and found Brandon at his battle station. It was no time for hesitation. Her fears and her difficulties were immediately before Colonel Brandon. He listened to them in silent despondence, sternly stroking his appendages—but her difficulties were instantly obviated, for with a readiness that seemed to speak the occasion, and the service pre-arranged in his mind, he offered himself as the messenger who should fetch Mrs. Dashwood. It was a decision as terrible as it was necessary: Though Brandon's departure would leave Elinor and Mrs. Jennings alone to defend the ship against Dreadbeard, his going was the surest and quickest way to bring Mrs. Dashwood hence.

"I can navigate those waters faster than any boat could sail it," he said.

Though she knew what emotional exertion Brandon required to so embrace the fishy part of his nature, Elinor made no resistance that was not easily overcome. She thanked him with brief, though fervent gratitude, and while he went to perform the elaborate stretching exercises necessary to prepare his body for such a lengthy swim, she wrote a few lines to her mother.

The comfort of such a friend at that moment as Colonel Brandon—or such a companion for her mother, how gratefully was it felt! A companion whose judgment would guide, whose attendance must relieve, whose friendship might soothe her! As far as the shock of such a summons *could* be lessened to her, his presence, his manners, his assistance, everything but his grotesque physical appearance, would lessen it.

He, meanwhile, whatever he might feel, acted with all the firmness of a collected mind, performed his stretches with the utmost dispatch, and calculated with exactness the time in which she might look for his return. Not a moment was lost in delay of any kind. After pressing her hand with a look of solemnity, and a few words spoken too low to reach her ear, Colonel Brandon leapt from the prow of the houseboat and began a sturdy, athletic crawl stroke to the south-southwest. Elinor went back into the cottage and up to her sister's room to wait for the arrival of the apothecary, and to watch by her the rest of the night. It was a night of almost equal suffering to both. Hour after hour passed away in sleepless pain and delirium on Marianne's side, and in the most cruel anxiety on Elinor's. The ideas in Marianne's fever-wracked brain were still, at intervals, fixed incoherently on her mother, and whenever she mentioned her name, it gave a pang to the heart of poor Elinor, who, reproaching herself for having trifled with so many days of illness, and wretched for some immediate relief, fancied that all relief might soon be in vain, that everything had been delayed too long, and pictured to herself her suffering mother arriving too late to see this darling child, or to see her rational.

She was on the point of sending again for Mr. Harris, or if *he* could not come, for some other advice, when the former arrived. His opinion, however, made some little amends for his delay, for though acknowledging a very unexpected and unpleasant alteration in his patient, he would not allow the danger to be material. He placed leeches all along Marianne's forearms, and laid the largest of the creatures directly on her inflamed eye— then, leaving the salutary bloodsuckers to do their work, he promised to call again in the course of three or four hours, and left both the patient and her anxious attendant more composed than he had found them.

With strong concern, and with many reproaches for not being called to their aid, did Mrs. Jennings hear in the morning of what had passed.

Her heart truly grieved. Marianne lay with her eyes closed, breathing shallowly, covered in the blood-sucking leeches that now represented her only hope of a return to health. The rapid decay, the early death of a girl so young, so lovely as Marianne, must have struck a less interested person with concern. On Mrs. Jennings's compassion she had other claims. She had been for three months her companion, was still under her care, and she was known to have been greatly injured, and long unhappy. The distress of her sister too, particularly a favourite, was before her—and as for their mother, when Mrs. Jennings considered that Marianne might probably be to *her* what Charlotte was to herself, her sympathy in *her* sufferings was very sincere.

Mr. Harris was punctual in his second visit, but he came to be disappointed in his hopes of what the last would produce. Even as he plucked free the leeches, fat from gorging on Marianne's diseased blood, it was clear that the remedy had failed. The fever was unabated, and Marianne only more quiet—not more herself—remained in a heavy stupor. Elinor, catching all his fears in a moment, proposed to call in further advice. But he judged it unnecessary: he had still another antipyretic to try, of whose success he was as confident as the last, and his visit concluded with encouraging assurances which reached the ear, but could not enter the heart of Miss Dashwood. Slowly, with the physician's customary deliberateness, he encased Marianne's body, from head to toe, in layer upon layer of slimy seaweed, leaving only a small slit at mouth-level for his patient to breathe.

"The salted leaves of kelp will draw the illness and fever from her," explained Mr. Harris. "And if she dies, her skin shall be smooth in death."

Elinor accepted the explanation, and was calm, except when she thought of her mother; but she was almost hopeless; and in this state she continued till noon, scarcely stirring from her sister's bed, her thoughts wandering from one image of grief, one suffering friend, to another. And what of Dreadbeard? Had it somehow escaped the attention of that infamous brigand that Mr. Palmer had departed? Could they be so fortunate, that he had decided to leave undisturbed this floating boat where it sat moored—along with the defenseless girls, one of them ill unto death, that sat upon it like ripe fruit, waiting to be plucked? Surely not—surely the monster was biding his time, toying with her, waiting to strike. Such considerations gave fresh misery to her reflections.

About noon, however, she began to hope she could perceive a slight amendment in her sister's pulse. She lifted up a tiny corner of the seaweed wrap from Marianne's face and looked at her left, unswollen eye. Seeing in it signs of life and intelligence for the first time in days, Elinor waited, watched, and examined Marianne again and again. Soon she hazarded to inspect the inflamed eye and found signs of life in it as well. Even Mrs. Jennings was forced to acknowledge a temporary revival, but she tried to keep her young friend from indulging a thought of its continuance—and Elinor told herself likewise not to hope. But it was too late. Hope had already entered, had caught the lip of her soul like a barbed hook; and feeling all its anxious flutter, she bent over her sister to watch—she hardly knew for what. Half an hour passed away, and the favourable symptom yet blessed her. Others even arose to confirm it. Her breath, her skin, her lips, all flattered Elinor with signs of amendment; and Marianne fixed her eyes on her with a rational, though languid, gaze. Anxiety and hope now oppressed her in equal degrees, and left her no moment of tranquility till the arrival of Mr. Harris at four o'clock—promptly he cut away the tight wrapping of dried sargassum; and his assurances, his felicitations on a recovery in her sister even surpassing his expectation, gave her confidence, comfort, and tears of joy.

Marianne was in every respect materially better, and Mr. Harris declared her entirely out of danger. He indulged in one more application of leeches, in order to be certain, which final treatment Marianne bore bravely. Even Mrs. Jennings allowed herself to trust in his judgment, and admitted, with unfeigned joy, the probability of an entire recovery.

Elinor continued by the side of her sister, with little intermission the whole afternoon, calming every fear, satisfying every inquiry of her enfeebled spirits, supplying every succour, and watching almost every look and every breath. The possibility of a relapse would in some moments occur to remind her of what anxiety was—but she saw, on her frequent and minute examination, that every symptom of recovery continued, and even her tumescent eye was beginning to return to its accustomed shape, and the layer of crust that had overlaid it had fallen away. Marianne, at six o'clock, sunk into a quiet, steady, and to all appearance comfortable, sleep, and Elinor silenced every doubt.

The time was now drawing on, when Colonel Brandon might be expected back; Elinor felt a stinging consciousness that she only had to keep them safe, only had to keep Marianne alive, until Brandon could return with their mother and the group of them could proceed to Barton Cottage, far from *The Cleveland*, far from fever, and far from Dreadbeard. As she sat with Marianne in the second-floor bedroom of the cabin, she imagined that she heard with every noise from without, every splash of tide against rock, the terrible sound of the pirate's silver boot heels on the foredeck.

The time could not pass quickly enough. By ten o'clock, Elinor trusted, or at least not much later, her mother would be relieved from the dreadful suspense in which she must now be travelling towards them. Oh! How slow was the progress of time which yet kept them in ignorance, and kept Elinor and Marianne within the prospect of danger they faced here!

At seven o'clock, leaving Marianne still sweetly asleep, Elinor joined Mrs. Jennings in the drawing-room to tea. Of breakfast she had been kept by her fears, and of lunch by their sudden reverse, from eating much; and the present refreshment, therefore, with such feelings of content as she brought to it, was particularly welcome. Together she and Mrs. Jennings ate an entire tuna, head to fin, including all interior organs; Mrs. Jennings saved the roe for Elinor to consume on her own, which she did, managing to enjoy the salty treat despite the welter of anxiety in which she waited.

The night was cold and stormy. The wind roared round the house-boat, tilting it violently back and forth in its moorings, and the rain beat against the windows. Marianne slept through every blast. The clock struck eight. Had it been ten, Elinor would have been convinced that at that moment she heard Brandon's strong crawl stroke cutting through the tide, swimming unerringly back to the houseboat; and so strong was the persuasion that she *did*, in spite of the *almost* impossibility of their being already come, that she raced out to the verandah and peered through the spyglass, to be satisfied of the truth. She instantly saw that her ears had not deceived her. Something was approaching, but it was not Brandon cutting through the waves with her mother upon his back; the object that approached from the western horizon was long, much longer than a swimming man, and it cut through the sea much faster than any man, even one with powerful face-flippers to propel him. As she stared through the spyglass, she heard the sound of oars beating against the waves.

Elinor's joy died in her breast. This was not Brandon and her mother—this was a ship. Dreadbeard was come.

Elinor swiveled the carronade and tried to fix aim on the fast-approaching enemy vessel; which boat, however, she soon noted seemed smaller than she would expect a three-masted pirate schooner. Judging that she would have better luck picking Dreadbeard and his men off at close range, once they had boarded—rather than trying to sink such a smallish craft with her untutored hand at a long gun—Elinor climbed quickly, hand over hand, down the trap to the hold, returning just as swiftly topside with Palmer's hunting rifle. Adopting a position in the shadow of the massive captain's wheel, she aimed the rifle at the gangplank of the houseboat, prepared to open fire as soon as the pirate crew climbed aboard.

Elinor squeezed her eyes shut and uttered a brief prayer as she crouched in the shadow of the wheel. It was not her choice to aim a rifle, nor to die aboard *The Cleveland* on this dark night—but she *would* defend her recovered sister. The sound of a boot heel at the end of the gangplank assured Elinor that the first of her unwelcome guests had made free to come aboard the boat. Her fingers grew sweaty around the trigger of the rifle. The heavy booted footfalls grew nearer.

She raised her gun, looked through the sight—and saw only Willoughby.

CHAPTER 44

ELINOR, STARTING BACK with a look of horror at the sight of him, did not lower her rifle. For one long second, her heart pounding and her head muddled, she considered the horrid possibility that Willoughby *was* Dreadbeard. Her hand remained on the trigger, and she even raised the barrel slightly—its action was suspended by his hastily advancing, and saying, in a voice rather of command than supplication,

"Miss Dashwood, don't shoot. For half an hour—for ten minutes— I entreat you to listen to me." He raised his hands in surrender, as did Monsieur Pierre, the orangutan, whom Elinor now saw at Willoughby's side, his hands held high over his head in a simian parody of Willoughby's supplicating stance.

"No, sir," she replied with firmness, "I shall *not* listen. Your business cannot be with *me*. Mr. Palmer is not aboard the boat."

"Were Mr. Palmer and all his relations at the devil, it would not have turned me from this gangplank. My business is with you, and only you."

"With me! Well, sir, be quick—and if you can, less violent."

"You, too," was his rejoinder, and, gathering his meaning, she slowly lowered the rifle, although she kept it grasped in her hands. "Sit down," he said, "and I will be both."

She hesitated; she knew not what to do. The possibility of Colonel Brandon's arriving and finding her there at the captain's wheel, in conversation with Willoughby, came across her. But she had promised to hear him, and her curiosity no less than her honour was engaged. After a moment's recollection, therefore, concluding that prudence required dispatch, and that her acquiescence would best promote it, she led Willoughby and his queer companion inside the cottage to the parlour, where they walked silently towards the table and sat down. He took the opposite chair, Monsieur Pierre squatted in the centre of the parlour rug, and for half a minute not a word was said by any of them.

"Pray be quick, sir," said Elinor, impatiently. "I have no time to spare. Pirates stalk this ship, I have great reason to fear, and I should return to my station at the captain's wheel."

He was sitting in an attitude of deep meditation, and seemed not to hear her.

"Your sister," said he, "is out of danger. The malaria is passed; I heard it from the apothecary's servant. God be praised! But is it true? Is it really true?"

Elinor would not speak. He repeated the inquiry with yet greater eagerness.

"For God's sake, tell me: Is she out of danger, or is she not?"

"We hope she is."

He rose up, and walked across the room.

"Had I known as much half an hour ago. But since I *am* here"— speaking with a forced vivacity as he returned to his seat—"what does it signify? For once, Miss Dashwood—it will be the last time, perhaps—let us be cheerful together. Tell me honestly: Do you think me most a knave or a fool?"

Elinor looked at him with greater astonishment than ever. She began to think that he must be in liquor; the strangeness of such a visit, and of such manners, and treasure hunters having a notorious fondness for spirits. With this impression she immediately rose, saying,

"Mr. Willoughby, I advise you at present to return to Combe—I am not at leisure to remain with you longer. Every moment we remain talking is a moment our enemies may take us unawares, which I cannot allow. Whatever your business may be with me, it will be better recollected and explained to-morrow."

"I understand you," he replied, with an expressive smile, and a voice perfectly calm. "And yes, I am very drunk."

But the steadiness of his manner, and the intelligence of his eye as he spoke, convinced Elinor that whatever other unpardonable folly might bring him to *The Cleveland*, he was not brought there by intoxication. She said, after a moment's recollection, "Mr. Willoughby, you *ought* to feel, and I certainly *do*—that after what has passed—your coming here in this manner, and forcing yourself upon my notice, requires a very particular excuse. By God, I would almost rather you *were* a pirate! What do you mean by it?"

"I mean," said he, with serious energy, "if I can, to make you hate me one degree less than you do *now*. I mean to offer some kind of explanation, some kind of apology, for the past. To open my whole heart to you, and by convincing you, that though I have been always a blockhead, I have not been always a scallywag, to obtain something like forgiveness from Ma—from your sister."

"Is this the real reason of your coming?"

"Upon my soul it is," was his answer, with a warmth which brought all the former Willoughby to her remembrance, and in spite of herself made her think him sincere. In the corner, Monsieur Pierre entered into a spirited liaison with an armchair.

"If that is all, you may be satisfied already—for Marianne has *long* forgiven you."

"Has she?" he cried, in the same eager tone. "Then she has forgiven me before she ought to have done it. But she shall forgive me again, and on more reasonable grounds. *Now* will you listen to me?"

Elinor bowed her assent. As Willoughby began to speak, she peeked briefly out the black-curtained window of the parlour, and, seeing no incoming vessel, allowed herself the ease to attend his story.

"I do not know," said he, "how *you* may have accounted for my behaviour to your sister, or what diabolical motive you may have imputed to me. Perhaps you will hardly think the better of me. It is worth the trial however, and you shall hear everything. When I first became intimate in your family, I had no other intention than to pass my time pleasantly while I was obliged to remain on the Devonshire coast. Your sister's lovely person and interesting manners could not but please me; and her behaviour to me almost from the first, was astonishing. At first I must confess, only my vanity was elevated by it. Careless of her happiness, thinking only of my own amusement, giving way to feelings which I had always been too much in the habit of indulging, I endeavoured to make myself pleasing to her, without any design of returning her affection."

Miss Dashwood, turning her eyes on him with the most angry contempt, stopped him by saying, "It is hardly worthwhile, Mr. Willoughby, for you to relate, or for me to listen any longer. Such a beginning as this cannot be followed by anything. Do not let me be pained by hearing anything more on the subject."

"I insist on you hearing the whole of it," he replied. "My fortune was never large, and I had always been expensive, always in the habit of associating with people of better income than myself. Every year since my coming of age had added to my debts. I was always searching for treasure and never finding it; always imagining it would be found the following year, always spending money freely with the expectation that it would be so. It had been for some time my intention to re-establish my circumstances by marrying a woman of fortune. To attach myself to your sister, therefore, was not a thing to be thought of—and with a meanness, selfishness, cruelty—which no indignant, no contemptuous look, even of yours, Miss Dashwood, can ever reprobate too much—I was acting in this manner, trying to engage her regard, without a thought of returning it. But one thing may be said for me: Even in that horrid state of selfish vanity, I did not know the extent of the injury I meditated, because I did not *then* know what it was to love. But have I ever known it? Well may it be doubted; for, had I really loved, could I have sacrificed my feelings to vanity, to avarice? Or, what is more, could I have sacrificed hers?"

He paused for a moment in his narrative; Monsieur Pierre laid his head in his master's lap and Willoughby indulgently scratched him.

"But I have done it. To avoid a comparative poverty, which her affection and her society would have deprived of all its horrors, I have, by raising myself to affluence, lost everything that could make it a blessing."

"Then you did," said Elinor, a little softened, "believe yourself at one time attached to her?"

"As surely as a piranha, once it has gripped its teeth into an explorer's plump leg, will hardly let go until sated or killed, nor did I think my heart would ever be released! To have resisted her attractions, to have withstood such tenderness! Is there a man on earth who could have done it? The happiest hours of my life were what I spent with her when I felt my intentions were strictly honourable, and my feelings blameless. Even then, however, when fully determined on paying my addresses to her, I allowed myself most improperly to put off, from day to day, the moment of doing it, from an unwillingness to enter into an engagement while my circumstances were so greatly embarrassed. I will not reason here—nor will I stop for *you* to expatiate on the absurdity, and the worse than absurdity, of scrupling to engage my faith where my honour was already bound. At last, however, my resolution was taken, and I had determined, as soon as I could engage her alone, to justify the attentions I had so invariably paid her, and openly assure her of an affection which I had already taken such pains to display. But in the interim of the very few hours that were to pass, before I could have an opportunity of speaking with her in private—a circumstance occurred—an unlucky circumstance, to ruin all my resolution, and with it all my comfort. A discovery took place." Here he hesitated and looked down, absently rubbing Pierre's furry stomach. "Mrs. Smith had somehow or other been informed, I imagine by some distant relation, whose interest it was to deprive me of her favour, of an affair, a connection—but I need not explain myself further," he added, looking at her with an heightened colour and an enquiring eye. "You have probably heard the whole story long ago. A seller of cakes—

an octopus—a girl left buried in the sand—"

"Yes, yes," returned Elinor, colouring likewise, and hardening her heart anew against any compassion for him. "I have heard it all. And how you will explain away any part of your guilt in that dreadful business, I confess is beyond my comprehension." The boat creaked wearily as it tossed in its mooring, and Elinor froze for a second, imagining she discerned the sound of a silvered boot heel pacing the deck outside; but the ominous noise was not repeated, and her heart after a moment unclenched.

"Remember," cried Willoughby, "from whom you received the account of my behaviour. Could it be an impartial one? I acknowledge that her situation and her character ought to have been respected by me. Her affection for me deserved better treatment, and I often, with great self-reproach, recall her tenderness. I wish—I heartily wish it had never been. But I have injured more than herself; and I have injured one, whose affection for me was scarcely less warm than hers; and whose mind was infinitely superior!"

"Your indifference is no apology for your cruelly leaving her in such circumstances, abandoned by your affection and buried neck-deep by the shore. You must have known that while you were enjoying yourself in Devonshire pursuing fresh schemes, she was reduced to the extremest indigence—or even worse. The tide might have swallowed her whole!"

"But, upon my soul, I did *not* know of her ultimate circumstances," he warmly replied. "I did not recollect that I had omitted to give her my address; and common sense might have told her how to find it out."

"Well, sir, and what said Mrs. Smith?"

"Good woman! She offered to forgive the past, if I would marry Eliza. That could not be—and I was formally dismissed from her favour and her house."

"This, I must mention, is exactly as I suspected—though my mother insisted it was a ghost who had cursed you."

"The night following this affair—I was to go the next morning—was spent by me in deliberating on what my future conduct should be.

The struggle was great—but it ended too soon. My affection for Marianne, my thorough conviction of her attachment to me—it was all insufficient to outweigh that dread of poverty. I had reason to believe myself secure of my present wife, if I chose to address her, and I persuaded myself to think that nothing else in common prudence remained for me to do. I have spent my life searching for treasure—I could not abandon one, once found. And so I went to Marianne, I saw her, and saw her miserable, and left her miserable—and left her hoping never to see her again."

"Then why did you call, Mr. Willoughby?" said Elinor. "A note would have answered every purpose. Why was it necessary to call?"

"It was necessary to my own pride. I could not bear to leave the Devonshire coast in a manner that might lead you, or the rest of the neighbourhood, to suspect any part of what had really passed between Mrs. Smith and myself—and I resolved therefore on calling at the shanty. The sight of your dear sister, however, was really dreadful; and, to heighten the matter, I found her alone. You were all gone I do not know where. I had left her only the evening before, so fully, so firmly resolved within myself on doing right! A few hours were to have engaged her to me forever; and I remember how happy, how gay were my spirits, as I rowed from your shack back to Allenham Isle, satisfied with myself, delighted with everybody! But in this, our last interview of friendship, I approached her with a sense of guilt that almost took from me the power of dissembling. Her sorrow, her disappointment, her deep regret, when I told her that I was obliged to leave Devonshire so immediately—I never shall forget it. Oh, God! What a hard-hearted rogue was I! I hid behind the portcullis of my diving helmet! I could not meet her eye!"

They were both silent for a few moments. Waves rattled the sides of the houseboat, and the old wood creaked again in the tide.

"Well, sir," said Elinor, who, though pitying him, grew increasingly impatient for his departure. "And this is all? If so then pray allow me leave to return to the deck, and my spyglass, and my watch for the hated Dreadbeard."

"My God—Dreadbeard, you say?"

The infamous name brought Willoughby to his feet, and seemed in an instant to clear his head and bring his eyes to full attention. "Miss Dashwood, think what you will of me—of my morals and of my depravity in my treatment of you and your relations—but I have spent my life in pursuit of buried treasures, and though I have never crossed paths with Dreadbeard, I have learned much about pirates. Come—let us booby-trap your boat."

Willoughby hurriedly strode out onto the verandah and from there down onto the foredeck. Asking firstly of Elinor where the hammocks were kept, he used them to rig neat mesh tiger-traps across each of the trap-doors.

"That notorious letter," he inquired of her, when they had travelled below-decks, where he splashed cooking oil across the locked door of the stores, so it could be lit to create an impassable wall of fire. "Did she show it you?"

"Yes, I saw every note that passed."

"When the first of hers reached me, my feelings were very, very painful. Every line, every word was—in the hackneyed metaphor which their dear writer, were she here, would forbid—a dagger to my heart."

Elinor's own heart, which had undergone many changes in the course of this extraordinary conversation, was now softened again—yet she felt it her duty to check such ideas in her companion as the last. "This is not right, Mr. Willoughby. Remember that you are married. Relate only what in your conscience you think necessary for me to hear." As she chastised him, she gingerly poked with the toe of her boot at the fake plank Willoughby had just rigged, through which a pirate's heavy boot would fall, sending him crashing into the quarterdeck.

"Marianne's note, by assuring me that I was still as dear to her as in former days, awakened all my remorse. I say awakened, because time and the delights of the Sub-Marine Station, had in some measure quieted it, and I had been growing a fine hardened rapscallion, fancying myself indifferent to her, and choosing to fancy that she too must have become in-different to me; talking to myself of our past attachment as a mere idle, tri-fling business, shrugging up my shoulders in proof of its being so, and silencing every reproach, overcoming every scruple, by secretly saying now and then, 'I shall be heartily glad to hear she is well married.' But this note made me know myself better. I felt that she was infinitely dearer to me than any other woman in the world, and that I was using her infa-mously. But everything was already settled between Miss Grey and me. To retreat was impossible. All that I had to do, was to avoid you both. I sent no answer to Marianne, intending by that to preserve myself from her further notice; and for some time I was even determined not to call in Berkeley Causeway. But at last, judging it wiser to affect the air of a cool, common acquaintance than anything else, I watched you all safely out of the docking station one morning, and left my hermit-crab shell."

"Watched us out of the house!"

"Even so. You would be surprised to hear how often I watched you, how often I was on the point of falling in with you. I have entered many a shop to avoid your sight, as the gondola glided past. Lodging as I did in Bond Causeway, there was hardly a day in which I did not catch a glimpse of one or other of you; and nothing but a prevailing desire to keep out of sight could have separated us so long. I avoided the Middletons as much as possible, as well as everybody else who was likely to prove an acquain-tance in common. If you *can* pity me, Miss Dashwood, pity my situation as it was *then*. With my head and heart full of your sister, I was forced to play the happy lover to another woman! Those three or four weeks were worse than all. Well, at last, as I need not tell you, you were forced on me; and what a sweet figure I cut! What an evening of agony it was! Aside from the feral lobsters that gouged a half dozen people to death, and I sad to not be in their number! Marianne, beautiful as an angel on one side, calling me Willoughby in such a tone! Oh, God! Holding out her hand to me, asking for protection from the armored beasts, asking me for an ex-planation, with those bewitching eyes fixed in such speaking solicitude on my face! And Sophia, jealous as the devil on the other hand, equally vulnerable to those hell-claws! Such an evening! I ran away as soon as I could, but not before I had seen Marianne's sweet face as white as death. That was the last, last look I ever had of her—the last manner in which she appeared to me. It was a horrid sight! Among many horrid sights from that evening, it was the most horrid of all! Yet when I thought of her to-day as really dying—of malaria, *and* yellow fever, *and* lupus—"

"No, not lupus."

"Really? Well, that's good."

"But the letter, Mr. Willoughby, your own letter; have you anything to say about that?"

"Yes, yes, *that* in particular. Your sister wrote to me again, the next morning after the lobster attack at Hydra-Z. You saw what she said. I was breakfasting at the Ellisons—and her letter was brought to me there from my lodgings. It happened to catch Sophia's eye before it caught mine— and its size, the elegance of the paper, the hand-writing altogether, immediately gave her a suspicion. Some had received some vague report of my attachment to a young lady in Devonshire, and what had passed at Hydra-Z had marked who the young lady was, and made her more jealous than ever. Affecting that air of playfulness, therefore, which is delightful in a woman one loves, she opened the letter directly, and read its contents. She was well paid for her impudence. She read what made her wretched. Her wretchedness I could have borne, but her passion—her malice—at all events it must be appeased. In short—what do you think of my wife's style of letter-writing?"

"Your wife! The letter was in your own hand-writing."

"Yes, but I had only the credit of servilely copying such sentences as I was ashamed to put my name to. The original was all her own—her own happy thoughts and gentle diction. But what could I do! I copied my wife's words, and parted with the last relics of Marianne. Her three notes—unluckily they were all in my pocketbook, or I should have denied their existence, and hoarded them forever—I was forced to put them up, and could not even kiss them. And the lock of hair—that too I had always carried about me, which was now searched by Madam with the most ingratiating virulence—the dear lock—all, every memento was torn from me."

Now they were finished in laying their traps and stood together again at the wheel, gazing out into the black of the nighttime sea. Monsieur Pierre gave a little monkey shake of the head, as if remembering the whole nasty business, and offering his beloved master every sympathy.

"I appreciate your able assistance in arming this craft, Mr. Willoughby, but you are very wrong—very blamable," said Elinor, while her voice, in spite of herself, betrayed her compassionate emotion. "You ought not to speak in this way, either of Mrs. Willoughby or my sister. You had made your own choice. It was not forced on you. Your wife has a claim to your politeness, to your respect, at least. She must be attached to you, or she would not have married you. To treat her with unkindness, to speak of her slightingly is no atonement to Marianne—nor can I suppose it a relief to your own conscience."

"Do not talk to me of my wife," said he with a heavy sigh. "She does not deserve your compassion. She knew I had no regard for her when we married. Well, married we were, and came down to Combe Magna to be happy, and afterwards returned to Sub-Marine Station Beta, before it was destroyed, to be gay. And now do you pity me, Miss Dashwood? Or have I said all this to no purpose? Am I less guilty in your opinion than I was before? Have I offered you a yellowed map, which you may follow to a forgiving place in your heart?"

"Yes, you have proved yourself, on the whole, less faulty than I had believed you. You have proved your heart less wicked, much less wicked. But I hardly know—the misery that you have inflicted—I hardly know what could have made it worse."

"Will you repeat to your sister when she is recovered, what I have been telling you? Tell her of my misery and my penitence—tell her that my heart was never inconstant to her, and if you will, that at this moment she is dearer to me than ever."

"I will tell her all that is necessary. But you have not explained to me the particular reason of your coming now, nor how you heard of her illness."

"On a fishing bank along the Thames, I ran against Sir John Middleton, and when he saw who I was—for the first time these two months—he spoke to me. His good-natured, honest, stupid soul, full of indignation against me, and concern for your sister, could not resist the temptation of telling me what he knew ought to—though probably he did not think it *would*—vex me horridly. As bluntly as he could speak it, therefore, he told me that Marianne Dashwood was dying of malaria, yellow fever—and I could have sworn he said, lupus, but if you say no, wonderful—at *The Cleveland*—a letter that morning received from Mrs. Jennings declared her danger most imminent—the Palmers are all gone off in a fright, etc. What I felt was dreadful! Thus my resolution was soon made, and at eight o'clock this morning I was preparing my kayak. Now you know all."

He held out his hand. She could not refuse to give him hers—he pressed it with affection.

"And you *do* think something better of me than you did?"—said he, letting it fall, and leaning against the wheel as if forgetting he was to go.

Elinor assured him that she did—that she forgave, pitied, wished him well—was even interested in his happiness—and added some gentle counsel as to the behaviour most likely to promote it. His answer was not very encouraging.

"As to that," said he, "I must rub through the world as well as I can. Domestic happiness is out of the question. If, however, I am allowed to think that you and yours feel an interest in my fate and actions, it may be the means—it may put me on my guard—at least, it may be something to live for. Marianne, to be sure, is lost to me forever. Were I even by any blessed chance at liberty again—were Sophia to meet with a giant octopus, say, and I not around."

Elinor stopped him with a reproof. "Octopi seem to play an important role in your adventures, Mr. Willoughby."

With a sheepish expression, Mr. Willoughby produced a long, slim cylinder from his pocket, marked along one side with a light sketch of an eight-armed figure.

"What—"

"'Tis an octopus whistle," Willoughby slyly explained; "specially designed to emit a sound pitched to draw their attentions, no matter the weather or water. I have found that being rescued from the clasping, eight-tentacled embrace of a giant octopus tends to create—in a lady—a certain affection—"

Elinor shook her head, unsure of the words to express disapprobation at such a device, and slipped the cylinder into her pocket.

"Well," he replied, "once more good-bye. I shall now go away and live in dread of one event."

"What do you mean?"

"Your sister's marriage."

"You are very wrong. She can never be more lost to you than she is now."

"But she will be gained by someone else. And if that someone should be the very he whom, of all others, I could least bear—but I will not stay to rob myself of all your compassionate goodwill, by showing that where I have most injured I can least forgive. Good-bye. God bless you—and—oh—one more thing—"

Without a further word, he removed from the sheath of his boot a razor-sharp dirk, and pressed its handle into Elinor's hand. And then he stumbled down the gangplank, his orangutan companion trailing behind, leapt into his kayak, and sailed away.

Elinor's stood swaying with the boat's rocking motion, her thoughts silently fixed on the irreparable injury which too early an independence and its consequent habits of idleness, dissipation, and luxury, had made in the mind and character and happiness of Willoughby. The world had made him extravagant and vain—extravagance and vanity had made him cold-hearted and selfish. From a reverie of this kind she was recalled by a most terrible sound—a long, harsh shriek, that she could not recognize until she looked through the spyglass—and would forever remember there-after as the sound emitted by an orangutan when it is run through with a cutlass.

For here at last, fulfilling her every terrified expectation, was *The Jolly Murderess*, six black flags fluttering darkly in the moonlight, sailing unerringly forward for *The Cleveland*, rapidly narrowing the hundred or so yards between the crafts. And here was a jolly-boat, its oars manned by two cruel-eyed brigands sent as an advance party, yet closer; it was this small vessel that had intercepted Willoughby's kayak. Elinor saw the limp body of Monsieur Pierre tossed like a ragdoll into the water; she saw the escaped Willoughby swimming furiously to shore. And she saw, as she again raised the spyglass from the jolly-boat to the ship itself, standing at the prow of *The Murderess*, the author of this latest and direst calamity—Dreadbeard himself.

The terrible pirate chieftain was massively tall, in a long and jet-black captain's coat, a cap of scarlet and gold tilted at a rakish angle back-wards on his big, bearded head, and a long mane of tar-black hair spilling from his hat and down his back. He stood beside the wheel, which was manned by a ragged, dirty-faced and hunched coxswain, who snarled and spat on the deck as he directed the ship on its course for *The Cleveland*. As for the hated captain, he stood stock still, his chest thrust forward, clutching in the fist of his left hand a gleaming double-edged cutlass, glinting like new-forged steel in the moonlight.

Elinor felt at once the ludicrousness of all Willoughby's trapdoors and netting, of any such trifling defenses; the tiny dirk he had handed her felt like a toy in her hand. Elinor trembled; *The Jolly Murderess* plowed the black water. The massive figure at the prow threw back his head and laughed—a loud, cackling, hideous bellow that rolled across the water towards her in terrible waves.

Dreadbeard had arrived.

CHAPTER 45

WHEN ELINOR RUSHED BACK inside the cabin and up the stairs to the bedroom of the unconscious Marianne, she found her just awaking, refreshed by so long and sweet a sleep. Elinor's heart, meanwhile, beat a rapid tattoo of terrified panic.

Peeking out the black-curtained window, she saw that the advance boat was nearly in boarding range of *The Cleveland*. She heard Dreadbeard's terrible laughter through the windows of the cabin, and then again, ever louder, nearer and nearer with every moment. The hideous sound threw her into an agitation of spirits which kept off every indication of fatigue, and made her only fearful of betraying her terror to her sister. "Go back to sleep, dear Marianne," she murmured in her ear. "Only sleep a while longer."

She raced back out onto the verandah, just in time to see the pair of foul mercenaries in their dinghy bump up against the hull and begin their ascent of the Jacob's ladder and onto *The Cleveland*.

"Avast, ye hearties!" they hollered as they climbed, "We be requestin' the pleasure of your company this fine evening!"

In Elinor's left hand she still clutched the little knife that Willoughby had pressed upon her—with her right she now snatched up Palmer's hunting rifle and aimed it at the gangplank; as soon as the kerchiefed head of the first invader appeared over the side, she squeezed the trigger. The force of the gun pushed Elinor backwards with tremendous force into the cabin-rail; and, furthering her distress, the shot missed entirely. The intended target, a lanky, filthy tar in a ragged, patched coat, laughed wickedly as the ball sailed harmlessly over his head. He hopped insouciantly over the side and advanced across the deck. Elinor backed up against the cabin-rail, squeezed off a second ball, and this time with greater success: the second pirate took the shot directly in his face as he appeared over the side rail; his head exploded in a burst of gore, and his body flew backwards into the sea.

But before she could rise to her feet, Elinor felt the calloused hands of the filthy first pirate at her neck, squeezing with brutal force; all the pain of the throat wound she had received from the sea scorpion recurred, only to be supplanted by the terrifying sensation of the air being choked from her body. She stared up into the dirty face of the pirate, and conceived with a desperate melancholy that this would be the last sight ever to greet her eyes. Oh, she wished she had granted her full attention, when gentlemen of fortune were the fashion in-Station, to the mock fights she had seen. Oh, how she wished she had some knowledge of how to repulse the cruel attentions of a pirate!

As if in answer to her desperate thoughts, she heard the bellowing voice of Mrs. Jennings: "Whittle! Whittle him!"

Indeed, such was a form of knowledge she knew well—and, moreover, she had the proper tool to hand: Willoughby's dirk, a hilted blade, five inches long, could most assuredly approximate a driftwood sculpting knife! She raised the dagger and began to cut away at the brigand's dirty grimace—one cut, then another, then another, a series of fierce slashes, imagining his hideous nut-brown face was nothing but a chunk of old driftwood she was shaping into a figurine.

As she slashed away, blood rained down out of the pirate's face directly onto hers; she spat his black blood from her mouth. Shortly, his grip relaxed, for she had stabbed the man to death. Mrs. Jennings, in her nightclothes and cap, rushed to her side and helped Elinor to her feet. "We must hurry," she sputtered. "We face—"

"Dreadbeard, dear. I know." She pointed to where *The Jolly Murderess* still sailed forward, now not more than thirty feet away; Dreadbeard still at the prow, cutlass in hand, seemingly unperturbed by the dispatch of his advance party. But then, as they watched, *The Murderess* stopped in its forward motion, and for a long moment simply sat in the water. Elinor thought for one joyful, fleeting second, that her adversaries were, for some blessed reason, preparing to turn and sail back out to sea. She raised the spyglass again, just in time to see Dreadbeard raise his huge cutlass overhead as a signal and let out an unholy shout; at which signal his crew—from their various positions, arrayed along the bow, huddled in the poop-deck, even hanging from the riggings—raised bows and let loose a bombardment of arrows.

Elinor and Mrs. Jennings ducked behind the captain's wheel as the deadly projectiles whizzed in a thick deadly blur around them.

"Surrender!" cried Dreadbeard's guttural voice from the prow of the *Murderess*. "Surrender—and mayhaps I'll spare ya keelhaulin', and only slit your throats and feed your guts to the sharks. You bein' ladies and all. Or then again, mayhaps I *won't*."

At this bit of piratical levity, his fellow mercenaries laughed in a ragged chorus.

Elinor summoned the courage to poke her head up from behind the wheel and shout, "We shall never—" only to have her sentence caught short by blinding pain as an arrow, one of a second round let loose by her adversaries, struck her in the arm. Mrs. Jennings then demonstrated that her apprehension of pirates was as keen as Elinor's, and her ability to fight them if anything more assured.

With a mighty wail she leapt to the guns and fired *The Cleveland*'s carronade with deadly accuracy; soon several of the enemy had fallen under a hail of round shot, collapsing mortally wounded to the deck. But the ship, even at that moment, resumed its forward progress as Dreadbeard's men threw the pieces of their former shipmates overboard.

"Closer, my dearies," shouted Dreadbeard from his place at the prow. "Who shall be my first dance partner, I wonder? I do so love the comp'ny of a lady."

It was then that Elinor remembered the whistle. Just as *The Jolly*

Murderess rowed near enough that she no longer required the spyglass to
see the leering faces of her foes, she produced from her pocket the long,
cylindrical penny-whistle that Willoughby had so shamefacedly handed
her only an hour before—though it seemed now like years gone by.

She blew it, and blew it again, and then again, knowing not whether
the device would prove effective; certain only that it was their only chance
at survival. And then, in a flash, from some inscrutable depth of the ocean,
a long, rubbery tentacle, bedecked with suction cups, snaked its way over
the side of the pirate ship and onto its fo'c'sle. In the next moment, another
tentacle appeared, and then another, and then a fourth. Soon *The Murderess*
was surrounded by a writhing school of eight-tentacled monsters, churning the black water, banging their great oblong heads against the hull, and
reaching their multitudinous tentacles into the galleys. The pirates called
out to each other in their mercenary cant, confused and fearful, as one by
one they were grabbed bodily by long, powerful tentacles and pulled into
the water. Elinor stood frozen, awestruck, the whistle still at her lips, as the
cephalopods did their grim work.

In several minutes time, the pirates had been vanquished—all, it
seemed, but for Dreadbeard himself, who still stood unbowed at the prow
of the schooner, his black eyes aglow. At his feet was a pile of chopped-
up tentacles, dispatched with a few swift blows of his gleaming cutlass;
under his foot was an octopus's shattered skull, which he had staved in
with the heel of his massive boot. He stared unerringly at Elinor, his cutlass high above his head, a virulent gleam in his eye, as the boat continued
to draw forward.

"What fascinatin' friends you've got, for a lass your age," smirked
Dreadbeard, kicking an octopus head overboard. "I am so *keen* to make
your acquain—aaaaah!"

Dreadbeard let out a horrid scream of pain and surprise as someone—or *something*—smashed him brutally with a length of plank on the
back of his massive shaggy head. The pirate captain reeled, giving the
stranger time to grasp the cutlass from his outstretched hand and, with a

single swift and powerful blow, chop off his head.

The hero was Colonel Brandon. Elinor hailed him heartily from the deck of *The Cleveland*, and he hailed her back, holding aloft the severed head of the fearsome Dreadbeard.

"Brandon? But that means—"

Elinor spun around on the deck of the houseboat, and beheld: "Mother!"

Mrs. Dashwood, whose terror, riding Colonel Brandon as he swam nearer and nearer the houseboat had produced almost the conviction of Marianne's being no more, had no voice to inquire after her, no voice even for Elinor; but *she*, waiting neither for salutation nor inquiry, instantly gave the joyful relief; "Marianne lives, mother! She lives! *And* we have vanquished the pirates! Happy day!"

Her mother, catching it with all her usual warmth, was in a moment as much overcome by her happiness, as she had been before by her fears. She collapsed into Elinor's arms, right there on the foredeck, and from that position the two watched as Colonel Brandon hacked the corpse of Dreadbeard to bits with an axe seized from the deck of the ship, and threw bits of his body, one by one, overboard to the octopi who had been of such able assistance. Colonel Brandon then leapt off the deck; in an instant, had swum the scarlet-flooded water and appeared beside them on the verandah of *The Cleveland*.

As *The Jolly Murderess* drifted slowly back out to sea, its peril decisively neutralized, Mrs. Dashwood was supported into the drawing-room between her daughter and her friend—and there, shedding tears of joy, though still unable to speak, embraced Elinor again and again, turning from her at intervals to press Colonel Brandon's hand, with a look which spoke at once her gratitude, and her conviction of his sharing with herself in the bliss of the moment. He shared it, however, in a silence even greater than her own.

As soon as Mrs. Dashwood had recovered herself, to see Marianne was her first desire; and in two minutes she was with her beloved child,

THE HERO WAS COLONEL BRANDON.

rendered dearer to her than ever by absence, unhappiness, and danger. Elinor's delight, as she saw what each felt in the meeting, was only checked by an apprehension of its robbing Marianne of further sleep—but Mrs. Dashwood could be calm, could be even prudent, when the life of a child was at stake, and Marianne, satisfied in knowing her mother was near her, and conscious of being too weak for conversation, submitted readily to the necessity of silence and quiet. Mrs. Dashwood *would* sit up with her all night; and Elinor, in compliance with her mother's entreaty, went to bed. But the rest, which one night entirely sleepless, and many hours of the most wearing anxiety, and pirate battle, seemed to make requisite, was kept off by irritation of spirits. Willoughby, "poor Willoughby," as she now allowed herself to call him, was constantly in her thoughts; she would not but have heard his vindication for the world, and now blamed, now acquitted herself for having judged him so harshly before. But her promise of relating it to her sister was invariably painful. She dreaded the performance of it, dreaded what its effect on Marianne might be; doubted whether after such an explanation she could ever be happy with another; and for a moment wished Willoughby a widower, and visualized Mrs. Willoughby being consumed by a great octopus, as the pirates had been so recently. Then, remembering Colonel Brandon, reproved herself, felt that to *his* sufferings and his constancy far more than to his rival's, the reward of her sister was due, and wished anything rather than Mrs. Willoughby's death.

Marianne continued to mend every day—her boils burst and healed, her cheeks cooled and her pulse calmed. The brilliant cheerfulness of Mrs. Dashwood's looks and spirits proved her to be, as she repeatedly declared herself, one of the happiest women in the world. Elinor could not hear the declaration, nor witness its proofs without sometimes wondering whether her mother ever recollected Edward. In turns they kept watch on the horizon for more pirates, and saw none. But Mrs. Dashwood, trusting to the temperate account of her own disappointment which Elinor had sent her, was led away by the exuberance of her joy to think only of what would increase it. Marianne was restored to her from a danger in which, as she now began to feel, her own mistaken judgment in encouraging the unfortunate attachment to Willoughby, had contributed to place her.

Only once in this generally joyful interlude did Elinor see a shadow pass over her mother's face—when she inquired as to the status of her *youngest* sister.

"Margaret . . ." said Mrs. Dashwood, with an anxious glance to Marianne, whom she clearly did not wish to trouble with any distasteful news, "Margaret remains on the island." When pressed on the meaning of this ambiguous reply, Mrs. Dashwood would only shake her head with a furrowed brow, and Elinor thought it best to let the issue drop.

And Mrs. Dashwood had yet another source of joy unthought of by Elinor. It was thus imparted to her, as soon as any opportunity of private conference between them occurred.

"At last we are alone. My Elinor, you do not yet know all my happiness. Colonel Brandon loves Marianne. He has told me so himself."

Her daughter, feeling by turns both pleased and pained, surprised and not surprised, was all silent attention.

"You are never like me, dear Elinor, or I should wonder at your composure now. Had I sat down to wish for any possible good to my family, I should have fixed on Colonel Brandon's marrying one of you as the object most desirable. And I believe Marianne will be the most happy with him of the two. If she can bring herself to forget, or tolerate, the mass of writhing tentacles upon his face."

Elinor passed this off with a smile.

"He opened his whole heart to me yesterday when we stopped to rest upon a slippery rock, midway from Pestilent Isle to here. It came out quite unawares, quite undesignedly. I could talk of nothing but my child, of course, and he could not conceal his distress; I saw that it equaled my own, and he made me acquainted with his earnest, tender, constant, affection for Marianne. He has loved her, my Elinor, ever since the first moment of seeing her."

Here Elinor perceived not the language nor the professions of Colonel Brandon, but the natural embellishments of her mother's active fancy, which fashioned everything delightful to her as it chose.

"His regard for her, infinitely surpassing anything that Willoughby ever felt or feigned, as much more warm, as more sincere or constant— whichever we are to call it—has subsisted through all the knowledge of dear Marianne's unhappy prepossession for that worthless young man! And without selfishness! Without encouraging a hope! The beauty of his heart, I aver, is in inverse proportion to the unbeauty of his face! No one can be deceived in *him*."

"Colonel Brandon's character," said Elinor, "as an excellent man, is well established."

"I know it is," replied her mother seriously. "His coming for me as he did, with such active, such ready friendship, willing even to wear a little saddle upon his back so I could ride more comfortably as he swam, is enough to prove him one of the worthiest of men."

"What answer did you give him? Did you allow him to hope?"

"Oh! My love, I could not then talk of hope to him or to myself. Marianne might at that moment be dying. But he did not ask for hope or encouragement. His was an involuntary confidence, an irrepressible effusion to a soothing friend—not an application to a parent. Yet after a time I *did* say, for at first I was quite overcome—that if she lived, as I trusted she might, my greatest happiness would lie in promoting their marriage; and since our arrival, since our delightful security, I have re-peated it to him more fully, have given him every encouragement in my power. Time, a very little time, I tell him, will do everything. Marianne's heart is not to be wasted for ever on such a man as Willoughby. His own merits must soon secure it."

"To judge from the colonel's spirits, however, you have not yet made him equally sanguine."

"No. He thinks Marianne's affection too deeply rooted for any change, and even supposing her heart again free, is too diffident of himself to believe, that with such a difference of age and disposition—and of course, there is the matter of the squishy—well, you know. He certainly is not so handsome as Willoughby—but at the same time, there is something much more pleasing in his countenance. There was always a something, if you remember, in Willoughby's eyes at times, which I did not like."

Elinor could *not* remember it—but her mother, without waiting for her assent, continued,

"I am very sure myself, that had Willoughby turned out as really amiable, as he has proved himself the contrary, Marianne would yet never have been so happy with *him*, as she will be with Colonel Brandon."

Elinor withdrew to think it all over in private, to wish success to her friend, and yet in wishing it, to feel a pang for Willoughby. She smiled a secret smile and ran her finger over the octopus whistle, still in her pocket.

CHAPTER 46

MARIANNE'S ILLNESS, though multifaceted and weakening in its kind, had not been long enough to make her recovery slow; and with youth, natural strength, and her mother's presence in aid, it proceeded so smoothly as to enable her to remove, within four days after the arrival of the latter, into Mrs. Palmer's dressing-room. She was impatient to pour forth her thanks to Colonel Brandon for fetching her mother; and bringing her hence so swiftly with such a strong steady crawl stroke; and for decapitating the fearsome Pirate Dreadbeard; and so he was invited to visit her.

His emotion on entering the room, in seeing the burst pustules that dotted her face and neck, and in receiving the pale hand—its fingernails yellowed and brittle from illness—which she immediately held out to him, were clear. In Elinor's conjecture, they must arise from something more than his affection for Marianne, or the consciousness of its being known to others. She soon discovered in his melancholy eye and the embarrassed little shuffle of his appendages as he looked at her sister, the probable recurrence of many past scenes of misery to his mind, brought back by that resemblance between Marianne and Eliza already acknowledged, and now strengthened by the wandering eye, the sickly skin, the posture of reclining weakness, the slow but steady streams of pus from various orifices, and the warm acknowledgment of peculiar obligation.

Mrs. Dashwood saw nothing in the colonel's behaviour but what arose from the most simple and self-evident sensations, while in the actions and words of Marianne, even as her words emerged in a hoarse croak, her vocal cords having been ravaged by infection, she persuaded herself to think that something more than gratitude already dawned.

At the end of another day or two, Marianne growing visibly stronger every twelve hours, Mrs. Dashwood, urged equally by her own and her daughter's wishes, began to talk of removing to Barton Cottage. On *her* measures depended those of her two friends; Mrs. Jennings could not quit *The Cleveland* during the Dashwoods' stay; and Colonel Brandon was soon brought, by their united request, to consider his own abode there as equally determinate, if not equally indispensable. At his and Mrs. Jennings's united request in return, Mrs. Dashwood was prevailed on to accept the use of his fully outfitted and newly refurbished pleasure yacht on her journey back, for the better accommodation of her sick child; and the colonel, at the joint invitation of Mrs. Dashwood and Mrs. Jennings, whose active good-nature made her friendly and hospitable for other people as well as herself, engaged with pleasure to redeem it by a visit at the shanty, in the course of a few weeks.

The day of separation and departure arrived; and Marianne, took a particular and lengthened leave of Mrs. Jennings, effusively professing her gratitude not only for nursing her back to health, but also for her part in fending off the pirates, whose attack and repulsion Marianne had only been told of after her constitution was more fully restored. She was so earnestly grateful, so full of respect and kind wishes as seemed due to her own heart from a secret acknowledgment of past inattention. Bidding Colonel Brandon farewell with a cordiality of a friend, she was carefully assisted by him onboard the pleasure yacht. Mrs. Dashwood and Elinor then followed, and the others were left by themselves, to talk of the travellers, and feel their own dullness; and Colonel Brandon immediately afterwards took his solitary way to Delaford.

The Dashwoods were two days aboard, and Marianne bore her journey without fatigue. They flew the captured flag of *The Jolly Murderess*, which, whether either by suggesting that they themselves were onboard that most feared of pirate vessels, or by giving fluttering evidence that they had destroyed it, kept all potential marauders at bay.

As they sailed into Sir John's archipelago and the choppy waters of Pestilent Isle, and entered on scenes of which every piece of shoreline brought some peculiar, some painful recollection, Marianne grew silent and thoughtful, and turning away her face from their notice, sat earnestly gazing through the window. Elinor, for her part, felt as she examined the old mudflats, the twisted trees, the familiar peak of "Mount Margaret" that something was decidedly altered in the landscape of their old homestead—as if something had somehow *shifted*—but she had not the luxury to reflect upon her impression. Her only priority was to monitor Marianne for any signs that the familiar sights would discomfit her, or restore her ill health by plunging her into a new depth of melancholy.

But Elinor could neither wonder nor blame; and when she saw, as the yacht was moored to their rebuilt wooden dock and she assisted Marianne down the gangplank, that she had been crying, she saw only an emotion too natural in itself to raise anything less tender than pity. Upon entering their common sitting-room, Marianne turned her eyes around it with a look of resolute firmness, regarding the dripping roof and weather-beaten windows as if determined at once to accustom herself to the sight of every object with which the remembrance of Willoughby could be connected. She said little, but every sentence aimed at cheerfulness, and though a sigh sometimes escaped her, it never passed away without the atonement of a smile. After dinner she would try her pianoforte. She went to it, but the music on which her eye first rested was a seamen's lament in six verses, procured for her by Willoughby, containing some of their favourite duets, one rhyming "a lassie so curvy" with "lay dying of scurvy" and bearing on its outward leaf her own name in his handwriting. That would not do. She shook her head, put the music aside, and after running over the keys for a minute, complained of feebleness in her fingers—and indeed, the minute action of running her hands over the keys had caused a brittle piece of fingernail to slide off and fall to the floor—and closed the instrument again; declaring however with firmness as she did so, that she should in future practice much.

Only when Marianne had retired to her old room for a well-needed rest, did Elinor venture to press again the question that had been on her mind since the yacht brought them within view of Pestilent Isle.

"Mother," she asked haltingly. "*Where* is Margaret?"

Mrs. Dashwood dissolved in tears, and at last gave her unhappy response: The girl had not been seen for several weeks; the night after Mrs. Dashwood penned her last missive to Elinor and Marianne, in which she had included the most distressing news of Margaret's depilation and the newly fang-like nature of her teeth, the girl had gone out again on one of her unannounced and unwarranted midnight walks—and, this time, never returned.

Mrs. Dashwood would fear the very worst, except for the strange incident she now relayed to Elinor—an incident which seemed to give assurance that the girl still lived, though it was a most unwelcome assurance, indeed. It seemed that on one rain-soaked recent night, Mrs. Dashwood had been woken, long past the stroke of midnight, by what she was quite certain was the voice of her youngest daughter, coming high and piercing across the rocky hills of Pestilent Isle, several times repeating the same distorted, bizarre phrase: *K'yaloh D'argesh F'ah!*

It was agreed that not a word of this would be imparted to Marianne, for fear of unsettling the course of her recovery. Indeed, the next morning produced no abatement in her happy symptoms.

"When the weather is settled, and I have recovered my strength," said Marianne, "we will take long walks together every day. We will walk to the dunes at the water's edge; we will travel to Deadwind Island and wander through Sir John's exotic gardens; we will again slog through the marshy fens and climb the lightning-scarred trees. I know we shall be happy. I know the summer will pass happily away. I mean never to be later in rising than six, and from that time till dinner I shall divide every moment between music and reading. I have formed my plan, and am determined to enter on a course of serious study. Our own library is too well known to me, to be resorted to for anything beyond mere amusement. But there are many works well worth reading at Sir John's estate; and there are others of more modern production which I know I can borrow of Colonel Brandon. I shall learn engineering; I shall study hydrology and biology and aeronautics; I shall endeavour to understand Mendel's principles and comparative zoology."

"But of what use will be such knowledge?" inquired Elinor with a smile meant to offer encouragement, but from which she could not hide a small measure of teasing.

"Someone," replied Marianne, looking away shyly, "will need to build Sub-Marine Station Gamma."

Elinor honoured her for a plan which originated so nobly as this; though smiling to see the same eager fancy which had been leading her to the extreme of languid indolence and selfish repining, now at work in introducing excess into a scheme of such rational employment and virtuous self-control. Her smile however changed to a sigh when she felt, still cosseted in her bosom, the octopus whistle, and remembered that promise to Willoughby was yet unfulfilled. Willing to delay the evil hour, she resolved to wait till her sister's health were more secure before she appointed it. But the resolution was made only to be broken.

They had been three days at home when the ever-present sea mist lifted enough for an invalid to venture out. Marianne, leaning on Elinor's arm, was authorized to walk as long as she could without fatigue, down the wandering lane that led inland from the shanty.

The sisters set out at a slow pace, and they had advanced only so far beyond the house as to admit a full view of the hill when Marianne calmly said, "There, exactly there, into that rolling brook, where the octopus set upon me—there did I first see Willoughby."

Her voice sunk with the word, but presently reviving she added, "I am thankful to find that I can look with so little pain on the spot! Shall we ever talk on that subject, Elinor? Or will it be wrong? I can talk of it now, I hope, as I ought to do."

Elinor tenderly invited her to be open.

"As for regret," said Marianne, "I have done with that, as far as *he* is concerned. I do not mean to talk to you of what my feelings have been for him, but what they are *now*. If I could be satisfied on one point—if I could be allowed to think that he was not *always* acting a part, not *always* deceiving me; but above all, if I could be assured that he never was so *very* wicked as my fears have sometimes fancied him, since the story of that unfortunate girl—"

She stopped. Elinor joyfully treasured her words as she answered, "If you could be assured of that, you think you should be easy." They paused in their walk to sit together on a large, jagged rock on the edge of mist-enshrouded little pool. "But how would you account for his behaviour?"

"I would suppose him only fickle. Very, very fickle."

Elinor said no more. She was debating within herself on the eligibility of beginning her story directly, or postponing it till Marianne were in stronger health. As they sat, the pool filled to a height of some inches with cloudy water, fed by some underground spring; in the next moment the water receded, revealing the muddy bottom of the basin. They sat for a few minutes in silence, during which time the pool emptied and filled again; the repetitive action of the water in the pond struck a familiar chord with Elinor, but she could not recall why. Perhaps it was nothing; perhaps it was only fancy. She could not forget that Margaret was missing, and wished with a pang of longing that her whole family might be safe and reunited.

"I am not wishing him too much good," said Marianne at last with a sigh, "when I wish his secret reflections may be no more unpleasant than my own. He will suffer enough in them."

"Do you compare your conduct with his?"

"No. I compare it with what it ought to have been. I compare it with yours."

"Our situations have borne little resemblance."

"They have borne more than our conduct. Do not, my dearest Elinor, let your kindness defend what I know your judgment must censure. My illness has made me think—and weep, and itch terribly, and have these weird feverish visions of parakeets pecking at my eyes—but it also made me think. Long before I was enough recovered to talk, I was perfectly able to reflect. I considered the past: I saw in my own behaviour, since the beginning of our acquaintance with him last autumn, nothing but a series of imprudence towards myself, and want of kindness to others. I saw that my own feelings had prepared my sufferings, and that my want of fortitude under them had almost led me to the grave. And I saw, as I have mentioned, whole great swooping flocks of multi-coloured parakeets, as vicious as they were colourful, descending on my eyes again and again. My illness, I well knew, had been entirely brought on by myself by such negligence of my own health."

"Your illness was brought on by mosquitoes."

"Yes, brought on by myself and also by the mosquitoes. But had I died, it would have been self-destruction. I did not know my danger till the danger was removed; but with such feelings as these reflections gave me, I wonder at my recovery—wonder that the very eagerness of my desire to live, to have time for atonement to my God, and to you all, did not kill me at once. Whenever I looked towards the past, I saw some duty neglected, or some failing indulged. Everybody seemed injured by me. The kindness, the unceasing kindness of Mrs. Jennings, I had repaid with ungrateful contempt. To the Middletons, to the Palmers, the Steeles—

At the mention of the Steeles, Elinor had a fleeting but distinct pain in her forehead—the five pointed symbol shot back into her mind's eye for one painful moment and then disappeared. *Why? Why again?*

The mist in the pond breathed out again, and then in. Marianne continued her oration.

"I had been insolent and unjust; with a heart hardened against their merits, and a temper irritated by their very attention. To John, to Fanny, yes, even to them, little as they deserve, I had given less than their due. But you above all, above my mother, had been wronged by me. I, and only I, knew your heart and its sorrows; yet to what did it influence me? Did I imitate your forbearance? No!"

Here ceased the rapid flow of her self-reproving spirit; and Elinor, impatient to soothe, though too honest to flatter, gave her instantly that praise and support which her frankness and her contrition so well deserved. Marianne pressed her hand and replied, "If I could but know *his* heart, everything would become easy."

Elinor, with a hand resting lightly on Willoughby's whistle, reflected on the propriety or impropriety of speedily hazarding her narration; and perceiving that as reflection did nothing, resolution must do all, soon found herself leading to the fact. She prepared her anxious listener with caution; related simply and honestly the chief points on which Willoughby grounded his apology; did justice to his repentance, and softened only his protestations of present regard. She described that as he spoke, Willoughby's appearance had seemed genuinely penitent, and Monsieur Pierre's as well. Marianne said not a word. She trembled, her eyes were fixed on the ground, and her lips became whiter than even sickness had left them. A thousand inquiries sprung up from her heart, but she dared not urge one. She caught every syllable with panting eagerness;

her hand, unknowingly to herself, closely pressed her sister's, and tears covered her cheeks.

Elinor led her towards home; and till they reached the door of the shanty, talked of nothing but Willoughby and their conversation together. As soon as they entered and tugged off their mud boots, Marianne with a kiss of gratitude and the words "Tell Mama" withdrew from her sister and walked slowly up stairs. Elinor would not attempt to disturb a solitude so reasonable as what she now sought; and so she turned into the parlour to fulfill her parting injunction. The conversation felt momentous; it felt like Marianne's very heart had shifted in her chest; indeed, it seemed to Elinor—even as she watched her sister trudge wearily up to her room—that the very island they stood on had moved beneath their feet.

CHAPTER 47

MRS. DASHWOOD DID NOT HEAR unmoved the vindication of the self-satisfied treasure hunter who had been her favourite. She rejoiced in his being cleared from some part of his imputed guilt. She was sorry for him; she wished him happy. But the feelings of the past could not be recalled. Nothing could do away the knowledge of what Marianne had suffered through his means, nor remove the guilt of his conduct towards Eliza. Nothing could replace him, therefore, in her former esteem, nor injure the interests of Colonel Brandon.

Had Mrs. Dashwood, like her daughter, heard Willoughby's story from himself—had she witnessed his distress, and seen the pitiable, semi-human expression upon the face of his orangutan, now sadly slain, it is probable that her compassion would have been greater. But it was neither in Elinor's power, nor in her wish, to rouse such feelings in another as had at first been called forth in herself. Reflection had given calmness to her judgment, and sobered her own opinion of Willoughby's deserts. She wished, therefore, to declare only the simple truth, and lay open such facts as were really due to his character, without any embellishment of tenderness to lead the fancy astray.

In the evening, when they were all three together, Marianne began to speak of him again—but it was not without an effort. Her unsteady voice plainly showed. "I wish to assure you both," said she, "that I see everything as you can desire me to do."

Mrs. Dashwood would have interrupted her instantly with soothing tenderness, had not Elinor, who really wished to hear her sister's unbiased opinion, by an eager sign, engaged her silence. Marianne slowly continued, "It is a great relief to me—what Elinor told me this morning—I have now heard exactly what I wished to hear." For some moments her voice was lost; but recovering herself, she added, and with greater calmness than before, "I am now perfectly satisfied, I wish for no change. Do you—do you hear that?"

Elinor could not deny that she *did* hear it, and could see by her mother's troubled expression that she heard it as well: the distinct sound of voices chanting together, but very lightly as though far off in the distance. She cocked her head for a moment, but the sound died away; Mrs. Dashwood wrung her hands and looked desperately to Elinor—Margaret was out there, somewhere on the island, they knew—and whatever the source of that chanting, it also held the key to her whereabouts.

The sound faded; Marianne, too caught up in her unburdening to linger on its mystery, continued. "In short, I never could have been happy with him, after knowing, as sooner or later I must have known, all this. I should have had no confidence, no esteem. Nothing could have done it away to my feelings."

"I know it—I know it," cried her mother, whose natural passion on the subject of her child's welfare was further riled by uncertainty of her youngest daughter's situation. "Happy with a man of libertine practices! With one who so injured the peace of the dearest of our friends, and the best of men! No, my Marianne has not a heart to be made happy with such a man! Her conscience, her sensitive conscience, would have felt all that the conscience of her husband ought to have felt."

Marianne sighed, and repeated, "I wish for no change."

"You consider the matter," said Elinor, "exactly as a good mind and a sound understanding must consider it. I dare say you perceive reason enough to be convinced that your marriage must have involved you in many certain troubles and disappointments. Had you married, you must have been always poor. His expensiveness is acknowledged even by himself, and his whole conduct declares that self-denial is a word hardly understood by him. His demands and your inexperience together, on a small, very small income, must have brought on distresses which would not be the *less* grievous to you—"

Elinor was interrupted by the noise, the same noise they had heard before, only louder this time, rolling across the hillside; and now the syllables were distinct enough to be heard: *K'yaloh D'argesh F'ah!*

"My God!" said Marianne now, her attention drawn for the moment from Willoughby. "That is the ghastly refrain that so agitated our dear Margaret—and indeed, where *is* Margaret?

Elinor, with a cautioning look to her mother, returned the conversation to its course.

"To abridge Willoughby's enjoyments, is it not to be feared, that instead of prevailing on feelings so selfish to consent to it, you would have lessened your own influence on his heart, and made him regret the connection which had involved him in such difficulties?"

Marianne's lips quivered, and she repeated the word "Selfish?" in a tone that implied—"do you really think him selfish?" Mrs. Dashwood, meanwhile, stared worriedly out the window, hoping or fearing to see what she knew not.

"The whole of his behaviour," replied Elinor, "from the beginning to the end of the affair, has been grounded on selfishness. It was selfishness which first made him sport with your affections; which afterwards, when his own were engaged, made him delay the confession of it, and which finally carried him from Barton Cottage. His own enjoyment was his ruling principle."

"It is very true. *My* happiness never was his object."

"At present," continued Elinor, "he regrets what he has done. And why does he regret it? Because he finds it has not answered towards himself. It has not made him happy. His circumstances are now unembarrassed. He suffers from no evil of that kind; and he thinks only that he has married a woman of a less amiable temper than yourself. But does it follow that had he married you, he would have been happy? He would then have suffered under the pecuniary distresses which, because they are removed, he now reckons as nothing. He always would have been poor; and probably would soon have learned to rank the innumerable comforts of a clear estate and good income as of far more importance than the mere temper of a wife."

"I have not a doubt of it," said Marianne, "and I have nothing to regret—nothing but my own folly."

"Rather say your mother's imprudence, my child," said Mrs. Dashwood, turning at last away from the window, for the chanting had again abated. "*She* must be answerable."

Marianne would not let her proceed; and Elinor, satisfied that each felt her own error, wished to avoid any survey of the past that might weaken her sister's spirits; she, therefore, pursuing the first subject, immediately continued:

"One observation may, I think, be fairly drawn from the whole of the story—that all Willoughby's difficulties have arisen from the first offence against virtue, in his behaviour to Eliza Williams. That crime has been the origin of every lesser one, and of all his present discontents."

Marianne assented most feelingly to the remark; and her mother was led by it to an enumeration of Colonel Brandon's injuries and merits, warm as friendship and design could unitedly dictate. Her daughter did not look, however, as if much of it were heard by her.

Elinor, according to her expectation, saw on the two or three following days, that Marianne did not continue to gain strength as she had done; but while her resolution was unsubdued, and she still tried to appear cheerful and easy, her sister could safely trust to the effect of time upon her health. Every day the pustules that marked her skin were healing, and the cool (though malodorous) sea winds that swept through the windows of Barton Cottage seemed to do her spirits well.

Elinor grew impatient for some tidings of Edward. She had heard nothing of him since the destruction of the Sub-Marine Station, nothing new of his plans, nothing certain even of his present abode. Some letters had passed between her and her brother, in consequence of Marianne's illness; and in the first of John's, which otherwise related the lingering after effects of his experiments in Station, including an insatiable appetite for grub worms, there had been this sentence: "We know nothing of our unfortunate Edward, and can make no enquiries on so prohibited a subject," which was all the intelligence of Edward afforded her by the correspondence, for his name was not even mentioned in any of the succeeding letters. She was not doomed, however, to be long in ignorance of his measures.

Their man-servant, Thomas, had been ordered one morning to row to Exeter on business. Later that afternoon, while serving a bowl of Mrs. Dashwood's latest culinary specialty—a lobster bisque served in the hollowed-out skull of a porpoise—Thomas offered the following voluntary communication: "I suppose you know, ma'am, that Mr. Ferrars is married."

Marianne gave a violent start, fixed her eyes upon Elinor, saw her turning pale, and fell back in her chair in hysterics. Mrs. Dashwood, whose eyes had intuitively taken the same direction, was shocked to perceive by Elinor's countenance how much she really suffered.

Elinor's mind was aflame; her entire spirit throbbed with distress. The five-pointed symbol, that totem of agony, returned at the servant's news in its most intense incarnation yet, twirling and throbbing in her mind's eye.

"Ah," she cried out, clutching with two hands at her skull. "The pain—"

Though desperate for further information, Elinor was unable in such a condition to ask Thomas for the source of his intelligence. Mrs. Dashwood immediately took that trouble on herself; and Elinor had the benefit of the information without the exertion of seeking it.

"Who told you that Mr. Ferrars was married, Thomas?"

"I see Mr. Ferrars myself, ma'am, this morning in Exeter, and his lady too, Miss Steele as was."

With every repeat of the name—Miss Steele—the pain recurred, amplified it seemed by its repetition.

"They was stopping at the door of the New London Inn. I happened to look up as I went by the chaise, and so I see directly it was the youngest Miss Steele."

Pain—the pain grew nearly unbearable. Elinor endeavored with all her ability to keep her attention upon the servant's story, so she could know of the fate of Edward.

"So I took off my hat, and she knew me and called to me, and inquired after you, ma'am, and the young ladies, especially Miss Marianne, and bid me I should give her compliments and Mr. Ferrars's."

"But did she tell you she was married, Thomas?"

"Yes, ma'am. She smiled, and said how she had changed her name since she was in these parts. She was always a very affable and free-spoken young lady."

"Was Mr. Ferrars in the carriage with her?"

"Yes, ma'am, I just see him leaning back in it, but he did not look up—he never was a gentleman much for talking."

Elinor's heart could easily account for his not putting himself forward; and Mrs. Dashwood probably found the same explanation.

"Was there no one else in the carriage?"

"No, ma'am, only they two."

"Do you know where they came from?"

"They come straight from town, as Miss Lucy—Mrs. Ferrars told me."

"And are they going farther westward?"

"Yes, ma'am—but not to bide long. They will soon be back again, and then they'd be sure to take a convenient and well-armored ship out to the islands, and call here."

Mrs. Dashwood now looked at her daughter; but Elinor knew better than to expect them. She recognized the whole of Lucy in the message, and was very confident that Edward would never come near them.

Thomas's intelligence seemed over. Elinor looked as if she wished to hear more.

"Did you see them off, before you came away?"

"No, ma'am—the horses were just coming out, but I could not bide any longer; I was afraid of being late."

"Did Mrs. Ferrars look well?"

"Yes, ma'am, but to my mind she was always a handsome young lady—and she seemed vastly contented."

Mrs. Dashwood could think of no other question, and Thomas and the tablecloth, now alike needless, were soon afterwards dismissed; Thomas returned downstairs to begin slicing up crayfish for to-morrow's breakfast.

Mrs. Dashwood and her daughters remained long together in a similarity of thoughtfulness and silence. Mrs. Dashwood feared to hazard any remark, and ventured not to offer consolation. She now found that she had erred in relying on Elinor's representation of herself; and justly concluded that everything had been expressly softened at the time, to spare her from an increase of unhappiness, suffering as she then had suffered for Marianne. Elinor, for her part, experienced such pain as if her head were captured in a vice.

She felt at last that it was appropriate to explain to her mother and her sister that the source of her pain was not merely the violent tugs upon her heartstrings occasioned by the information regarding Edward and the new Mrs. Ferrars; she finally told them of the odd symbol that had first appeared in her mind about the time of the Steeles' first arrival among them in the islands; she further explained how it had re-occurred inter-mittently in the months since; and how, finally, she had glimpsed it one other place only—on the lower back of Lucy Steele, when they changed clothes after the Fang-Beast's attack.

"I am at sea, my dear," said Mrs. Dashwood with a puzzled expres-sion. "What can it mean? What connection can there be between this recurring pain in your brain, and this girl?"

"I shall tell you what it means." Sir John suddenly stepped into the shanty, looking very serious indeed; Mrs. Jennings stood beside him, wringing her hands together.

"What it means," Sir John continued, "is that she is not a girl at all. She is a sea witch! And Mr. Ferrars is in the gravest danger."

CHAPTER 48

"SEA WITCHES WANDER THE EARTH when it suits them, but their true habitation is in undersea grottos, where they live and thrive for many centuries," said Sir John with a grave look. "But they are not an immortal race, contrary to what is commonly said of them. Indeed, the rest of us might well be counted safer if they *were*—since the only certain way for a sea witch to prolong its foul existence is by consuming human bone marrow, which is therefore, to them, the most precious of elixirs. Hence their occasional appearance, in the guise of attractive human women, among the terrestrial world—where they make love to an un-knowing man, marry him unawares, and then, when the opportunity presents itself, kill him and suck out his marrow."

Elinor and Mrs. Dashwood heard this oration in stunned silence, struggling to reconcile the picture in their minds of charming Lucy Steele, who had lived among them for so many months, with this new picture, of a devil-spirit who had emerged from a watery cavern to drink the juice of human bones.

"And what of the *elder* Miss Steele," wondered Marianne. "How could she not know that her sister had been replaced by a sea witch?"

"It is impossible that she did *not* know," Sir John answered, "For a sister to a sea witch is certain to be a sea witch herself."

"And yet, Anne Steele did not find a man to marry her!" protested Mrs. Dashwood.

"As I said, the witches take the *physical form* of human women," explained Sir John. "There is nothing they can do about their personalities."

Elinor, consumed with concern for Edward, and hoping to find some justification for disbelieving Sir John's counsel, inquired as to how he had arrived at his dire conclusion. "It is the five-pointed symbol you described, and its accompanying distress," came the reply. "Certain sensitive souls can sense their presence of sea witchery; they come to sense the distinctive presence of a witch, and it causes them a searing, throbbing pain, precisely as you have described it."

As if to confirm this conclusion, the pain returned to Elinor again, and she was overcome by a twisting pain, that gripped her body from her head to her guts. *Edward—Edward*—was all she could think.

"If your friend has indeed been so fool enough to wed a sea witch," Sir John concluded, "then she has already come upon him sleeping, snapped his bones, and feasted upon the precious white fluid within as if it were mother's milk."

Elinor realised—even as fresh waves of pain coursed through her body—that the hope she had harboured, in spite of herself, that something would occur to prevent Edward's marrying Lucy, was grounded in some instinctual understanding of the horrid danger that his engagement posed; if only resolution of his own, some mediation of friends, or some more eligible opportunity of establishment for the lady, had arisen to assist the happiness of all, and prevent his being turned into an immortality-preserving snack for a sea witch! But he was now married, and thusly doomed. Except—

"Wait a moment," she managed to say. "If the pain and sensitivity you mention function as a sort of alarm of a witch's foul intentions—"

"As indeed it does."

"Why am I, even now, wracked by it—if Lucy Steele has already found her mark, and consumed him?"

Sir John, for once unsure of his answer, was trying to fashion one when Mrs. Dashwood beckoned them both to the window. The figure of a man clambering from a skiff, just tied to the dock, drew her eyes to the window. He approached their gate. It was a gentleman—it was Colonel Brandon! But why would Colonel Brandon, who had swum so nobly to Marianne's rescue and, they thought, shed his embarrassment of his fishier qualities, now arrive onboard a skiff? No—it was *not* Colonel Brandon— neither his air—nor his height—and no mucous-dripping tentacles. Were it possible, she must say it must be Edward. She looked again. He was at the bottom of the steps now. She could not be mistaken. It *was* Edward. Intact! And here!

The pain evaporated from her mind, but still Elinor was over-whelmed. She moved away and sat down. "I *will* be calm; I *will* be mis-tress of myself."

She saw her mother and Marianne change colour and whisper a few sentences to each other. She would have given the world to be able to speak—and to make them understand that she hoped no coolness, no slight, would appear in their behaviour to him; but she had no utterance, and was obliged to leave all to their own discretion.

No further syllable passed aloud. They all waited in silence for the appearance of their visitor. His footsteps were heard climbing the rickety wooden steps of the gravel path; in a moment he was in the passage, and in another he was before them.

His countenance, as he entered the room, was not too happy, even for Elinor. His complexion was white with agitation, and he looked as if fearful of his reception, and conscious that he merited no kind one. "My God!" muttered Sir John. "He is half consumed!" But a closer inspection revealed that he was walking upright and breathing normally, which would be impossible if several of his bones had been snapped and sucked upon.

Mrs. Dashwood, uncertain of the social requirements of a situation in which an acquaintance is newly married, but (unknowingly so) to a witch of the deep, met him with a look of forced complacency, gave him her hand, and wished him joy.

He stammered out an unintelligible reply. Elinor's lips had moved with her mother's, and, when the moment of action was over, she wished that she had shaken hands with him too. But in the next moment she resolved that she could not let her friend not know the truth about the woman he had wed. Elinor, resolving to exert herself to caution her old friend, though fearing the sound of her own voice, now said:

"There is something we must tell you about Mrs. Ferrars! Some most terrifying information, so you best brace yourself."

"Terrifying information? About my mother?"

"I meant," said Elinor, taking up some work from the table, "terrifying information about Mrs. *Edward* Ferrars."

She dared not look up—but her mother and Marianne both turned their eyes on him. He coloured, seemed perplexed, looked doubtingly, and said, "Perhaps you mean—my brother—you mean Mrs. *Robert* Ferrars."

"Mrs. Robert Ferrars!" was repeated by Marianne and her mother in an accent of the utmost amazement; and though Elinor could not speak, even *her* eyes were fixed on him with the same impatient wonder. He rose from his seat, and walked to the window, apparently from not knowing what to do; took up a pair of scissors that lay there, and while spoiling both them and their sheath by cutting the latter to pieces as he spoke, said, in a hurried voice, "Perhaps you do not know—you may not have heard that my brother is lately married to—to the youngest—to

Miss Lucy Steele."

His words were echoed with unspeakable astonishment by all but Elinor, who sat in a state of such agitation as made her hardly know where she was.

"Yes," said he, "they were married last week, and are now at Dawlish."

Elinor could sit no longer. She ran out of the room, and as soon as the door was closed, burst into tears of joy, which at first she thought would never cease. Edward, who had till then looked anywhere, rather than at her, saw her hurry away, and perhaps saw—or even heard, her emotion; for immediately afterwards he fell into a reverie, which no remarks, no inquiries, no affectionate address of Mrs. Dashwood could penetrate, and at last, without saying a word, quitted the room, and went for a happy walk along the beach—leaving the others in the greatest astonishment and perplexity on a change in his situation, so wonderful and so sudden.

Marianne, though, ventured to add one note of concern: "Doesn't this mean, however, that Robert Ferrars will be, or has already been, consumed by the sea witch?" But none present felt that possibility was much to be concerned with, or regretted.

CHAPTER 49

UNACCOUNTABLE AS THE CIRCUMSTANCES of his release might appear to the whole family, it was certain that Edward was free; and to what purpose that freedom would be employed was easily pre-determined by all. For after experiencing the blessings of *one* imprudent engagement, contracted without his mother's consent, as he had already done for more than four years, nothing less could be expected of him in the failure of *that*, than the immediate contraction of another.

His errand on Pestilent Isle, at the rickety house known as Barton Cottage, was a simple one. It was only to ask Elinor to marry him—and considering that he was not altogether inexperienced in such a question, it might be strange that he should feel so uncomfortable in the present case as he really did, so much in need of encouragement and fresh air. He paced on the beach for a full five minutes, as Mrs. Dashwood peeked at him through the bay window. She once shouted "Watch out!" and would later relate that Elinor's moment of great happiness was nearly undone before properly contracted, when a giant bivalve mollusk tried, and barely failed, to snap itself shut around his unprotected ankles.

How soon he had walked himself into the proper resolution, however, how soon an opportunity of exercising it occurred, and how he was received, need not be particularly told. This only need be said—that when they all sat down to table at four o'clock, about three hours after his arrival, he had secured his lady, engaged her mother's consent, and was not only in the rapturous profession of the lover, but one of the happiest of men. His situation indeed was more than commonly joyful. He had more than the ordinary triumph of accepted love to swell his heart, and raise his spirits. He was released without any reproach to himself, from an entanglement which had long formed his misery, from a woman whom he had long ceased to love, and who (he was now informed) was an immortal and evil spirit, who had emerged from a cave many fathoms below sea level to secure a victim, from whom to suckle the very stuff of life for her own diabolical use. He was brought from misery to happiness—and the change was openly spoken in such a genuine, flowing, grateful cheerfulness, as his friends had never witnessed in him before.

His heart was now open to Elinor, all its weaknesses, all its errors confessed, and his first boyish attachment to Lucy treated with all the philosophic dignity of four and twenty.

"When first I met her, Lucy appeared everything that was amiable and obliging. She was pretty too—at least I thought so *then*; and I had seen so little of other women, that I could make no comparisons, and see no defects. I did at times notice, now that I think of it, that her eyes, on odd occasions, would flash the deepest, most crimson red, and that when she laughed at a jape, she would cackle rather alarmingly. Considering everything, therefore, I hope, foolish as our engagement was, foolish as it has since in every way been proved, it was not at the time an unnatural or an inexcusable piece of folly.

"And now," he concluded, his eyes firmly affixed on Elinor's beaming countenance, "I feel that the world has shifted under my very feet."

There was a long silence, in which all present realised that Edward's choice of phrase, if accidental, bore a literal as well as a figurative accuracy; the room had, in fact, shifted beneath their feet; and even as they all adjusted to this slight but discernible tilt, it jerked in the other direction, and they all were thrown violently to the ground.

"My God!" cried Sir John, emerging from the instinctual barrel roll he had gone into at the room's first moving, and standing with legs spread far apart, firmly balanced himself against the alarming angle of the floor.

"Goodness," echoed Mrs. Jennings from under the tea table. "What is happening?"

"*It is beginning,*" came a raspy voice from the doorway of the cottage, and all eyes turned to find young Margaret—although no longer did she look young, nor even like a girl at all—but like a fearsome, troll-like creature of the darkness: Her head pin-bald, her cheeks caked with dirt, her eyes squinting against the daylight.

"Margaret!" said Mrs. Dashwood with a wail. "My darling!"

At her approach, with arms outstretched, Margaret hissed like a snake, baring razor-sharp teeth at her mother. "Come no closer, woman of earth! Leviathan wakes—we must be girded for its waking!" And then, throwing back her head and screaming in a loud, unnatural voice, "*K'yaloh D'argesh F'ah! K'yaloh D'argesh F'ah!*"

This ejaculation received the predictable startled reaction; all present exchanged concerned expressions, before they were distracted as the house trembled once more, and tilted dramatically, from forty-five to eighty-five degrees in the opposite direction. Mrs. Jennings rolled wildly out from under the table and slammed with a resounding thud against the pianoforte.

"It was all true," Sir John moaned. "Palmer warned me—I wouldn't listen—it is all true!"

"K'yaloh D'argesh F'ah! K'yaloh D'argesh F'ah!" shouted Margaret again.

Elinor, having tumbled from the heights of happiness into a miasma of terror—and from one end of the parlour to the other—found herself now staring wide-eyed out the southerly aspect of the cottage. There she saw Mount Margaret, a streak of grey-black smoke pouring forth from its top, while all along the craggy hillside hideous troll-like creatures crawled like insects towards the summit.

"What?" she cried out to Edward, who was bleeding copiously from a cut he had received in the first roll of the room. "What is happening?"

This was the last phrase anyone was able to emit for a long time. In the next instant, the entire house and all inside it, were lifted a hundred feet up in the air, and tossed into the sea.

*   *   *

Elinor surfaced in the cold, choppy waters off of the Devonshire coast, grasping for a scrap of furniture on which to secure herself, and thinking longingly of the Float-Suit she had worn in Sub-Marine Station Beta. Bits and pieces of Barton Cottage were borne past her by the agitated churning of the water: wood beams from the doorframe, several steps from the rickety wooden staircase; the piano bench; her collection of driftwood sculptures—all of it so much sea-borne rubbish now, as, she feared, was she herself.

And then—straight ahead of her—Elinor saw the most horrible sight her vision had yet comprehended. Pestilent Island, her home, was lifting itself out of the water—in a long, fluid motion the four-mile sweep

THE LEVIATHAN LOOKED THIS WAY AND THAT, ITS GARGANTUAN EYES
ROLLING WILDLY.

of the island rose and rose and rose, revealing beneath the surface the ir-
refutable aspect of a *face*—it was a beast of impossible size, and the island
that had been their home was merely the head—no, merely the *crest* of the
head. Up it rose, with sea-water streaming down around it on all sides, a
wall of mighty waterfalls crashing into the ocean.

The whole fearsome head lifted itself from the water, and a pair of
huge rolling eyes, surveyed the horizon line; two barbed and scaly claws,
each as big as a battleship, set to thrashing about in the water. The
Leviathan looked this way and that, its gargantuan eyes rolling wildly, as
a blast of steam shot upwards from the blowhole on the very crest of its
head—what Elinor now realised they had called Mount Margaret for all
these many months. The whole head was dotted here and there with flexing, viscous gill-like slits and holes; it was one such gill-set, she thought,
where she and Marianne had sat and talked last of Willoughby, where she
had watched the mist roll in and out of the pond, one minute facet of the
massive operation of the Thing's respiratory system. The pool had not
seemed to breathe, it *did* breathe.

As she watched, the Leviathan brought one gigantic claw down into
the water, scooped up a school of monstrous tuna, each one as big as a
cow, and tossed them into its maw like peanuts.

The island was awake, and it was *hungry*.

Elinor swam. She swam as fast as she could, kicking and paddling,
setting her eyes for Allenham, the next island in the chain, though she
knew it to be four miles, and too far a swim for her to make; and could
not she hope to outswim the creature that, simply by outstretching its gigantic front claw, could scoop her up in an instant.

Where were her mother and Marianne? Had the Leviathan already
consumed them, like it had those tuna? And *where* was her dearest Edward?

On she swam, banishing all thoughts, thinking only of breathing, of
swimming—of survival.

What a rapid turn of events this day had wrought! First, that great
change which a few hours had wrought in the minds and the happiness

of the Dashwoods! And now this—a race for life, to stay ahead of the sleep-hungered Leviathan that once had been her home.

On she swam, until her arms grew tired and her head grew heavy; the impossibility of her task weighed on her as much as her heavy woolen frock; she would never make it. With despair she began to feel a powerful tidal pull beneath her—though there was no undertow, not out here, miles from shore. Glancing back over her shoulder she confirmed her fear: The monster had brought its snout down to the water line and opened its mouth, and was simply sucking in sea-water. The water was rushing into its insatiable mouth, and dragging Elinor with it. She fought the undertow with all her ability; she kicked furiously, battling the tidal force with all the strength in her body.

"That's it!" shouted a voice. "Those are the calves I love!"

She turned her head, raised it from the water, and beheld her dear Edward, swimming beside her. He held out his hand to her, and she hers to him; just by touching, their energies combined, and each felt their individual power increase. They swam that way, as one swimmer, stroking simultaneous, towards the safety of the schooner.

A schooner? Indeed—for here was Mr. Benbow, with the familiar scowling face and feathers tied in his beard, calling from the prow of the *Rusted Nail!*

"Ahoy!" he called, as his mates appeared; there was Mr. Palmer and One-Eyed Peter and Two-Eyed Scotty and gentle Billy Rafferty—and even Mrs. Palmer, laughing cheerily with babe in arms. The crew lustily cheered Elinor and Edward forward, urging them on with foul-mouthed piratic exhortations. In a moment the pair pulled free of the monster's tidal force; in another instant they were climbing the ropes and ladder tossed from the bow, and were aboard the schooner.

"Hard to port, Peter!" called Mr. Benbow. "Hard to port and steady as you go. We must escape this island-turned-fiend, or we'll all be swimming in its dank digestive juices by sunset!"

Marianne, Mrs. Dashwood, and the rest had already been plucked from the sea, and in a quarter hour's time, they had sailed clear of the Devonshire coast and the Leviathan. All were wrapped in blankets, seated with cups of hot grog on the fo'c'sle of the *Rusted Nail*, listening to Mr. Palmer's solemn-voice explanation of what they had just witnessed.

"What my wife insists on calling *drollery*," said he, "and what others call *bitterness* or *dyspepsia*, I can call what it is in truth: The kind of desperate soul-deep melancholia that comes from having looked into the dark eye of time and seen the darkest secrets of the earth.

"It was on a sea journey, some half dozen years after I left His Majesty's service to go adventuring with Sir John and his crew, in search of whatever tribal curse it was that affected the Alteration. We ran aground on a patch of rock several hundred nautical miles north-northwest of the Tasmanian shore. There we lived for fourteen terrible months, sacked out on rocks, under makeshift tents we stitched from pieces of our ravaged sail; by day we wandered, hunting wolves and apes for food; at night we slept, at constant peril from the lash of the wind and the sting of a thousand different species of mosquito and night crawler.

"One day I found a cave; from within its depths, I saw a pair of gleaming eyes inside, and heard a queer chanting. Wearied by tedium of our island life, and certain regardless that my life would soon be meeting its end, I saw no risk in venturing after the source of the mystery. And so I decided to explore the cavern—how bitterly I have wished, every subsequent day, that I had decided otherwise!

"After travelling only a few yards within the cave, I was seized all at once by what felt like a thousand grasping hands and pulled to the dirt floor. The things that assaulted man—for *things* I was certain they were, merciless beasts, though later I would find that they were men—chanted as they dragged me into the cave-floor, chanted with one horrible voice: *K'yaloh D'argesh F'ah! K'yaloh D'argesh F'ah!*

"All the hair was shaved from my body; with bits of flint they filed my teeth to sharpened points. At last I was left alone, naked, trembling and bleeding, with one that acted as the leader. I need not tell you how startled I was when he began to speak in English, though his voice was raspy as if out of practice."

Palmer explained that the man was a member of a tribe of subterranean cave-men, who had once dwelt above ground like other human races, but now lived in caverns below the earth's surface, and worshipped a pantheon of cruel and hidden monster-gods called the *K'yaloh*. The *K'yaloh* were an ancient race, older than man, older than beast, older than the Alteration, older than time itself. They laid in slumber, waiting for the day of waking. When they woke, all that we know would be destroyed.

"*K'yaloh D'argesh F'ah*," the leader told Palmer. "Leviathan slumbers, but day will come of wakening."

"The tale of my escape, and of my journey home, is long," Palmer concluded. "But it is not a tale worth telling, because, well, because nothing is worth anything. If I am quiet—if I am droll—it is because since that day, life has held little interest. For how could it—what purpose is there in pursuing the trivial amusements of man?"

"*K'yaloh D'argesh F'ah*," he repeated slowly. "Day will come of wakening."

He glanced backwards at their churning wake, back towards the swirling waters where once Pestilent Isle had sat. "Day has come."

* * *

It must be that there is something in the hearts of human beings, some natural fluid perhaps, that insists on happiness, even confronted with the most powerful arguments against it. For having heard Mr. Palmer's tale, and not doubting its veracity, the Dashwoods continued in their happy excitement at the engagement that had unfolded, just before the Leviathan woke from its ageless slumber. Indeed, Mrs. Dashwood, too happy to be comfortable (and additionally sleeping on One-Eyed Peter's bunk, which he had gallantly ceded to her) knew not how to love Edward nor praise Elinor enough, how to be enough thankful for his release without wounding his delicacy, nor how at once to give them leisure for unrestrained conversation together, and yet enjoy, as she wished, the sight and society of both.

Marianne could speak *her* happiness only by tears. Comparisons would occur—regrets would arise—and her joy, though sincere as her love for her sister, was of a kind to give her neither spirits nor language. "Arrrgh," she could only say, taking inspiration from the pirates that surrounded her. "Arrgh."

But Elinor—how are *her* feelings to be described, as she sat on the rear deck of the *Rusted Nail*, staring back at the open horizon where her home had once been? From the moment of learning that Lucy was married to another, that Edward was free, to the moment when she plunged into the ocean and had to swim as fast as ever she had to keep from becoming monster-food, she was everything by turns but tranquil.

But when she found every doubt, every solicitude removed, compared her situation with what so lately it had been—saw him honourably released from his former engagement, saw him instantly profiting by the release, to address herself and declare an affection as tender, as constant as she had ever supposed it to be—and then saw how both of them, together, outswam and survived an ancient beast that was as big, literally, as some island nations—she was oppressed, she was overcome by her own felicity—it required several hours to give sedateness to her spirits, or any degree of tranquility to her heart.

They were aboard the *Rusted Nail* for a week, in sorting out the details of what would come next for them all, which was felicitous from Elinor's perspective—for whatever other claims might be made on him, it was impossible that less than a week should be given up to the enjoyment of Elinor's company, or suffice to say half that was to be said of the past, the present, and the future—for though a very few hours spent in the hard labour of incessant talking will dispatch more subjects than can really be in common between any two rational creatures, yet with lovers it is different. Between *them* no subject is finished, no communication is even made, till it has been made at least twenty times over. They spoke of the various pirates with whom they were surrounded, they watched the minnows trail happily behind the boat, they wondered at how long the Thing had slumbered, and where it would next lie its massive head, and for how long; when these topics had been exhausted, they began upon them again.

It was shortly thereafter that Colonel Brandon arrived, swimming swiftly alongside the *Rusted Nail* and hailing to be allowed aboard, which permission was most expeditiously granted. Edward was delighted, as he really wished not only to be better acquainted with him, but to have an opportunity of convincing him that he no longer resented his giving him the living of Delaford. "Which, at present," said he, "after thanks so ungraciously delivered as mine were on the occasion, he must think I have never forgiven him for offering."

Now he felt astonished himself that he had never yet been to the place. But so little interest had been taken in the matter, that he owed all his knowledge of the lake, the village, and the monsters that menaced it, to Elinor herself, who had heard so much of it from Colonel Brandon, and heard it with so much attention, as to be entirely mistress of the subject.

One question after this only remained undecided, between them, one difficulty only was to be overcome. They were brought together by mutual affection, with the warmest approbation of their real friends; their intimate knowledge of each other seemed to make their happiness certain—and they only wanted something to live upon. Edward had two thousand pounds, and Elinor one, which, with the Delaford lighthouse, was all that they could call their own; for it was impossible that Mrs. Dashwood should advance anything; and they were neither of them quite enough in love to think that three hundred and fifty pounds a year would supply them with the comforts of life. Edward was not entirely without hopes of some favourable change in his mother towards him; and on *that* he rested for the residue of their income.

As for Colonel Brandon, he generally swam alongside the ship for most of the day; and clambered aboard in the morning, early enough to interrupt the lovers' first tête-à-tête before breakfast.

A three weeks' residence at Delaford, where, in his evening hours at least, he had little to do but to calculate the disproportion between six and thirty and seventeen, had brought him aboard the *Rusted Nail* in a temper of mind which needed all the improvement in Marianne's looks, all the kindness of her welcome, and all the encouragement of her mother's language, to make it cheerful.

It would be needless to say, that the gentlemen advanced in the good opinion of each other, as they advanced in each other's acquaintance, for it could not be otherwise. Their resemblance in good principles and good sense, in disposition and manner of thinking, would probably have been sufficient to unite them in friendship, without any other attraction; but their being in love with two sisters, and two sisters fond of each other, made that mutual regard inevitable and immediate, which might otherwise have waited the effect of time and judgment. Edward had no judgment against Brandon's bizarre appearance; he considered it merely an outward affliction analogous to his own inward affliction, that is, his shyness of manner; some are marked within, he reflected, and some without.

A letter from town, which a few days before would have made every nerve in Elinor's body thrill with transport, now arrived to be read with less emotion than mirth. Mr. Dashwood's strains were solemn. Mrs. Ferrars was the most unfortunate of women—poor Fanny had suffered agonies of sensibility—and he considered the existence of each, under such a blow, with grateful wonder. Robert had been consumed bodily on their wedding night. When they had come to the honeymoon suite the morning after the wedding, they had found no Robert whatsoever, only a pile of bones, each cracked in two, with the marrow utterly sucked out. And Lucy sitting atop the gruesome pile, gorged and sated, her eyes glazed with animal delight, cackling lightly to herself; her skin had returned to its original colour, a thorough-going and revolting sea green.

Even with what occurred, Mrs. Ferrars could not forgive Robert his offense; she only had trouble deciding which sinner to condemn more thoroughly—her son, for marrying a woman with no independent means, or the woman, for eating him. Neither of them were ever again to be mentioned to Mrs. Ferrars; and even, if she might hereafter be induced to forgive her son, his wife should never be acknowledged as his widow, which would prove to be an easy directive with which to comply, for the following day she returned to her undersea cavern, somewhere deep below the Pacific Ocean.

John concluded that "Mrs. Ferrars has never yet mentioned Edward's name," and seemed to suggest, further, that Mrs. Ferrars, now that her eldest had been so horribly dispatched, was inclined to feel a renewed sympathy towards her youngest, who had been so poorly used. This determined Edward to attempt a reconciliation.

Thus Edward Ferrars and Colonel Brandon quitted the *Rusted Nail* together at the coast of Somersetshire. They were to go immediately to Delaford, that Edward might have some personal knowledge of his future home, and assist his patron and friend in deciding on what improvements were needed to it; and from thence, after staying there a couple of nights, he was to proceed on his journey to town.

CHAPTER 50

AFTER A PROPER RESISTANCE on the part of Mrs. Ferrars, just so violent and so steady as to preserve her from the reproach of being too amiable, Edward was admitted to her presence and pronounced to be again her son. Her family had of late been exceedingly fluctuating. For many years of her life she had had two sons; but the crime and annihilation of Edward a few weeks ago, had robbed her of one; the literal annihilation of Robert had left her for a fortnight without any; and now, by the resuscitation of Edward, she had one again. Any further resuscitation of Robert was impossible; he was a bag full of broken bones, and even the bag his mother refused to acknowledge.

In spite of his being allowed once more to live, however, Edward did not feel the continuance of his existence secure, till he had revealed his present engagement; for the publication of that circumstance, he feared, might give a sudden turn to his constitution, and carry him off as rapidly as before. With apprehensive caution, therefore, it was revealed, and he was listened to with unexpected calmness. Mrs. Ferrars at first reasonably endeavoured to dissuade him from marrying Miss Dashwood, by every argument in her power—she told him, that in Miss Morton he would have a woman of higher rank and larger fortune; and enforced the assertion, by observing that Miss Morton was the daughter of a great engineer with thirty thousand pounds, while Miss Dashwood was only the daughter of a private gentleman who had been eaten by a shark; but when she found that, though perfectly admitting the truth of her representation, he was by no means inclined to be guided by it, she judged it wisest, from the experience of the past, to submit—and therefore, after such an ungracious delay as she owed to her own dignity, she issued her decree of consent to the marriage of Edward and Elinor.

With an income quite sufficient to their wants thus secured to them, they had nothing to wait for after Edward was in possession of the lighthouse; the ceremony took place in the church on Deadwind Island early in the autumn. It was a lovely affair, with a penguin theme; Sir John hosted ably, apologising to the guests for the absence of his wife—whom he so wished might one day come back, that he was known to sit up nights, a cup of rum in hand, staring out the window of the estate, watching the sea for her return.

Edward and Elinor were visited on their first settling by almost all their relations and friends. Mrs. Ferrars came to inspect the happiness

THE CEREMONY TOOK PLACE ON THE SHORES OF DEADWOOD ISLAND EARLY IN
THE AUTUMN.

which she was almost ashamed of having authorized; and even the Dashwoods were at the expense of a journey from Sussex to do them honour.

"I will not say that I am disappointed, my dear sister," said John, popping a grub worm in his mouth from the small dirt-filled bag in which he carried them. "*That* would be saying too much, for certainly you have been one of the most fortunate young women in the world, as it is. But, I confess, it would give me great pleasure to call Colonel Brandon brother. His property here, his place, his house, everything is in such respectable and excellent condition!"

Elinor's marriage divided her as little from her family as could well be contrived; for her mother and sisters spent much more than half their time with her, since they now had no proper home of their own, their island having turned out to be the skull of a giant sea monster, and were now living in a tent on the grounds of Sir John's home on Deadwind Island. Mrs. Dashwood was acting on motives of policy as well as pleasure in the frequency of her visits at Delaford; for she felt earnestly that island life was no longer healthy for Margaret, who had, since the Leviathan's waking, begun a slow, difficult recovery to her old self—her hair was growing back out, and she had begun again to speak in halting sentences. Frequent visits to Delaford also served Mrs. Dashwood's wish of bringing Marianne and Colonel Brandon together; precious as was the company of her daughter to her, she desired nothing so much as to give up its constant enjoyment to her valued friend; and to see Marianne settled at the mansion-house was equally the wish of Edward and Elinor. They each felt his sorrows, and their own obligations, and Marianne, by general consent, was to be the reward of all.

With such a confederacy against her—with a knowledge so intimate of his goodness—with a fast-fading horror of his nauseating appearance—with a conviction of his fond attachment to herself—what could she do?

Marianne Dashwood was born to an extraordinary fate. She was born to overcome an affection formed so late in life as at seventeen, and with no sentiment superior to strong esteem and lively friendship, voluntarily to give her hand to another! And *that* other, a man who had suffered no less than herself under the event of a former attachment; whom, two years before, she had considered too old to be married; who turned away at times from his own face in the mirror, so cursed was it to look upon—and who still suffered on occasion the smallest case of cartilage rot!

But so it was. Instead of falling a sacrifice to an irresistible passion, as once she had fondly flattered herself with expecting—instead of remaining even forever with her mother, and finding her only pleasures in retirement and study towards designing a superior Sub-Marine Station, as afterwards in her more calm and sober judgment she had determined on—she found herself at nineteen, submitting to new attachments, entering on new duties, placed in a new home, a wife, the mistress of a family, and the patroness of a village. She found, in the event, that his face was not the only region of his physiognomy that could be described as multi-appendaged, and she found that fact to carry with it certain marital satisfactions.

Colonel Brandon was now as happy, as all those who best loved him, believed he deserved to be; in Marianne he was consoled for every past affliction, even for that affliction which had so defined his life. Her regard and her society restored his mind to animation, and his spirits to cheerfulness; and that Marianne found her own happiness in forming his, was equally the persuasion and delight of each observing friend. Marianne could never love by halves; and her whole heart became, in time, as much devoted to her husband, as it had once been to Willoughby.

Willoughby could not hear of her marriage without a pang; and his punishment was soon afterwards complete in the voluntary forgiveness of Mrs. Smith, who, by stating his marriage with a woman of character as the source of her clemency, gave him reason for believing that had he behaved with honour towards Marianne, he might at once have been happy and rich.

That his repentance of misconduct, which thus brought its own punishment, was sincere, need not be doubted—nor that he long thought of Colonel Brandon with envy, and of Marianne with regret. But that he was forever inconsolable, that he fled from society, or contracted an habitual gloom of temper, or died of a broken heart, must not be depended on—for he did neither. He lived to exert, and frequently to enjoy himself. His wife was not always out of humour, nor his home always uncomfortable He resumed his constant searching for treasure, digging up with new maps, outfitting new schooners, and training new dogs.

For Marianne, however—in spite of his incivility in surviving her loss—he always retained that decided regard which interested him in everything that befell her, and made her his secret standard of perfection in woman; and even though in later years he obtained a new octopus whistle and used it liberally, many a rising beauty would be slighted by him in after-days as bearing no comparison with Mrs. Brandon.

Among the merits and the happiness of Elinor and Marianne, let it not be ranked as the least considerable, that though sisters, and living almost within sight of each other, they could live without disagreement between themselves, or producing coolness between their husbands; all lived in contented proximity—except for nights when they were awoken, in their separate establishments, by a cold and unmistakable sound, echoing across the countryside: *K'yaloh D'argesh F'ah! K'yaloh D'argesh F'ah!*

THE END